THE PREQUEL:

IT HAPPENED HERE

A Novel By John Kingston

THE PREQUEL:

IT HAPPENED HERE

A Novel By John Kingston

AN ALTERNATIVE TRUE HISTORY

Copyright © John Kingston 2017

VOLUME ONE OF THREE

ISBN: 978-0-9955703-0-6

9 780995 570306

STATEMENT

With the exception of Mr. Michael Randle, Mr. John Wrighton and Mr. Lawrence "Larry" Questad all characters appearing in this work are fictitious. Any resemblance fictitious characters bear to real persons, living or dead, is purely coincidental.

DEDICATIONS

I WISH TO THANK DOCTORS PHILIPPE RIBET , ROBERT GREENBAUM AND ESPECIALLY MR.STEPHEN EDMONDSON FOR GIVING ME A 'SECOND CHANCE' IN MAY 2007 AND THE OPPORTUNITY TO FINISH THIS WORK.

MY PERSONAL GRATITUDE TO MR. SHERIF HABASHI, DR. NEIL KITCHEN AND PROF. MICHAEL GLEESON FOR SAVING THE LIFE OF MY YOUNGER DAUGHTER, LAURA.

TO EVERYONE, AND ESPECIALLY MY DEAR FRIEND ROGER BALL, FOR THEIR HELP AND SUPPORT IN MY JOURNEY THROUGH LIFE.

INDEX

VOLUME ONE

THE PREQUEL:
IT HAPPENED HERE
AN ALTERNATIVE TRUE HISTORY
INTRODUCTION

FROM PRESIDENT KENNEDY`S INAUGURAL ADDRESS,

FRIDAY JANUARY 20TH 1961:

"...In the long history of the world, only a few generations have been granted the role of defending freedom in its hour of maximum danger. I do not shrink from this responsibility; I welcome it. I do not believe that any of us would exchange places with any other people or any other generation. The energy, the faith, the devotion which will light our country and all who serve it, and the glow from that fire can truly light the world."

(The Times, Monday 25th November 1963)

CHAPTER 55.

An Act to make exceptional provision for the Protection of the Community in cases of Emergency.

A.D. 1920.

[29th October 1920.]

BE it enacted by the King's most Excellent Majesty, by and with the advice and consent of the Lords Spiritual and Temporal, and Commons, in this present Parliament assembled, and by the authority of the same, as follows :

1.—(1) If at any time it appears to His Majesty that any action has been taken or is immediately threatened by any persons or body of persons of such a nature and on so extensive a scale as to be calculated, by interfering with the supply and distribution of food, water, fuel, or light, or with the means of locomotion, to deprive the community, or any substantial portion of the community, of the essentials of life, His Majesty may, by proclamation (hereinafter referred to as a proclamation of emergency), declare that a state of emergency exists.

Issue of proclamations of emergency.

No such proclamation shall be in force for more than one month, without prejudice to the issue of another proclamation at or before the end of that period.

(2) Where a proclamation of emergency has been made, the occasion thereof shall forthwith be communicated to Parliament, and, if Parliament is then separated by such adjournment or prorogation as will not expire within five days, a proclamation shall be issued for the meeting of Parliament within five days, and Parliament shall accordingly meet and sit upon the day appointed by that proclamation, and shall continue to sit and act in like manner as if it had stood adjourned or prorogued to the same day.

2.—(1) Where a proclamation of emergency has been made, and so long as the proclamation is in force, it shall be lawful for His Majesty in Council, by Order, to make regulations for

Emergency regulations.

1

A.D. 1920.
securing the essentials of life to the community, and those regulations may confer or impose on a Secretary of State or other Government department, or any other persons in His Majesty's service or acting on His Majesty's behalf, such powers and duties as His Majesty may deem necessary for the preservation of the peace, for securing and regulating the supply and distribution of food, water, fuel, light, and other necessities, for maintaining the means of transit or locomotion, and for any other purposes essential to the public safety and the life of the community, and may make such provisions incidental to the powers aforesaid as may appear to His Majesty to be required for making the exercise of those powers effective :

Provided that nothing in this Act shall be construed to authorise the making of any regulations imposing any form of compulsory military service or industrial conscription :

Provided also that no such regulation shall make it an offence for any person or persons to take part in a strike, or peacefully to persuade any other person or persons to take part in a strike.

(2) Any regulations so made shall be laid before Parliament as soon as may be after they are made, and shall not continue in force after the expiration of seven days from the time when they are so laid unless a resolution is passed by both Houses providing for the continuance thereof.

(3) The regulations may provide for the trial, by courts of summary jurisdiction, of persons guilty of offences against the regulations; so, however, that the maximum penalty which may be inflicted for any offence against any such regulations shall be imprisonment with or without hard labour for a term of three months, or a fine of one hundred pounds, or both such imprisonment and fine, together with the forfeiture of any goods or money in respect of which the offence has been committed : Provided that no such regulations shall alter any existing procedure in criminal cases, or confer any right to punish by fine or imprisonment without trial.

(4) The regulations so made shall have effect as if enacted in this Act, but may be added to, altered, or revoked by resolution of both Houses of Parliament or by regulations made in like manner and subject to the like provisions as the original regulations; and regulations made under this section shall not be deemed to be statutory rules within the meaning of section one of the Rules Publication Act, 1893.

56 & 57 Vict.
c. 66.

(5) The expiry or revocation of any regulations so made shall not be deemed to have affected the previous operation thereof, or the validity of any action taken thereunder, or any penalty or punishment incurred in respect of any contravention

or failure to comply therewith, or any proceeding or remedy in A.D. 1920.
respect of any such punishment or penalty.

3.—(1) This Act may be cited as the Emergency Powers Short title
Act, 1920.

(2) This Act shall not apply to Ireland.

and application.

Printed by Eyre and Spottiswoode, Ltd.,

for

William Richard Codling, Esq., C.B.E., M.V.O., the King's Printer of
Acts of Parliament.

(The Stationary Office Ltd.)

Public Order Act, 1936.

[1 EDW. 8. & 1 GEO. 6.   CH. **6.**]

ARRANGEMENT OF SECTIONS.

A.D. 1936.

13

CHAPTER 6.

An Act to prohibit the wearing of uniforms in
connection with political objects and the maintenance by private persons of associations of
military or similar character; and to make
further provision for the preservation of public
order on the occasion of public processions and
meetings and in public places.

A.D. 1936.

[18th December 1936.]

BE it enacted by the King's most Excellent Majesty,
by and with the advice and consent of the Lords
Spiritual and Temporal, and Commons, in this present
Parliament assembled, and by the authority of the same,
as follows :—

1.—(1) Subject as hereinafter provided, any person
who in any public place or at any public meeting wears
uniform signifying his association with any political
organisation or with the promotion of any political
object shall be guilty of an offence :

Provided that, if the chief officer of police is satisfied
that the wearing of any such uniform as aforesaid on
any ceremonial, anniversary, or other special occasion
will not be likely to involve risk of public disorder, he
may, with the consent of a Secretary of State, by order
permit the wearing of such uniform on that occasion
either absolutely or subject to such conditions as may be
specified in the order.

Prohibition
of uniforms
in connec-
tion with
political
objects.

1

A.D. 1936
———

(2) Where any person is charged before any court with an offence under this section, no further proceedings in respect thereof shall be taken against him without the consent of the Attorney-General except such as the court may think necessary by remand (whether in custody or on bail) or otherwise to secure the due appearance of the person charged, so, however, that if that person is remanded in custody he shall, after the expiration of a period of eight days from the date on which he was so remanded, be entitled to be discharged from custody on entering into a recognisance without sureties unless within that period the Attorney-General has consented to such further proceedings as aforesaid.

Prohibition of quasi-military organisations.

2.—(1) If the members or adherents of any association of persons, whether incorporated or not, are—

(*a*) organised or trained or equipped for the purpose of enabling them to be employed in usurping the functions of the police or of the armed forces of the Crown; or

(*b*) organised and trained or organised and equipped either for the purpose of enabling them to be employed for the use or display of physical force in promoting any political object, or in such manner as to arouse reasonable apprehension that they are organised and either trained or equipped for that purpose;

then any person who takes part in the control or management of the association, or in so organising or training as aforesaid any members or adherents thereof, shall be guilty of an offence under this section :

Provided that in any proceedings against a person charged with the offence of taking part in the control or management of such an association as aforesaid it shall be a defence to that charge to prove that he neither consented to nor connived at the organisation, training, or equipment of members or adherents of the association in contravention of the provisions of this section.

(2) No prosecution shall be instituted under this section without the consent of the Attorney-General.

(3) If upon application being made by the Attorney-
General it appears to the High Court that any association
is an association of which members or adherents are
organised, trained, or equipped in contravention of the
provisions of this section, the Court may make such order
as appears necessary to prevent any disposition without
the leave of the Court of property held by or for the
association and in accordance with rules of court may
direct an inquiry and report to be made as to any such
property as aforesaid and as to the affairs of the association and make such further orders as appear to the
Court to be just and equitable for the application of
such property in or towards the discharge of the
liabilities of the association lawfully incurred before the
date of the application or since that date with the
approval of the Court, in or towards the repayment of
moneys to persons who became subscribers or contributors
to the association in good faith and without knowledge
of any such contravention as aforesaid, and in or towards
any costs incurred in connection with any such inquiry
and report as aforesaid or in winding-up or dissolving the
association, and may order that any property which is
not directed by the Court to be so applied as aforesaid
shall be forfeited to the Crown.

(4) In any criminal or civil proceedings under this
section proof of things done or of words written, spoken
or published (whether or not in the presence of any
party to the proceedings) by any person taking part
in the control or management of an association or in
organising, training or equipping members or adherents
of an association shall be admissible as evidence of
the purposes for which, or the manner in which,
members or adherents of the association (whether
those persons or others) were organised, or trained, or
equipped.

(5) If a judge of the High Court is satisfied by
information on oath that there is reasonable ground for
suspecting that an offence under this section has been
committed, and that evidence of the commission thereof
is to be found at any premises or place specified in the
information, he may, on an application made by an
officer of police of a rank not lower than that of
inspector, grant a search warrant authorising any such
officer as aforesaid named in the warrant together with

A.D. 1936, any other persons named in the warrant and any other
officers of police to enter the premises or place at any
time within one month from the date of the warrant, if
necessary by force, and to search the premises or place
and every person found therein, and to seize anything
found on the premises or place or on any such person
which the officer has reasonable ground for suspecting
to be evidence of the commission of such an offence as
aforesaid :

Provided that no woman shall, in pursuance of a
warrant issued under this subsection, be searched except
by a woman.

(6) Nothing in this section shall be construed as
prohibiting the employment of a reasonable number of
persons as stewards to assist in the preservation of order
at any public meeting held upon private premises, or the
making of arrangements for that purpose or the instruction of the persons to be so employed in their lawful
duties as such stewards, or their being furnished with
badges or other distinguishing signs.

Powers for
the preser-
vation of
public
order on the
occasion of
processions.
3.—(1) If the chief officer of police, having regard
to the time or place at which and the circumstances in
which any public procession is taking place or is intended
to take place and to the route taken or proposed to
be taken by the procession, has reasonable ground for
apprehending that the procession may occasion serious
public disorder, he may give directions imposing upon
the persons organising or taking part in the procession
such conditions as appear to him necessary for the
preservation of public order, including conditions pre-
scribing the route to be taken by the procession and
conditions prohibiting the procession from entering any
public place specified in the directions :

Provided that no conditions restricting the display
of flags, banners, or emblems shall be imposed under this
subsection except such as are reasonably necessary to
prevent risk of a breach of the peace.

(2) If at any time the chief officer of police is of
opinion that by reason of particular circumstances
existing in any borough or urban district or in any part
thereof the powers conferred on him by the last foregoing
subsection will not be sufficient to enable him to prevent

serious public disorder being occasioned by the holding   A.D. 1936.
of public processions in that borough, district or part, he
shall apply to the council of the borough or district for
an order prohibiting for such period not exceeding three
months as may be specified in the application the holding
of all public processions or of any class of public procession
so specified either in the borough or urban district
or in that part thereof, as the case may be, and upon
receipt of the application the council may, with the
consent of a Secretary of State, make an order either
in terms of the application or with such modifications
as may be approved by the Secretary of State.

This subsection shall not apply within the City of
London as defined for the purposes of the Acts relating
to the City police or within the Metropolitan police
district.

(3) If at any time the Commissioner of the City of
London police or the Commissioner of police of the
Metropolis is of opinion that, by reason of particular
circumstances existing in his police area or in any part
thereof, the powers conferred on him by subsection (1)
of this section will not be sufficient to enable him to
prevent serious public disorder being occasioned by the
holding of public processions in that area or part, he may,
with the consent of the Secretary of State, make an order
prohibiting for such period not exceeding three months
as may be specified in the order the holding of all public
processions or of any class of public procession so specified
either in the police area or in that part thereof, as the case
may be.

(4) Any person who knowingly fails to comply with
any directions given or conditions imposed under this
section, or organises or assists in organising any public
procession held or intended to be held in contravention
of an order made under this section or incites any person
to take part in such a procession, shall be guilty of an
offence.

4.—(1) Any person who, while present at any   Prohibition
public meeting or on the occasion of any public pro-   of offensive
weapons at
cession, has with him any offensive weapon, otherwise   public
than in pursuance of lawful authority, shall be guilty   meetings and
processions
of an offence.

A.D. 1936.
—

(2) For the purposes of this section, a person shall not be deemed to be acting in pursuance of lawful authority unless he is acting in his capacity as a servant of the Crown or of either House of Parliament or of any local authority or as a constable or as a member of a recognised corps or as a member of a fire brigade.

Prohibition of offensive conduct conducive to breaches of the peace.

5. Any person who in any public place or at any public meeting uses threatening, abusive or insulting words or behaviour with intent to provoke a breach of the peace or whereby a breach of the peace is likely to be occasioned, shall be guilty of an offence.

Amendment of 8 Edw. 7. c. 66.

6. Section one of the Public Meeting Act, 1908, (which provides that any person who at a lawful public meeting acts in a disorderly manner for the purpose of preventing the transaction of the business for which the meeting was called together, or incites others so to act, shall be guilty of an offence) shall have effect as if the following subsection were added thereto—

" (3) If any constable reasonably suspects any person of committing an offence under the foregoing provisions of this section, he may if requested so to do by the chairman of the meeting require that person to declare to him immediately his name and address and, if that person refuses or fails so to declare his name and address or gives a false name and address he shall be guilty of an offence under this subsection and liable on summary conviction thereof to a fine not exceeding forty shillings, and if he refuses or fails so to declare his name and address or if the constable reasonably suspects him of giving a false name and address, the constable may without warrant arrest him."

Enforcement.

7.—(1) Any person who commits an offence under section two of this Act shall be liable on summary conviction to imprisonment for a term not exceeding six months or to a fine not exceeding one hundred pounds, or to both such imprisonment and fine, or, on conviction on indictment, to imprisonment for a term not exceeding two years or to a fine not exceeding five hundred pounds, or to both such imprisonment and fine.

6

(2) Any person guilty of any other offence under A.D. 1936 this Act shall be liable on summary conviction to imprisonment for a term not exceeding three months or to a fine not exceeding fifty pounds, or to both such imprisonment and fine.

(3) A constable may without warrant arrest any person reasonably suspected by him to be committing an offence under section one, four or five of this Act.

8. This Act shall apply to Scotland subject to the following modifications :— Application to Scotland.

(1) Subsection (2) of section one and subsection (2) of section two of this Act shall not apply.

(2) In subsection (3) of section two the Lord Advocate shall be substituted for the Attorney-General and the Court of Session shall be substituted for the High Court.

(3) Subsection (5) of section two shall have effect as if for any reference to a judge of the High Court there were substituted a reference to the sheriff and any application for a search warrant under the said subsection shall be made by the procurator fiscal instead of such officer as is therein mentioned.

(4) The power conferred on the sheriff by subsection (5) of section two, as modified by the last foregoing paragraph, shall not be exercisable by an honorary sheriff-substitute.

(5) Subsection (1) of section three of this Act shall in its application to a burgh have effect with the substitution of references to the magistrates of the burgh for references to the chief officer of police, and any reference to the powers conferred by the said subsection shall be construed accordingly.

(6) In subsection (2) of section three and in .subsection (3) of section nine of this Act for references to a borough or urban district and to the council thereof there shall be substituted respectively references to a burgh and to the magistrates thereof.

B

A.D. 1936.

——

Interpreta-
tion, &c.

11 & 12
Geo. 5. c. 31.

9.—(1) In this Act the following expressions have
the meanings hereby respectively assigned to them, that
is to say :—

> " Chief officer of police " has the same meaning as
> in the Police Pensions Act, 1921;

> " Meeting " means a meeting held for the purpose of
> the discussion of matters of public interest or for
> the purpose of the expression of views on such
> matters;

> " Private premises " means premises to which the
> public have access (whether on payment or
> otherwise) only by permission of the owner,
> occupier, or lessee of the premises;

> " Public meeting " includes any meeting in a public
> place and any meeting which the public or any
> section thereof are permitted to attend, whether
> on payment or otherwise;

> " Public place " means any highway, public park
> or garden, any sea beach, and any public bridge,
> road, lane, footway, square, court, alley or
> passage, whether a thoroughfare or not; and
> includes any open space to which, for the time
> being, the public have or are permitted to have
> access, whether on payment or otherwise;

> " Public procession " means a procession in a public
> place;

> " Recognised corps " means a rifle club, miniature
> rifle club or cadet corps approved by a Secretary
> of State under the Firearms Acts, 1920 to 1936,
> for the purposes of those Acts.

(2) The powers conferred by this Act on the Attorney-
General may, in the event of a vacancy in the office
or in the event of the Attorney-General being unable
to act owing to illness or absence, be exercised by the
Solicitor-General.

(3) Any order made under this Act by the council
of any borough or urban district or by a chief officer
of police may be revoked or varied by a subsequent order
made in like manner.

(4) The powers conferred by this Act on any chief
officer of police may, in the event of a vacancy in the

office or in the event of the chief officer of police being A.D. 1936.
unable to act owing to illness or absence, be exercised
by the person duly authorised in accordance with directions given by a Secretary of State to exercise those
powers on behalf of the chief officer of police.

10.—(1) This Act may be cited as the Public Order   Short title
Act, 1936.   and extent.

(2) This Act shall not extend to Northern Ireland.

(3) This Act shall come into operation on the first
day of January nineteen hundred and thirty-seven.

PRINTED IN ENGLAND BY SWIFT (PRINTING & DUPLICATING), LTD., FOR
HARRY PITCHFORTH
Controller of Her Majesty's Stationery Office and Queen's Printer of Acts of Parliament

(The Stationary Office Ltd)

ELIZABETH II

1964 CHAPTER 38

An Act to amend the Emergency Powers Act 1920 and make permanent the Defence (Armed Forces) Regulations 1939. [10th June 1964]

BE IT ENACTED by the Queen's most Excellent Majesty, by and with the advice and consent of the Lords Spiritual and Temporal, and Commons, in this present Parliament assembled, and by the authority of the same, as follows:—

1. In section 1(1) of the Emergency Powers Act 1920 (by virtue of which Her Majesty may by proclamation declare that a state of emergency exists if at any time it appears to Her that any action has been taken or is immediately threatened by any persons or body of persons of such a nature and on so extensive a scale as to be calculated, by interfering with the supply and distribution of food, water, fuel or light, or with the means of locomotion, to deprive the community, or any substantial portion of the community, of the essentials of life), for the words from " any action " to " so extensive a scale " there shall be substituted the words " there have occurred, or are about to occur, events of such a nature ".

Amendment of s. 1(1) of Emergency Powers Act 1920.
10 & 11 Geo. 5 c. 55.

2. The Defence (Armed Forces) Regulations 1939 in the form set out in Part C of Schedule 2 to the Emergency Laws (Repeal) Act 1959 (which regulations enable the temporary employment in agricultural work or in other work, being urgent work of national importance, of members of the armed forces of the Crown to be authorised) shall become permanent.

Defence (Armed Forces) Regulations 1939 made permanent.
7 & 8 Eliz. 2 c. 19.

3.—(1) This Act may be cited as the Emergency Powers Act 1964.

Short title and extent.

(2) Section 1 of this Act shall not extend to Northern Ireland.

PRINTED BY PERCY FAULKNER, C.B.
Controller of Her Majesty's Stationery Office and Queen's Printer of Acts of Parliament

BHAGAVAD-GITA, THE SONG OF GOD.

BEFORE THE BATTLE OF KURUKSHETRA. EXTRACTS FROM THE CONVERSATION BETWEEN ARJUNA AND SRI KRISHNA. THE SANSKRIT WORD KALA CAN, I UNDERSTAND, MEAN EITHER TIME OR DEATH.

THE ORIGINAL SANSKRIT TEXT FROM CHAPTER ELEVEN IS FOLLOWED BY THE AUTHOR`S LIBERAL AND FREELY ADAPTED VERSION OF OTHERS`ERUDITE TRANSLATIONS:

TEXTS 32 TO 34 INCLUSIVE:

TEXT 32

श्रीभगवानुवाच

कालोऽस्मि लोकक्षयकृत् प्रवृद्धो
लोकान् समाहर्तुमिह प्रवृत्त: ।
ऋतेऽपि त्वां न भविष्यन्ति सर्वे
येऽवस्थिता: प्रत्यनीकेषु योधा: ॥३२॥

THE LORD GOD SAID: I AM TIME GROWN OLD, DEATH, THE DESTROYER OF WORLDS, HERE TO DESTROY YOU ALL. EVERY SOLDIER ON BOTH SIDES WILL DIE, BUT YOU, THE PANDAVAS, WILL SURVIVE.

TEXT 33

तस्मात्त्वमुत्तिष्ठ यशो लभस्व
जित्वा शत्रून् भुङ्क्ष्व राज्यं समृद्धम् ।
मयैवैते निहताः पूर्वमेव
निमित्तमात्रं भव सव्यसाचिन् ॥ ३ ३ ॥

ARISE! PREPARE FOR BATTLE AND FAME.DEFEAT YOUR ENEMIES AND ENJOY THE FRUITS OF VICTORY. I HAVE PREORDAINED THEIR DEATHS AND YOU, ARJUNA, THE EXPERT ARCHER, WILL BE MY INSTRUMENT OF DESTINY .

TEXT 34

द्रोणं च भीष्मं च जयद्रथं च
कर्णं तथान्यानपि योधवीरान् ।
मया हतांस्त्वं जहि मा व्यथिष्ठा
युध्यस्व जेतासि रणे सपत्नान् ॥ ३ ४ ॥

GREAT VALIANT WARRIORS INCLUDING DRONA, BHISMA, JAYADRATHA AND KARNA HAVE ALREADY BEEN CONDEMNED BY ME. FIGHT, KILL THEM! **BE NOT CONCERNED BY YOUR CONSCIENCE WHEN YOU VANQUISH THEM IN BATTLE!**

PSALM FIFTY-ONE

Have mercy upon me, O God, after Thy great goodness

According to the multitude of Thy mercies do away mine offences .

Wash me thoroughly from my wickedness and cleanse me from my sin.

For I acknowledge my faults: and my sin is ever before me.

Against Thee only have I sinned, and done this evil in thy sight: that Thou mightiest be justified in Thy saying, and clear when Thou are judged.

Behold, I was shapen in wickedness: and in sin hath my mother conceived me.

But lo, Thou requirest truth in the inward parts: and shalt make me to understand wisdom secretly.

Thou shalt purge me with hyssop, and I shall be clean: Thou shalt wash me, and I shall be whiter than snow.

Thou shalt make me hear of joy and gladness: that the bones which Thou hast broken may rejoice.

Turn Thy face from my sins and put out all my misdeeds.

Make me a clean heart, O God and renew a right spirit within me.

Cast me not away from Thy presence: and take not Thy Holy Spirit from me.

O give me the comfort of Thy help again: and stablish me with Thy free Spirit.

Then shall I teach Thy ways unto the wicked: and sinners shall be converted unto Thee.

Deliver me from blood- guiltiness, O God, Thou that art the God of my health: and my tongue shall sing of Thy righteousness.

Thou shalt open my lips, O Lord: and my mouth shall shew Thy praise.

For Thou desirest no sacrifice, else would I give it Thee: but Thou delightest not in burnt–offerings.

The sacrifice of God is a troubled spirit: a broken and contrite heart, O God, shalt Thou not despise.

O be favourable and gracious unto Zion: build Thou the walls of Jerusalem.

Then shalt Thou be pleased with the sacrifice of righteousness, with the burnt- offerings and oblations: then shall they offer young calves unto Thine altar.

THE LATIN TRANSLATION OF PSALM FIFTY-ONE, WHICH IS REPRODUCED BELOW, IS THE BASIS OF GREGORIO ALLEGRI`S MAGNIFICENT, MULTI VOICED MISERERE MEI

Miserere mei, Deus: secundum magnam misericordiam tuam.

Et secundum multitudinem miserationum tuarum,dele iniquitatem meam.

Amplius lava me ab iniquitate mea: et a peccato meo munda me.

Quoniam iniquitatem meam ego cognosco: et peccatum meum contra me est semper.

Tibi soli peccavi , et malum coram te feci : ut justificeris in sermonibus tuis , et vincas cum judicaris.

Ecce enim in iniquitatibus conceptus sum:et in peccatis concepit sum: et in peccatis concepit me mater mea.

Ecce enim veritatem dilexisti : incertia et occulta sapientiae tuae manifestasti mihi.

Asperges me hysopo , et mundabor : lavabis me , et super nivem dealbabor.

Auditui meo dabis gaudium et laetitiam : et exsultabunt ossa humiliata.

Averte faciem tuam a peccatis meis: et omnes iniquitates meas dele.

Cor mundum crea in me, Deus: et spiritum rectum innova in visceribus meis.

Ne proiicias me a facie tua: et spirtum sanctum tuum ne auferas me.

Redde mihi laetitiam salutaris tui: et spiritu principali confirma me.

Docebo iniquos vias tuas: et impii ad te convertentur.

Libera me de sanguinibus , Deus, Deus salutis meae : et exsultabit lingua mea justitiam tuam.

Domine, labia mea aperies: et os meum annuntiabit laudem tuam.

Quoniam si voluisses sacrificium, dedissem utique: holocaustis non delectaberis.

Sacrificium Deo spiritus contribulatus: cor contritum , et humiliatum , Deus , non despicies.

Benigne fac, Domine,in bona voluntate tua Sion:ut aedificentur muri Ierusalem.

Tunc acceptabis sacrificium justitiae,oblationes, et holocausta : tunc imponent super altare tuum vitulos.

(https://en.m.wikipedia.org/wiki/Miserere-(Allegri)#Sources)

TRANSCRIPT OF THE QUEEN`S CHRISTMAS MESSAGE, WEDNESDAY,DECEMBER 25TH, 1963.

Since my last message of Christmas greetings to you all, the world has witnessed many great events and sweeping changes, but they are already part of the long record of history. Now, as ever, the important time for mankind is the future; the coming years are full of hope and promise and their course can still be shaped by our will and action.

The Christmas message of peace on earth, goodwill toward men, remains the same; but we can only achieve this if we are all truly ambitious for what is good and honourable. Humanity can only make progress by determination and concerted effort.

One such concerted effort has been the campaign to free the world from hunger. I am very happy that the people of the Commonwealth have responded so generously to this campaign. Much has been achieved but there is still much to do and on this day of reunions and festivities in the glow of Christmas let us remember the many undernourished people, young and old, scattered throughout the world.

All my family joins me in sending every one of you best wishes for Christmas and may God`s blessing be with you in the coming year.

(BBC Caversham Park)

RULE BRITANNIA, a song by Thomas Augustine Arne, 1740

When Britain first at Heav`n`s command

Arose from out the azure main;

This was the charter of the land,

And guardian angels sang this strain;

Rule, Britannia! Britannia, rule the waves:

Britons never will be slaves.

The nations not so blest as thee,

Shall in their turn to tyrants fall;

While thou shalt flourish great and free,

The dread and envy of them all .

Rule, Britannia! Britannia, rule the waves:

Britons never will be slaves.

Still more majestic shalt thou rise

More dreadful from each foreign stroke;

As the loud blast that tears the skies,

Serves but to root thy native oak .

Rule, Britannia! Britannia, rule the waves:

Britons never will be slaves.

Thee haughty tyrants ne`er shall tame,

All their attempts to bend thee down

Will but arouse thy generous flame;

But work their woe, and thy renown.

Rule, Britannia! Britannia, rule the waves:

Britons never will be slaves.

To thee belongs the rural reign;

Thy cities shall with commerce shine;

All thine shall be the subject main,

And every shore it circles thine .

Rule, Britannia! Britannia, rule the waves:

Britons never will be slaves.

The Muses, still with freedom found,

Shall to thy happy coast repair;

Blest Isle! With matchless beauty crowned,

And manly hearts to guide the fair .

Rule , Britannia! Britannia, rule the waves:

Britons never will be slaves.

DER RING DES NIBELUNGEN: GOTTERDAMMERUNG

VON RICHARD WAGNER

VOLLSTANDIGER KLAVIERAUSZUG

VON KARL KLINDWORTH

AN EXCERPT FROM ACT THREE,SCENE TWO,
A WOODED PLACE ON THE RHINE,
GUNTHER'S HALL .

SIEGF.

die Lo - - he durch - schritt ich,
I *passed* *through* *its* *fire,*

etwas beschleunigend.

und fand zum Lohn
and found *for prize*

(In immer grössere Verzückung gerathend.)
(*sinking more and more into a state of ecstasy.*)

Immer etwas mehr zurückhaltend.

schla - - - fend
sleep - - - *ing,*

ein won - - ni - ges Weib
a *wo* - - *man* *fair,*

Gemächlich im Zeitmass.

pp dolce espressivo

in   lich—   —ter Waf—fen Ge—wand.
all   clad   in glit—ter-ing mail.

Den Helm löst' ich der herr-lichen Maid; mein Kuss   er—   weck—   —te sie
The helm I loosed from the glor-i-ous maid,   my   kiss   a—   —woke   her from

kühn:___   oh!   Wie mich brünn-stig da   um—schlang der
sleep:___   ah,   then like flames of fire   en—fold-ed   me

(Zwei Raben fliegen aus einem Busche auf,
kreisen über Siegfried, und fliegen dann,
*(Two ravens fly up out of a bush, circle
over Siegfried, and then fly away*

schö—   —nen Brünnhil—   —de Arm!
beau—   —teous Brünnhil—   —de's arms!

(In höchstem Schrecken aufspringend.)
(springing up in greatest dismay.)

GUNTH.

Was hör' ich!
What saith he?

Lebhaft.

GUNTH.   297

dem Rheine zu davon.)
towards the Rhine.)
HAG.
Erräth'st du auch die-ser Ra - ben Geraun'?
Those ra-vens' speech! canst thou read it a-right?
più f
(Siegfried fährt heftig auf, und blickt, Hagen den Rücken zukehrend, den Raben nach.)
SIEGF. (Siegfried stands up suddenly and, turning his back to Hagen, looks after the ravens.)
(Hagen stösst seinen Speer in Siegfried's Rücken.)
(Hagen thrusts his spear into Siegfried's back.)
HAG.
Ra-che rie-then sie mir!
Vengeance is their de - cree!
ff
P.
(Siegfried schwingt mit beiden Händen seinen Schild hoch empor, um ihn nach Hagen zu werfen: die Kraft verlässt ihn; der Schild entsinkt ihm rückwärts; er selbst stürzt über dem Schilde zusammen.)
(Siegfried swings his shield on high with both hands, as tho' to throw it upon Hagen: his force fails him; the shield falls backwards and he himself falls down on the shield)
(Gunther und die Mannen stürzen sich über Hagen.)
(Gunther and the Vassals rush towards Hagen.)
fff
4 Mannen (welche vergebens Hagen zurückzuhalten versucht.)
4 Vassals (who have in vain tried to hold Hagen back.)
Hagen, was thu'st du?
Hagen, what dost thou?
2 andere Mannen.
2 other Vassals.
Was thatest du?
What deed is that?
Mässig langsam.
etwas nachlassend.
f
dim.

HAG.

Hagen, was tha - thestdu?
Hagen, what deed is that?

Mein - eid
False - hood's

räch' ich!
payment!

(Hagen wendet sich ruhig zur Seite ab, und verliert sich dann über der Höhe, wo man ihn langsam durch die anbrechende Dämmerung von
(Hagen turns quietly away and then is seen through the gathering twilight slowly moving up the height, over which he disap-

(Gunther beugt sich, schmerzergriffen, zu Siegfried's Seite nieder.—
Die Mannen umstehen theilnahmvoll den Sterbenden.)
*(Gunther bends down, stricken with grief, at Siegfried's side.—
The Vassals stand round the dying man filled with sympathy.)*

Sehr langsam

dannen schreiten sieht.)
pears.)

(Siegfried, von zwei Mannen
sitzend erhalten, schlägt die
Augen glanzvoll auf.)
*(Siegfried, held by two Vassals
in a sitting position, opens his eyes.)*

SIEGF.

Brünnhil - de!
Brünnhil - de!

und feierlich.

26809

41

SIEGF.

bie-tet mir Gruss!
greeteth me there!

(Er sinkt zurück und stirbt.— Regungslose Trauer der Umstehenden.)
(He sinks back and dies.— The rest stand round him in sorrow without moving.)

(Die Nacht ist hereingebrochen.— Auf die stumme Ermahnung Gunther's erheben
(Night has come.— At Gunther's mute command the Vassals raise Siegfried's

Mannen Siegfried's Leiche, und geleiten sie, mit dem Folgenden, in feierlichem Zuge über die Felsenhöhe langsam von dannen.)
corpse and during the following, carry it away in a solemn procession over the height.)

Feierlich.

THE OPENING OF, AND EXTRACTS FROM

CHANCELLOR ADOLF HITLER`S ADDRESS TO THE REICHSTAG,

BERLIN, APRIL 26th 1942

RECORDED BY THE FOREIGN BROADCAST MONITORING

SERVICE, FEDERAL COMMUNICATIONS COMMISSION.

"The 11th of December of 1941 when I last spoke to you it was my privilege to lay before you an account of the course of events of the preceding year.   In their historical magnitude and lasting political significance they are such as may not be recognized to the full extent for centuries to come.   After a few weeks the suppression of the uprising in Belgrade which had been instigated by Britain and Moscow, Europe for the first time in perhaps centuries to come became aware of the common danger from the East, upon the successful warding off of which the very existence of the whole of our continent had so often before depended. For many people the causes of this terrible war into which we were forced in 1939, began to be more clearly recognized, for this war did not bear the characteristics of the previous conflicts among the European nations to which we were accustomed.   To an ever increasing degree it began to be generally realized that the reasons for this conflict were no longer to be sought in the usual interests even if plausible of the various nations, but that in reality it was one of those elementary struggles which shaking the foundations of the world but once in a thousand years, introduce a new millennium...

When on the third of September, 1939, after Germany had made countless efforts in the cause of peace, France and Britain declared war on the New Reich, after these states had shoved Poland into the foreground by giving her authority to act as a means of starting the conflagration, one was compelled to doubt the common sense of a world, which instead of averting the terrible misfortune of such a mad war literally forced this catastrophe to happen without any apparent reason.

Now we all know that ever since the internal disruption of the European states Britain had entered into a conspiracy based upon a political doctrine which saw in the disintegration of the continent the essential conditions for the prosperity and growth of the British Empire. No doubt this thought which dominated British policy was in itself very alluring. While Europe was exhausting her strength in numerous internal wars, Great Britain succeeded in burning [?, Author's note]up a world-wide structure with a minimum of sacrifice of blood. The title of "Empire" was given to this structure deserved to be compared with that of imperial Rome as little as an international business concern for the creation of cultural values.

It is an overestimation of the British statesmanship as well as of the political and military capacities of the British to assume that these are the causes for the decay of Europe. Here the origin of the condition is confused with its exploitation. For Europe's decay is due partly to the natural senility of the continental power pre-eminent after the collapse of the Roman Empire, and partly to the deterioration of the elements which had provided the Western centre of that time with its racial and constitutional foundation.

 The dissension between the classical Roman conception of the state on the one hand ,and the no less imperial claims of the Roman church on the other brought about the gradual destruction of the foundations of the central state in Europe. To this was added the profound earnestness with which the world then treated questions which were suited to involve Europe in endless internal religious status, while the same problems are today recognized as being completely unimportant as far as the state is concerned, and treated accordingly.

Thus, the collapse of the old German Empire and consequently of the centre of the dominant internal European organization was just as little brought about by the British as the collapse of Rome was brought about by the Germanic tribes. In both cases, however, internal conditions of weakness resulted in situations which enabled external forces to intervene, thus imposing a new course on the history of the world for many centuries to come...

Only a fool can overlook or deny the fact that, like every political organizing process, this process too confers its benefits on the human race, but it is just as foolish to assume that the British Empire could forever maintain the so-called balance in Europe. The racial elements of this continent linked together by blood and outlook who were striving to establish unity could not in the long run be prevented from combining. It was, moreover, completely foolish to assume that on the appearance of a danger forming an equal threat to the existence of all the people in Europe they could prevent the union of the countries thus threatened...

With whomever England allies herself, she will see at the end of this war her allies stronger than she is herself or ever will be. Her arch-capitalists and the Bolshevist statesmen may greet each other with the greatest possible deceptive friendship, her archbishops may embrace the bloody spectre of Bolshevism as fervently as possible, the more lies, deception and corruption have to be used in order to hide the unnatural coalitions of this Empire from her own people or from humanity, the less they will be able to deceive the nations with a vision and to hinder the natural progress of a forced historical development.

There is a wise proverb which says that the gods strike blind those whom they wish to destroy. I do not know whether every Englishman today still thinks that Britain acted with wisdom and inspiration when she declined the innumerable proposals for an understanding which I have made since 1933. Nor do I know whether every Englishman today is as convinced that it was wise to refuse my offer of an alliance renewed as late as September 1st 1939, and to repudiate my peace proposals at the conclusion of the campaign in Poland and France...

The hidden forces which incited England already in 1914, in the First World War, were Jews...

In this tremendous and truly historical uprising of the nations we are all now taking our part, some of us as leaders, others as actors or performers. On one side we find the exponents of democracy, that is Jewish capitalism with all its deadweight of obsolete political theories and parliamentary corruption, its out-moded social order, the Jewish brain trust, the Jewish newspapers, stock exchanges and banks, a concern of mixed political and economic profiteers of the worst order, arm in arm with the Bolshevist state. Those powers of a perverted humanity are ruling, over them the Jew, who brandishes a bloody scourge in Soviet Russia...

That I am determined to do everything in this direction in order to do justice to these problems, you, my old party comrades will not doubt. However, there's one thing I shall expect, namely that the country will give me the authority to immediately intervene and take personal charge whenever unconditional attention is not paid in the service of great and vital tasks. The front and the homeland, transportation administration, and our agriculture [?] must obey only one thought and that is to win the victory...

But if in England the idea should prevail of carrying on air warfare against the civilian population with new methods, then I should right now to state the following to the whole world: Mr. Churchill began this warfare in May, 1940. For four months I warned him and waited. Then the time came in which I was compelled to act. The person who was alone responsible for this kind of fighting began to complain. Even now my waiting is no weakness. Let this man not complain and whine again when I find myself compelled to give an answer which will bring very much suffering upon his own people.

From now on I shall repay blow with blow until this criminal himself and his work are crushed."

(http://www.ibiblio.org/pha/policy/1942/420426b.html)

FROM PSALM 146, VERSE THREE:

ג. אַל תִּבְטְחוּ בִנְדִיבִים בְּבֶן אָדָם | שֶׁאֵין לוֹ
תְשׁוּעָה:

"DO NOT PUT YOUR TRUST IN PRINCES, IN MORTAL MEN, WHO CANNOT SAVE."

SIR O. MOSLEY TO SUE B.B.C. FOR LIBEL

(THE TIMES, PAGE 13, THURSDAY JANUARY 3RD 1963)

A writ claiming damages for libel has been issued by Sir Oswald Mosley, leader of the Union Movement, against the B.B.C. and Mr. Paul Fox, a member of the B.B.C. television staff. The alleged libel is in a letter written by Mr. Fox.

Н.С.Хрущев
Доклад на закрытом заседании
XX съезда КПСС
24-25 февраля 1956 г.

Культ личности и классики марксизма

Товарищи!

В отчетном докладе ЦК КПСС XX съезду и ряде выступлений делегатов съезда, а также ранее, на пленумах ЦК КПСС, уже много говорилось о культе личности и его вредных последствиях.

После смерти Сталина, ЦК партии начал постепенно, но настойчиво проводить политику разъяснения того положения, что для марксизма-ленинизма является непозволительным и чуждым особо выделять какое-либо отдельное лицо, превращая его в сверх человека, наделенного сверхестественными качествами, приближающими его к божеству. Предполагается, что такой человек все знает, за всех думает, может делать абсолютно все и является непогрешимым в своих поступках.

Вера в возможность существования такой личности, и, в особенности, такая вера по отношению к Сталину, культивировалась среди нас в течение долгих лет.

Целью настоящего доклада не является тщательная оценка жизни и деятельности Сталина. О заслугах Сталина при его жизни уже было написано вполне достаточное количество книг, брошюр и работ. Роль Сталина в подготовке и осуществлении Великой Октябрьской Социалистической Революции, в Гражданской войне и в борьбе за построение социализма в нашей стране известна во всем мире. Всем это прекрасно известно. Сейчас мы имеем дело с вопросом, который имеет огромное значение для партии не только в настоящий момент, но будет иметь и в будущем. А именно — с вопросом о том, как постоянно рос культ личности Сталина, культ, который стал на определенной стадии своего развития источником целого ряда чрезвычайно серьезных и грубых извращений партийных принципов, партийной демократии и партийной законности.

Так как еще не вполне достаточно полно осознают практические отрицательные последствия культа личности, а также огромный вред, причиняемый нарушением принципа коллективного руководства партией и сосредоточение огромной, практически неограниченной власти в руках одного человека — ЦК КПСС считает абсолютно необходимым ознакомить XX съезд Коммунистической Партии Советского Союза с имеющимися в нашем распоряжении и относящимися к данному вопросу материалами.

Разрешите мне, прежде всего, напомнить вам, как строго классики марксизма-ленинизма клеймили всякое проявление культа личности. В письме к немецкому политическому деятелю Вильгельму Блоссу Маркс писал:

«Из-за моей антипатии к какой бы то ни было разновидности культа личности, я никогда не придавал гласности, во время существования Интернационала, многочисленные письма, которые я получал из различных стран и в которых особо выделялись мои заслуги, что всегда обижало меня. Я далее никогда не отвечал на них, за исключением тех случаев, когда я хотел отчитать автора подобного письма.

Энгельс и я присоединились к тайному обществу коммунистов при условии, что все содержавшиеся в уставе этого общества положения, допускавшие возможность суеверного почитания каких-либо авторитетов, будут исключены из этого документа. Впоследствии, Лассаль поступил совершенно противоположным образом. Несколько позднее Энгельс писал: «Как Маркс, так и я всегда были против какого-либо публичного проявления культа личности, за исключением тех случаев, когда это было действительно необходимо. И больше всего мы выступали против таких проявлений по отношению к нам самим».

Также хорошо известна чрезвычайная скромность, которой отличался великий гений революции — Владимир Ильич Ленин. Ленин всегда подчеркивал роль масс, как творцов истории, а также направляющую и организовывающую роль партии, как живого и созидательного организма и роль ее Центрального Комитета.
Марксизм не отрицает роли лидеров рабочего класса в руководстве революционным движением.

Придавая большое значение роли руководителей и организаторов масс, Ленин в то же самое время безжалостно клеймил всякие проявление культа личности, неумолимо сражался с чуждой марксизму теорией о «герое» и «толпе», выступая против всех попыток противопоставить «героя» массам и народу.
Ленин учил, что сила партии состоит в ее неразрывной связи с массами, в том, что за партией стоит народ — рабочие, крестьяне и интеллигенция.

«Только тот сможет победить и удержать власть в своих руках, — говорит Ленин, — кто верит в народ, кто окунается в источник вечно живой созидательной деятельности народа».

Ленин с гордостью говорит о коммунистической партии большевиков, как о вожде и учителе народных масс; он постоянно призывал выносить все наиболее важные вопросы на рассмотрение сознательных трудящихся и их партии. Ленин говорил: «Мы верим в это, мы видим в ней мудрость, честь и совесть нашей эпохи».

Ленин всегда категорически выступал против всех попыток, направленных на принижение или же умаление руководящей роли партии в структуре советского государства. Он выработал большевистские принципы партийного руководства и нормы партийной жизни, подчеркнув, что высшим принципом партийного руководства является коллективность. Уже в дореволюционные годы, Ленин назвал Центральный Комитет партии коллективом руководителей, а также стражем и толкователем партийных принципов. «Во время между съездами, — указывал Ленин, — Центральный Комитет охраняет и толкует партийные принципы».
Подчеркивая роль ЦК партии и его значение, Владимир Ильич отмечал: «Наш ЦК представляют собой в высшей степени сплоченный и авторитетный коллектив».

В то время, когда Ленин был жив, ЦК партии являлся действительным воплощением принципа коллективного руководства партией и страной. Будучи воинствующим марксистом-революционером, всегда непоколебимым в принципиальных вопросах, Ленин никогда не навязывал насильно своих взглядов товарищам по работе. Он всегда пытался убедить, терпеливо разъясняя другим, почему он пришел к тому или иному мнению. Ленин всегда тщательно следил за тем, чтобы соблюдались нормы партийной жизни, чтобы устав партии действовал на деле, чтобы съезды и пленумы ЦК происходили в должное время.

ЛЕНИН О СТАЛИНЕ

В дополнение к великим заслугам В. И. Ленина, выразившимся в победе рабочего класса и трудящихся масс, в победе нашей партии и в проведении в жизнь идей научного коммунизма, его необычайный ум выразился также и в том, что он вовремя заметил в Сталине ряд отрицательных качеств, которые позднее привели к весьма печальным последствиям.

Боясь за будущее партии и Советского Союза, В. И. Ленин дал Сталину абсолютно правильную характеристику, указав при этом на необходимость устранения Сталина с поста Генерального Секретаря. При этом Ленин указал, что Сталин является чрезвычайно жестоким человеком что он недостойно относится к своим товарищам, что он капризен и злоупотребляет своей властью.

В декабре 1922 года, в письме к партийному съезду, Владимир Ильич писал:

«Став Генеральным Секретарем партии, товарищ Сталин сосредоточил в своих руках огромную власть, и я не уверен в том, что он всегда будет в состоянии использовать эту власть, с необходимой осторожностью».

Это письмо — политический документ огромного значения, известный в истории партии как политическое завещание Ленина, — был распределен среди делегатов XX съезда КПСС. Вне всякого сомнения вы его уже неоднократно читали и будете еще перечитывать не один раз. Я прошу вас обратить внимание, в какой форме Владимир Ильич выражал свое волнение о будущности партии, народа, государства, о будущем руководстве партии.

Владимир Ильич говорил:

«Сталин слишком груб, и этот недостаток, вполне терпимый в среде и общениях между нами, коммунистами, становится нетерпимым в должности Генсека. Поэтому я предлагаю товарищам обдумать способ перемещения Сталина с этого поста и замены его другим человеком. Этот человек, прежде всего, должен отличаться от Сталина в основном тем, что он должен обладать большим терпением, большей лояльностью, большей вежливостью и более внимательным отношением к товарищам, быть менее капризным и т. д.».

Этот документ, оставленный Лениным, был доведен до сведения делегатов XII съезда партии, которые тогда обсуждали вопрос о смещении Сталина с должности Генерального Секретаря. Однако делегаты съезда решили оставить Сталина на посту, надеясь, что Сталин примет во внимание критические замечания Владимира Ильича и будет в состоянии побороть свои отрицательные качества, вызывавшие у Ленина такую серьезную тревогу.

Товарищи! Съезд партии должен быть ознакомлен с двумя новыми документами, которы подтверждают характеристику Сталина, данную ему Лениным в его политической завещании. Этими документами являются письма Надежды Константиновны Крупской Каменеву, который возглавлял в то время Политбюро, а также личное письмо Ленина к Сталину.
Сейчас я зачитаю вам эти документы.

Письмо Н. К. Крупской:

«Лев Борисович! Из-за короткого письма, которое я написала под диктовку Владимира Ильича с разрешения врачей, Сталин позволил себе совершить вчера по отношению к мне необычайно грубую выходку. Я не первый день в партии. В течение этих всех тридцати лет я никогда не слышала ни от кого из товарищей единого грубого слова. Дело партии и Ильича является для меня не менее дорогим, чем для Сталина. В настоящее время я нуждаюсь более, чем когда бы то ни было в контроле над собой. О чем можно и чем нельзя говорить с Ильичем, я знаю лучше, чем какой-либо врач, так как я знаю, что его волнует и что нет. Во всяком случае, я знаю это лучше Сталина. Я обращаюсь к вам к Григорию, как к близким товарищам В. И. и прошу вас защитить меня от грубых вмешательств в мою личную жизнь, а также от скверных ругательств и угроз. У меня нет никаких сомнений в том, каким будет единогласное решение Контрольной комиссии, которой Сталину, по всей вероятности, нравится грозить мне. Однако у меня нет ни силы, ни времени, которые мне было бы необходимо затратить в связи с этой ссорой. Кроме того, я живой человек, и сейчас мои нервы напряжены до предела.

Н.Крупская

Надежда Константиновна написала это письмо 23 декабря 1922 года. Два с половиной месяца спустя, в марте 1923 года, Владимир Ильич написал Сталину следующее письмо:

Письмо В. И. Ленина:

«Товарищу Сталину;
Копии: Каменеву и Зиновьеву.
Дорогой товарищ Сталин!
Вы разрешили себе грубо вызвать мою жену к телефону и грубо отчитать ее. Несмотря на тот факт, что она сказала Вам, что она согласна забыть о сказанных Вами словах, тем не менее она рассказала о случившемся Зиновьеву и Каменеву. Я не собираюсь забывать так легко о том, что делается против меня, и мне кажется, что мне здесь не нужно подчеркивать тот факт, что все, что делается против моей жены, я рассматриваю, как бы если это делалось лично против меня. Поэтому я прошу Вас тщательно взвесить, предпочитаете ли Вы взять Ваши слова обратно и извиниться, или же Вы предпочитаете разрыв между нами взаимоотношений. (Шум в зале.)

Искренне Ваш
Ленин
5 марта 1923 года.

SPECIAL REPORT TO THE 20TH CONGRESS OF THE COMMUNIST PARTY OF THE SOVIET UNION

(Closed session, February 24-25, 1956)

By Nikita Sergeyevich Khrushchev, First Secretary, Communist Party of the Soviet Union

Comrades! In the Party Central Committee's report at the 20th Congress and in a number of speeches by delegates to the Congress, as also formerly during Plenary CC/CPSU [Central Committee of the Communist Party of the Soviet Union] sessions, quite a lot has been said about the cult of the individual and about its harmful consequences.

After Stalin's death, the Central Committee began to implement a policy of explaining concisely and consistently that it is impermissible and foreign to the spirit of Marxism-Leninism to elevate one person, to transform him into a superman possessing supernatural characteristics, akin to those of a god. Such a man supposedly knows everything, sees everything, thinks for everyone, can do anything, is infallible in his behavior.

Such a belief about a man, and specifically about Stalin, was cultivated among us for many years. The objective of the present report is not a thorough evaluation of Stalin's life and activity. Concerning Stalin's merits, an entirely sufficient number of books, pamphlets and studies had already been written in his lifetime. Stalin's role of Stalin in the preparation and execution of the Socialist Revolution, in the Civil War, and in the fight for the construction of socialism in our country, is universally known. Everyone knows it well.

At present, we are concerned with a question which has immense importance for the Party now and for the future -- with how the cult of the person of Stalin has been gradually growing, the cult which became at a certain specific stage the source of a whole series of exceedingly serious and grave perversions of Party principles, of Party democracy, of revolutionary legality.

Because not all as yet realize fully the practical consequences resulting from the cult of the individual, [or] the great harm caused by violation of the principle of collective Party direction and by the accumulation of immense and limitless power in the hands of one person, the Central Committee considers it absolutely necessary to make material pertaining to this matter available to the 20th Congress of the Communist Party of the Soviet Union.

Allow me first of all to remind you how severely the classics of Marxism-Leninism denounced every manifestation of the cult of the individual. In a letter to the German political worker Wilhelm Bloss, [Karl] Marx stated: "From my antipathy to any cult of the individual, I never made public during the existence of the [1st] International the numerous addresses from various countries which recognized my merits and which annoyed me. I did not even reply to them, except sometimes to rebuke their authors. [Fredrich] Engels and I first joined the secret society of Communists on the condition that everything making for superstitious worship of authority would be deleted from its statute. [Ferdinand] Lassalle subsequently did quite the opposite."

Sometime later Engels wrote: "Both Marx and I have always been against any public manifestation with regard to individuals, with the exception of cases when it had an important purpose. We most strongly opposed such manifestations which during our lifetime concerned us personally."

The great modesty of the genius of the Revolution, Vladimir Ilyich Lenin, is known. Lenin always stressed the role of the people as the creator of history, the directing and organizational roles of the Party as a living and creative organism, and also the role of the Central Committee.

Marxism does not negate the role of the leaders of the working class in directing the revolutionary liberation movement.

While ascribing great importance to the role of the leaders and organizers of the masses, Lenin at the same time mercilessly stigmatized every manifestation of the cult of the individual, inexorably combated [any] foreign-to-Marxism views about a "hero" and a "crowd," and countered all efforts to oppose a "hero" to the masses and to the people.

Lenin taught that the Party's strength depends on its indissoluble unity with the masses, on the fact that behind the Party follows the people -- workers, peasants, and the intelligentsia. Lenin said, "Only he who believes in the people, [he] who submerges himself in the fountain of the living creativeness of the people, will win and retain power."

Lenin spoke with pride about the Bolshevik Communist Party as the leader and teacher of the people. He called for the presentation of all the most important questions before the opinion of knowledgeable workers, before the opinion of their Party. He said: "We believe in it, we see in it the wisdom, the honor, and the conscience of our epoch."

Lenin resolutely stood against every attempt aimed at belittling or weakening the directing role of the Party in the structure of the Soviet state. He worked out Bolshevik principles of Party direction and norms of Party life, stressing that the guiding principle of Party leadership is its collegiality. Already during the pre-Revolutionary years, Lenin called the Central Committee a collective of leaders and the guardian and interpreter of Party principles. "During the period between congresses," Lenin pointed out, "the Central Committee guards and interprets the principles of the Party."

Underlining the role of the Central Committee and its authority, Vladimir Ilyich pointed out: "Our Central Committee constituted itself as a closely centralized and highly authoritative group."

During Lenin's life the Central Committee was a real expression of collective leadership: of the Party and of the nation. Being a militant Marxist-revolutionist, always unyielding in matters of principle, Lenin never imposed his views upon his co-workers by force. He tried to convince. He patiently explained his opinions to others. Lenin always diligently saw to it that the norms of Party life were realized, that Party statutes were enforced, that Party congresses and Plenary sessions of the Central Committee took place at their proper intervals.

In addition to V. I. Lenin's great accomplishments for the victory of the working class and of the working peasants, for the victory of our Party and for the application of the ideas of scientific Communism to life, his acute mind expressed itself also in this. [Lenin] detected in Stalin in time those negative characteristics which resulted later in grave consequences. Fearing the future fate of the Party and of the Soviet nation, V. I. Lenin made a completely correct characterization of Stalin. He pointed out that it was necessary to consider transferring Stalin from the position of [Party] General Secretary because Stalin was excessively rude, did not have a proper attitude toward his comrades, and was capricious and abused his power.

In December 1922, in a letter to the Party Congress, Vladimir Ilyich wrote: "After taking over the position of General Secretary, comrade Stalin accumulated immeasurable power in his hands and I am not certain whether he will be always able to use this power with the required care." [1]

This letter -- a political document of tremendous importance, known in the Party's history as Lenin's "Testament" -- was distributed among [you] delegates to [this] 20th Party Congress. You have read it and will undoubtedly read it again more than once. You might reflect on Lenin's plain words, in which expression is given to Vladimir Ilyich's anxiety concerning the Party, the people, the state, and the future direction of Party policy.

Vladimir Ilyich said:

"Stalin is excessively rude, and this defect, which can be freely tolerated in our midst and in contacts among us Communists, becomes a defect which cannot be tolerated in one holding the position of General Secretary. Because of this, I propose that the comrades consider the method by which Stalin would be removed from this position and by which another man would be selected for it, a man who, above all, would differ from Stalin in only one quality, namely, greater tolerance, greater loyalty, greater kindness and more considerate attitude toward the comrades, a less capricious temper, etc."

This document of Lenin's was made known to the delegates at the 13th Party Congress, who discussed the question of transferring Stalin from the position of General Secretary. The delegates declared themselves in favor of retaining Stalin in this post, hoping that he would heed Vladimir Ilyich's critical remarks and would be able to overcome the defects which caused Lenin serious anxiety.

Comrades! The Party Congress should become acquainted with two new documents, which confirm Stalin's character as already outlined by Vladimir Ilyich Lenin in his "Testament." These documents are a letter from Nadezhda Konstantinovna to [Lev] Kamenev, who was at that time head of the Politbiuro, and a personal letter from Vladimir Ilyich Lenin to Stalin.

I will now read these documents:

"LEV BORISOVICH!

"Because of a short letter which I had written in words dictated to me by Vladimir Ilyich by permission of the doctors, Stalin allowed himself yesterday an unusually rude outburst directed at me.

This is not my first day in the Party. During all these 30 years I have never heard one word of rudeness from any comrade. The Party's and Ilyich's business is no less dear to me than to Stalin. I need maximum self-control right now. What one can and what one cannot discuss with Ilyich I know better than any doctor, because I know what makes him nervous and what does not. In any case I know [it] better than Stalin. I am turning to you and to Grigori [Zinoviev] as much closer comrades of V[ladimir] I[lyich]. I beg you to protect me from rude interference with my private life and from vile invectives and threats. I have no doubt what the Control Commission's unanimous decision [in this matter], with which Stalin sees fit to threaten me, will be. However I have neither strength nor time to waste on this foolish quarrel. And I am a human being and my nerves are strained to the utmost.

"N. KRUPSKAYA"

Nadezhda Konstantinovna wrote this letter on December 23, 1922. After two and a half months, in March 1923, Vladimir Ilyich Lenin sent Stalin the following letter:

"TO COMRADE STALIN (COPIES FOR: KAMENEV AND ZINOVIEV):

"Dear comrade Stalin!

"You permitted yourself a rude summons of my wife to the telephone and a rude reprimand of her. Despite the fact that she told you that she agreed to forget what was said, nevertheless Zinoviev and Kamenev heard about it from her. I have no intention to forget so easily that which is being done against me. I need not stress here that I consider as directed against me that which is being done against my wife. I ask you, therefore, that you weigh carefully whether you are agreeable to retracting your words and apologizing, or whether you prefer the severance of relations between us.

"SINCERELY: LENIN, MARCH 5, 1923

(Commotion in the hall.)

(http://agitclub.ru/spezhran/hruzev1.htm)

THE PREQUEL: IT HAPPENED HERE

AN ALTERNATIVE TRUE HISTORY

PROLOGUE

The roots and origin of the new World Order were a direct result of the aftermath of the 'Cuban crisis' in nineteen sixty-two and the actual catalysts were the PLANNED assassination of the young United States President on Friday November twenty-second nineteen sixty-three by TWO assassins and then, three days later, the equally dramatic and meticulously prepared massacre in central London.

In the United Kingdom, events then focused around Harold Wilson, a politician whose career and reputation had been the subject of much speculation and conjecture, whilst accusations of his loyalty and the POSSIBLE infiltration of the Labour Party by extreme left wing, even Communist agents persisted ,but ultimately it was his actions following either extraordinary pressure, blackmail, or, if his detractors had been correct about his true loyalties, his betrayal and treason. But he is no longer alive to defend his soiled reputation and actions for his execution for High Treason have, for some, conveniently closed any review of THEIR later actions or his real reasons.

These revelations, and others, now follow in YOUR journey of discovery.

ONE

Monday 31 December 1962

Dawn

55. 500639, 38. 515491

He sat precariously on the corner of the bed listening to the guard outside of his bedroom who was singing to himself an old peasant tune. He had not slept well for nearly three months and he had developed a new routine which only partially compensated for his lack of sleep.

His feet searched and found his slippers which they wriggled into and he cautiously walked to the door where his dressing gown hung from a peg. There was just about enough light seeping through the gap at the bottom of the door for him to successfully don the dressing gown which his wife had furtively purchased through a firm in Helsinski, a facility that was forbidden to the overwhelming majority of his fellow countrymen.

It was only when he was in the dacha that he was able to live a relatively normal life and access to his staff gave him an insight into the lives of his fellow countrymen. He listened with great interest and reflected on the hopes and unfulfilled expectations which he and his associates in the Kremlin either were unaware of, or ignored, since they were more concerned with the modernisation and expansion of their military forces. The people hoped that an avalanche of consumer goods would one day become available, especially fridges and cars, but above all that food, in abundance and a greater variety, would fill the shop shelves.

He opened the bedroom door and the guard immediately sprung to attention, but relaxed when a gentle movement of his leader's hand signalled his wishes.

The guard saw the man quietly walk along the corridor, briefly pausing outside of two adjacent bedrooms, which that night were occupied by four very important visitors, but then as the man walked past the stairs a young officer, undoubtedly on his first posting, was shocked by the man's presence and stood rigidly to attention, his body frozen half in surprise, the other half uncertain of the expected protocol. With unnecessary courtesy the man knocked before entering the last door in the corridor which housed the permanently occupied communications centre and even as the door was opened the unmistakeable mechanical sounds of the equipment, printing out messages or deciphering encrypted messages, could be heard.

Like the guard, the three occupants immediately stood to attention, but were silently put at their ease to continue their duties.

He collected a small pile of deciphered messages which he perused, making certain that he annotated each message with his signature. None of the messages were of any consequence unlike those that he had received some three months before when for some thirty-six hours, before returning to Moscow by helicopter, the dacha and the communications room had literally been the centre and focus of power in the Soviet Union.

Simultaneously the four men were each enticed by the magnificent aroma of coffee and the wonderful smell of freshly baked bread which wafted into the room as the door was carefully opened by the chef followed by his baker who delivered two trays of cups, saucers and plates accompanied by two jugs of coffee, cream, finely granulated white sugar and fresh milk whilst the baker produced two gargantuan loaves, a black bread and a rye bread whilst one plate was covered with soft, almost runny butter and the other, golden honey.

The guard, who had been outside the bedroom, entered and was offered a chair whilst the First Secretary of the Communist Party of the Union of Socialist Soviet Republics stood watching the men, who like wild beasts, tore the bread apart, but since the loaves had just been taken from the oven the men were nearly burned and cursed in a jovial friendly manner whilst the First Secretary smiled in envy.

The chef looked at the man, understood his unspoken wishes and left the room, returning shortly afterwards with a lemon tea together with a small plate on which a number of irregular lumps of brown sugar were littered.

Outside, the novice guard had not flinched, immobile and uncertain of his orders, when the baker came out to him and the callow youth gingerly followed the baker into the communications room where he had no alternative but to stand next to the most powerful man in the Soviet Union.

Nikita Khrushchev truly enjoyed the company of his staff who were a safety valve in a world of danger and intrigue, for in truth the reason that he had not slept well for some three months was because he was insecure and frightened. What his nemesis had called the 'Cuban crisis' had been approved by the Presidium but its disastrous outcome had been blamed on him and a clique led by Leonid Brezhnev was waiting to pounce and it would need all the experience, guile and cunning that he had learned at the feet of his old boss to withstand the coming struggle.

Secondly, and he allowed himself to smile, he was under a rigid diet, imposed by his ultimate boss and if she caught him again, as she had some three weeks before, eating his favourite bread, butter and honey, then the wrath of her anger would reach out to everyone in the room and he knew that they knew her thoughts. He loved his wife very much.

He walked back to the bedroom, once more pausing outside the two bedrooms where his very special guests lay fast asleep, then entered the bedroom carefully, succeeding in not disturbing his wife and lay on the bed, supine, his mind actively considering his options as sleep overcame him.

TWO

Morning

They were woken by the joyous and boisterous sounds of children laughing, giggling, running and jumping on the wooden floor in the corridor outside of their bedroom. He saw the smile on her face and gently caressed her cheek but noticed the concern etched on her forehead. Instinctively he knew that she was worried about the safety of their four grandchildren for this was the very first time ever that they had all stayed together in the dacha. He had frequently warned and again recently reminded the commanding officer of the elite KGB troops that if any of his four grandchildren were staying in the dacha or were in the surrounding gardens, that his troops must empty their weapons. On one occasion the order had not been obeyed and such was his immense power and authority that the previous commanding officer had been summarily dismissed. He hoped, rather optimistically, that none of his beloved grandchildren would antagonise any of the innocent guards before entering their grandparent's bedroom.

Soon the "ritual" would begin. This was his greatest pleasure and joy. All the years of loyal service to the Party and the gradual accumulation of influence and power were as nothing when balanced against the supreme pleasure of being a grandparent. They were both excited for his wife knew how her husband looked forward to the expressions of love that came from the three boys and his adored granddaughter. In preparation for the "ritual" he pulled the duvet towards him, exposing his feet and both husband and wife jointly pretended to be asleep.

They heard the door open accompanied by the muted sounds of giggling. The four children entered in single file led by the eldest, a boy of fourteen followed by his younger sister some five years younger than him; behind her, followed their cousin, coincidentally some five years younger than her and finally his brother rather less than eighteen months of age, who had only recently mastered the art of walking. They congregated at the end of the bed where the eldest began to tickle the soles of his grandfather's feet but without success; he was followed by his sister who was more successful, as her grandfather was unable to stop his feet twitching and then her younger cousin completed the task as their grandfather, unable to control himself, deliberately bellowed like a giant in a child's fairytale:

"Who has woken me from my slumber?!"

At which moment all the children burst into laughter except the youngest who was unused to the game and he began to cry, running around the bed into his grandmother's open arms.

It was a very happy home.

He had set aside the rest of the morning to play with his grandchildren, but his wife Nina had decided that it was too cold outside for her husband or the children to play in the snow. They played in the large reception room with toys, games, and with their grandfather acting as a horse upon whom they rode. They exhausted him. Their energy seemed infinite, his finite and after an hour or so he conceded , sitting on a chair and asking his grandchildren to let him rest. It was at that moment, both conveniently and fortunately, that the door opened and three of his private staff entered the room. If an observer had not been previously aware or had not been warned about their appearance or did not know their history, he might have recoiled in shock, even callously describing them as grotesque, but to the grandchildren, in their innocence, who had been brought up in their company, their appearance was accepted as normal.

In 1945, at the end of the Great Patriotic War, he had decided to use his power as a member of the Politburo to help some of the true heroes of the Soviet Union, a few amongst many millions of those who had suffered in the defence of the Motherland. The first had fought in the great tank battle of Kursk, a tank captain, his T 34 had received a direct hit from a German Tiger tank and his crew had been instantaneously killed; he managed to escape from the tank but had been viciously and cruelly burnt on his face and body. The second had fought in the desperate defence of Moscow when the Teutonic hordes had reached the outskirts of the city and all seemed lost. He had valiantly remained at his post but suffered extreme frostbite losing most of his nose, some fingers and one thumb. The third man had fought in the defence of Stalingrad not knowing that the chief political officer would one day become his master and finally his friend.

He sat on the veranda, which stretched the whole length of the dacha, in a wicker chair which supported his spine, alleviating the occasional bouts of painful sciatica and his consequent cries of pain which were sometimes misconstrued by those around him as belligerence or anger. He was wearing his old grey trench coat, a reminder of the Civil War, when as a young political officer he had liberated the coat from a white officer, prior to the man`s execution. He wore his Panama, given to him as a gift by his wife, and was covered with thick woollen blankets to keep out the cold

This was the first time in many months that he felt alone with his thoughts, even though he knew that discreetly positioned were KGB officers, who would be instantaneously ready to protect him in the event of any difficulties. Another member of his staff tactfully came up to him and such was their rapport that the man knew that his master wanted some lemon tea which he promptly brought, together with some lumps of sugar and a small samovar full of hot water. Of all his staff this man had the most interesting history and, it was hoped, that the eldest grandchild would soon be ready to learn at first hand the true nature of war and not the glorified propaganda of films and books. The man had, as a student, volunteered to fight for the Republican cause in the Spanish Civil War where he had been recruited by the N K V D and schooled in the Spanish art of execution.

Unfortunately his patriotism and loyalty were cynically abused and he was used as a tool against their political enemies, especially the P.O.U.M. and it is certain that following the arrest, imprisonment and torture of Andres Nim that he executed the Spanish patriot in a prison outside of Madrid. Discarded by the N K V D (he was fortunate not to have been executed by them) he enlisted for military service on his return to the Motherland and ended his wartime service as an anonymous pawn used as fodder in the defence of some insignificant map reference in the Caucasus. Mentally and physically broken with T.B. it was only the fortunate intervention of his new patron which saved him and allowed him to rebuild his life.

The veranda faced North West and in the distance, some eighty to ninety kilometres away, lay Moscow and the centre of government. The estate was surrounded by a vast pine forest which stretched in places to a depth of five to ten kilometres and with a single exit and entrance which meandered through the pine forest to an auxiliary road which ultimately joined a main arterial road directly leading to the capital. The perimeter of the estate circumscribed by the edge of the unrelenting pine forest was defined by a wide road built to be able to carry at least two heavy lorries passing in opposite directions and was permanently cleared of snow by specially adapted lorries, which continually circulated, maintaining a clear pathway, whilst within the perimeter were well maintained lawns interspersed by orchards of apple and cherry trees which were temporarily largely hidden by layers of pristine snow. The picturesque view was spoiled by a concrete island perhaps the size of half a football pitch from which a pathway led to the dacha. Behind the residence lay a building designed to appear as a large farm yard barn where cars, used by the residents of the dacha, lorries which were used specifically to maintain the roads and vehicles for the benefit of the KGB were garaged. The estate was not only a secret location but also a place of secrets. Only the ground floor and the first subterranean level of the "barn" were used, the lower levels remaining a closely guarded secret ,for their existence and purpose would only be disclosed in the event of mortal peril to the occupiers of the dacha and their immediate family. The remainder of the ground floor and the first lower level were utilised as canteens, leisure and accommodation facilities for the officers and troops .Access to at least three lower levels by lift or a stairway was via the officers quarters and it was believed, but never discussed even in hushed tones, that there was an escape tunnel which led to a clearing deep in the forest.

From his vantage place he could both see and hear some off duty soldiers playing an impromptu game of basketball on the naked concrete circle and he felt a sense of jealousy that they were young, full of vitality and oblivious to the bitter winter as, without exception, they had discarded their military trench coats and some had even partially stripped off parts of the tops of their uniforms. Every few minutes, as reliable and regular as a metronome, a small detachment of guards led by an officer would march past the veranda and the officer would ceremoniously salute him.

He had two appointments that afternoon, the first would be to review the twice weekly intelligence report compiled specifically for his eyes only (whilst other members of the Presidium would receive a similar but edited version), the second meeting had only recently been arranged and was completely unofficial and concerned two army officers who had been arrested on the grounds of treason. He had asked to see them, and since they were being taken to Moscow, a minor detour and a short interruption, would not be recorded.

Khrushchev had not only been a witness to history but also had been part of history. His mind wandered back to 1919 when as a young political officer in the Red Army he had been present at a speech made by Nikolai Bukharin (then the editor of *Izvestia*) and he had been spellbound both by the power of his oratory and his intellectual arguments. Soon afterwards he had been spotted by Lazar Kaganovich who had promoted and sponsored his career, recognising his administrative qualities and above all his loyalty to the Party Because of his ability and loyalty, in 1932 he was elected secretary of the Moscow City Party Organisation and later the same year became the first secretary. Six years later, in 1938, he would become a candidate member of the Politburo [the former name of the Presidium] and the following year a full member.

And then, following the turmoil after the death of the "Boss" and the brief rule of Malenkov and Molotov, he was elected First Secretary. He then began a journey which he now realised contributed to his decision to make what was a seminal and crucial speech to the Twentieth Congress. He went to the *untainted* archives` of the N K V D [which by then had been reorganised and re titled, the KGB] and verified his worst fears that Andres Nim, Secretary of the P.O.U.M., had been arrested and ultimately executed by the N K V D because of the organisation`s anti Stalinist position.

He remembered.

If he had learnt only one quality of leadership from the" Boss "it was to keep his friends close to him and his potential enemies even closer.

He remembered that phone call .

His thoughts then went back nearly a quarter of a century when he accompanied the leadership to an event held at the Moscow Art Theatre on its fortieth anniversary, sometime in the autumn of 1938 [in fact, the date was 27 October-author`s note] when, as it was usual, a group photograph was taken and next to him was the evil dwarf, Nikolai Yezhov and next to him the theatre`s director Y. Boyarsky; both of whom, within twelve months, would be purged. And was it there, or another place or time when, in the company of the intellectual giant Boris Pasternak, that the great man had seen Beria and had almost been sick in his presence?

The secret police had existed prior to the revolution and had been used against its future leaders by representatives of the autocratic Tsar, especially in 1905, but since the overthrow of the Mensheviks by Lenin`s Bolsheviks it had become an even more powerful instrument of totalitarian authority. Whether it was the Cheka or its successors, the G. P.U., the O.G.P.U., the N K V D or now the current body of power, the KGB, it was still an instrument of terror, fear, oppression, and occasionally corruption. Its leaders, whether they were Felix Dzerzhinsky, Genrikh Yagoda [purged, and of course executed, for failing to indict Bukharin] Nikolai Yezhov [who carried through the Purge with manic fervour and who himself was purged] or finally the odious and incorrigible Lavrenti Beria (a perverted sexual deviant who he himself had seen commit frottage in public and had shamelessly used his own N K V D staff to cruise the streets procuring 'suitable 'female company) were not the standard bearers of the Socialism that Lenin and his associates(most now dead ,murdered in Stalin's terror) had fought for.

He remembered that phone call and the desperate, humiliating pleas of Nikolai Bukharin.

He understood that he was about to be arrested for treason and could Nikita approach the' Boss' to plead his case?

He was concerned that whilst his phone might not be tapped, that Bukharin's phone would be constantly monitored. In a cynical attempt to shake off his caller he promised to make one phone call on his behalf, but did not say that the phone call would be to Stalin's right-hand man Lazar Kaganovich and that his 'ONLY' intention was to protect his own neck.

An hour later, unexpectedly, he heard the doorbell ring and answering the door found that it was Bukharin. He realised that he was becoming enmeshed in a situation which could end his career and since it was becoming nearly impossible to communicate with the man who was now irrational, he arranged for his chauffeur to immediately take the man home and he again telephoned his mentor Kaganovich and recommended that Bukharin be immediately detained on the grounds not only of the potential danger to himself but also to the state, a course of action which when drawn to the attention of Stalin was received with great approval and laughter.

Nikolai Bukharin would soon be arrested, physically and mentally broken, convicted of treason and then executed but worst of all, despised by the nation.

Suddenly he was woken by the gentle hand of one of the members of his staff who reminded him that lunch was now ready and in order that he could prepare for his grandchildren's departure but also his two meetings.

As he entered the kitchen, without embarrassment, he went up to his wife and kissed her on her cheek, ignoring all those sitting at the table who were mainly his staff, except two KGB soldiers who had been invited by his wife, since they had been on duty that morning in the hallway outside of the bedroom ,and had, as she discovered, suffered the butt of the grandchildren`s mischievous games.  One of the soldiers looked in disbelief at the arrival of this man, the focus of his duties and the most powerful man in the nation; his fellow conscript continued, oblivious to anyone`s arrival, as he was writing to his girl friend who lived and studied in the capital city. Alerted by his associate he instinctively looked up and, galvanised, shot up and stood to attention. The man gestured with his hand and the soldier meekly and cautiously sat down not knowing where to hide his face or how to react to the situation. He therefore did not see the master of the house take a bowl of hot borscht full of boiled potatoes and a small plate upon which was heaped a pile of kasha, sit at the corner of the table and silently enjoy his repast, also consuming, with great relish a meagre portion of warm black bread that his wife permitted him to eat but without *ANY* butter or honey.

His wife kindly offered and took the young man`s letter to be posted in a special communications facility exclusive to the Presidium thereby accidentally by-passing the military censor, and unwittingly, by that simple act of kindness endangering the lives of her grandchildren but also changing the course of world history.

THREE

Afternoon

73 18 N to 73 24 N, 54 30 E to 55 10 E

The four grandchildren returned to Moscow in an official party Zil limousine, complete with curtains, driven by a KGB chauffeur and accompanied by two female KGB officers, whose main responsibility was to look after the youngest grandchild.

At the front and rear of the small cavalcade were two anonymous four-door saloon cars in which KGB officers sat, guarding the limousine. The children's grandfather observed a tear in his wife's eye as she did not know when the children could return because of their education or more important of all, because of his busy schedule.

At the entrance to the main living room stood two guards each cradling a loaded A.K. 47, they promptly stood to attention as the man walked past, opened the door for him, which he entered and he positioned himself close to a blazing fire.

He had expected and emphatically requested the prompt delivery of the two prisoners' personal files but also, and more importantly, the dossier concerning their activities including the report regarding certain military activities which were not only highly sensitive but were currently a state secret. He personally was aware of the latest developments but it was to be the subject of a long term policy decision that the Presidium was not yet ready even to review. He called an assistant, they briefly spoke and he settled down to rest or if possible doze off [a rare event in view of his busy life] until the arrival of the courier.

How long he had rested for he would never know, but when he was gently woken he felt refreshed and enthusiastic, eager to investigate the men`s special interests and intentions.

They had fought, as tank commanders, in the cauldron of hell which was the battle of Kursk. They had not only inspired their officers and men, but their bravery had been beyond any degree that the Party or the nation could demand or expect; Marshall Zhukov had personally pinned on each man the highest honour that a grateful nation could bestow. Before the war they had been contemporaries at a military academy where their lecturer had been the legendary and virulently anti Semitic former nobleman Mikhail Tukhachevsky and under his guidance they specialised and learned the techniques that their mortal enemy would soon call "the blitzkrieg", the rapid deployment and use of tank formations. Later Tukhachevsky would become Deputy People`s Commissar of Defence but along with his friend Army Commander Yakir, Commander of the Kiev Military District they would both be arrested, tried for treason and executed along with other leading members of the military hierarchy.

He already knew that one of the two had been marked out for a potential career in the diplomatic corps, as he was fluent in English (or would become so with further tuition), most likely as a military attache in London or Washington but he had been reprimanded and discreetly warned in view of his overt and vociferous support for the disgraced military hierarchy. But that was just over a quarter of a century before and his record also showed his foolishness openly criticising Stalinism when, even after the death of the Generalissimo in nineteen fifty- three, it was still highly dangerous, but his career had prospered and he was now an advisor to. He temporarily paused and remembered that some months before he had come across a report from this man, warning, in the most unequivocable terms, the dangers of a confrontation with the United States if missiles were based in Cuba. The discovery of the men's interest in a separate ,highly secret and sensitive area naturally gave serious grounds for concern and his independent opinions were dangerous in a nation that only accepted uniformity and adherence to the Party line.

FOUR

The behaviour and actions of the couriers was predictable; one carried an anonymous briefcase which was physically attached by a chain to his wrist, whilst the other two men had duplicate sets of keys to unlock the briefcase from the courier and to unlock the first of two locks located on the briefcase itself.

Even the Premier and First Secretary of the Communist Party of the Soviet Union had to sign a receipt for the documentation and would have to sign again when the documentation was returned to the couriers, such was the sensitivity of the information. The three men would always, he observed, be standing at ease, but their attention would unerringly be fixed on the papers that the First Secretary was perusing after he had opened the second lock. The compilers knew their reader well, because the presentation was always brief, succinct and double spaced so that annotations, comments and requests could be inserted. Occasionally he would ask for copies, or in certain instances further in depth reports which would normally arrive within 24 hours of his requests.

The first part was the now regular report on the current Nuclear testing programme. Between December 22nd and 25th there had been eleven successful detonations at Semipalatinsk and Novaya Zemlya including on December 24th, a detonation of twenty four point two megatonnes. He immediately realised that with the anticipated delivery of the new generation of Intercontinental Ballistic Missiles [the SS 11 series-author's comment] he could stand face to face with Kennedy, and not be threatened or blackmailed.

The second report related to the meeting less than two weeks before between Kennedy and the British Prime Minister Harold Macmillan in Nassau, Bahamas where, and it was public knowledge in the West, they had discussed the sale of the ballistic missile system, Polaris A3 P, to the United Kingdom. He was not naive. The report was, in effect, essentially a summary of information that was openly available in the West from such newspapers as *The New York* or *London Times* and he would await a subsequent report which should confirm any secret arrangements or protocols. In the meantime he penned an annotation to the report requesting *IMMEDIATELY* [His capitals- the author] full detail of the current state of their own submarine missile programme.

If the Americans and their British allies could launch a fleet of vessels without a Soviet response then the balance of power would shift inexorably to Kennedy. Research and development would have to be accelerated, let alone the theft from the United States of sensitive technological information and he could see a noose being tightened around the neck of the Soviet Union as a fleet of nuclear powered submarines could lurk undetected beneath the Atlantic, Pacific and Arctic seas waiting the orders of Kennedy and the psychopathic warmongers in the Pentagon, to throttle and strangle Socialism.

The next document was entirely new to him. How the information was obtained did not concern him, only its accuracy, because he and his predecessors and undoubtedly their opponents, through surrogates, waged an undeclared war to protect their own secrets and to uncover their enemy's more prized possessions. They had made an intelligence breakthrough and obtained information regarding a new British military aircraft code-named B.A.C. T. S. R. 2 - a tactical, strike and reconnaissance plane - with potentially outstanding performance capabilities. In documentation attached to the report, it listed its anticipated performance parameters and a further document analysed its potential capability against the Warsaw Treaty nations and the Soviet Union. It was recommended that action be taken politically, economically, and by any other means to delay or even to have the programme cancelled . The reader made brief notes on the documents requesting, as soon as possible, not only a copy for his records, but more specific information in order that a political decision could be made.

The penultimate document confirmed that information had reached Moscow concerning a leading figure in the Chinese government who had sensationally indicated his intention to defect to the Soviet Union. His identity was secret and only known to the ambassador in Peking. He could bring with him Information regarding future Chinese military intentions especially in the field of their nuclear weapons programme.

The reader smiled, for he knew something that no one else in the Soviet Union knew; that was the identity of the man, for some six months before the Soviet ambassador to Peking has sought a private meeting with the First Secretary on an unscheduled visit to Moscow. Marshall Lin Piao, designated by Chairman Mao himself as his 'Heir', had indicated his intention to defect but such a successful action would have major political repercussions and it was decided to wait until the man had actually defected before adopting a political posture [Readers may not know that the Marshall's plane was shot down and he was killed trying to escape to the Soviet Union sometime in 1971 and it is now believed by American Sinologists that this event caused a schism between the two powers] .

The final document was most unexpected. The Naval attache at the London Embassy had begun a "relationship" with a young lady who coincidentally was having a carnal [the reader understood the implication of the phraseology] association with a British Cabinet Minister and it was hoped that this could be potentially highly valuable. The reader was about to close the file when he noticed a hand written pencil note made by one of the compilers who must have had a sense of humour. It referred to an old Russian saying:

' When a Cossack drops his trousers his brains fall out into his pants.'

He could not control himself. He burst out laughing at which stage the three officers averted their eyes, pretending not to see or hear what had just happened while one of his staff rushed into the room alerted by the unusual outburst and in response the master said

"Even I am allowed to laugh at matters of State."

He completed the transfer of documentation back to the three couriers and awaited the delayed arrival of the courier with the files relating to the two prisoners and their alleged treason.

He was in the same room where a few hours before had been filled with the laughter and joy of his grandchildren and where he exhausted himself playing. The short winter's day had ended, darkness had descended and he prepared both himself and the room for his second and final meeting . He had deliberately kept the lighting low as he had recently found the glare of artificial lighting stressful, though the dancing flames emitted by the fire relaxed him and therefore he had instructed his staff to stoke up the fire.

He saw no benefit in chastising the overdue courier on his tardiness since it would serve no purpose and he had far more important problems to consider. He would use the time before the men's arrival to read not only their biographies, but also to read the details of the allegations of their treachery and treason. He had no obligation towards them, as ultimately they were just two of literally tens of thousands of serving officers in the three branches of the military forces, however he felt a commitment in view of their bravery in battle and their contribution to the final victory. Perhaps, just perhaps ,he could learn from them what their proposed treachery was and if it could be turned to his own advantage and if not, they could be disposed of, not even by a signature on a piece of paper, but by a few words spoken to one special member of his staff.

Such were their reputations and the previous preliminary reports that he had read, that he was already aware of their backgrounds, especially of one because of an overseas connection. But before he was able to read the two files the men were brought into the room, each one handcuffed on both wrists to a guard on either side of them. Undoubtedly both the guards and their captives had expected their destination to be ,most likely, a prison or military barracks where the tried and trusted methods of interrogation would be efficiently pursued, not an elegant, almost pre revolutionary private residence where a man had his back to them and was apparently enjoying the warmth of a blazing fire.

As he turned towards them ,they were all ,without exception, both guards and prisoners, shocked at the identity of the man for, even in the subdued lighting, his identity was absolutely self evident. He looked at the prisoners and was immediately shocked by their appearance for the programme of interrogation and dehumanisation had, if only unintentionally, begun. The methods that awaited them would be cruel, vicious, callous and inhuman and already the initial stages were carved and hewn in their appearances.

They had not shaved for some ten days or so; their hair was dishevelled and their clothing, dirty and unkempt. Not only that, he felt nauseous such was the smell of defecation and excreta as one of the men must have just urinated in his trousers. They were also displaying, most significantly, the signs of sleep deprivation and he remembered, because Lavrenti Beria had, on more than one occasion regaled him, with obvious pleasure and sadistic relish, details of how the prison guards, when the prisoners were allowed a temporary respite to sleep would not only adjust the clock setting and vary the meal times but prematurely wake them to disorientate them still further. He wanted time to read the men's biographies and endeavour to superficially peruse and absorb the essential elements of the dossiers. He immediately instructed the guards to release the men who were be taken to the officers quarters to be shaved (he had no intentions of letting them shave themselves as they might commit suicide), showered and provided with suitable clothing befitting their rank and status. Finally they should be given strong black coffee-without sugar.

He might initially deal with them in a more humanitarian manner because it was important to learn the answers to his enquiries and such an unexpected approach might surprise and destabilise them enough to make at least one of them cooperate, anyhow once the interrogators got hold of them, rigorously enforcing the regime of sleep deprivation and applied not only disorientation techniques, but also Beria's method of unrelenting, continuous interrogation, they wouldn't last more than a few days . Perhaps the threat or even the implied threat might loosen their tongues. He looked at the prisoners and as a parting message stated, without malice, but emphatically and chillingly:

"It is alleged that you have committed treason and it is only through my intervention that you are still alive, however you may leave this room later this evening and at my whim, without the formality of due process I could have you murdered like rabid dogs, such is the precariousness of your situation."

As the prisoners left the room he briefly spoke to one of his staff who immediately left the dacha in order to return to his home to make a special collection. In the meantime he was able to read not only their service records, biographies and a synopsis of their alleged crimes but also was able to plan how he would question them.

It was evident from the files that the intelligence services had been extremely concerned with the nature and seriousness of the men's actions. Each file was headed not only with the two men's identities but also their target and cover names, which were respectively, Alexander and Constantin, and he decided initially once and once only that he would address them by their first names but subsequently he would speak to them using their target names as this could magnify the seriousness of their situation. It was 'Alexander' who intrigued him the most. There were, undoubtedly, a number of army officers fluent in the English language but it was a hiatus in his wartime service that was of interest not only to him, but also to one of the investigating officers. From 1943 to 1944 for a period of some fourteen months, not only were his whereabouts, but also his career records, were either hidden by a veil of secrecy or it was possible that the administrators had failed to correctly maintain and update his file. The same investigating officer was also interested in his visits to Finland and his meetings with an Englishman which had been photographed; what was also interesting and thought provoking was the accidental discovery of an apparently misfiled photograph which appeared to be some twenty years old showing the prisoner with an attractive female and most surprisingly ,a man looking strangely like a younger version of the second man in the recently taken photo in Finland.

He stood between the two men and the blazing fire whose flames flickered and danced and in order to emphasise his power, four or perhaps five of his staff were strategically positioned in the room to protect their master in the unlikely, but possible event, that any one or both men might become violent but this did not arise. From then on, though even he could not see into the future, their destinies would become inextricably intertwined. He would appeal to their acceptance of reality and not to some noble, idealistic but ultimately doomed action. Again he spoke in chilling but realistic and pragmatic terms:

"Your conviction for treason, as you must know, will not only ultimately result in your execution but also dire consequences for your families. Evidence includes not only photographs but transcriptions of telephone conversations and of your clandestine meetings which were overheard or recorded. I could immediately authorise your continued (and final) journey to Moscow where you would be incarcerated and interrogated and I believe you are aware of the techniques that would be used. However brave you might be, you would both finally succumb. You will shortly have the option to accept this valiant but futile option. You will never see me again and you will most likely die not only wondering why you made such a sacrifice but how your families would suffer, not knowing the reason for their humiliation. If you cooperate and cooperate completely and openly I might be lenient and also convert your predicament into something more than a pyrrhic victory. As a sign not solely of my sincerity but of my power to protect you I am prepared to destroy some of the incriminating documentation. I intend leaving this room for a very short while to give you one opportunity to make a final and irrevocable choice."

When he returned to the room his intuition anticipated that the most interesting of the army officers, 'Alexander', would not only be the spokesman but the de facto leader, representing a consensus of their joint opinions, but also as their spokesman, explaining and defending their situation. It was therefore a surprise when 'Constantin' put himself forward to voice their position :

"Not only do we require certain guarantees, but certain conditions, especially the protection of our families and we must be permitted, within the confines of this room, to freely express, without censorship and pressure, our motives, which include adherence to the political philosophy which forms the foundation of what we define as Marxist-Leninism and what we believe is the Presidium`s continuing betrayal of that philosophy by its perpetuation of the practices of Stalinism and the evils associated with his period as First Secretary. What you call treason is what we call patriotism. You threatened us with the consequences of our actions warning us that we would be incarcerated and tortured and would have to endure that which is spoken of in the most hushed of tones, the conveyor belt. And you, both Premier and First Secretary of the Communist Party appear to have learned nothing following the suffering of the people in the Great Patriotic War and of the many people whose lives were ruined by Stalin's terror including our mentor Mikhail Tukhachevsky and the military hierarchy .They, like us, were not traitors but true patriots."

Years in the shadow of Stalin's ruthlessness had tempered his patience and forged within him an instinct for silence and, when convenient or usually when prudent, acquiescence; they had expressed his own thoughts on the direction of the nation and above all a return to the values and idealism that had been extinguished following the death of Lenin, the assassination of Kirov and the ultimate ascent to power of the Georgian psychopath and these men were undoubtedly not even aware of his speech to the Twentieth Congress and his hopes for his grandchildren's future which symbolised the future of the U.S.S.R. Now was not the time to embrace them and to express his support for their joint hopes. He was unable to admit the truth of their argument because for him, at this moment in time, the immediate future was his own survival.

"You speak of events in our recent history, ignorant of the bacillus that had infected the body of our Motherland. Had you looked at yourselves in a mirror before I ordered your physical cleansing you would have seen yourselves for what I believe you have become, traitors. You were once the elite of the elite, admired by your troops and the defenders of the nation. I saw men in the Lefortovo, innocent men, absolutely broken by the system, their bodies emaciated as yours are becoming, ulcerated ,bruised and deformed by the absence of any medical treatment and still even then knowing that their trials would be a travesty of justice, they still had a reservoir of dignity and wisdom to deny their interrogators .

Furthermore I cannot accept your joint interpretation of the Presidium's philosophy and you have made fundamental errors both in your analysis of Marxist-Leninism and of our nation's future direction. You would be best served by openly explaining what I clearly see is not only what our Party ideologists would condemn as your political heresy, but also your treason, for you were planning a military action which I now believe would not only jeopardize the security of the nation but the authority of the Party. No doubt one of you (he again expected the one identified as 'Alexander' to represent the other) will fully explain and describe what I am coming to the preliminary conclusion is some immensely impractical plan."

'Alexander' began to speak, softly and confidently: what he had to say was expressed concisely, without emotion, but went straight to the core of the plan only after which he expanded on the substance. His expertise and broad knowledge justified and confirmed the First Secretary's anticipation of his abilities: no wonder his military students or even his fellow officers appreciated his lectures but above all his expertise. And then he changed the thrust of his presentation. He alluded to two additional non military options and the structure and

76

undoubted shock of the initial military attack. He appeared embarrassed, even ashamed, as if the scenario was in contradiction to the medieval laws of chivalry and therefore dishonourable. But the First Secretary was suddenly electrified and excited by the plan. The planning department had *NEVER* proposed such an operation and he now understood why they were so interested in an area of military technology and combat which was essentially secret; not only that, the two political options would, if successfully executed, give him and the Presidium an advantage and initiative which could be battle winning. This new dimension, coupled with an earlier comment regarding the nuclear threshold could be, with refinement, a plausible and practical option.

Their initial work, suitably harnessed, was already taking on a dimension of feasibility and reality in the mind of the First Secretary. The nuclear threshold was the most dangerous stage of this or any confrontation; the rhetorical remark that the presenter had made earlier now seemed an established fact, which was that the enemy would undoubtedly not resort to tactical nuclear weapons against the occupied territory of its allies and that their destabilised opponents would, most likely, be receptive to clandestine secret diplomatic overtures giving Soviet forces and their allies the opportunity to continue their advance and expansion westwards pending a negotiated and favourable settlement. He asked himself if such an operation could be planned and executed without the knowledge of the Presidium by a close group of trusted associates and then to present the Presidium with a fait accompli. His political opponents would immediately be rendered impotent and he could purge them without the crude methods that had been employed by the 'Boss', furthermore, though it was irrelevant, the two traitors were now superfluous to his requirements and they would have to be disposed of, since he would not now wish the K G B to get hold of them and extricate knowledge of the meeting. Only the question of 'Alexander`s' history and the two photographs still intrigued him and he wished to resolve this minor irritation.

Khrushchev saw 'Constantin' as an opportunist who would be prepared to sacrifice his associate to advance his situation. He had seen the sycophants surrounding the 'Boss', ever attentive to his demands and whims, hoping that it would advance their political careers. He was, without doubt, dangerous.

If he had the time and inclination, he would test his analysis, but in the meantime he would arrange for members of his staff to take him to the barracks to be fed while he questioned 'Alexander'. He was to discover within this man not only personal qualities that made him unique but would bind them together.

FIVE

He glanced at the two photographs, compared them once again and beckoned one of his ever attentive staff to collect the photos and hand them to 'Alexander', together with the sheet of typed paper which he had previously noted and marked as important. He requested 'Alexander' to examine the photographs carefully, waited for him to peruse the documents, and then asked him:

"Why did you go to Arzamas-16, officially on an inspection tour, but accompanied by an unidentified and unscheduled companion that you compelled the Jew, the Yid, David Abramovich Fishman not to make any reference to his presence and specifically requested access to both the warhead production and the assembly lines of thermonuclear weapons in the Oblast [district- author's note] of Sarova ,Nizhniy Novgorod?"

'Alexander' did not flinch .He looked at the First Secretary, then looked down again at the two photographs. His answer was honest if not unexpected.

"Because I wanted, if it was possible, to see the achievements of Soviet science, technology and industry."

"If this is your answer, who is the man in the two photographs and who is the girl? "

"She is, no I'm sorry, she was an N K V D agent, but I have not seen her. "

He clearly stopped himself as if the information was either very personal or some inhibition precluded him from divulging any further facts.

The First Secretary could not hide his irritation and growing anger at the man's apparent reticence and lack of cooperation explaining the background and facts behind the photographs. His patience draining away, it generated a confrontational and unambiguous demand for the man's cooperation.

"You seem reticent to explain the background to the first photo which only confirms my suspicions and intuition that your co -conspirator and motives are not in the best interests of the Party and furthermore your access to Arzamas-16, one of the nation's most secret locations, appears in itself grounds for treason and the person or persons who gave you access have put themselves in grave peril."

A brief, uneasy silence descended. It was clear that there were certain events during the Great Patriotic War which even a Presidium member was unaware of. The First Secretary would have no alternative but to instigate the ultimate sanction in the absence of the man's complete cooperation.

"Mr. First Secretary and Premier, after the battle of Kursk and my award from the hands of Marshall Zhukov himself, I received a summons from Moscow and I assumed that I was to be reassigned, hopefully to a new front line position, driving the Nazi barbarians from the soil of our Motherland. Indeed, I was extremely confident, because Marshall Zhukov was greatly impressed by our achievements and I assumed wrongly, that my summons was as a result of his personal interest.

Entering a room, I was confronted by a long table at which six men sat. I was particularly drawn to one man in the middle of the group; he was highly decorated and from his dress uniform (and I incidentally still remember his exact opening words -Your valiant recklessness smashing the Nazi tank formations) I recognised his rank as that of a Major General . An officer seated adjacent to him also congratulated me on my award and then asked me how I wanted to serve the nation. I assumed that this was a preamble to my new appointment on the front line and I responded enthusiastically that I wished to serve my nation and the Party in any way and looked forward to active front line duty. It was then that one of the two men at the far end of the table asked me in excellent English-but with a distinct American accent- if I was prepared to serve the nation, utilising my previous phrase :

'In any way.'

My response was naive, and I answered in the affirmative, without a second thought; it was then that I recognised the uniform of the   N K – V D.

He continued, again in excellent English, and whilst I heard what he said I did not comprehend the ramifications of his statement.

 "You have been selected to join a secret operation in the Ukraine with immediate effect and our friends in the army command have agreed to your temporary transfer; Lavrenti Beria himself was drawn to you personally, both by your bravery and above all your knowledge of English . From now on you are under the command and authority of the N K V D who will be represented by my assistant who is sitting next to me and who incidentally is conversant in English, but is not as fluent as you. Until such time as your mission has been completed, which we estimate to be in twelve to eighteen months time, everything which now takes place is top secret, and you must not approach any of your associates or family or ever discuss your posting. You are to be congratulated on having been chosen to be involved in an operation which will have far-reaching consequences for the benefit of the nation. Later today, you will be introduced to your fellow officers, a female N K -V D officer, the other a British diplomat who was temporarily seconded by the British Embassy here In Moscow to our army."

The man and his associate rose from their chairs, walked round the table, shook my hand and then confirmed with sincerity their excitement that they would be working with such a hero of the Soviet Union and one who they hoped would inspire all those involved in the operation to fulfil the hopes and demands of their comrade ,Beria. It was only then that the first shiver, yes shiver of concern was felt, as I realised that I would be under the watchful eye of a man with a frightening reputation.

I glanced round at the Army Major General and I could see in his eyes and in his face that he was powerless to intervene and that he had no option but to acquiesce to the demands of the N K V D. Sometimes a picture is worth a thousand words and his face and eyes expressed my position and predicament.

Subsequent events moved swiftly and within an hour or so, I had been introduced to the very young woman officer and the English diplomat. Although I only had recently been married I found her most sensuous and physically attractive and had to immediately control my emotions as I realised that her first loyalty would be to the Party and Lavrenti Beria whilst mine, of course ,and it goes without saying, for me ,to my marriage vows . Our conversation switched effortlessly from Russian to English, but not as though we were each testing the other`s command of this foreign-language but if it was natural for us to converse in such a way. It was clear that she was dedicated to the Party and her position as a representative of Beria; she admitted, or let slip, that she was unaware of the nature of the posting and her responsibilities, however she was excited to be involved in what was an unusual and clandestine operation .

I found the man taciturn and reserved but even then I suspected and was subsequently proved correct in my analysis that he was not only most amiable and friendly but extremely supportive of the Russian people and their traditions, though as regards socialism and the political policies of Stalin he was most guarded and definitely quiet which probably explained my original summation of his personality.

She had a distinctive American accent, whilst his was tinged with a slight, but identifiable Muscovite accent which he soon lost.

The following morning, we were taken by a limousine, to an apparently barely used railway station, where we boarded the last carriage of a line of some four or five carriages and as we boarded I noticed also embarking were about fifty N K V D. troops ."

He digressed for a moment, glanced at the First Secretary and commented:

"When you travel by train I assume it is in extreme luxury and comfort, however when I returned to Moscow to be interviewed, the standard of the compartment was antiquated, tired, and the seats uncomfortable because the springs underneath were broken. Our compartment was, in comparison, luxurious. We were constantly interrupted by waiters entering the compartment obsequiously and dutifully enquiring our requirements for food or drink and confirmed that our lunch would be served shortly, and even provided, before we went into the dining salon, which was incidentally used exclusively by the four of us , with expensively produced menus the like of which I have never seen before or since.

The fourth member of our luncheon quartet brought with him a thick brown envelope which he flamboyantly placed underneath his buttocks for safety and proceeded to peruse his menu. I then made a judgement about this man which was also to be proved accurate: he was as overwhelmed by the environment as I was and, as I later confirmed, was the girl though the Englishman hinted that he had previously experienced such decadent pleasures. We ate magnificently. Since I may not live past tonight I will not give you the pleasure of my memories. At the end of the feast and I choose that word accurately, our future commanding officer announced that he now intended to open, read and note the orders which his superiors had prepared, and that he would meet us back in the compartment when he was ready. About an hour or so later he returned, his breath expelling the odour of foreign whisky which served as further confirmation of my assessment that he was not used to the availability of the best food and drink and he had taken advantage of the situation.

He announced, with bravado, that the orders initially confirmed his status as Camp Commander and that furthermore, as we were all under N K V D authority, that meant ultimately he had the right, without trial, to authorise the death penalty for reasons which would become apparent shortly and for the purpose of the operation that we should speak only in English and restrict ourselves to Russian in private meetings, when only the four of us were present. He ominously then stated that from now on we were incommunicado and that we would not be permitted to receive or send any correspondence to the outside world. There would be one radio in his office tuned to Moscow and we were permitted at any time to listen to the official Soviet stations but not to any foreign stations. He then explained the purpose of the camp and our responsibilities .It was now clear why we had been chosen.

The English diplomat protested in a most quintessentially British manner and in response he was advised that the orders were comprehensive and that Moscow had taken into account his commitment to the British embassy and promised that special arrangements would be put in place, however this turned out to be a worthless promise."

The First Secretary was fascinated and mesmerised by the man's story, the events so interested him that he sat as if at the fireside of an ancient Shaman, recounting with great emotion, some old traditional story that had been passed down from generation to generation.

'Alexander' spoke falteringly, frequently hesitating, sometimes returning to previous statements, either to correct an error or to amplify or clarify a statement or observation that he might have previously made. The reason for this style of delivery was simply because he was drawing on memories nearly twenty years old that he had suppressed in consequence of the two warnings, the first given in Moscow and the second in the railway carriage by the newly appointed Camp Commander. Furthermore the Premier, with an incisive intuition borne both by experience and wisdom, sensed that there were personal reasons which 'Alexander' directly mentioned or alluded to; but it was the story of the events that fascinated the Premier.

He always affectionately referred to the camp as the' Town', the inmates as the residents and their work, as their employment. How long he took to tell the story was never timed for in reality he described a patchwork of anecdotes or descriptions of aspects and events of life in the camp which the Premier used to build up a picture of the history of the location. But one crucial fact became clear and that was the specific purpose of the camp was successfully achieved. Whether or not the inmates believed the explanation for their presence or they became reconciled to the inevitable is now unimportant. What is important to the narrative is that Lavrenti Beria's demands were completely fulfilled.

The Premier detected an element of great emotion as 'Alexander' spoke of the final days of the camp when the Camp Commander addressed the inmates (he was never heard, either in public or in the privacy of the administrative complex, ever to describe them as residents) and reminded them of the promise that had been made when the camp was opened and when they had arrived from various locations, some plucked from labour or penal camps in the 'Gulag' and whose *ONLY* crime was that they were, furthermore they were all healthy and above all well fed. If anything their diet was too good. There was a sense of optimism, even joy. Some had become even more committed to the cause of Socialism and would not take advantage of the promise whilst others looked forward to the future with great expectation and the fulfilment of the promise.

But there was more: 'Alexander' told the First Secretary what had ultimately happened to him and the Englishman, but of the girl, her fate was unknown though he believed she returned to Moscow.

The First Secretary, like an excited child, interrupted the orator demanding to know what excuse was given for his absence of fourteen months or so and additionally he remembered to ask who obtained the authority for him to visit Arzamas-16.The answer to the former was somewhat of an anticlimax.

The cover story was credible but of course untrue. During the return journey to his comrades after he had supposedly left Moscow, he had been temporarily seconded to help relieve Soviet troops who had discovered a minor concentration camp. Unfortunately he had contracted typhus and had been hospitalised in a military sanatorium, recuperating and regaining his weight and strength. To the other question his answer was evasive and clearly intended to protect the identity of his sponsor and he succeeded in his deception for it was the event in the Ukraine that had seized the First Secretary's interest.

If emboldened by the First Secretary's enthusiastic response to his narrative he used the opportunity to make one further and final revelation.

"Mr. First Secretary, I have one more fact to reveal and it concerns what you have described as an ineffective and unoriginal plan .This plan was conceived at my request by the man that I have consistently described as the Englishman and I have not, as yet, told you of the events that followed his departure from the camp , his reception on his return to England and of the subterfuge that protected him, much of which I learned of after we met up again, years after the war. I appeal to your compassion or, as the nation's leader, to look upon my actions or the actions of my comrade as misguided patriotism since he was unaware of the origin of the military and political plan.

But the decision had already been made: based not on the principles of justice or fairness but of pragmatism and his need to plan an operation so unexpected, ruthless and devastating that its consequences would overwhelm both the nation`s enemies and his political foes at home who believed that soon they would usurp and end his political career and any influence in the Presidium.

SIX

Evening

Nina had gone to bed earlier than usual and he had dismissed most of his staff other than two specially trusted members, whose skills would be required that night. The prisoners were in the officers` quarters and had undoubtedly been well fed in accordance with his instructions and although denied strong alcohol should have been supplied with Georgian wine. They had unwittingly opened new vistas for him and he was mentally busy planning how he could convert their concepts into a viable scheme without arousing the suspicions of those members of the Presidium who he sensed were contemplating or even planning his political demise . A number of decisions had already been made and he realised that once he had begun he would cross the Rubicon and there could be no turning back.

The prisoners were now in the custody of his elite KGB guard who had been instructed to deliver them, not to the originally intended destination in the Moscow area but to a military aerodrome where they would be temporarily held, pending further instructions. Whilst the two men would be held 'incommunicado' their immediate families would be taken into protective custody again also pending the Premier`s further instructions. These actions symbolised that the Rubicon had been crossed.

About an hour or so into the journey East ,one of the First Secretary's staff , who had been requested to accompany the two men in order to verify that his Master`s requirements were complied with, asked that the convoy be halted as he wished to answer a call of nature, mentioning a secluded location some ten to fifteen minutes away, adjacent to an isolated but strategically located fuel station , appropriately positioned to service long distance lorry traffic .

When they reached the location , the station had closed for the night but there was one single lorry presumably waiting for the station to open in the morning. The man asked if

"Anyone wanted to go for a pisch?"

Suggesting to 'Constantin' that it might be a good idea to relieve himself of the near full bottle that he had drunk, to which he received a positive answer .

The car exited the road and drove to the side of the unlit office behind which was a rudimentary urinal.' Constantin' and the First Secretary`s two representatives, one of whom carried a torch, exited the car, however they found the urinal securely locked and bolted; ignoring the situation the man put the torch in his pocket, opened his trench coat, undid his belt and dropped his trousers before pisching over a metre ahead of himself. 'Constantin' imitated his predecessor and physically indicated his intention to outdistance his opponent and proceeded to undress in a like manner. As he put his hand to his organ and began to outperform his opponent (by perhaps half a metre or so), the first contestant deftly moved behind the defenceless man, raised both hands, as if imitating some anachronistic or archaic religious act, and then dropped a garrotte across the man`s throat, nimbly pulling the wooden bars as close together as possible to exert the maximum tension, the same as he had done, with great personal satisfaction, less than a decade before when he executed Lavrenti Beria [who had anticipated a bullet in his neck and was grovelling and urinating as he lost control of his functions].

The blood exploded from an artery somewhere near the victim`s throat, as he automatically but vainly struggled, whilst the second man firmly holding his right arm was doused with a combination of urine and blood. Resistance was both futile and short, the executioner let go the pressure after perhaps a minute or so and the lifeless corpse collapsed in the snow in such a position that like a macabre epilogue his protruding tongue appeared to lick his own blood and urine which stained the pristine snow. The assistant left the site and ambled over to the lorry, without a care in the world, and beckoned the hearse to follow him.

The lorry, with its extra passenger and the deceased, reached the outskirts of Moscow and a steel foundry, where the body was unceremoniously consigned to the blazing furnace and oblivion, following in the footsteps of the man who had, on the orders of Stalin himself ,overseen the development of the first Soviet Nuclear explosion on August 29th 1949.

Nikita Sergeyevich Khrushchev, First Secretary and Premier of the U.S.S.R. and of course, by definition, member of the Presidium, but above all a loving husband and proud grandfather, sat alone in his wife`s kitchen sipping his lemon tea amidst the silence. As if subconsciously, he looked up to a shelf positioned above that luxury of the decadent West, a large joint refrigerator and deep freezer and immediately recognised his beloved first wife's collection of old pre revolution cookbooks battered and well thumbed, and if he remembered correctly, her little drawings to remind her – and others – what dishes to avoid or which ones to be altered, always clearly specifying the measures to be used or added. He reminisced. He had been rewarded with two happy marriages but still could not reconcile himself to the cruelty of life and how, as his career advanced, that she had been taken from him.

This mood of nostalgia suddenly opened the door to another half forgotten and perhaps corrupted memory.

All those years ago he had been sitting in his apartment in Moscow, just as he was now, sipping his lemon tea when the telephone rang and he spoke to Nikolai Bukharin. He thought it strange that a humble glass of lemon tea could spark from the depths of his mind such ancient and above all trivial memories.

He looked up at the clock, stared into infinity and calculated that his orders, or certainly the first part, should have just been achieved.

It had been a long day and he felt the necessity for sleep. For the first time in three months he would sleep well and tomorrow by the Gregorian calendar it would be New Year's day, nineteen sixty-three. He very briefly wondered what his destiny would be and quickly fell into a deep relaxing slumber, sleeping the sleep of the innocent.

Outside , the bitter Siberian wind pressed ever Westwards.

THE PREQUEL:IT HAPPENED HERE

AN ALTERNATIVE TRUE HISTORY

THE END OF DEMOCRACY

THE DECEPTION

January 23rd 1963

ONE

The bitter Siberian wind pressed ever Westwards, relentlessly endeavouring to invade and occupy any orifice or space which would succumb to its invisible, frigid tentacles. Sir Hugh Stephenson had prudently located a position where he was both partially shielded, not only from the worst extremes of the wind but also, if there were any late night travellers, from any investigation of his presence. His back to the wind, he afforded himself further protection by raising the velvet collar of his exquisitely tailored, elegant, black woollen coat, covered his head with his favourite bowler hat and rather inelegantly placed his gloved hands inside the coat pockets thereby very slightly stooping.

Standing at the corner of Prince Consort Road and Exhibition Road he looked North to the Alexandra Gate and beyond to the blackness of Hyde Park and Kensington Gardens. Soon he would, by necessity, return to the 'safe' house that had been so promptly and without question provided for him, by his friends in the secret organisation M I 6. His thoughts concentrated on the recent event outside of Moscow and, more surprisingly, his own involvement. He was brought back to reality when, most unexpectedly, he heard the sound of singing coming ever closer to him. He automatically moved back one step, hiding himself in the shadow of a building, slightly reorienting his line of vision and saw coming towards him, on the other side of the road, a group of young revellers following the vanguard of a raised Union Jack and singing, with great gusto and fervour, repeatedly the first and only the first verse of Rule Britannia. He searched for his Hunter but was unable to read the dial, however he logically estimated that the time was around three a.m. He was gripped both by surprise at their rather late (or conversely, their very early) act of patriotism which filled him with pride and hope in the next generation which would lead his country. Their parents' generation had answered the call to duty and had kept alight the flame of freedom and liberty but he hoped that even now in such a dangerous world it would not be necessary to call upon their children to again make the supreme sacrifice.

Slowly, with the combination of wind direction and the Doppler shift, the strains faded into oblivion and silence.

'Rule, Britannia! Britannia, rule the waves: Britons never will be slaves.'

Sir Hugh Stephenson was the Chairman of The Joint Intelligence Committee, a body shrouded in secrecy whose responsibility was the evaluation of intelligence and above all the assessment and analysis of such information in order that senior Government Ministers, especially including the Prime Minister and the heads of the three armed forces could be advised and guided in their decisions.

The press was gagged by the imposition of a 'D' notice that effectively banned the public disclosure of the very existence of this body, however the Committee, and the composition of its membership, was a well known fact not only to the Intelligence community and the Country's allies but apparently also to the Warsaw Pact nations and more especially to their political master, the Soviet Union. Unconfirmed, but anecdotal evidence suggests that The Daily Express journalist Chapman Pincher (a specialist writer on Intelligence and defence matters) used to, whenever he met Hugh Stephenson, doff his trilby and in good faith and more particularly in acknowledgement of his position address him as Mr. Chairman.

The journey to the 'safe' house was short but he was temporarily exposed to the full force of the wind which had increased in intensity and severity so much so that when he reached his destination his cheeks felt raw as if they had been slashed by a blunt razor blade. He was already aware of the essential outline of the previous week's event and he had excused himself from the diplomat's monologue and report and above all the machine gun like rat-a- tat-tat of his secretary's aged, but in her hands, or should it be sensitive finger tips?, Underwood typewriter.

As he climbed the few steps to the entrance of the mansion block of flats his mind focused on some of the background facts which might put into perspective the report and observations that he would shortly review and analyse. Since the autumn and what he coined 'The Cuban Adventure' both the United States and The Soviet Union seemed to have realised that the proximity and potential of a thermonuclear holocaust had not only narrowly been avoided but was shown to be frightfully inevitable in the absence of diplomatic communication and compromise .Furthermore Britain`s irrelevance as a 'super power' had been painfully exposed since negotiations had been conducted between the two real super-powers without even the hint or even an informal request for the intercession or involvement of Her Majesty`s Government. This, therefore ,was the reality of world power confirmed by a recent article in *The Times* which reported that Moscow Radio had announced that *Pravda* would soon publish the text of President Kennedy`s message to First Secretary Khrushchev of December 18th.

The Chairman of the Soviet Communist Party was, at heart, a realist and pragmatist, for earlier in the month *Pravda* had also reported, following his visits to Poland and then the German Democratic Republic (East Germany), where he had made a speech to the Congress of the East German Socialist Unity Party, that:

'War will devastate both sides. Seven hundred million victims of first nuclear blow.'

Khrushchev had been influenced by his immediate, if only short term predecessor, Malenkov, who had stated publicly in March 1954 of the hydrogen bomb, in those chilling ominous tones of *HIS* predecessor Stalin, that:

'...A new World War, given modern weapons, would mean the destruction of World civilisation.'

If only to confirm his analysis and the irony of the situation, whilst his official position was in effect perhaps the ultimate advisor to Her Majesty`s Prime Minister, *The Times* had reported on New Year`s day that Moscow Radio, in a further announcement, that First Secretary Nikita Khrushchev had sent a message to Prime Minister Harold MacMillan:

'That the New Year would see the ending of all Nuclear weapons tests for all time.'

If a sense of realty had finally gripped the three World leaders then perhaps the 'arms race' and the insane expansion of nuclear weapon production might be reduced or even halted and then his work, his contribution, would have been worthwhile and not in vain. But above all his experience, his duty, and most important of all, his objective caution would mean that his advice and counsel would always favour the National self interest.

TWO

The night porter dutifully opened the old mature double oak doors with that now long since dead genuine show of respect and courtesy, fleetingly observing the bitterly cold weather and he returned to his well thumbed copy of *Picture Post*. The block of flats was luxurious, elegant, but above all, for the purposes of Sir Hugh Stephenson, discreet and convenient as it was no doubt for his friends and old school chums also for their requirements. He decided that some exercise might enhance his circulation and proceeded to ignore the lift and take the stairs to the fourth floor which he reached but his effort only confirmed the reality of his age and diminishing physical powers.

Outside of the apartment sat a solitary sentinel immersed in the previous day's *Daily Telegraph* and the crossword. His undoubted military training and relative youth combined with a respect for his superiors brought him to attention as he formally acknowledged the visitor. He spoke through the door, presumably to an associate, possibly using some coded word or phrase (this was, of course, M I 6 territory) to confirm all was well and when the door opened revealed another security officer similarly attired in a lounge suit and smoking a highly flavoured cigarette which he promptly attempted to extinguish, however the visitor was able to interrupt the man's actions so he was able to continue his pleasure.

The diplomat's statement had apparently been completed, the contents of a brown envelope translated and also the deafening and nauseating sound of the archaic, but highly effective typewriter had ceased. His secretary was in the kitchen discussing that most British of topics - the weather - whilst the diplomat with professional tact and actual experience, though delivered with hyperbole, was describing the current extreme Moscow weather. They were both enjoying an old fashioned English cup of tea which Stephenson then partook, admiring the excellent quality and classic design of both the cup and saucer and although, whilst superficially engaging himself in the irrelevance of the conversation, he was mentally focusing on the report which he could see laying on the dining room table. Excusing himself, he proceeded both to count and tally not only the original multi paged document, but also the carbon copies. Having verified the count he called in the officer, gathered up the sheets of used carbon paper and instructed the man to use his cigarette to ignite the paper and when the act had been completed he signalled him and to the man's surprise to actually crush the burnt remnants thereby destroying absolutely any possible evidence.

Cars were summonsed, which regretfully took some fifteen minutes or so to arrive (much to Stephenson's annoyance since it had been a very long day and night), when on their arrival he suggested to his secretary to recover from her labours and to return to work the following Monday.

He advised the diplomat that unfortunately the charade of his incapacitation would, by necessity, have to continue for a few days more when he promised that he could return to his family, but continuing the impression that he had been repatriated under a cloud following an accident. The offer, or actually the hint that after a few months he would receive a 'plum' posting elsewhere (probably Washington), was enough to ameliorate the situation. Stephenson then finally took the opportunity both to read the original and to make some notes and annotations on the sole carbon copy of the report.

The report was in three parts. The first described the contact, the second, the message (including the diplomat's general comments) and the final part, a translation of the accompanying document in Cyrillic:

Travelling on an approved route towards the embassy's dacha, chauffeured by a security officer, they both simultaneously became aware of a broken down car with one tyre lying in the road adjacent to the vehicle which was not only jacked up but because of its position effectively and efficiently blocked the road making it impossible to make an evasive manoeuvre. Sitting in the front left seat (it was a standard English right hand drive vehicle specially engineered at the Rover factory to cope with the extreme winter conditions) he felt his driver both automatically and instinctively lean over, open the glove compartment and take out a revolver.

Three men were standing behind the disabled vehicle and one, the shortest, walked round the car towards them and as he reached them he signalled that they should open the passenger's window and it was then that the diplomat saw, with revulsion, that the man appeared to have no nose. The man smiled as if he knew instinctively why the passenger was distressed and began to speak, first in Russian and then briefly in English. The diplomat was emphatic about the messenger's status; he was clearly no more than as he was described, a messenger, and certainly not a plenipotentiary. Indeed he was confident that the man could not understand English as the part he spoke in English seemed to be delivered without emotion or comprehension as to its meaning . The Russian was spoken in the accent of an uncouth, unsophisticated factory worker(the diplomat's verbatim comments) or more accurately an agricultural labourer, but it was the contents of the message that was important.

The messenger surprisingly addressed him by name. That initial contact immediately summonsed up the diplomat's realisation that the whole event had been meticulously planned and executed, indeed in retrospect he again realised that he did not even have time to contemplate that the scenario was a prelude either for an assassination or kidnapping attempt. The man began what was clearly a well rehearsed speech, but the delivery lacked the eloquence or inspiration of the trained or natural communicator. Such were the absence of those skills or mastery of the statement that on more than one occasion he back tracked to correct himself or to 'fill in' parts that he had omitted and wished to include:

'His master (a phrase which he repeated with fondness and respect) wished to pass on to Mr. [sic] Hugh Stephenson and his associate and friend, Sir Kenneth Strong a confidential and personal message.

Whatever our political differences, our Intelligence staff have an honourable if grudging respect both for their integrity and comprehension of the global state of power. We are aware of Sir Kenneth's war time association and relationship with the now former United States President 'Eisenhower', the man who opened 'The Second Front' and therefore permitted our glorious troops to begin their inexorable march Westwards to avenge the rape and pillage of the Motherland and perhaps he could convey sincere wishes to the former Commander in Chief for a long and healthy retirement.'

To the diplomat and to the select few readers of the report this statement could only have come from one of the highest ranking members of the ruling Presidium if not from The First Secretary himself.

As if to confirm the reader's conjecture, the messenger continued:

'My identity and the fact of my unusual contact and the origin of the document that my messenger will shortly deliver to you must, by obvious necessity, remain confidential as will further contact when I hope an additional document to supplement the first will verify my sincere intentions . You may accurately confirm my identity but for our mutual best interests please do not pursue this avenue of enquiry.'

And if with some sense of wilful humour, the messenger, and the diplomat was clear in his analysis of the man's demeanour, stated that, without emotion for he obviously did not realise the ramification of his words:

'You must really look after your secrets; anyone can get hold of them!'

The messenger then stopped for some moments as if to emphasise that the nature of his oration was to continue on a different course and he shortly resumed.

'My representative will hand to you, to be given personally to Mr.[sic] Stephenson and no one else, a document that I only received within the last fourteen days; whilst it will interest many in our military high command it is of little concern to me. I will make indirect contact one more time, but for security purposes that will be the final contact.'

The diplomat then concluded his report with a tragic observation.

"The messenger then handed over an envelope which you now have. As you know it was only opened in your presence earlier this evening, or was it early morning such has been the strain of the last few days that events and time seemed to have merged? When the man delivered the envelope I saw for the first time that his hand was horribly mutilated. He had lost not only his thumb but also two fingers and the remaining two fingers were used like a claw. He could, and I speak with compassion, have been a character from a Wagnerian Opera, a dwarf, a Nibelung from Nibelheim who had emerged from the subterranean world of Das Rheingold. "

Hugh Stephenson was only superficially interested in the man`s observations for he was reading the translation of the three page document. The sender was right; perhaps his humour was somewhat arcane and perverse but what he had said was true. British security was like a sieve. The document concerned a still partially secret but not now secret project that he himself only knew about in the vaguest terms. The subject was an advanced tactical, strike and reconnaissance aircraft with the title -B.A.C.T.S.R.2!

The messenger retraced his steps through the fine, powdery, pristine snow towards the supposedly disabled vehicle, the imprints displaying evidence of his unnatural gait. Suddenly, without warning, the chauffeur gunned the engine into life, reversed, turned round and hurriedly began the journey back towards Moscow and safety.

An eerie silence pervaded the cabin of the vehicle for a minute or so until the diplomat acknowledged the driver`s initiative which was the sole and only option and in an authoritative tone first thanked the driver for his action and then, commensurate with his status, advised the man, if he needed telling, that he should forget all about the incident and if questioned confirm that he had sensed a mechanical fault which now seemed either to have rectified itself, or he was wrong in his judgement.

The following day a meeting was arranged with the ambassador, who admitted great interest in the innocuous brown envelope, but agreed that irrespective of the sender's identity that the fewer the better that were aware of the existence of the envelope and far more important, the contents, the safer for all concerned. It was recommended that both the diplomat and the security officer be immediately repatriated on the false and spurious grounds that the former had been involved in a 'liaison' with a Russian youth and to enhance the scenario a rumour was to be circulated in the rarefied atmosphere of the diplomatic community in Moscow that his return followed a foolish and indiscreet incident. The Ambassador stressed that possibly, no likely, that the men's departure, back by Swissair via Switzerland would be noted by the originator of the message.

THREE

Hugh Stephenson welcomed his dear friend Kenneth Strong to his London Club and suggested that they immediately talk, such was the importance of the matter that he had briefly and very discreetly mentioned by telephone earlier the same day. They settled in the library, both convenient for its tranquillity and now especially as it was empty, undoubtedly because those members present (and their guests) had been drawn to the restaurant, for Stephenson understood a superb Scottish rib of beef, or as he had a particular preference, underdone racks of lamb were being served that evening. Anyway, the pleasures of the epicurean menu would be delayed such was the importance of the recent event in Moscow since affairs of national security would have to take precedence.

Strong read the copy, noting his host's notes and annotations and added his own notes in the green ink which was his trademark. When it came to the translation of the document, Stephenson could visibly see anger and shock welling up in the emotions of his old friend and associate.

For a man with the reputation and experience of Sir Kenneth Strong his initial comments were most unexpected and above all unpredictable:

"I am pleased that as yet we have not dined. It is clear that penetration of some of our most important secrets has been deep and prolonged. I could not have asked for a more comprehensive and critical analysis of the G.O.R.339 project. The sieve has leaked so much that our friends in M.I.5 and M.I.6. will have, in my long experience, an impossible task identifying the fountain from whence this cornucopia of knowledge flowed."

The waiter brought him a second Whisky and soda (an unusual act for whilst he did not follow the Temperance movement he was known for his frugal eating and drinking habits). He continued as if the opportunity to sip his drink had been used to consider the appalling state of events:

"As regard the contact, I personally suggest that you take no immediate action or even, as I suspect, go to Harold. Events in Moscow and Washington are moving inexorably towards a Nuclear Test Ban Treaty. I conclude that this is some form of contact to accelerate or promote negotiations. If you are informed of a further approach or a not dissimilar contact, please feel free to contact me at home, and as you know, at any reasonable time, unless I am playing bridge, in which case I will be incommunicado. Please can I decline your kind invitation for supper as I have to go to Gower Street to see some of our mutual friends and acquaintances about the Cabinet Minister and his indiscretion."

Stephenson dined alone, surrounded by an abnormally high volume of noise from the unusually vocal assembly of diners. The rack of lamb, slightly pink, was both succulent and excellent.

FOUR

Sir Kenneth was concerned with the depth of information about the history of the project, summarised in the three pages of a five page memo. Less than ten days later he heard again from his friend as a second contact had been made and the final two pages of the memo delivered as evidence of the sender's status.

The 'T.S.R.2'flew and ultimately only three aeroplanes were built before the project was cancelled but these events were in the future and subject to different political and other pressures, however it is illuminating to consider the total five page document.

As early as 1956 the Soviet Union was aware that The Ministry of Supply was working with the English Electric Company to develop a new fighter-bomber and in March 1957 it was known that the matter had been formalised in the General Operational Requirement 339. Crucially for Britain's enemies the specification required a supersonic all weather aircraft able to operate at high altitude at Mach Two plus, with a short take off capability and from a non concrete runway! What seemed to concern the Soviet analysts was also the requirement that the aircraft should be capable of delivering tactical nuclear weapons at low altitude and the report emphasised, in capital letters, in all weathers.

Development of the project accelerated in December 1958 when the veil of secrecy was partially lifted in the House of Commons during a statement and in January 1959 Vickers Armstrong together with the English Electric Company received the official public 'go ahead' under a new designation, Operational Requirement 343.

What had clearly concerned Sir Kenneth was the obvious and intense effort of the Soviets identifying and verifying the performance specifications which resulted in urgent plans for counter measures specifically including a new generation of ground to air missiles even more accurate and with a greater range than the version which had successfully destroyed the American spy plane, the U2, in 1960.

Even before Sir Kenneth began his security enquiries a second confrontation took place, again outside of Moscow, which was designed to change the course of history.

The Ambassador feigned not only astonishment but also total ignorance when he heard the junior diplomat`s account of the events, subsequently confirmed and verified independently by his chauffeur and security officer. Indeed the scenario was, for all intent and purposes, identical to the earlier event, the differences being the location and a new messenger, though, of course all these facts were not known to the diplomat and his driver who terminated the confrontation by emulating his predecessor`s actions, hurriedly exiting the scene, returning post haste to Moscow. This time the new messenger was described as a war veteran, heavily scarred on his face, the only visible part as he was wearing a leather and woollen cap with ear muffs. No reference was made to an earlier encounter, the same type brown coloured envelope was handed over with, unbeknownst to the recipient, the same request as to its destination and the message. When the ambassador heard the summary and of course not in any way disclosing his knowledge of an earlier meeting he realised the strategic importance of the situation.

The Ambassador took the initiative suggesting that the two men temporarily remain in the embassy compound whilst he took instructions from 'London' though this time he also contacted an old and trusted acquaintance, Sir Ivone Kirkpatrick, in the most discreet of terms, who, with great wisdom and experience suggested, coincidentally. that his best advice was to approach the two most trustworthy and competent men in London, Sir Hugh Stephenson and Sir Kenneth Strong!

The two men, together with the unopened and priceless envelope taped to the chauffeur`s thigh close to his groin, were shepherded back to the United Kingdom again via Switzerland by an obliging and cooperative group of Swiss diplomats who were able to skilfully avoid any heavy handed approaches that might have interfered with their charges.   No cover story was disseminated to explain a further repatriation of embassy employees and they ultimately finished their journey being debriefed in the same flat in Kensington.

FIVE

The appointment to meet the Prime Minister was made for the morning following the debriefing and translation of the latest 'gift'.

Harold MacMillan deftly raised the bone china tea saucer, sat back in his preferred leather armchair that had also been the favourite chair of Sir Winston Churchill, lifted the cup and imbibed the excellent brew of blended tea.   He had developed a precision of reasoning and eschewed the habit of his less intelligent predecessors who had on certain occasions argued by the use of banal slogans and summarised his thoughts and demands logically, succinctly and with the absolute minimum of irrelevant commentary.

"I first of all agree with Sir Kenneth [a mark of respect] that there has been a degree and history of penetration of our aviation project and as such confirm that the action that you have already instigated, through the appropriate departments, be carefully monitored.   The four men that have successfully been repatriated from the Soviet Union – the two diplomats and two security officers - must be again thanked for their initiative, however whilst the final decision will rest with the Foreign Secretary and his advisors I think it wise, in the national interest, that at least for the next year or so that they be quarantined in the U.K. Whilst we both appreciate that this may appear as a stain on their reputations and consequently on their careers I believe that a quiet meeting with the F.S. will resolve any misunderstandings that they may have conceived.

That said I would like you to leave me the report of the second meeting only which I will read at leisure and I will ask that you adjourn to discuss the whole affair with the Foreign Secretary as we both know that he will undoubtedly ask a number of probing questions. Perhaps in an hour or so you can collect the report and I look forward, in a week or so time, to see you again, along with Sir Kenneth - unless he is again playing bridge - to have a very quiet chat together with the Foreign Secretary and to discuss the recommendations of two men who are held in such esteem by their nemeses."

The P.M. sat back in the leather armchair, relaxed, first finished the cup of tea, read the report and then moved on to other matters of state.

In conjunction with the first 'encounter' the sender's identity was unquestionably self–evident, but it was his offer which was tantalisingly seductive. The Prime Minister's thoughts kept returning to the contents of the report.

Surprisingly it had begun with an admission of fear but then had referred to the ideological conflict which formed the basis and grounds of the so called struggle between Capitalism and Socialism, that is 'The Class Struggle'. The ultimate consequences of this confrontation, war, could result in an escalation which if unchecked might end in an uncontrollable cataclysm with an unparalleled devastation of civilisation such as was conceived by Malenkov in 1954.

The author was prepared to immediately divulge that in the late autumn or early winter-probably about the second or third week in November-that the Warsaw Treaty nations led by the German Democratic Republic and Poland intended to carry out apparently offensive manoeuvres which in reality were defensive actions planned by the two member states and supported by other member nations to test not only their battle readiness but more important their equipment under the strain and stresses of pseudo combat conditions. The fear was that this scenario might be misinterpreted as an act, or prelude to war.

In view of the 'Cuban disaster' (The Prime Minister immediately noted the word disaster as being an implied statement of the true interpretation of the outcome, when a more bland or even neutral description would have sufficed), the Soviet Union believed it not only important to secretly announce this forth coming war game but to suggest that representatives of N A T O, the United States, France and the United Kingdom be invited to witness the manoeuvres and also within certain limitations, the preparations.

The author understood that the battle scenario was an unexpected, surprise and unprovoked attack against East Germany by N A T O (the P.M. assumed that the erroneous translation of the German Democratic Republic was that of the diplomat and certainly not that of the messenger or the actual author) which punched its way to the Polish border creating a long but narrow corridor where it was held in anticipation of a Soviet Union non nuclear counter strike. Since the initial unsuccessful defence of the D.D.R. would subsequently result not only in an escalation and a dramatic increase in military activity, in the author's mind (suddenly the P.M. noted with great interest), the Soviet Presidium feared, like an uncontrollable fire, that unless the West was given prior notification of the 'War Games' the simulated fire would explode into a real conflagration.

Thus the initial stage of the deception had begun: the seeds of an immense lie sown in the minds of the men whose primary responsibility was the defence of the Realm and on behalf of their allies, the symbolic defence of freedom and liberty, the central part, the kernel of President Kennedy's inaugural speech on January the twentieth 1961.

SIX

Already two of the three super – powers (but not yet super–states) existed, the Soviet Union and the United States. By land mass and actual military power the United Kingdom continued to decline. The third super–power, China, was a sleeping giant. Founded only as recently as 1949, the culmination of virtually half a century of strife ending in a victorious civil war against the Nationalists under Chiang Kai Shek and his political party, the Kuo Min Tang.

Early in the twentieth century the last dynasty and its boy Emperor were overthrown and replaced by a Republic which was weak and unable to govern or maintain effective central control, resulting in the rise of Warlords alongside which an ongoing struggle continued between the Communists and the Nationalists with the latter all but destroying the former who managed to escape in what is now known as 'The Long March' in nineteen thirty-four. However a further, even greater, peril was to afflict the prostrate, exhausted and hungry nation when the country was invaded by the Japanese whose period of occupation was marked by a regime of callous sadism, including at a place known as 731 where prisoners were subjected to biological weapon tests and even more dreadful, their infection by various fatal diseases .

With the defeat and expulsion of the Nationalists in 1949, the Communists could begin their policy of rebuilding the country which was literally reborn, being purified and cleansed of those capitalist elements such as the despised and hated land owners and the business classes including moneylenders who were seen and perceived as 'diabolical leeches' by the leadership under the enigmatic leader, Mao Tse Tung.

China was making an enormous effort to modernise, symbolised by its secret effort to develop its own atomic bomb, so that in early 1963, both President Kennedy and First Secretary Khrushchev would have been aware of the work, though unaware that development was focused on what was to be the test site in the Province of Sinkiang in the region known as Lop Nor. The first test explosion took place in October 1964 and this investigative work will disclose for the first time the personal involvement of the First Secretary and his bribe of fissionable material to further his deception plan.

China was militarily hemmed in, to the North and West, by its assumed ideological, political and military ally, the Soviet Union, who was both wary and uncertain of the long term intentions of their enigmatic and cryptic neighbours, and to the East, the United States, whose dominant hegemony in the Pacific Ocean was enforced by a navy of immense and awesome power and with strategic bases in both Japan, who had been defeated by their occupiers in 1945, and Formosa, the home of the ousted Nationalist leader Chiang Kai Shek and his political party, the K.M.T.

It has been said that the United Kingdom and the United States, allies for approximately a hundred years, were divided by a common language, English, however Britain's decline and the rise of the United States, can be traced back to the First World War, then the 'Great Depression' and finally 'exhaustion' and virtual financial bankruptcy, following the Second World War.

The late nineteen twenties and above all the nineteen thirties were a period when extremism flourished, symbolised by the confrontation of Communism (and Socialism) against Capitalism, though in the United States, whilst there were groups of the 'Left' and 'Right' there was also a strong isolationist movement gaining inspiration and support from perhaps the Nation's greatest living hero, Charles Lindbergh, the aviator and the first man to fly the Atlantic solo.

In Europe and specifically Italy and Germany, right wing parties gained power. In Italy,Fascists under a demagogue, Benito Mussolini and in Germany, the National Socialists, under a charismatic orator, Adolf Hitler, anti democratic and anti communist whose rabid anti-Semitism can partially be traced to the fact that many of the revolutionaries in Russia were Jews though in certain cases they were 'lapsed' or no longer 'practising. In France and Great Britain right wing organisations sprung up, independent of their more successful foreign contemporaries but in part modelling and apeing themselves on the

Fascists and the Nazis as they were better known, fundamentally in their political programmes but also in their uniforms. Impetus for their creation and national support was first based on their In Europe and specifically Italy and Germany, right wing parties gained power. In Italy, Fascists under a demagogue, Benito Mussolini and in Germany, the National Socialists, under a charismatic orator, Adolf Hitler, anti democratic and anti communist whose rabid anti-Semitism can partially be traced to the fact that many of the revolutionaries in Russia were Jews though in certain cases they were 'lapsed' or no longer 'practising'. In France and Great Britain right wing organisations sprung up, independent of their more successful foreign contemporaries but in part modelling and apeing themselves on the Fascists and the Nazis as they were better known, opposition to the creation of the Communist state in Russia (founded in November 1917 by Lenin), the failed attempt at the end of the First World War in Germany to emulate the events in Russia but also and especially in the United Kingdom, the 'tidal wave' of economic failure that followed the disastrous collapse of the main stock exchange of the United States, on 'Wall Street', New York, at the end of October 1929 which resulted in the 'Great Depression'.

In the United Kingdom, there arose a number of right wing movements, most prominently the National Union of Fascists ,led by a former M.P., Oswald Mosley, not only charismatic and plausible to his growing army of followers, but who was a dangerous demagogue, however the natural conservatism of the British people and the growing realisation of the true nature of his intentions, combined with the increasing threat of militarism from expansionist Germany under Hitler, lost him support which ebbed away to the democratic parties of the less extreme right, centre and left. Mosley seemed a spent force even being interned at the beginning of the Second World War with his wife, in view not only of their rabid politics, but also more importantly, because of their support and known connection with the Country's enemy, Adolf Hitler.

At first the war, although called the Second World War, was mainly confined to the European 'arena' and only became 'global' in December 1941, following an unprovoked atack on the United States by the Japanese who then allied themselves with Fascist Italy and Nazi Germany. Britain promptly allied themselves with the United States to form the United Nations subsequently receiving much needed aid.

Such was the Machiavellian nature of European politics that, like magnetism, but for purely cynical reasons, the two opposing political philosophies of Communism and National Socialism had earlier made a non aggression pact in 1939 (which paved the way for the European war) but the *pact* was broken in June 1941 (actually on the twenty second) when Germany invaded Russia. By the end of nineteen forty-one the anathema between Capitalism and Communism was temporarily halted by the three major powers who united in the common cause to defeat and destroy Hitler and his philosophy of National Socialism.

By May 1945 the goal had been achieved in Europe and in August 1945 the United States ,supported by Great Britain, defeated Japan who were finally brought to their knees when they were hit twice within four days by a new and hitherto secret super weapon that had been developed in absolute secrecy, the atomic bomb. The United Kingdom who had been the torch bearer of freedom and democracy, was both exhausted and financially bankrupt but was recognised as the moral leader of the now free world, however true power, that is military and industrial strength now resided in the might of the Soviet Union and in the United States, then the sole possessor of the atomic bomb.

At the beginning of 1963, fundamentally the situation had not altered, though the war time alliance of the 'Big Three' had dissolved into their original political orientations; militarily all three powers now possessed an even more deadly weapon in the hydrogen bomb and were all devising new systems to deliver the weapon such as intercontinental ballistic missiles which were originally land based but beginning to be submarine launched.

This was therefore the world that Sir Hugh Stephenson saw in his privileged position and probably dreaded bequeathing to the next generation. He would soon receive a summons that even he wanted to believe was the precursor and fore runner to a new, more peaceful world, that would succeed the frightening world that he inhabited.

SEVEN

Dawn had already broken and the night porter, reaching the end of his arduous twelve hour shift, awaited with anticipation the tray from the kitchen which carried the excellent and delicious breakfast for which the Club was renowned. He exited the reception area and walked to the half ajar front door, noted the aftermath of the overnight rain, looked unsuccessfully for the overdue newspaper delivery boy and turned around with that military discipline which age had not yet overcome when suddenly he heard the sound of cracking paper. Looking down he saw a small envelope, damp from the rain and partially jammed underneath the bottom of the door. He bent down, felt a pain in the base of his back and immediately, quietly and with due respects to his surroundings uttered a silent curse and noted the addressee's name. Fleetingly he wondered when the letter had been delivered as he was always, when on duty, ever vigilant and attentive but could not remember dozing off, even for a moment ,however he, placed the envelope in the cubby hole allocated to Sir Hugh Stephenson, adjacent to the partitions for a number of M.Ps. of different loyalties and close to the special section for members of the aristocracy and the 'Fourth Estate'. The event and its memory left his mind until a week later he was summonsed to the office of the General Manager and in his company was Sir Hugh and another gentleman, who he recognised as an occasional visitor but whose identity was unknown to him.

Unusually for a Club with such a membership list and reputation what followed seemed out of all proportion to the actual event. When he recounted the interrogation to his immediate family (It was not, by any definition, a conversation) he was overwhelmed by the three men's interest in the provenance of the envelope.

"No, he had not dozed off, or worst still fallen asleep at his post."

Thinking aloud, which amazingly appeared to destabilise not only the General Manager but also Sir Hugh Stephenson and the visitor, who visibly reeled in obvious confusion, he conjectured that it might have been left by a departing member or a guest and accidentally knocked to the floor. Such was his inspired thought that this comment ended the enquiry and no more was ever heard by him on the subject.

EIGHT

The Foreign Secretary read a translated copy of the correspondence whilst the Prime Minister imposed upon Sir Kenneth Strong for both guidance and tuition to improve his poor game of Bridge realising, in fact, that his heavy work load and commitments would preclude him from improving his weak game.

'Intriguing and fascinating' was the comment from the F.S, whilst the P.M. responded with that air of assured confidence and authority that:

'The identity of the author seems indisputable.'

However the two visitors were somewhat less than confident in their joint assessment, for on the other hand it could all be a plan with some devious alternative intention and should be treated as such.

The P.M. was most concerned that a man of Stephenson 's status and most important of all, with knowledge of many State secrets, should not only be allowed out of the Country but was to meet, in the verbatim words of the original " Cyrillic" letter:

'A Red Army officer who had distinguished himself at the great tank battle of Kursk, who was an expert in tank warfare and who was authorised and permitted to give details of the proposed autumn manoeuvres.'

The letter explained that the nature of the 'contact' meant that it was not possible, at that time, to send a diplomat or someone from their Intelligence service but Mr.(sic) Stephenson would find the man, who had been additionally selected in view of his command of English, not only sincere, but an able messenger, as he would also confirm on what basis the author of the three 'contacts' would finally permit the arrangement to proceed. It was suggested that Mr. Stephenson and only Mr. Stephenson was acceptable and the Soviet army officer who would introduce himself as 'Alexander' and would request and be handed back the original of the two letters, in Paris, on a specified date at a restaurant in Montparnasse, La Coupole which was not known to the author of the letter but had been suggested as a suitable venue and location.

The author continued, though the following concluded the letter:

'That no doubt you or your associates and advisors will be concerned with your own personal security and safety, but be assured that no harm is intended and if any malicious action was intended I feel certain that there would have been adequate opportunity in London. If you wish to delay or relocate the venue, do not turn up to the meeting but leave a message at the reception that you have been delayed, though I regret to advise that to rearrange the meeting may prove to be difficult.'

If the truth was known Hugh Stephenson was secretly excited by the whole event, because he had never been directly involved in the shadowy world of intrigue and as he was to admit to his dear friend, Sir Kenneth Strong, after he successfully completed the assignment, the closest he had been to this world was the summary of agents 'reports and the recent novels of a former Second World War associate (well actually the connection was more tenuous than close), Ian Fleming.

Discreetly, Sir Kenneth explained in the broadest and vaguest terms to the head of M.I.6. that the P.M. required Hugh to meet a potential Soviet defector (at which moment 'C's' ears pricked up in interest) and it was requested that 'C' contact his opposite number in Paris to arrange some form of saturation cover in the event of any unforeseen problems or difficulty. To create totally an element of drama and absolutely unnecessary melodrama, in the event of matters getting out of hand, a cover story was already prepared that Hugh Stephenson had unexpectedly suffered a heart attack (fatal or otherwise depending on the outcome).

The meeting went off successfully without a hitch, the terms of the arrangement were clearly offered and ,in principle, accepted. However Hugh Stephenson regretted, that as the appointment began after the busy lunch hour, the best of the oysters had been consumed .

NINE

First Secretary Nikita Khrushchev began his journey on December thirty-first nineteen sixty-two and it was only then that he began to comprehend the complexity of his task. The deception had to succeed on two different but inter-connected fronts: militarily ,the United States, N A T O and her allies including especially the United Kingdom and domestically, his potential and actual rivals in the Presidium especially the scheming President Brezhnev and although now no longer a member of the Presidium but still an influential figure, his former mentor and long time friend but still an unrepentant, implacable Stalinist, Lazar Kaganovich .

Of the two fronts the former would be the most simple to organise since it was only necessary to present a scenario which was superficially credible but fulfilled the preconceived ideas of those who were to be deceived, to specially include, at the foundation of the deception, justification and an explanation of the intended increased military activity of their Warsaw Treaty allies and, at home, if only to fore stall any probing enquiries, to create a 'policy' that was not only believable but feasible and could even be presented to the Presidium as a 'fait accompli' requiring only their retrospective agreement and as an additional bonus their appreciation of his actions .

The Union of Soviet Socialist Republics was a net importer of wheat and not only was this a financial drain on the wealth of the nation but was a noose around the neck of the people which the Capitalists could tighten in the same way that the United States had tightened the blockade around Cuba, forcing the Presidium into a humiliating climb down only a few months earlier. A policy of increased wheat and grain production in the Ukraine (of course not mentioning to the nation that it was in truth to cover the deficit of the cancellation of imported grain) would be welcomed by the people and be misinterpreted by those abroad who constantly monitored Soviet domestic policy.

The true purpose reopening a number of redundant factories would, in accordance with the original plan as presented to him on December the thirty-first, conveniently facilitate the production of organo – phosphates and the manufacture of some eighteen hundred Yak 2 planes, which even he knew were essentially obsolete but would be justified and explained as a low cost method to broadcast, in bulk ,the fertiliser. Not only that, the further necessity to train low grade pilots could be utilised to use the elite of the new entrants to be trained as part of a reservoir of crews to man the new generation of planes which were now 'off the drawing board', close to the end of their development stage and had been approved for production.

Whilst a small group of planners under the overall command of 'Alexander' laboured in their isolated and secret redoubt to convert the theoretical concept into an operational plan , he had authorised the reopening of various redundant or 'moth–balled 'chemical factories. Instructions to change production from organo-phosphates would be issued by secret orders from the K G B for perhaps his greatest achievement had been to bring the Commander in chief of the General Staff, freed of stifling political control, and the head of the K G B into his confidence with the promise of a military campaign to expand and strengthen the borders of the nation and of their allies.

Diplomatically, other than the need to arrange for his Warsaw Treaty allies to press forward in the mass production of the aircraft and pilot training, was the tacit approval of his presumed ally and fellow socialist, Mao Tse Tung. He therefore drafted a secret message to his ambassador in Peking, who incorrectly believed the message was to warn the 'Great Helmsman' that there was a traitor in the highest echelons of power and to identify Lin Piao.

His choice of emissaries was, of course, restricted by the overriding need to limit knowledge of his intentions and the widening programme of action to as few as possible and his selection, which under conventional circumstances would have been viewed not only as bizarre but possibly contemptuous, ultimately was not only inspired but achieved in total all the First Secretary`s requirements.

The personal message was, having stripped off its superfluous personal greetings, a statement of his real intentions, his need for cooperation and the price that he was prepared to pay, without at any time mentioning or even hinting at the information that was in his or even in the ambassador`s knowledge.

TEN

The offer to 'Alexander' was ,without doubt, both unexpected and totally acceptable, though he was not in a position to demand or request any additional or modified terms, however it fulfilled the vacuum in his life. He could be reunited with his immediate family, though, by virtue of his work his family would be isolated in the secret retreat which they did not know was near the ever expanding subterranean complex in the Yamantau mountain.

Additionally he had to travel to Paris and deliver a message in English to a courier.

He would be accompanied by two KGB officers (a husband and wife team) who had been specially chosen and recommended by the head of their organisation, primarily, as they were multi lingual and had previously served in Paris (and would not be distracted by the hedonistic and decadent Capitalist environment) and were highly inventive should there be an attempt to kidnap their charge, since the integrity of their British opposite numbers was in doubt in view of the known number of attempts not only to infiltrate the Motherland but also to cause mayhem and distrust wherever their shadow and skullduggery reached.   Whilst their charge was aware of his supervision he was not informed that the rendez vous was being encircled by agents and representatives of the KGB and other East European allies solely to protect his life and limb .

His instructions and orders were simple and clear. He was first to identify the British representative and to assist him he would be given two photographs of the man, one of which was a full facial shot apparently taken at long range, the other possibly an extract of a more comprehensive shot which seemed to be part of a larger, wider image possibly originally incorporating figures either side of him, which he could even hand over, but it was absolutely necessary, if the meeting was to proceed, that he had to collect a five page document which he was allowed to peruse but was not permitted to read in depth. Presumably his superiors assumed that the honesty of the courier was unimpeachable and that he would keep his side of the agreement.

Once the exchange had been completed he was then instructed to deliver the substance of the report on the nature of the military exercise and that under no circumstances must he hint or imply that, in fact, he was in charge of the planning group, and that he should indicate that the operation was the initiative and concept of both Polish and East German planners.

It was even suggested, for the first time ever, that representatives from the (and these were apparently his exact words according to the report of Hugh Stephenson)' other side' unofficially view both the build up to the 'War Games' but also to watch the unfolding action.

There were a limited number of preconditions that Stephenson would think both not only reasonable but sensible, taking into account all the current circumstances. All the approved representatives would have to dress in East European civilian outfits that would be supplied by their hosts, that no photographic records could be taken (however local military photographers would be on hand with express and absolute instructions and indeed permission to record whatever they were requested to photograph or film) and that finally the arrangement had to remain a secret as public knowledge of this unique arrangement might be misconstrued , misrepresented or even used for propaganda purposes by either side.

Hugh Stephenson arrived prematurely, just as the bulk of the Parisian workers were ending their long lunch hour or two and were drifting back to their offices and shops. A few tables seemed to be lingering over extended luncheon breaks and a number of visitors wandered in possibly on the off chance of a table, some of whom must have been recommended by word of mouth, which Hugh always believed was the best advertisement for a restaurant or a show or play. However he was not solely looking at his fellow diners or the ebb and flow of new guests for he reminded himself that had been advised by his dear friend and associate, Sir Kenneth Strong, that in view of his chairmanship of a secret committee and his knowledge of many State secrets, that the P.M.`s and the F.S.`s concern was that he would be, and in Sir Kenneth`s own words, adequately protected and that he should enjoy the superb cuisine without any worry for his own safety. Indeed the Prime Minister had in the past, but unfortunately not recently, been a regular visitor and concurred that oysters should be ordered and form the centre piece of his meal.

Unfortunately life can be cruel. With that Gallic charm of resigned indifference, the waiter, probably recognising the man as yet another 'Roast Bif', announced that the best and therefore the most expensive variants had been consumed, but he could still recommend other less expensive oysters, though his customer should order promptly as there seemed to be an abnormally high demand that day. Hugh resigned himself to the inevitable and following a superb simply boiled but exquisitely cooked lobster and a fine well composed fresh salad he had,for him, the piece de resistance, ten, but not an Anglo -Saxon dozen oysters which slid down his throat, tantilising his heightened senses.

As he sipped his coffee he accidentally glanced at his Hunter and realised with the passing of time well spent and more importantly with the time differential that his appointment was imminent. The restaurant had thinned out, there were only a dozen or so diners remaining and he conjectured if any were watching him for his own protection, or if conversely their focus and concern was with the messenger.

"Mr. Stephenson? "The questioner looked across from the other side of the table.

Since, sometimes, initial impressions can forge or undermine a relationship or in this case an association, Hugh`s first reaction was of surprise as the man was surprisingly tall (he estimated six foot one to two) which seemed rather large for one who had allegedly fought inside a cramped T34 at the legendary Battle of Kursk .

He carried himself with a bearing and deportment instilled by all military organisations irrespective of loyalty, class, nationality or language.

He wore a suit but he appeared uncomfortable, not only because, to the sophisticated and trained eye, it was ill fitting, but to Hugh Stephenson, who had the knowledge and more importantly the access to some of the finest gentleman`s tailors, the quality of the material was also, to say the least, poor.  If anything it brought out his true nature , sympathy and a genuine desire to ease the man`s discomfort. He stood up, confirmed his identity in the affirmative and raised his right hand to shake the man`s hand, which afterwards he regretted as the army officer`s grip was strong and resolute, and when he subsequently reported on the meeting he described the handshake as comparable to the probable vice like grip of a Russian Bear. He instantaneously decided to put the man at ease asking if he had eaten, suggesting the dish 'of the day' but his response, unfortunately, whilst courteous, was clearly guarded as if it was a prelude to a bizarre kidnapping attempt.

In an amicable, but clearly organised way, the Russian asked for the return of the five page document which was handed over together with the two envelopes which were neatly folded and which he placed in his left hand pocket. To complete the transaction he offered to Stephenson, who was caught by surprise, the two photographs by which he had simply identified the British courier. Of course those persons more adept in the ways of intelligence had copied the five pages of the report on the B.A.C.T.S.R.2 and even the envelopes, first using the standard method of photography and then using the latest system of American technology, the Xerox photocopying machine. Of the two photographs, British Intelligence was later never definitively able to confirm the location or when the pictures had been taken since, regretfully, Hugh Stephenson was a creature of habit and his dress code and conservatism restricted his outfits.

Only once before in his life had 'Alexander' ever seen, held or had the pleasure to hold and enjoy such a grand and exquisitely produced menu and he was confused and lost in the maze of such a lengthy list made even more confusing by the fact that it appeared exclusively in French and he believed, wrongly, that the waiter had assumed that he was indeed French, when unfortunately the truth was probably more acidic as the waiter was symbolically expressing his French patriotism and cultural superiority. A dish caught his eye and with a slight oral baroque flourish requested (since, presumably, it had a Russian over tone) Chicken Kiev. Moments later Hugh Stephenson, with a quiet tone of support, congratulated him not only on an excellent and patriotic choice but then suggested, in the presence of the waiter ,that he commence his repast with the chef's ever reliable but truly Gallic achievement of French onion soup which was received by the waiter as an acknowledgement of the superiority of French cuisine and Britain's humble place in gastronomy. Whether the Englishman's intervention or guidance was that of a true knight in armour it was received with appreciation and helped to break the ice of a delicate meeting.

Taking the initiative and in hindsight perhaps, with an air of bravado, Mr. Stephenson then asked the Russian who was clearly relishing his soup:

"How many agents are protecting you, because I don't recognise any from my side and I was warned before coming here that YOUR side might attempt to kidnap me but it would appear that I am on my own and at your mercy? "

The response was as honest and surprising as if the Russian had been as worried as his English host:

"Actually I am as concerned as you are for I also was warned before my departure from Moscow that the British Secret Service could not be trusted as they were viewed as perfidious, devious and dishonourable.

They simultaneously scanned around the restaurant, ignored the romantic dalliances of the two Parisians(who were, of course, the married K G B agents), the equivalent of three tables distance away, as they were in a different world and jointly announced, even harmonising their conclusion:

"On the contrary, I believe that I am at the mercy of your secret agents wherever they may be."

That brief phrase symbolised the breaking of the ice and the invisible barrier of distrust that had initially divided the two men. Hugh Stephenson asked and was permitted to open a small notebook writing with a fine lead pencil and made notes of the message but also of those personal comments which in themselves were seemingly irrelevant but in their overall context confirmed the good faith of the information that was passed to him. In reality little more of substance was added: 'Alexander' confirmed he had been surprisingly selected to travel abroad, because, he had been told, that his command of English and his practical knowledge of tank warfare and tactics combined with the limited technical information that his superiors had supplied to him meant that he was qualified to give a report.

But he did also confirm the anticipated location of the three sites where the East Germans and Poles probably intended to centralise their tank formations and he interestingly mentioned the proposed use by both Poland and the German Democratic Republic` of their civilian fleet of YAK 2s which would be used for agricultural crop spraying in the summer months, as spotter aircraft.

If the conditions demanded by his superiors were acceptable they could meet again, in some two weeks time, at the Nuclear Test Ban Treaty Conference and confirm their agreement.

For 'Alexander', as far as he knew, the meeting in Paris was to be his only involvement, but he had enjoyed not only the company of an English gentleman (carefully NOT mentioning that this was NOT for the first time!), but also once in his life, the thrill and excitement of the world of espionage. However, on reflection, he preferred the tension and life and death struggle of the battlefield and now in his middle age the theory and planning of defensive tactics against their nation`s perceived enemies and with a sigh of wishful hope he added:

"If you represent the true nature of the British people perhaps, just perhaps, this can be the start of cooperation and not confrontation ."

Hugh Stephenson was genuinely touched by the man`s sentiments, laying down his now well used pencil and suggesting:

"I propose in the spirit both of cooperation and friendship that for possibly the first time ever the British Intelligence Service, whoever and wherever they may be, for apparently they are clearly invisible, knowingly and willingly pay for my guest, a representative of that mighty army which helped cleanse Europe of the evil of National Socialism and probably, as an unwitting agent of some secret Soviet organisation, which no doubt is manipulating all these events."

'Alexander' never revealed his real name but felt for the first time in many weeks relaxed and at ease with himself and the recent turmoil which had changed the course of his life. Hugh Stephenson was fascinated with his guest's reminiscences about the titanic Battle of Kursk and his meeting with the legendary Marshall Zhukov, whilst 'Alexander' nearly accidentally mentioned the subsequent events but stopped himself, excitedly ending his wartime memories detailing his involvement in the final push on Berlin. As he was reading the menu again, this time at the insistence of his host, like the knockout punch of a heavy weight boxer or more appropriately for one who enjoyed the intellectual challenge and logic of chess, like an unexpected sealed adjournment move of devastating consequences from a chess master of the rank of Botvinnik or Tal, he suddenly recalled the past.

The fate of his friend Mandel Goldburgh, for his selfless act had most likely saved his friend's life. Then his mind wandered, uninhibited by the boundaries of time and space and this crucial meeting which would enable him to be reunited with his family. But had SHE received the promotion that had been promised to her or was it, as in many cases, just a fraudulent incentive to motivate her?

Inexplicably the menu had, like a catalyst, reignited memories long since hidden and forgotten; the beautiful and sublime memory of the various smells that he had experienced, how they lingered like an early morning mist but unlike the mist the different fragrances enhanced and enriched his senses.

However he had to face the true purpose of the camp and not the facade and above all the promises made to the 'Residents' given by him, Natalia and Goldburgh and was it all part of a grand deception? Now he was again, at the behest of his political masters, laying the seeds of possibly a new, greater deception. What would be the consequences of his actions and above all should he risk the future happiness of his family and finally, like the man opposite him, was he being secretly monitored or was that yet another deception? His mind computed the various options, weighing them on a balance of moral, ethical and pragmatic dilemmas. He would take a chance. His responsibility to the many crossed the barriers of national loyalties and outweighed his own personal demands.

As they rose from their chairs, after the host had paid for the meal and, as is the custom, the guest thanked his host, the Russian peculiarly and rather oafishly lifted his foot which he placed on the chair and commenced to tie his shoe laces and at the same time blocking the path of his host. It was then, as Stephenson was literally face to face with his guest, that the man, deliberately, with the intention of avoiding the potential prying eyes of any witnesses who might still be in the room, endeavoured to catch the attention of his host and he moved his head from side to side as he opened his mouth to silently express the word, no.

Their two paths would only cross one more time as YOU, the reader, will learn; but immediate, more imminent events would be dramatically influenced both by the deception and more significantly by Stephenson misunderstanding his guest's basic error of social etiquette.

ELEVEN

"As safe as The Bank of England" announced Sir Kenneth Strong as he accosted his friend some one hundred yards from the restaurant, simultaneously hailing a black Citroen taxi which had been waiting to be beckoned.

Hugh Stephenson relied heavily on his pencilled notes to recount his guest's statement. They, that is Stephenson, Sir Kenneth and two senior intelligence officers from M I 6 sat in what was commonly known as a 'secure room' in the bowels of the embassy. The man who would have to advise the P.M. was requested to make an immediate oral statement which was conveniently tape recorded and then the two M I 6 officers begun to dissect each and every part of the original statement with intense forensic probing to clarify the intentions of the Soviet messenger. But in the end the four men agreed and concurred that the offer, the conditions and above all intentions appeared genuine. However the junior of the two high ranking officers with great intuition and foresight proposed that the whole offer could be part of a deception which masked a wider ,more devious plan, and continued with apologies to his superiors that in his opinion and allowing himself to conjecture, conceived that the whole plan could just be an illusion, a shield, to attack Western Europe. Stephenson was in an invidious position as ultimately and finally as the chairman of the Joint Intelligence Committee he would have to advise the P.M. The same 'junior 'officer harked back to the breach of etiquette and the man's actions at the moment of their departure that Sir Hugh had specially mentioned and subsequently clarified in the debriefing. It was agreed that more than probably it was an error, a faux pas, exposing the man's lack of social breeding; perhaps a pompous way of explaining his act but in effect most likely, the simple best explanation.

Hugh Stephenson had one question to ask that had dominated his thoughts since he entered the restaurant and the subject had been raised by his guest. Where and when had they infiltrated British agents into the restaurant to protect him? It was the senior of the two officers who responded with a reply which undermined his confidence in his own Country's intelligence services.

The response and the ensuing conversation was brief and illuminating.

"Well actually there was no one in the room. We had a couple of 'Frenchies' from the Deuxieme Bureau that our Parisian associates provided for us and we understand they had a magnificent time in the kitchen, holed up in the head chef's office, consuming the most excellent oysters that they had ever eaten since we also guaranteed their expenses."

"And the other side?"

"Well no one saw them. Knowing the KGB they were, most likely, ensconced on the other side of the road in one of the first floor offices observing everything through binoculars."

"What would have happened if they tried to kidnap me?" Enquired a frustrated and increasingly disillusioned expert in International relations.

"Only the Hebrews in Israel go in for that sort of thing. Eichmann was special to them and gentlemen have an understanding. We don't kidnap them and vice versa. Can you imagine the chaos and diplomatic ramifications if either side actively begun such a policy in the other's back garden? Any way with all the cuts being made because the country has 'never had it so good' we honestly couldn't afford to saturate the restaurant with our agents, and think of the bill. You had a wonderful lunch, the French enjoyed their oysters and we had a baguette each."

Sir Hugh Stephenson prepared a long detailed report and his conclusions which he personally handed to the F.S.as the P.M. was otherwise busy. No reference was made to cuts in the budget of the Intelligence Services but he covered himself, at the suggestion of Sir Kenneth, and recommended, even underlining in red ink, that ultimately he accepted the bona fides and sincerity of the messenger but N A T O forces including the U.S. and United Kingdom should be put on Amber Alert to balance the most unlikely deceit and treachery of the Warsaw Pact forces.

TWELVE

Vasily Chuikov watched his wife delicately undo the stitching of his best civilian jacket, taking care not to tear the satin lining, at which moment he got up and walked into the dining room (a small but separate room containing a dinner table which, dependant on the size of his guests, could accommodate eight thin people or at best six more corpulent bodies), avoiding the table and made for an isolated item of furniture diplomatically concealed or perhaps enhanced by a plush velvet drape that in truth had seen better days. Lifting the front of what must have, at one time, formed part of a curtain, he exposed a standing safe which he quickly opened using a dial on the front. Once opened he withdrew a bundle of papers and took out a small box whose contents seemed to be entirely composed of cotton wool, however he took from the box a tiny plastic container the size of a postage stamp and as thick as ten kopek coin. He returned to the kitchen where he very carefully handed the item to his wife who encased the plastic item in some tissue paper and she then sewed the whole object between the lining and the woollen cloth.

When she had finished they both sat in silence, their eyes never meeting as if they both felt too frightened or ashamed to discuss the truth. Then, as if to confront their worst fears, she looked directly at her husband and spoke as if their very lives were at risk.

"Only once did you ever talk about what you called' thinking the unthinkable'. You also spoke at the same time about a foreign book, the translation of which you had read and I remember that for a few days you kept on repeating the same phrase as if its very title had obsessed you and caused you to doubt your own professional ability and competence. I remember that phrase :

'Will the survivors envy the dead?'

I am frightened! What does your comrade in arms want?"

Her husband was unable to answer his wife as he could give no rational explanation or justify the unusual conditions of his host's invitation but he could not refuse either his dear friend and the most important man in the Soviet Union. He kissed his wife with a passion which was usually the domain of young lovers and held her in his arms, an embrace that he might never repeat.

His chauffeur had been instructed not to take his official Army limousine which would automatically bear unique registration plates, but to use an anonymous civilian registered car that might be used by an up and coming member of the Party and not the Commander in chief of the Army. He felt uncomfortable in civilian dress, yet another of his host`s demands, and finally to increase his anxiety whilst he was accompanied in a separate vehicle containing his obligatory bodyguard there were only two of them also dressed in civilian clothes, much to their obvious irritation. They reached the dacha much more than an hour later having negotiated the meandering unlit road which they had no alternative but to use, arriving at the side entrance almost but not quite unnoticed.

He was met by his host`s wife who ushered him into the kitchen where he was confronted by two of his host`s personal staff.

She looked at him and was surprised, no shocked, to see his grey and ashen face contorted in fear.

"Vasily, my dear, have you seen a spectre or a ghost? Nikky" – She suddenly realised that she had committed an indiscretion and immediately asked the two men to leave the room as she wished to privately speak to her husband`s old comrade in arms but above all his dearest friend.

"My husband is reading some state papers and will be with us shortly. But why are you wearing such drab civilian clothes when you should be wearing your full military regalia? Nikky is very proud of you but more important how your leadership, valour and final decisive victory at Stalingrad helped to promote his career in the Presidium. You are so ashen faced. Is it your dear wife, is she well?"

"Nina, first of all I will not mention to your dear Nikita, that in public you called him by his pet name that only your closest family can call him, but it is a matter that frightens both myself and my wife as we fear the First Secretary`s invitation is a prelude to my arrest, such were his strange and unusual requirements for my visit and our fear was so great that my wife sew a phial."

She gently put her finger to his lips, stopped him finishing his sentence and began to calm and reassure him.

"Dearest Vasily if I thought that my husband, in my home, intended such an evil and dishonourable deed I would have no qualms but to impose upon him the severest act of cruelty that you could imagine. I would put him back on a strict diet, however on second thoughts he would be so irritable that his associates in the Kremlin might wish to oust him ,if only for peace and quiet, or worst still he might declare war, unilaterally, and attack West Germany. I therefore think, on balance, that your wisdom and common sense will calm him."

Thus the most powerful man in the Soviet Union, when confronted by his apparent lack of consideration and tact in the privacy of his own home, appeared to understand the depth and extent of his strange and unusual demands, apologising profusely and insisting, without delay, that his dear and old friend immediately telephone his wife to assure her, not only of his safety, but, that his comrade in arms regretted any misunderstanding.

Indeed the following day, most unexpectedly, she received a bouquet of such magnitude and exquisite composition, whose fragrance was nearly, in her own word, divine, that on her husband`s later return, that they jointly burst into tears of joy.

The two men dined well but frugally. They started with a Jewish dish that had been introduced to them by Lazar Kaganovich. They called it by its Russian name, Ptchia, avoiding the Yiddish name of Fusnogge, but they both enjoyed the earthiness of the calves-foot jelly. Then followed Spiegel Carp in a rich green jelly and to finish blintzes with sour cream. They had begun the second bottle of vodka when the demeanour of the host changed inexplicably.

"My dear friend, what I have to tell you may affect our relationship for ever. When I made what you and your wife misconstrued as some unusual demands, it was solely to protect you. I have decided, late this autumn, using the front of Warsaw Treaty manoeuvres to attack and liberate West Germany and if the plan is successful to continue the momentum into France, Belgium and Holland. This is my decision and, my dear old Comrade, is not known to the Presidium but only to a very, very few members of the army and the head of the KGB, angry at the constant assertion of political control by the Party. "

Khrushchev stopped for an appreciable time then continued.

"You realise what the consequences could be for me, Nina, let alone the Party and the nation."

He continued, explaining his political reasons, part of the background, the furtive manner in which the most able and competent members of the planning bureau had been assigned to organise the operation and finally the plan which would be the vanguard of the assault on Western Germany. No mention was made of the two operations in the United States or the United Kingdom, however he stated that the catalyst that would ignite the military operation was close to finalisation and when the two non military actions had been successfully completed then, on his authority, and he stressed again, on his authority alone he would 'ignite the fuse.'"

THIRTEEN

Nikita Khrushchev was alone in his private office in the Kremlin, apparently conducting matters of State, but his outward appearance of calm determination and concentration masked his true mental condition as his mind continuously wandered back to his real concerns and the fact that temporarily, at least, his fate rested in the hands of others, though they were his trusted allies. However, in the final analysis, if his plans were uncovered before they had been successfully implemented or if they failed ,then he and he alone would incur the wrath and revenge of the Presidium and above all Leonid Brezhnev. Perhaps his state could be compared to the titanic stresses and strains of the friction between two tectonic plates passing each other as vast underground forces exerted their power in an effort to relieve themselves of their pent up potential energy .

Weeks later, in an atmosphere of euphoric success, he looked back on this period of both doubt and concern as he justified to himself and himself alone, by the dubious argument that for all men of destiny the supreme test of leadership was to conquer one's self doubt because in the final analysis, he was only answerable to himself and not his followers.

Already the strands of the labyrinthine plan were combining in his favour. He had received a report of 'The Paris' meeting accompanied by a supplementary annex which essentially, excluding some minor omissions and a few insignificant errors or corruptions was a verbatim transcript of the encounter, so accurate as if a stenographer was not only present but was in fact figuratively sitting at the same table.

He never enquired as to the method or methods involved, leaving the techniques to the experts, but the truth was, as British Intelligence suspected ,simply that their opposite numbers had been located on the other side of the street, in a first floor office using powerful binoculars but more importantly using experts in lip reading. This, combined with a 'bonus' of some two hundred and fifty U.S. Dollars each to the waiter and the sommelier to pass on anything that they may have overheard, was adequate.

But the litmus test would be the acceptance by the British of the offer.

The approach was made ,as mentioned, at the next meeting of the Nuclear Disarmament Treaty negotiations and then it became the responsibility of the puppeteers in the K G B to prepare and manipulate carefully selected officers in the military hierarchy of the D.D.R.to organise the reception and the deception of the N A T O, American and French delegates.

The K G B was beginning to take a more active role in the many strands of the conspiracy, thereby relieving the First Secretary of those minor administrative procedures for which a bureaucracy was better able to fulfil. Most important of all the K G B had set up in Milan, incidentally not far from La Scala, a private limited company (the First Secretary was not, of course, expected to understand such a bourgeois definition, but would readily grasp or comprehend its structure of anonymity) and adequately capitalised (yet another Capitalist function which again the First Secretary would again not understand or care about).

Its staff, ignorant of its true purpose and cunningly employed because of their knowledge and historical connections with various international film production companies, had negotiated and arranged with a highly respectable and prominent theatrical costumiers in London, the production, to very specific requirements, of thirty uniforms for delivery in London at a venue to be confirmed no later than October first and furthermore the commission was supplemented by an additional lucrative fee for an introduction to a specialist vehicle producer to supply, no later than November first, five lorries specially livered and with particular distinctive registration plates, again for delivery in London but at a different location.

Payment had been made by the London subsidiary of a highly respectable bank based in West Germany but the origin of the payment had been cloaked in a series of transfers (each subject to a 'handling' fee of usually half of one percent - an effective and superficially ethical procedure to buy, at a price, the professional silence of the banks) and through a 'chain' of leading eminent legal firms mainly based in Switzerland. Thus the origins of the payments were hidden and the nature of the uniforms mentioned, in passing, as being required for an Italian–German film co production which *MIGHT* begin production either in the U.K.in late autumn or more likely in the spring but with filming in Italy.

Khrushchev's confidence was raised when he was informed that the crucial foundation of the plan had been set in motion. At some risk to their anonymity and deep cover the head of North American Intelligence operations was specially activated. There was absolutely no reason why American Intelligence could ever suspect this person since they vociferously and financially supported the Republican Party and above all a strong military posture against 'Commie' aggression whilst operating a highly successful chain of travel agencies in the

United States, Canada and Mexico, thus allowing the real nature of their operation to proceed without suspicion .

The K G B had allocated the enormous sum of five hundred and fifty thousand U.S.Dollars for this most crucial part of the whole plan but expected(and even 'budgeted' to recover ninety percent of their outlay, that is five hundred thousand dollars which, by a convoluted and tortuous path, would ultimately be transferred to another cell in the United States, to be recycled and most likely used as bribes to unbutton as many secrets of the next generation U.S. military aircraft). Nikita Khrushchev was elated by these developments but did not realise or connect the first cell to information that he had recently learned.

For his overall plans to reach fruition it was essential that a satisfactory and prompt agreement be made with the Chinese .A 'delegation' had been sent some ten days before by an indirect route, and to avoid any connection with him. Thus the party of six people was described as a trade and technical delegation specialising in an area that the Chinese were becoming not only interested but also concerned, that is their increasing population and their desire to create a nationwide contraceptive programme , possibly based on a chemical additive to the water supply.

The tension and stresses that raged within him were partially caused by the delay awaiting the outcome of his representatives' meeting with Chairman Mao, a man that he considered not only inscrutable but partially, in consequence, unpredictable. He had again decided crucially to maintain a high level of secrecy and in consequence not to send an elite member of his Diplomatic Corps choosing instead three members of his own staff, two of whom he had previously used, with some success ,to convey messages via diplomats based in the British Embassy. This was a calculated gamble on his part for he realised their limitations and fallibility: each one had, in reality, memorised a portion of the message and as such, even if they individually reviewed their own portion ,could not comprehend the sum of the whole ,but in any case their loyalty to their master and their naivety would maintain the security of the message. He hoped that the Great Helmsman would be persuaded not solely by his offer but as a man of the soil by the sincerity of the almost childlike honesty of the three men.

The message -excluding the preamble-of courteous best wishes to the leader of the most populous nation on earth and to the Great Helmsman who was leading the peasants and factory workers towards the Utopia of Socialist equality, was blunt and contained a bribe , a gift, to cement the proposed arrangement .

In the greatest secrecy an elite Soviet planning group was organising a non nuclear first strike led by a Warsaw Treaty vanguard against West Germany and her N A T O allies. Of course the great Satan, the United States, would no doubt come to the aid of her allies along with her lap dog ,the British, however contingency plans had already been incorporated in the operation to minimise their joint contribution, indeed such was the scheme of action that it was hoped that the decaying structure of British power and global influence could finally be overthrown and its ever diminishing Empire left open to conquest as the Japanese had unsuccessfully attempted just over twenty years before.

The First Secretary visualised a new world order dominated by three super states; the Soviet Union whose sphere of influence would incorporate the West European peninsula , the Mediterranean basin and the oil rich Middle East, whilst China's hegemony would encompass the Far East including such former areas of British influence as Hong Kong and Singapore. He anticipated, but was not certain, that the United States would cling on to the islands that made up Japan and again, for strategic purposes ,they would also support Mao's arch nemesis , Chiang Kai Shek in Taiwan. The United States would undoubtedly make up the last member of the new triumvirate , probably absorbing former territories of the British Empire within its sphere of influence and diplomatically 'shafting 'the British Government (Chairman Mao was, according to one of the three emissaries, confused at the meaning of this word and asked his official translator to exactly translate the word. A smile was then observed on the face of the man, a rare occurrence) .

For his part ,on behalf of the Presidium , he offered complete freedom of action by his comrade in arms and liberator of the formerly oppressed masses to take any action now or in the future in what he geographically described as East- Asia. He then referred to the military confrontation over autonomy in the Ussuri river area which should now be regarded as an unfortunate misunderstanding ,or even a breakdown in communications ,and once a mutually beneficial agreement had been made they would withdraw their forces from the region.

For strategic purposes , his military planners required either landing rights or preferably access to aerodromes close to their joint border, especially in Manchuria, able to accommodate about forty long range bombers carrying a variety of weapons(Khrushchev was careful not to specify the nature and potential power of the bomb load). In return for this sign of friendship he was prepared to make an unusual gift of unquantifiable value .Soviet Intelligence had been aware, for some time, of the Chinese nuclear weapons programme and he wished their scientists and engineers well in their labours. Once they had successfully exploded their first test weapon he was prepared to authorise the delivery ,over the course of twelve or eighteen months or so, of enough Uranium and Plutonium to power up to twenty-five bombs. He understood that this would total about one hundred kilos which he was advised would come from their existing stock of reprocessed first generation nuclear weapons.

He would be able to meet Chairman Mao or Secretary Chou En Lai within days of the Chairman`s provisional agreement.

Whilst the First Secretary trusted his ambassador in Peking, since they and they alone shared the precious nugget of knowledge of the intended treachery of Lin Piao, the ambassador was not in the limited circle of those that were aware of the proposed plot that would be seen in the eyes of the Presidium as treachery. It was therefore necessary for patience and the return of the travel weary and exhausted delegation, who on their return, were unable to give an objective report, not only of the Chairman`s response to the message but also to the presentation and unique delivery. These were frustrating days for Nikita Khrushchev as he waited for some form of reply from the Chairman which, in hind sight, came swiftly, clearly exposing the great interest of the Chinese leader. It came in a bellicose request from the Chinese ambassador, not for an appointment with the appropriate Ministry but with the First Secretary himself concerning China`s anger at Soviet aggression in the Ussuri river region.

This was now the time for the First Secretary to extend his programme of deception and subterfuge.

President Leonid Brezhnev had interrupted a meeting of little consequence to respond to Khrushchev`s urgent hand written memo which appeared pregnant with information of the highest importance to the Party and the nation and he was not to be disappointed. Nikita Khrushchev showed him the ambassador`s message, which gave no indication that it was in response to his delegation`s recent visit and cynical offer. Khrushchev asked his fellow Presidium member his thoughts on the minor confrontation on the Ussuri river between armed forces of the two nations and what price would buy peace, maintain goodwill between the two countries and above all to consider if the region had any strategic military value or if there was any potential for mineral wealth that they or, in years to come, their successors might regret their predecessors `abrogation of their responsibilities. Presented with such an unexpected situation Brezhnev was unable to give an objective or even coherent response , allowing the First Secretary to recommend that:

"As he intended to leave within twelve or so hours, could his dear comrade return perhaps within nine to ten hours following his in depth enquiries?"

Leonid Brezhnev returned punctually at the due time and it was self evident that he had risen to the First Secretary's challenge as he delivered a presentation supported by obscure documentation to confirm that this barren, isolated and seemingly insignificant area was indeed necessary for the long term interests of the Party and should not be cheaply discarded .He wished his superior well on his journey and awaited his report on its outcome.

Nikita Khrushchev initially travelled by military aircraft, then by helicopter and finally, by lorry to an isolated, inconsequential venue on the edge of the Gobi desert, a place chosen by his host who turned out to be Mao's deputy, the erudite and astute Chou En Lai. After the meeting, when Khrushchev reported the events to the Presidium, listing a farrago of lies about the agenda that had been discussed, the only honest comment that he mentioned was the insane and utterly unreasonable location for such a high level of discussions and negotiations which seemed consistent with the Chinese concern for secrecy and disregard for the health of a man of his age.

The essence of the lie was Chairman Mao's anger at his Socialist partner's imperial expansion into an area which the Chinese people regarded as their sovereign territory, not only that, but the struggle of the People's army to defend their borders might mean an even more violent confrontation. The real truth was more pragmatic, cynical and Imperialistic. Both Mao and Chou wished Khrushchev success in the liberation of, and victory in, the West; furthermore the gift of the highly prized, almost magical Plutonium and Uranium (what Chou did not realise was that Khrushchev would siphon off, through the 12th Main Directorate – the body responsible for the decommissioning of obsolete nuclear weapons - the prized material) was a symbol of the trust and friendship which bound the two nations. Lastly Chou suggested, with almost Machiavellian deceit, that to confuse the Americans, the irrelevant and unimportant 'confrontation' on the Ussuri river be continued and even internationally publicised .

The brief meeting concluded with the exchange of two items of confidential information. Khrushchev warned Chou that he had received unconfirmed reports that the American C.I.A. were financing American and international climbing expeditions to the Himalayas with the secret condition that the triumphant teams would install on the conquered mountains, including Mount Everest and K2, highly sophisticated 'weather'monitoring devices which, in reality, were radiation monitors, able to analyse the fallout from the future, and he hoped successful Chinese test and subsequent tests.

Chou, on his part, noted with inscrutable interest the clearly previously unknown item of intelligence and in response confirmed that Chairman Mao was currently unavailable, fulfilling a long standing arrangement and at that very time was in a clandestine meeting with the North Vietnamese leader Ho Chi Minh, which explained his unfortunate absence, negotiating a political and military programme not only to infiltrate South Vietnam, but also to commence military action to ultimately bring down the essentially military cabal in Saigon, reunite the people and unify the peninsular. And, if as an afterthought, Chou mentioned with a tone of unemotional detachment that in order to destroy national support for American intervention, a long term strategy was and had been developed to insidiously undermine American support by the dissemination of anti war and pro peace propaganda and biased arguments by 'spontaneous' peace movements based initially inside United States universities and subsequently flowing outwards through the Intellectual elite and thence, if possible, via what had been described as the caring left wing Democrats in the Hollywood entertainment industry, who would unknowingly erode and finally destroy the nation`s will to support their government`s military plans.

The true purpose of the exercise was known to no more than thirty people, including, at maximum, only about five Polish and East German officers in the military hierarchy, of whom four were known to have been killed in a single lucky counter-strike by West German fighter-bombers. In the intelligence community most likely only three men, including the feared spymaster, Markus 'Mischa' Wolf, who had been especially requested by the head of the KG B to monitor any political or unusual military action in the West.   Wolf had been promised, symbolically, the head of his arch rival and opposite number, the former Nazi and now West German spymaster, Reinhard Gehlen.

In the Soviet Union the total number involved was about eight or nine, but certainly excluding Khrushchev`s mentor, the arch Stalinist and Jew, Lazar Kaganovich, the remainder, the bulk, being members of the military including the one man that Khrushchev not only knew intimately but could trust for his absolute loyalty, judgement and above all his ruthless attention to the challenge, his former military ally on the Volga at Stalingrad, Commander of the Sixty–second Army, now Marshall of the Soviet Union and Commander in chief of the Soviet Land Forces,Vasily Chuikov, however the circumstances surrounding the recruitment of his great ally is indicative of not only the secrecy which enveloped the clandestine venture but also sheds a light on the continuing paranoia and fear which still gripped all stratas of the nation and was a bitter legacy of the Stalin era and the Purges.

Thus a formidable organisation which included both the head and deputy head of the KGB and the elite team of planners led by 'Alexander' though small in number, was more than adequate and competent to set in motion the plan.

FOURTEEN

By the end of August nineteen sixty–three all the elements of the conspiracy were in place, though certain parts were ongoing, especially the crucial American operation which was being meticulously prepared, the catalyst ,which would trigger the whole plan. The head of the K G B, Vladimir Semichastny was absolutely confident and adamant that there was adequate time to organise the final threads of the plot. 'Sleepers' had yet to be activated ,and in consequence had never been operational, and since the head of North American Intelligence had never been in direct contact with them it had been agreed to utilise the capitalist system to investigate three sleepers to obtain an in depth resume of their present situation, especially any weaknesses which might make them vulnerable if, when activated ,they refused to cooperate. For some years the leader had indirectly monitored their whereabouts and through various attorneys instructed three different firms of private detectives to investigate the three men on the spurious but plausible grounds that they were being investigated on behalf of an aggrieved partner for acts of adultery or, as well, when applicable, their business background on behalf of a potential new business partner. Such was the apparent urgency of the instructions from the different firms of attorneys and the high price that they were readily prepared to pay the private detectives that the information including bank account numbers was quickly gathered and was sufficient to put pressure on the subjects, though only two men were ultimately selected in view of the venue of the intended operation, their proximity to that site and finally, coincidentally, their financial vulnerability.

The 'British' venture was proceeding on time, with delivery of the uniforms and the vehicles estimated by the manufacturers to be a few days earlier than as contractually agreed. Introduced again by the ever helpful theatrical costumiers (no doubt encouraged by a further commission from the film production company in Milan), three short term tenancies were arranged through different estate agents, one lying on the Essex and Suffolk borders, the second outside of Flitwick in Bedfordshire and the final site on the other side of the Thames near Kilnbrook in Kent. There was one other important matter to be arranged but it was decided to delay the arrangement until a few days before needed, to avoid, or minimise any disclosure of the adventure.

Earlier doubts or lack of confidence had been swept aside on the twentieth of June when the 'Hot Line 'had been installed and became operational both in the Kremlin and the White House, giving the First Secretary the ability and facility not only to communicate directly with the President but more importantly, to abuse the whole principle and the purpose of the new communication system.

Warsaw Treaty troops had been sent into the countryside as in previous years to help gather in the harvest and to give the soldiers a temporary break from the rigours and boredom of military service but their officers were surprised at a wave of gossip, rumour and conjecture which seemed to sweep through their men like a virulent plague, concerning the possibility of manoeuvres allegedly scheduled for the late autumn or more likely early winter.

Such was the strength and persistence (and widespread currency) that a general notice was finally issued from the High Command in the German Democratic Republic confirming that a major military manoeuvre was to commence in mid November to test the readiness of the Warsaw Treaty forces.

Only one other contingency concerned the First Secretary and he resolved to rectify what he considered to be an error of his own judgement. The planners were meticulously following the brilliantly conceived operation of Viktor Kashkarov (who still was only known to the conspirators as 'Alexander') though what it had lacked in military substance (which was why the planners were currently specially involved preparing the actual organisation of the operation), it was immensely detailed and analytical in dealing with the consequences of the political and subsequent military actions. A logical, unemotional review of the overall plan and especially of the two political acts revealed a bold and devastating hammer blow and the anticipated chaos would *UNDOUBTEDLY* result in the complete destabilisation of the enemies of Socialism which was why he had embraced the whole plan.

However he had deviated from the original concept and had incurred the dissatisfaction of the planners when he had earlier agreed and then notified them of a fait accompli by involving the navy and the Pacific submarine force in an action rashly forced upon him by the Commander in Chief of the navy, in pursuit not only of personal glory but more likely to give the navy a victory to rank alongside the great achievements forged by the Red Army during the Great Patriotic war. It was the consequences of the action which worried Khrushchev for the return was miniscule in proportion to the adverse consequences. Therefore after some considerable thought he realised that he could convert possible failure into a scheme of great deviousness possibly even indirectly involving his political foes and hastening their eclipse.

A major statement would be made by him at the next closed meeting of the Presidium early in September.

FIFTEEN

The summer of nineteen sixty–three was, for the people of Western Europe and especially also of the United States and her northern neighbour, a period of increasing prosperity and leisure. The traumas and social upheaval consequent to, and following the Second World War, were receding into the mists of history whilst new landmarks were being created. In Stockholm, Sweden, the more culturally orientated holiday makers marvelled at the recently raised wooden battleship, the Vasa, now publically on exhibition, whilst further North West, in the forests of Northern Norway athletes Harold Groenningen and Gergement Eggen diligently and conscientiously prepared themselves for the following winter`s World Skiing championships and their special discipline of cross country skiing.

In London a great dual track and field meeting had recently ended between the World`s leading power, the United States and their smaller and less formidable rival, the United Kingdom. The two day event witnessed by sell out crowds saw three world records and for the excited throng the sight of a heavily built black sprinter, Robert 'Bob'Hayes, who demonstrated his magnificent ability which many considered would bring him a Gold medal in the Olympics to be held the following year in Tokyo, Japan.

This then was but a brief snap shot of a world that did not know that war and conquest was being plotted against them and their values and that soon their world, that less than twenty years before many of them had fought to preserve, would soon end.

It was about this time but certainly before the end of September that Nikita Khrushchev completed his plans and irrevocably set in motion the series of actions which he calculated would secure his position and would, as a secondary result, change the global political map, finally terminating the illusion and the slender hold that Britain held on world power and influence.

It was temporarily convenient for the First Secretary not only to be humble but also, by clearly drawing the Presidium's attention to the Cuban Debacle which verbatim, were his own and exact words, that he was able to both gauge and sense the degree of dissatisfaction and the number of members whose attitude would expose their possible support for his removal as First Secretary. He began by stating a self evident truth that the Soviet Union could not consider itself to be a truly global power unless it was self sufficient and it was not only vulnerable but economically weak if it continued to be an importer of wheat, indeed the drain of 'hard currency' meant that other more important purchases were delayed to the detriment of economic expansion and above all the defence of the nation and her Socialist allies.

Later the tone of his statement and the manner of his delivery changed, surprising some of those present; he spoke with that didactic manner which was usually the prerogative of the intellectual elite in their support and validation, if validation was indeed necessary, of Marxist–Leninism, appearing also pedantic and doctrinaire, ending with what he also called 'the millstone' around their necks. He then announced with both pride and confidence the fact that on his authority as First Secretary he had ordered an urgent programme to produce adequate supplies of organo – phosphates and to broadcast the fertilisers, the production of a large number of antiquated, slow but highly effective Yak 2 aeroplanes and he intended to also make available both fertilizers and planes to their Warsaw Treaty allies. He sensed an ambiguous and contradictory response to his revelation but managed to obtain their overwhelming agreement when he produced a series of economic forecasts (suitably biased, as was typical with any forecast or projection, of a five year plan). Of course he knew by the time that the report was analysed and scrutinised that the conflagration would have consumed his opponents. Or himself, if his plans failed.

He continued, again surprising those present, by thanking and praising the man who he distrusted most and who had, by his outspoken attitude, earlier shown his anger at the First Secretary's unilateral actions ordering the production both of chemicals and planes. President Brezhnev was surprised at the praise heaped upon him by the Premier, who had referred to the advice and information that he had quickly collated in respect of the disputed area adjacent to the Ussuri river but above all the importance placed on the confrontation by Chairman Mao, continuing the web of lies and deceit which he had previously disseminated. No mention was made of the intended political and military action that was planned as Khrushchev calculated that he could use these events as evidence of the Imperialistic, expansionist intentions of the untrustworthy Chinese.

He concluded his report with two items.   The first, carefully constructed to create a humorous and ambiguous interpretation (which might even bring out the licentiousness in the body politick of such a geriatric group) and to alert the members of the Presidium to the perfidiousness of the British and the second, to obtain a mandate and permission for naval manoeuvres in the Pacific.

John Profumo had resigned as the British Minister of War amidst a scandal of epic proportions. All this was known to the Presidium and reported in their twice weekly intelligence reports some time before. What they did not then know, but was about be revealed to them, was the revelation of the military information that the man had divulged and which was passed to their diplomat by their mutual lover. Khrushchev had hoped for some intelligence from this corrupt and venal liaison (He avoided the use of the word 'ménage' as he wished to retain an air of gravity since he sensed that the decadence of the whole affair might convulse him into uncontrollable laughter) and he announced with great solemnity that:

" During penetration of the woman involved in the scandal by the now disgraced politician, it had resulted in him disclosing, probably as an act of bravado and arrogance, the operational programme of the British V- bomber force, but more important, confirmation of their primary and secondary targets.   Such knowledge meant that the erection (Khrushchev apparently emphasised this word, barely able to retain a posture of gravitas) and construction of various anti aircraft defences could be scaled down or even cancelled at a major saving to the defence budget. As regards the naval manoeuvres in the Pacific this was not to be an infringement of American hegemony but an attempt during the current expansion and modernisation of the Soviet's naval power to assess their latest capabilities."

SIXTEEN

Nikita Khrushchev sat alone in the kitchen of his dacha, reviewing the success of his deceptions. Brezhnev had exposed himself as a dangerous adversary and the potential focus of those who sought to usurp his power whilst Lazar Kaganovich had confirmed his obsolete and anachronistic worship of Stalin and of Stalinism. He located a piece of blank paper and the remainder of a pencil, no doubt used by his wife, and began to effortlessly, and fluently write, without reference to previous versions, what was to be a near definitive version of an ultimatum. When he finished the draft he summonsed a member of his staff who neatly cut the document vertically into three pieces and then proceeded to hide the sheets in one of the old cookery books, disposing of the previous version meticulously in the manner specified by his master. Outside, day was turning into dusk and the weather was slowly changing from the glorious warmth of late summer to the pleasant coolness of early autumn. However the changes in seasons and climate, whilst a harbinger of winter, were but a prelude to.war!

SEVENTEEN

Outside, day was turning into dusk and the weather was slowly changing from the glorious warmth of late summer to the pleasant coolness of early autumn. Mandel Goldburgh was immersed, in his own words, in the warmth and glow of sublime pleasure and emotional ecstasy. He had borrowed from a friend not only his record player but more importantly recordings of all six of the Bach Brandenburg Concertos and was currently in some Buddhist Nirvana enjoying the magnificent, stirring and beautiful fifth work.

He then decided, on the spur of the moment, to make his regular visit to London, located his diary, vacillated, but then settled on the end of November and with anticipation, entered an appropriate note for the long week end beginning Friday November twenty-second. Whilst the museums, art galleries and libraries of Manchester and the surrounding towns of the North-West satisfied his intellectual and cultural interests he had discovered, following many pilgrimages to the British Library, that it had not only a unique atmosphere and environment but its very existence stimulated his desire and craving for knowledge and wisdom.

This perhaps was at the centre and focus of the man himself. His interest in certain esoteric and arcane subjects reflected not only his personality but the unspoken and secret hopes and passions that only he understood. In truth he felt unfulfilled, as if life and events had thwarted his destiny. Since his return from the Soviet Union during the war, his life, whilst being modestly comfortable had in reality been empty and worthless, furthermore he felt unable to influence the lives of others as he stood and watched the inexorable rise of Harold Wilson. This was a situation that he found both ambiguously satisfying and at the same time frustrating since he perceived that the man was an opportunist and did not possess his own profound qualities of wisdom and compassion, however he pursued his goals in the hope that destiny or the Islamic-Arabic concept of Kismet might, by unknown or even random occurrences, open a door to a destiny that would fulfil his dreams but more importantly, permit him to be part of the flow of events to create a better, more compassionate society.

Although he believed in the brotherhood of man, universal freedom and equality he was not that naive or to express himself more crudely ,stupid, not to recognise the natural, if not inborn fallibility of man himself. The methods to fundamentally change the very fabric of society or more specifically a nation could not be achieved solely by agreement or the democratic will as expressed by the ballot box, only by an elite, a meritocracy, or an oligarchy who had a clear plan and objective but always and absolutely a moral and ethical responsibility to the nation and the people.

But this was the paradox and above all the contradiction in his argument. If the democratic process was eliminated without reference to society in general then what right had the oligarchy or the meritocracy to assume that their ultimate goal was acceptable to those upon whom a new order had been or would be unilaterally imposed?

War! He had spent twelve months of his life drawing up a plan so diabolical in its execution that he felt not only ashamed of his creation but nauseous when he thought of the suffering that would follow. He had felt a moral obligation to create a military operation of devastating force only because the request had come from a special friend, the man whose foresight and sacrifice had saved his life. He had been given a second chance and was able to begin his life again having figuratively cleaned the slate of his past mistakes. Financially, a shrewd investment under strange circumstances and miscellaneous agreements which appeared as 'pensions' or dividends meant that he did not have to work and could pursue a life of modest upper middle class standards - but not of their values and norms- without the concern of penury.

He visited London some four, or occasionally five times a year, the centre piece of his journey and the high point of the visit being his attendance at the British Library and his access to some of the most beautiful and almost sensuous volumes whose leather bound works gave off odours of almost addictive power. But there was another less honourable reason for each and every visit, the almost messianic loyalty and support for the man who was now leader of the Opposition and probably the next Prime Minister, was a camouflage to hide a loyalty which had its roots and origins in an agreement made nearly a quarter of a century before. Of course Wilson did not know or even suspect that one of his loyal supporters and constituency workers was, in effect, and in reality, a spy, which accounted for one of his various incomes along with other pensions.

A contrived chance meeting ,after the War, appeared in retrospect, like a weakly constructed plot in a not too well written novel by an author whose inflated self opinion was greater than the quality of his writing. Anyway he had joined the local Labour constituency party and over a period ingratiated himself, by his help, cooperation and his unswerving loyalty to the local M.P., Harold Wilson.

He also was to revive his association and genuine friendship with the man who had saved his life and who was expected to climb the hierarchy of military power in the Soviet Union and to rekindle that connection it was suggested that he write to him at the address that had been given when they separated. It took over two years from the time of his correspondence being posted, to when, surprisingly, he received a reply.

Their paths never knowingly crossed and he never received any communication from his controller. With a regular and consistent frequency his post office account was credited every quarter with an amount that every year, without exception grew, without the necessity of any demand for its increase. In return his only obligation was to pass on any information whilst he was in London. The method was simple and unerringly regular, without deviation. Always on a Friday and on no other day, even in an emergency, he was to telephone a particular number from any London telephone box and to then identify himself by his full name and his mother's maiden name. The operator was invariably female and American and without exception most formal and professional in demeanour and tone. Once, for no other reason than courtesy and good manners, when he detected the accent of the Mid-West - a region that had once been his home he commented appropriately but was immediately rebuffed. The procedure was that seemingly, by the magic of modern science and technology (subjects that Harold Wilson seemed obsessed with and was a regular mantra in his ideology, if he really had an ideology), he was transferred, most likely to a recording device where he first repeated his identification after which he then dictated his report. As Harold Wilson's career advanced and as his association with the man drew closer and information changed from secondary source gossip and trivia to primary source and sometimes golden nuggets of inside information, Goldburgh noticed that the quarterly payments seemed to increase exponentially.

These increases coincided with the unexpected equest from his friend, when they met in Finland, to conceive and develop both a military and political strategy to liberate West Germany from the perceived Communist view point, of American domination.

He had spent twelve valuable months of great effort and application planning a unique strategy and more importantly researching all the probable consequences of such an operation. When he delivered the document it was received with obvious gratitude and thanks but no further reference was made, not even when, deviously and clandestinely, and as a shock to him, he was smuggled into the Soviet Union for the first time since nineteen forty-four with his dear friend and taken on a journey of tiring and exhausting duration to an ultra secret location to view the industrial complex of Arzamas -16.

It was only, as their two paths diverged, that he enquired, with sincere gratitude for such an unexpected experience, which he had assumed was in recognition of his own endeavours, that he was told that it had been organised by an old family friend for all his work over the last few years.

Such was the cornucopia of information that he had available that the next time he visited London he found it both convenient and necessary to make, uniquely, two telephone calls from two different telephone boxes to transmit his message, however, for the first and only time he wondered where was the ultimate destiny of his information .

EIGHTEEN

NOVEMBER 19th 1963

At about the same time that Goldburgh was finalising the arrangements for his forthcoming and imminent visit to London, the team of inspectors were making their third, final and longest visit to various holding camps of East German and Polish forces seemingly randomly scattered across Eastern Germany but close to the West German border.

There were, in total, three visits by the body of officials selected by N A T O, France and the United States to inspect and review, under the helpful assistance and cooperation of their Warsaw Treaty hosts, preparations for the latter's forthcoming late autumn or early winter manoeuvres. In reality the representatives of the hosts were dominated by Soviet Army officers especially chosen not solely for their command of English, which unofficially became the common language of communication, but also because of their experiences in the Great

Patriotic War which made them excellent social hosts in the amicable atmosphere which was intended deliberately to encourage fraternisation and to divert as much as possible any inquisitive enquiries.

At first the visitors felt uncomfortable in the civilian suits that had not only been provided for them but had been individually tailored (and gave them ,in the words of one fashion conscious West German officer, the appearance of East German Politburo members) but mainly because they felt en masse, that their military status and above all the very nature of their work demanded that they should be correctly attired.

It was necessary that the East German, Polish and Soviet liaison officers were unaware and ignorant of the true, intended purpose of the so called exercises. Indeed they genuinely believed, because it was the core of their military philosophy that the sole purpose of the exercise was to check and scrutinise the capability and state of the Warsaw Treaty Organisation to contain, halt and repulse an attack that was unexpected and unprovoked by a perfidious and nefarious enemy whose actions were not only preconceived but also premeditated and meticulously pre planned, in fact symbolic of the very nature of the so called capitalist Western democracies.

The caution and mistrust exhibited by both sides echoed an earlier meeting which had taken place, unbeknownst to the representatives of the 'Western' allies and their hosts, some months before inside a Parisian restaurant, which would repeat the joint realisation of shared and common interests and values but this time none of the participants knew or even suspected that the embryonic erosion of long held prejudices would end in a callous betrayal.

The first meeting had been arranged with the intention to break down the barriers of mistrust and caution that was ingrained in the participants and this was partially achieved by selecting from both sides officers who had previously served in Berlin and had, in the course of their duties, communicated with their opposite numbers, especially at the crossing points thus reuniting some old associates.

Overwhelmingly important was the 'West's' voracious appetite and desire for knowledge and information about any aspect of military activity behind the *Iron-Curtain*, even to confirm and verify news or information that had been obtained or gleaned from diverse sources. The first meeting, before the barriers begun to be eroded, was best described by a West German officer when he alluded, most cunningly and with an element of callous *déjà–vu,* to the similar situation that *MUST* have taken place, when after the most cynical and hypocritical of any agreement in history, the pact signed by Molotov and Von Ribbentrop in the summer of nineteen thirty-nine, when German Gestapo and Soviet N K V D officers met for the first time to discuss matters of mutual concern. The West German officer continued, with an air of regret and even guilt, surmising that no doubt the subject of their mutual interest was the rape of Poland and how they intended to wipe the symbolic blood from off of their hands.

The team of inspectors had also been alerted, not only to the possibility of what was euphemistically known as 'The Honey Trap' (not a new method of corruption and undue influence, but one most effectively used by the sinister Markus Wolf), but to the more likely possibility that their hosts might, no, more likely would endeavour to mislead and deceive the delegation .

The Inspectors were introduced to the 'War Games' by the unveiling of a large wall map of West and East Germany and Poland before one of the liaison officers explained the logic behind what they were all to shortly witness:

"The 'West' would launch an unprovoked and unexpected thrust into the German Democratic Republic using its tank force to punch a wide salient supported by an umbrella of fighter support, endeavouring to penetrate eastwards as far as possible to the Polish border and beyond before an anticipated defensive wall of regular Polish forces would stem and halt the advance after which Soviet forces, backed by fighter planes could counter attack and repel the invaders."

An entirely new dimension was added when an East German officer gave a short speech to emphasise the belief that ,whilst as a group, the Warsaw Treaty nations regarded the people of Western Europe as 'peace loving', they anticipated in the scenario of the 'War Games', that the political leaders in the West and especially in the United States would prevaricate and deliberately delay a cease fire citing some national or international event not directly connected with the ruthless military adventure. Surprisingly, the potential use of tactical nuclear weapons was not mentioned at that time.

The Western intelligence officers were then given an in depth analysis and demonstration of the proposed counter offensive. Their hosts then apologised for the brevity of the lunch which was to follow, explaining that their 'friends and guests' would soon be transported by a fleet of military helicopters to one of the tank parks that were being raised in preparation for the manoeuvres, as they would act as the incoming Western invasion force.

The location of the venue was not specified and in hindsight an approximate reckoning was not calculable since, most inconveniently, the windows of the transport helicopters were blacked out (the reason given was that the paint used was a newly developed compound devised to give passengers some protection against the blinding flash of a nuclear detonation) and the fleet of helicopters varied not only their velocity but also made what was considered to be unnecessary course changes, which were promptly explained as training strategies to simulate the evasion of enemy anti aircraft batteries and the more feared hand held rocket devices believed by intelligence officers to be in the armoury of the 'West'.

On arrival they were then chauffeured in a convoy of Zil limousines to what was clearly an old but well established military complex where they estimated were parked some two hundred or so T-54 tanks. Even before the guests were able to mention their interest to have a close examination of the 'chariots' their hosts not only offered an intimate viewing of any tank but offered the experience of a ride under combat conditions.

For some of the visitors it was not only an infantile treat, but for the technicians an unrivalled opportunity to view its opponents' main battle wagon. The apparent sincerity of their hosts and their honesty and openness was clearly evident when they answered the probing technical enquiry of one eagle eyed and clearly observant English intelligence officer who had spotted an even newer T55 with an innovative modification that was not known to the military services in the West. There then followed a candid description of the previously secret P.A.Z. system.

The innovation was the formerly secret P.A.Z. nuclear contamination detection and filtration system, combined with an improved air filtration system to seal the tank from contaminated outside air. A technical description of great complexity followed but this showed to the visitors the clear sincerity and *bona–fides* of their hosts.

Following a nuclear blast, and it was now clear that the Warsaw Treaty leadership expected an early escalation across the nuclear threshold and that the Americans would abundantly use tactical battlefield nuclear weapons, to protect the crew, the on board RBZ/1M gamma ray detector system, once triggered, would turn off the engine ,thereby alerting the crew and turn on an overpressure system which would keep out external radioactive air (In hindsight neither the hosts nor their guests realised the potential possible alternative use of the system as a temporary facility).

NINETEEN

The next and second visit took place about a month later giving the visitors ample opportunity not only to digest and analyse what they had observed - and been told - but to consider any potential options that could be utilised by their hosts that had not been taken into account by their own planners and strategists. Since no programme had been agreed they realised that any disclosures were entirely subject to the whim and good faith of their opposite numbers.

They were not to be disappointed. On their return they were showered with a cascade of information and access to weapons and information that before these events could only be dreamed of or more usually gleaned from various sources but usually in fragments, sometimes of dubious provenance or whose veracity was suspect, which was then assembled like a jigsaw puzzle usually creating an imperfect, distorted image or inaccurate summary of the subject under scrutiny. They observed hangars and more chillingly hardened silos under construction, the former clearly designed to protect their aircraft however the hardened silos appeared to be in an early stage of construction but the subsequent consensus was ominous, generally that the sites were for a new intermediate range ballistic missile. The realisation that a 'Western' sneak assault could wipe out their planes or

in the near future hit their missiles before launching was obviously in the minds of the Warsaw Treaty planners, but these excavations had unearthed a secret which for no reason than the pursuit of pure knowledge the hosts wished to display.

The visitors had specially been brought to this location because excavations had accidentally unearthed what was an archaeological military treasure site, as the base had been in the Great Patriotic War (it was, by custom, never designated the Second World War) a Nazi aerodrome operating the advanced Me-163 Komet and the amazing Arado Blitz 234 Bomber. The visitors were then given virtual carte blanche to inspect not only the partially built hardened silos and hangars but more importantly their precious contents, the latest generation M.I.G. and Sukhoi fighters.

Access to the cockpits was promptly granted despite the muted and passive protestations of the guards who were clearly concerned that there were so many visitors, but above all the language spoken was not German or Russian but English and even worse that the dominant accent was American. The inevitable request arose generating much confusion and even consternation in their hosts` rank. Two Soviet officers departed, returning about an hour later clearly elated and in respect of one of the officers bearing a broad grin.

"Yes, two of the visitors could be taken up the following day in the two seater Sukhoi though their qualifications and experience on high performance jets would be crucial in their selection!"

They were then shepherded across the main runway passing six or eight obsolete, apparently new Yak 2 piston engine propeller driven planes languishing at the end of the runway. Most of those present including the hosts paid little attention to this anachronism of twentieth century flight except one American who rhetorically asked:

"If this was to be your secret weapon in the event that hostilities broke out?"

He received no discernible response other than muted laughter from most of those present.

The excavations had unearthed what had initially appeared to be a bunker whose origin could not be traced in any archives or subsequently by the few remaining men or officers who had served at one time or another on the base. When the only entrance had been located and opened they were confronted ,not unexpectedly, by a deserted and derelict room containing the remnants, in varying degrees of decay, decomposition or rust of the typical contents of an administrative room and as such the building was closed and marked for demolition.

Both by chance and luck, as they were removing the contents, a concealed entrance was noticed, highlighted by the flaking, in a regular pattern, of the green paintwork. When the door, which was jammed, was ultimately opened they were confronted by a scene only comparable to the opening of a Pharaoh`s tomb and with great pride they wished to show the discovery to the visitors.

What was uncovered and in near pristine condition was an operations room which, from the documentation that had been examined, was rudely and urgently evacuated, most likely as it was in the path of the advancing Red Army forces. Along one wall was the communication section including a number of four rotor Enigma enciphering machines (and in boxes, some of which were still unopened, unused spare rotors), a portable telephone exchange and what the commentator described as the jewel in the crown, a ten rotor *Geheimschreiber*!). The final destiny of the room and above all its contents, most of which still had yet to be catalogued, would rest with powers above them, however in years to come, the exhibit might reach the 'West'. They all had a cursory journey through the room even reading or perusing the many documents and of the few that were viewed the overall impression was of impending doom and desperation.

They retraced their steps across the runway, passing the neatly assembled YAK 2s, however their numbers had increased by four more planes and three of the pilots were lazily standing around the recently landed craft. The pilots were young, very young, perhaps only just out of their teens, their deportment and attitude typical of young men everywhere. They adopted the posture and demeanour of complete confidence and experience, which, of course, had not been tested, but probably only gleaned by the minimum of practical experience.

The same American officer, who had previously rhetorically asked his hosts about their intended use, noted with inspired interest that the latest arrivals had both underneath the wings and on the sides of the fuselage, as befits the antiquity of the planes, control wires leading from fitted racks to the cockpit. In the background an English officer clearly and distinctly offered the cryptic description and eponymous title, Heath Robinson.

The officer pursued his enquiries as he felt obliged to investigate the whole matter and asked the purpose of the modifications but the young men appeared reticent to answer the enquiry, most likely because they must have sensed or even overheard many of the group, including some of the hosts, speaking in English. The most senior Soviet officer interrupted the enquiry and with an authoritarian bark compelled anyone of the three to give a full complete answer. The reply was an anti climax, as the explanation for the use of the plane was as an agricultural crop sprayer and to distribute organo – phosphates the following spring to increase wheat production. Thus it seemed such a simple and satisfactory answer. Such was his sincerity and spontaneous explanation that the assembled party moved on blinded to the true purpose which, of course, was not known to any of those present.

The next day was, for most of the visitors, the highlight, as three, not two officers were given literally the surprise of their careers for three Tupolev TU 28P, NATO designation "Fiddler" fighters had been specially flown in and three lucky, but highly experienced officers, were whisked across East Germany, Poland and into the Soviet Union at Mach 1.4 and for the whole group their visit ended that evening with mutual agreement to reconvene in late September or early October for a third and final reconnaissance before the manoeuvres began.

Thus, like your author, are men deceived by blind trust in others.

By the end of September no communication had been received to confirm an arrangement but on or about October tenth one of the West German officers in Bonn received a brief apologetic telephone call from an East German counterpart genuinely regretting the lack of contact and confirming that for reasons not known to him all the events had been postponed for some two to three weeks but he personally promised that he would not delay any future arrangements. Nothing transpired until the beginning of November when a formal invitation and an apologetic hand written post script was received confirming that they should be ready for the Tuesday , November the nineteenth, a few days before the rescheduled exercises were now due to commence and that special arrangements had been made (which partially explained the delay) and they would actually view the operation from a command and control centre on the Polish / German border and that additionally some of the observers could join the actual exercises but they should bring adequate winter clothing to supplement the clothing supplied already by their hosts.

The trap , previously suitably baited, had unwittingly been prepared by the naive and ignorant assistance offered in good faith by the hosts which ultimately would result in the deaths of all the observers by an unlikely hand.

TWENTY

On Thursday, November nineteenth Eighteen sixty-three, President Abraham Lincoln made a short speech at the dedication of a National Soldiers' Cemetery at Gettysburg, Pennsylvania.

After the brief speech a reporter from the *Chicago Tribune* telegraphed a prophetic sentence:

"The dedicatory remarks of President Lincoln will live among the annals of man."

'Four score and seven years ago our fathers brought forth on this continent a new nation, conceived in liberty, and dedicated to the proposition that all men are created equal.

Now we are engaged in a great civil war, testing whether that nation, or any nation so conceived and so dedicated, can long endure.

We are met on a great battlefield of that war.

We have come to dedicate a portion of that field, as a final resting place for those who here gave their lives that that nation might live.

It is altogether fitting and proper that we should do this.

But, in a larger sense, we can not dedicate , we can not consecrate, we can not hallow this ground.
The brave men, living and dead, who struggled here, have consecrated it, far above our poor power to add or detract.

The world will little note, nor long remember what we say here, but it can never forget what they did here.

It is for us the living, rather, to be dedicated here to the unfinished work which they who fought here have thus far so nobly advanced.

It is rather for us to be here dedicated to the great task remaining before us-that from these honoured dead we take increased devotion to that cause for which they gave the last full measure of devotion- that we here highly resolve that these dead shall not have died in vain- that this nation, under God, shall have a new birth of freedom-

and that government of the people, by the people, for the people, shall not perish from the earth.'

One hundred years to the exact same day there began a series of events that ,like the then on going Civil War would test both a new ,yet unelected President, and the people of the *UNITED* States.

Tuesday, November nineteenth was *THE* pivotal day of the conspiracy and for Nikita Khrushchev it was then necessary to widen knowledge of the *TRUE* purpose of the 'War Games',involving others and potentially jeopardising the whole operation.   The Rubicon was physically crossed when three independent but inter – related events took place, each thousands of miles from the others in different time zones but each crucially dependant on both of the others.   The final outcome was essentially based on events in the United States and Great Britain.

He was woken by two of the most beautiful acts of mother nature which reminded him of his secret and nearly forgotten youth.   Whether it was the birds in the trees singing, as dawn broke, or vaulting over the horizon, the Sun illuminating his bedroom and the lustre of the sun flakes dancing and cavorting across the room might well have caught his half opened eyes and awoken him, he did not know, but it was the tranquillity of his home that was such a rare occurrence. His wife was still asleep and even more beautiful than when he first met her. Soon his home would be inundated with the joyous happy sounds of his two teenage daughters and the noises of a normal Dallas family preparing for the day ahead and jousting for priority outside of the second bathroom.

In the tranquillity of his sanctuary he remembered that *today* was extremely special both for him and *his* country.   One hundred years ago the President had spoken to the nation to heal a great wound but more importantly had uttered simple words of great truth which made him proud to be an American.

Being the third Tuesday of the month he knew that his regular schedule would change, even though he was not a creature of habit: tonight he would join his friends for a few beers, a barbeque, pool and conversation without the interruption of their wives or partners.   His wife would first drop off the two girls at their High School and then he would be left at his office whilst she returned to the small, but very happy home, which was beginning to burst at the seams, before she began her daily routine.

Whilst he had slept well he could not control his thoughts because he was waiting for the post and *THAT* letter. His attorney,who incidentally he would meet that evening, had intimated to him that unofficially he had been advised that all was in order, that the financial and back ground investigations had been completed and he would receive the letter of authority within a few days. He had not told anyone for fear of rejection and failure. He had even began to dream of the benefits that would accrue following his application. Many of his contemporaries or associates would undoubtedly purchase the most gaudy and ostentatious automobiles that Detroit could construct or ,and for a moment he was tempted, one of those predatory Jaguar XK150s that were exquisitely designed ,sculptured and shaped and personified the nature of the beast. He stopped dreaming and brought himself back to the real world and decided that he would purchase a hand built personalised hunting rifle to replace his mass produced but essentially effective Italian 6.5millimetre model 91/38 Mannlicher-Carcano.

He gazed transfixed at his wife, she was truly the most beautiful woman that he had ever seen, more beautiful and erotic than when they had first met in Calabasas all those years ago. The truth that had been hidden and the bodyguard of lies that protected him had allowed their relationship to flourish but if even accidentally the truth was discovered not only would it destroy him but probably undermine the trust that had, with maturity, cemented and strengthened their bond of love and their companionship.

Sometimes those ancient events seemed unreal, as if he had only dreamed them. They were ethereal, being acted out behind a mist that not only shrouded them from the inquisitiveness of others but even made him doubt their veracity, as fleetingly he endeavoured to revive dim memories not only of his childhood and youth but more important, of the war and finally *THAT* place. He had even forgotten how to speak his mother tongue except that one time when, at his daughters` High School,one of the teachers began to speak in the language of Tolstoy and Pasternak, making crucial errors of syntax and grammar, nearly compelling him to discard very close on to twenty years of deceit and deception and to go over to the pedant and in his acquired tongue reprimand him and show him the errors of his way. But the discipline that had ruthlessly been imposed upon him controlled any rash acts and he did not allow the facade to crumble, even for one brief moment.

The post arrived and like a ravenous beast he devoured the pile of envelopes leaving only the subject of his absolute and exclusive interest , correspondence from the heart of the United States military, the Pentagon. He scanned the contents as if it was a summary of his exam results, only concerning himself with the substance of the body of the inelegantly constructed and dry statement of fact. Yes, yes, yes, he had been approved as an official contractor to the United States military and with immediate effect could tender for the construction of various forms of military buildings only in the Continental United States and not elsewhere. He had achieved his ambition.

His site manager would soon arrive and he resolved to tell him the exciting news and to show his appreciation to his administrative staff, as well as the contractors, he decided to give them all, on Friday, the day off with *DOUBLE* pay in recognition of their valued support and because the President, *HIS* President was visiting his home town. He had said his President, but in truth he was a committed and proud Republican but this young man (in reality a contradiction of facts since Kennedy was older than him) had stood up to Khrushchev and the insidious Communist anti democratic expansion of the Soviet Union.

He knew he was an American in every way except by birth and the illegal way that he had entered the United States, however it was unnecessary to prove either to himself or others his loyalty to the symbol of his homeland, the Stars and Stripes.

The day was spent in the company of his site manager and the man's pick up truck as they visited the five on going construction sites and on each the gratitude of his employees was confirmed, that without pay, most would put in a Saturday shift to partially recover the time lost for the Friday bonus.

Over a hurried lunch they briefly discussed the future and their joint hopes for the anticipated expansion of the firm. He was dropped off at the office, showered, changed into something casual that his wife had selected for him and proceeded to attack the pile of paper work that always seemed to mount up and accrue in any office or ,as his friends would say, in any business, as he awaited a telephone call from any one of his friends, to confirm their arrival time when he would be collected.

It was about the time that he anticipated a call, that the telephone rang and as was customary, since it was his private and(though it sounded more impressive than the fact)unlisted number, that he answered with his first name since the caller would have only been one of his family members or as was convenient, the bank vice president who had been very supportive, or finally and most likely, one of his circle of friends. But the voice was feminine, sensual with the texture of liquid wild honey or the decadent sweetness of a pomegranate rich in its' succulent juice. But she spoke in an alien tongue and he recognised only two words, his birth name and her name! She stopped, waited for him to respond and in the absence of any acknowledgement or oral emotion, she continued but this time in English, speaking slowly and clearly as if it was important for both of them to understand her message:

"My dearest Yuri, it is, Natalia ,who willingly gave herself to you and who still even to this day cherishes and yearns for your body that gave to me your seed, a sign and symbol of our love and trust in each other, but I now grieve that I can never repeat what was in the past as I know that you are committed to another.

But I now call upon you to fulfil your duty to the Motherland and repay the trust that was put in you when we were both young. We have, like guardian angels, watched over you since you arrived in California where you made your first home and, as we taught you, learned the devious, immoral capitalist arts and built a new life for yourself.

You are to perform one deed on behalf of *YOUR* Motherland and if you wish, you and your family will then be taken home to where your roots and family lie, to be greeted as a hero, or if you so wish you may stay in this land where the strong devour the weak and the principles of comradeship and equality have been forgotten by a people who are consumed by the worship of materialism and self interest."

He gathered and collected his thoughts, figuratively staggered to his feet like a boxer recovering from a near knockout blow and tried to answer her. His response was surprisingly coherent and articulate despite the circumstances, unlike those of a shell shocked boxer.

"It is nearly twenty years since we last fleetingly saw each other and, as ordered, went in different directions. You returned to Moscow and the N K V D; If you had entered the United States and if your yearning for me was so strong why did you not contact me ?"

Suddenly an inner strength swelled up inside him and he felt confident that he could rebut her plans and restore his life and the security and safety of his secret. He continued, his mind recovering from the surprise blow, the fog dissolving in his brain.

"My loyalty to the Motherland was tested two decades ago and our love and trust in each other was, I believed, forged in the woods and consummated by our joyous union.

Did it mean nothing to you or is the love of the Party a more powerful emotion that transcends and overwhelms your feelings for me? I have nothing to offer the Party after all these years since the qualities and strength of youth have, with the duration of time, been sapped, and all I now am is but an empty vessel of my former self."

His earlier silence was reciprocated as if she did not expect such a determined and resolute reply to her approach, indeed he thought, momentarily that he had rebutted her approach and that his secret and in consequence his future,was secured.

The silence continued for a few more moments until she replied with a devastating response, which in reality was the only response she could have given and was undoubtedly the prepared reply to him.

"Yuri, you have been chosen and awoken because you possess one special quality that makes you suitable, unique and perfect for the task that has been granted to you. Indeed, the inheritors of the plans that Lavrenti Beria created and bequeathed to the Party have honoured you with the sacred duty and when completed, you can return, forever, to your new life and we will also reward you financially. But beware, our masters also have within their power the ability to destroy you just as they are able to continue and maintain the secrecy and deception of which you are just a part."

Suddenly the euphoria of success evaporated and a chilling almost frightening wave of fear overwhelmed him as she continued and concluded her remarks.

"You have two teenage daughters and you have very recently been accepted by the Pentagon to tender contracts on behalf of your company. You should not have broken your cover and nearly exposed yourself. The Pentagon is only really concerned with firms , like yours, that can complete the work, on time, but above all to the contract price. Go to meet your friends where you will receive a packet but do not open it in front of them. Go to what your friends, in their all male environment call the john. You will receive a sign not only of good faith, but of the power that could be unleashed against you. Sleep well tonight, you have nothing to fear if you perform this one deed. I will contact you on Thursday morning."

The phone went dead. He was inundated with various and sometimes conflicting thoughts but paramount amongst them was the shock not only of her contact but her intimate knowledge of his business affairs.

He thought that perhaps she could be bought off, like Danegeld, but that was unlikely; perhaps she could be tricked into exposing herself? He could confess to the authorities who would probably be lenient, for other than illegally entering the country he had committed no crime and had paid all his taxes. And if she was not arrested? She knew about the girls!

Suddenly the telephone rang again. It served as a double shock for it withdrew him from the almost frantic worries that had suddenly engulfed him and back to reality and also surprised him. It was one of his circle of friends, who apologised for the delay but commented on the fact that he had not been able to get through earlier since the number was tied up!

Little was said by the two friends as they circumnavigated the last of the commuter traffic leaving central Dallas and he had lost the enthusiasm to tell his friend, who usually was most interested in his career, of the most exciting news which he hoped would change and improve his family's standard of living. His thoughts were focused on one matter and that matter only. The sign or whatever it was ,which could affect his whole future.

His circle of friends were well known at the bar that was perhaps their spiritual home or more likely a refuge from their responsibilities as husbands and parents. It was an oasis of tranquillity where, for a short while, the burdens of duty and the troubles of life could be briefly discarded.

The owner called him over and explained that shortly before an anonymous visitor that he did not know and therefore recognise had hurriedly called in and requested that a small package be passed to him. The owner further commented that he assumed, wrongly, that he was a business associate or even an acquaintance since he must have known of the impending visit.

He rushed into the john, entered a cubicle, sat down and cautiously began to open the package, careful not to damage the contents. Just as he was about to peer inside the opened packaging he realised that the door had been unlocked and was ajar; he stood up and lunged forward, securing the door and continued his task. The document was in Cyrillic, tattered but fastidiously preserved. It was his identity card. He could go to the authorities with this document. They would now listen to his, what seemed improbable, story and they could help him. But her offer, her request, perhaps he should at least listen to her, perhaps she could be bought off! The girls and his beloved wife had to be protected at all costs.

For a short time afterwards he even managed to forget the pressures that could suffocate and destroy him. The eight or so friends were so excited when he told them of his business success and when, with patriotic fervour, he mentioned that he was giving all his employees the day off on Friday, because *HIS* President was coming to Dallas they, in different ways, commented upon his patriotism and loyalty to the flag. He even allowed himself the honour to pay for all the drinks that evening, requesting a special toast to John and Jackie.

But he could not sleep that night or on the following evening, disturbing his wife constantly and even after they had physically joined together he was still unable to sleep, explaining to his exasperated wife that he could no longer hide his excitement about his future business plans.

The telephone did not ring. Perhaps she had gone away and he could resume his life. The staff would be in shortly and certainly she would not dare contact him and risk being overheard. He was about to unlock the main office door when his worst nightmare was realised. He lifted the receiver and heard her voice, still silkily sensual and creamy smooth but also emphatic and absolutely intransigent.

Her instructions were comprehensive and absolute and even the timings were specific. She ended her demands and requirements with an unsolicited promise and warning.

"Yuri, we will never meet, though I am now permitted to speak again to you one more time. If our masters had been kind then perhaps we would have been together as man and wife. You will be given all the documents that could identify you and disclose your origins. Spend the money cautiously but before that think of your target as a wild animal in the forests where you grew up: have no emotion."

TWENTY-ONE

Tuesday, November nineteenth was to be a long day for the First Secretary and he deviously organised his official appointments and balanced the exact locations of his meetings so that he was at all times close to his private office but more importantly nearby to his scrambled personal telephones. He was due to receive two highly confidential calls, the first at approximately mid day from the Commander in Chief of the navy and the latter about nine hours later from the head of the K G B.

Both telephone calls would confirm matters of marine intelligence: the former to confirm the assembly of a marine armada at a point some two hundred and twenty nautical miles off of the Californian and Oregon coast and the latter, the arrival and disembarkation of passengers from a Polish registered vessel somewhere in the London Thames estuary.

An adventure, described by the head of the K G B, when acquainted with the operation, as perhaps the most callous and despicable coup d`etat that he had ever been involved in, even taking into account the undermining of democratic governments in Eastern Europe after the Second World War, but he was reminded that the purpose of the plan was to destabilise the British government as the initial operation was only the second part of a far wider scheme.

He had additionally organised his diary to enable him, if necessary ,to cancel any one or all three meetings comprising delegations from three Republics of the Union. The first was typical of his day to day routine but was politically important for him , as the First Secretary, and for the Presidium because they were able to control and more importantly monitor political opinions and economic trends literally at the 'coal face' which in this case was completely true since the delegation represented coal miners from the Urals. They had been allocated the usual ninety minute period but Khrushchev was most astute and experienced in this type of situation. He would deliberately allocate a whole two hour 'slot' which could always be aborted in the event of a more urgent matter arising.   He had honed and perfected the hypocritical art, no ability, which globally must be practised by consummate politicians of different nationalities and more important of all,of diverse persuasions and opinions, which was the ability and the acquired art to appear absolutely interested in their visitors problems and the substance and minutae of their presentation, when in reality their minds and attention was elsewhere, only absorbing and filtering specific matters such as worker satisfaction and methods to increase production quotas.

Occasional interruptions of the delegation to ask for clarification of particular points would appear to strengthen the opinion of the delegation that their presentation was being sown on fertile ground. Always, without exception, the First Secretary would end the formal part of the meeting by insisting that on their return they should submit a full report together with a brief summary of the whole which in reality he might read but then refer the contents to the appropriate Ministry for an in depth analysis. To conclude the meeting he would usually then escort the Party to one of the private dining rooms where he would finally take his leave,citing, as if the matter was a state secret, his wife`s insistence that he adhere to a rigid diet.

It was imperative that he be close to the telephone and to maintain his privacy. He completed his other two routine meetings and remained magnetised to his office. At six- thirty he was galvanised into action when one phone burst into life and answering with a cold dictatorial tone he was shocked but pleasantly surprised to hear the voice of his only grand daughter who was enquiring into his health and wishing to learn when she could see him next. He managed to control his taut emotions, end the conversation without distressing her because the extended delay had metaphorically made him like a stretched rubber band, the tension so extreme that the band and of course his patience might snap at any moment. He was beginning to form the opinion that the excessive delay would portend and heralded potentially the most extreme bad and unsatisfactory news.

Indeed when he received the first call a little before 10 p.m. he instinctively knew there was a major problem :the almost timid, apologetic tone of the Commander in Chief, the same man who only a few months before had audaciously requested a naval dimension to the adventure and who had stood before the First Secretary and assured him in absolute terms of his ability and competence to organise and above all fulfil his grandiose plan.

The truth was unpalatable and could only result in a catastrophe. Only eleven type 629 diesel powered submarines had left their bases in the Pacific region early in November, because not enough trained engineers were available to complete various minor modifications that were deemed necessary.

Furthermore, of the eleven vessels that had begun the vast trans-Pacific odyssey, two had only been partially loaded, one with one missile and the other with two, instead of the full capacity of three missiles which were each on the other nine vessels and finally, whilst en route, the fleet had encountered technical problems with the normally reliable diesel engines (possibly due to the workload on the engines).

The Commander in Chief was proud to report that four vessels had, by nineteen fifty five hours (Moscow time), reached their destination (the exact coordinates were confirmed and noted by Khrushchev) carrying a total compliment of eleven missiles. Khrushchev thanked the man for the information and confirmed, as previously agreed, that no action should commence until and only after his authority had been given.

It was clear, self evident and above all imperative that the operation be aborted and his alternative plan, a chess sacrifice, be implemented along with a personal sacrifice by the Commander in Chief of the navy himself!

Until such time as the two operations in the United States and the United Kingdom had been satisfactorily completed he would stay his hand but make certain that the Commander be available to make his contribution to the deception.

TWENTY-TWO

The two, thin ribbons of land on the North and South banks of the River Thames from the City of London as they snake eastwards through that area known as 'Docklands', towards The Thames Estuary and finally into The English Channel have not only been the site of mercantile trade but also the location of crime and hedonistic pleasures since Roman times; indeed such locations as Deptford and Southwark have been prominent and historical references or illusions appear in the works of Chaucer and Shakespeare. Undoubtedly the fierce independence and disrespect for authority could explain the rise of Socialism, Trade Unionism and Communism in what is still commonly referred to as the' East End', resulting in nineteen forty five, in the election of a Communist M.P.,Phil Piratin, for the Constituency of Mile End , Stepney, though he lost the seat in nineteen fifty partially through boundary changes when the seat became Stepney (Incidentally, though not directly relevant to this work, but to continue this factual report, readers should note, or already be aware that the author was *INDIRECTLY* related to this politician, but not by blood).

In such an environment it would not be difficult, and it was proved a formality, to recruit political supporters with strong left wing sympathies to assist the cause and the ideals of Socialism. The identity and in consequence the background of the man who promoted the operation through trusted representatives is still shrouded in mystery however one name has been put forward by two people (one a former member of the Communist Party and the other, now dead, an M I 5 officer, for a short time seconded to the ultra secret section, Department F4) and that person was the Trade Union official, Jack Jones.

On Tuesday, November nineteenth, nineteen sixty-three,a Polish vessel, the *DRAWA* arrived at Gravesend from Szczecin. The property of the Polish Steamship Company and therefore ultimately the Polish Government, she had been built in Gdansk in 1958 with a weight of 480tons gross and in her hold she carried what would soon be the instrument of death and political chaos. Eighteen specially selected and trained Spetsnaz GRU troops (Glavnoye Razvedyvatel`noye Upravleniye) mainly recruited from shock troops originally trained and allocated, in the event of war ,to destroy U.S. weapon systems such as the Lance, Sergeant and Pershing missiles, reportedly reaching up to over four hundred miles inside enemy territory. In addition to their military skills they had been chosen for their ability to speak, not fluently, but to be able to communicate in German, English and possibly French. But as a final quality, was the proven capability to use their initiative and be able to travel off the land.

Early on the twentieth, the eighteen men dressed as manual labourers disembarked, under cover of darkness, and were met by three vans liveried with the names of well known and respectable vegetable wholesalers. The men and two containers, each perhaps symbolically the size but heavier than a full coffin, were loaded onto the vans and they then departed to a destination only confirmed by their group`s leader who along with his deputy were the only two aware of the operation and even then they had been briefed and handed documentation only hours before the boat`s departure.

They reached their destination at about four a.m., some miles North of their base in order to maintain their secrecy and some twenty minutes later a coach arrived, to collect the men and their valuable cargo, but in the darkness no one could discern the prominent and grandiose title of
...

The Anglo–Italian and West German Film Corporation of Milan.

Doubling back on themselves, following a tortuous route through dark, deserted country roads they reached their destination, a deserted, rented short term base outside of Flitwick, which was to be their headquarters until the following Sunday evening.   The coach was garaged in a barn whilst the troops prepared for a long wait which was to interspersed with limited manoeuvres in an adjacent field.

TWENTY-THREE

He was unable to sleep, as his mind relentlessly and with unremitting application mulled over and worried, both about the unknown, exact task that he was demanded and expected to fulfil, but also his desire to again hear her voice. His wife lay beside him, unaware and oblivious of his thoughts, as he also both tossed and turned and fantasised about Natalia, creating a symbolic image of her luscious lips as a dilated, enlarged and inviting vagina that he would enter and satisfy both their wildest emotional and physical desires.

He wandered downstairs carefully avoiding turning on any lights which might awaken the home`s occupants and cautiously negotiated the hallway before entering the kitchen after which he gently closed the door and only then turned on the kitchen lights, which for a few moments half blinded him such was their intense luminosity. The kitchen table reminded him of the chaos and illogical randomness following an explosion. His daughters` study books lay in disorder.  He saw Shakespeare`s Hamlet precariously tottering on the edge of the table and tucked inside as an aide memoire was a reference note...

ACT 1, SCENE IV,LINE 23.

He inquisitively opened the book (remembering that he was totally ignorant of the works of the Bard and indeed barely knew of his existence before his arrival in the United States), found the reference and slowly began to read:

So, oft it chances in particular men...

He read, then reread the quotation and speech and on the third occasion begun to comprehend its meaning. But his situation was not the result of his personality, it was clearly the circumstances of many diverse and inter -reacting events. He put down the thin volume and again rummaged through the chaos and disorder of his other daughter's school papers, alighted on her Shakespearean work, Julius Caesar, and again if perhaps by coincidence, she had also left a reference which he busily pursued, since being unable to sleep, he had time on his hands. The reference was circled with doodles and other indecipherable symbols which led him to believe that her mind and her interests were not in the field of English Literature...

ACT 4,SCENE 111,LINE 217.

There is a tide in the affairs of men...

Again, he read, reread and again reread the quotation, suddenly savouring the analogy of his position with the character's observation. Perhaps, he thought, that this was an omen for *HIS* good fortune and his chance to convert the ill timed and unfortunate imposition on his new life to his advantage; it was, in the final analysis, his future against his victim, who in any event would not suffer, as his shot would be immediately fatal, such was his confidence in his ability.

He awoke, finding himself back in his own bed, again admiring the radiant beauty of his wife, strangely refreshed and anxious to leave for work , but this was not an act of urgency, but of enthusiasm. What had begun and viewed as a repugnant and abhorrent act, had, by a logic and selfish justification for his own desire to survive and prosper, become an act of self preservation, his own.

The previous anxiety and tension, but above all the ominous anticipation of her call were now submerged in his new confidence and hopes for the future. She called, conveniently, as if she was aware that their conversation would not be over heard by the staff, who in any case had yet to arrive, and indeed the conversation, no for this was not a dialogue as she dominated the call and minimised his involvement, conveniently ended just a few moments before the first of the staff arrived.

He listened, both captivated by the sensuous, silky and seductive tones of her voice but as well by the almost logical and efficient manner in which she presented her instructions as if the taking of a human life was but an administrative action of daily occurrence and routine.

Today, Thursday, in accordance with her instructions, he would commence the inexorable series of actions which unbeknownst to them both would change the course of history. After the event he would receive all the documentation that had been accumulated during his life in the Soviet Union and would be free to dispose of all or any of the records including his birth certificate. She astonished him when, incidentally, she listed the numbers of his personal and the firm's bank accounts even offering to confirm the balances up to a week before and finally as evidence of her knowledge of his family's affairs summarised details of his two daughters' lives at High School. The inference was crystal clear that his rejection of her demands would directly affect his family.

Later that day he was to organise a new post office box facility, ostensibly to receive mail in anticipation of future Pentagon contracts and communications, for on the first of each month, beginning December he would be mailed $five thousand in used notes for a period of thirty-six months and she felt certain that with the initiative and commercial flair that he had accumulated in his new homeland that he would be able to hide this income and use it to the benefit of his family or his firm. The money would be mailed in a particular type of easily identifiable envelope and that at the beginning of each month he should personally collect the mail including the envelope. Tomorrow, Friday, he would meet her representative and be shown a specimen, but later that morning, the Thursday, he should take time off from the office and whilst arranging the new post office box facility, he should rehearse the itinerary that had already been previously outlined to him.

He wanted to say so much to her about the past and even the future, if only once ,not realising the consequences of such an association, but she dominated the conversation because the reality was her commitment to her masters and the success of her mission.

At about nine forty -five he called in the firm's accountant and asked him if he could arrange to open up a new post office box account and have the information and documentation ready for him by the early afternoon , as he was shortly leaving and would be back by three p.m, or so. Punctually at ten fifty, as she had instructed, he left the office and followed a pre determined route into the centre of Dallas. It was, in truth, the most direct and easiest to follow though she had specified a diversion which, including a stop, added some fifteen minutes to the overall time. He found himself in a menswear shop and ,as instructed, asked for a pair of men's cotton gloves, when on receipt of the request, the assistant, a somewhat indiscreet man, answered him by remarking that the previous day, the shop had been visited by a most stunning and elegant woman who had suggested that the following day a friend would call in to collect and pay for the gloves. He was somewhat surprised when the assistant enquired if the lady was in fact his wife and for a moment the camouflage of his secret and true origin was briefly lifted when he honestly stated, though the answer could be misinterpreted, that :

"She was a very old and dear colleague and friend."

He continued the pre planned journey, arrived at the second destination ,and briefly stood on what was known locally as the grassy knoll, looked up to a specific building and the sixth floor, which was not coincidental, for on the Friday she would stand virtually at the same spot and unlike the other onlookers she would discreetly turn in the direction of the same building and with her camera, fitted with a powerful but not too ostentatious long range lens, capture the dramatic evidence of two men at a sixth storey window. He moved on, as instructed, the next part of his journey taking him to an hotel which was well known to him and indeed he was known to the management for he sometimes recommended business associates to use the hotel such was its central location and good value . He used the journey to reconnoitre, to locate any potential waste food bins or even public waste paper bins for a purpose that was patently clear.

After he had completed his assignments he found a friendly diner, had a burger and a vanilla shake and then took a taxi to one of his building sites, engaged the site manager in a brief conversation and to complete his meandering journey engaged a second taxi back to his office where he made it his business to confirm with his accountant details of the new post office box number .

TWENTY-FOUR

Surprisingly, despite the magnitude and enormity of the task ahead he slept well, but woke a bit earlier than usual, managing to eat with the family, which was not unusual , but not a regular occurrence.

The family bid its adieux and he left for work and on reaching his destination, as instructed, took from the glove compartment, his small but effective revolver which he was licensed to carry. He spent nearly two hours using the solitude and tranquillity to catch up on his ever growing mountain of paperwork until ten fifty when he left the office, locked up and made certain that in his pockets were the pistol and the pair of cotton gloves.

He arrived outside of the Texas School Book Depository within a minute or so of the time calculated for the journey, even though the mass of onlookers far exceeded his expectations and had hindered his journey. He entered the building with an air of confidence and was unchallenged. He climbed the six flights of stairs with the last vestiges of his youth and did not pass anyone else either ascending or descending. He walked to a nondescript door, knocked twice and heard what he assumed was a heavy box being moved from the other side of the door. He heard the door being unlocked and he stood back to be acknowledged (but not greeted) by a thin faced man of insignificant appearance.

There, by the window, as promised, and it could have been his own rifle, was the Mannlicher- Carcano91/38 6.5millimetre Italian rifle. As he carefully and deliberately put on the cotton gloves he signalled to his assistant, without saying a word, to bring the instrument of death to him, observing that the man`s fingers clearly were positioned to make a number of identifiable prints. The assassin sat on a conveniently placed chair, out of view of the assembled crowds six floors below, noted that the man was again barricading the door with a partially filled box, and after checking that the rifle was unloaded he proceeded to check the firing mechanism before positioning himself near the window.

He mentally prepared himself for the hunt and the kill. For a few minutes he allowed himself to be back in the forests of his youth, along with his now long dead father : soon a pack of wild wolves would pass by and he would then have but a few well controlled moments to release three or maybe four shots to down his quarry. Two would be enough, a third shot probably an unnecessary bonus.

The papers and television had for some days published details of the route that the Presidential cavalcade would follow and the vehicles would enter Elm Street giving him an excellent line of vision in which to hit the pack of wolves.

He got off three shots successfully hitting both the leader of the pack and his adjacent companion. Without *ANY* emotion, he turned away from the window, handed the rifle back to its custodian, walked to the door, dragged the box away from the door which he then opened with his still gloved hands, looked at the man for a brief instant and then departed, finding the descent less exhausting than the earlier ascent. On reaching the ground floor, as suggested to him, he half turned, to give a false and erroneous impression that he was entering the building, for in fact, he must have exited the building literally moments or seconds before the first investigators began to swarm to and into the building. He had successfully completed the first two parts of his instructions: the kill and then the exit. He was carried along by the shocked crowd and was unable to exactly follow the prescribed route, but as the crowds dispersed and thinned he got back on course, spotting in an alley a large commercial waste bin, partially open, in which he disposed of one of the two gloves. Shortly before he reached his destination he slipped the other glove which still, very slightly, exuded the odour of cordite, into a trash can outside of the rear of a diner.

He arrived at the hotel some seven or eight minutes late, went to the reception, where he was instantaneously recognised, and asked for a room. He was addressed with great courtesy by the receptionist who asked "If he wanted the room for the night or just for the afternoon? "

To which, slightly taken aback by such a formal but friendly enquiry, he replied:

'It 's terrible out there. God knows what has happened. There's rumours that Kennedy has been hit! Probably just for a couple of hours only. I'll let you know. Is there anything to sign for or pay?'

The receptionist addressed him by his name and with great respect and possibly looking to the future, assured him that undoubtedly they would satisfactorily resolve the matter.

He took himself to the room not knowing that he was being followed by his contact who had arrived shortly before him and who had strategically placed himself close to the reception area in order to identify and follow him.

159

After having relieved himself he took off his tie,loosened his shoes and he sat on the edge of the bed awaiting his contact's approach and it was not long before there was a knock on the door.

He could not hide his surprise or pleasure on seeing the courier: he had not seen his compatriot and fellow sleeper since they had said their good byes before going their separate ways almost twenty years before. They smiled at each other, shook hands and then. clasped each other in a bear hug of friendship. A torrent of conversation followed, interspersed with laughter and nostalgia. Then, as though their minds were one, in harmony and resonance, they started speaking in their mother tongue . For both men this was the first time in nearly twenty years and at first they were both slow, unsure and faltering as distant memories were revived. They spoke of the camp , but not of the girl, of their lives and of his success and his friend's struggles. Perhaps he could help his friend but to preserve their joint secret the association had to be discreet?

The courier announced that he was carrying certain documents which were contained in an envelope which he would shortly produce but in the meantime he was instructed to obtain the Post Office box number for contact purposes. He also understood that his friend:

"Might have a pair of gloves which he should hand over as a formal means of identification", to which he received the unfortunate reply that:

"They had been disposed of as he had been specially instructed to dispose of the pair separately."

His old friend authoritatively responded that:

"In fact, that was what he had really been told to expect and that he was also told that his contact would have with him a small pistol."

Yuri placed the pistol on the table as he emphatically remarked that:

"It would be unwise for them to be seen together, however he could be contacted via the Post Office box number for social or business purposes but initial contact should be delayed for at least six to nine months."

The courier strangely asked to be excused, went to the toilet, relieved himself and returned to the room still drying his hands on a towel. He walked past the sitting assassin and suddenly, with unexpected speed, grabbed the pistol from off the table wrapping the towel around the barrel and encasing his hand and without interrupting the rhythm, shot from very close range his friend in the temple killing him instantly. Yuri slumped forward accompanied by a small fountain of blood which soon subsided. The executioner, if in anticipation, stepped aside to avoid being drowned in the man`s life blood. He then indifferently and without any apparent respect for the man manipulated the pistol into his fingers and as if to apologise for his deceit and treachery, said:

"Goodbye my dear friend, It was either your life or mine!"

TWENTY-FIVE

Her promise and integrity was confirmed when he returned to his own motel room where he was surprised to see, adjacent to a fat ,plain unsealed envelope, a quart bottle of his favourite Vodka, which normally he could not afford to buy, and when he did he always ended the session regretting his foolishness.

She had contacted him four days earlier and the shock of hearing Russian and his real name of Oleg completely destabilised him and it was only when she began to speak to him in English and identified herself that he regained, like a gyroscope, his balance. He had never earned $seventy-five thousand and her offer was irresistible. He had driven down from Wichita, Kansas, the previous day, on the '35', through Oklahoma and passed Oklahoma City arriving in Dallas, exhausted, in the early evening.

The room had been prepaid for two nights, and he was so tired that even after an invigorating shower he had succumbed to sleep but woke early realising that on his arrival he had overlooked to look inside the fridge, as specially instructed, where as promised was an envelope which he had to give to his contact but was to recover after he had executed him. There was, as promised, another but this time bulging unsealed envelope which he nervously delved into. It was $fifteen hundred in $twenty used notes. And when he returned home there would be a further $five thousand in his toolkit in the garage. How she knew all these little facts was unimportant. He would soon have money in his pockets and there was a woman at the bar he frequented who knew how to open her legs and give him the pleasure that he enjoyed.

But the instructions were clear and specific. He was not to leave the room but to request reception, for a $twenty tip, to bring to him breakfast and at eleven forty-five he was to leave his room and walk to a hotel which would take forty-five minutes and wait in the reception room until just before one p.m. when his contact would arrive and he was to follow him to his room *WITHOUT* communicating with him or being noticed. After killing him he was to clear up and whilst in the room he was to be absolutely careful *NOT* to leave any finger prints and, If possible ,he should endeavour not to draw the staff's attention to his presence.

On return to his own motel he should deposit the envelope which he had recovered and place the document in the fridge in exactly the same place as he had found it. He was to 'check out', citing his shock and distress at the day's events.

His auto, bearing out of State Kansas plates, was freed from the car park as the guard raised the barrier and in response he saluted the man with the opened bottle from which he look liberal and generous swigs, ignoring a slight difference to the normal taste.

He decided to stop off at Purcell , South of Norman, on the '35' for a steak dinner and a few drinks at a bar that he knew was very 'lively' and might be suitable for an overnight stop for he had plenty of greenbacks.

They came from behind a parked, articulated rig and he had just about enough time to screw the bottle cap on to the already half full bottle and grab some strategically placed chewing gum. He was about to enter the Interstate when the two Highway Patrolmen stopped his vehicle. They were stopping all 'out of State' registered vehicles and checking the drivers and their vehicles, recording the information. He had nothing to hide and the search was conducted with speed and courtesy. As he drove off, one of the officers suggested he stop drinking immediately because the roads were being heavily policed but he continued drinking, ignoring the officer's wise counsel.

He was ordained never to reach his destination for she and her superiors would never allow him to live and perhaps, probably, inevitably tell his story and the bait of discreet monthly payments over four years was never intended to be honoured. Whether it was the poison that had been furtively introduced into the bottle or the volume of liquor that he had consumed is now unimportant. Shortly after he exited the Interstate for Purcell he must have lost control and hit, head on, a lorry transporting fuel and the ensuing conflagration reduced his human body to ashes far quicker and effectively than a crematoria. But a decade later, by persistence and luck, both Yuri and Oleg would be connected by a simple mistake that they had been warned not to commit.

TWENTY-SIX

The Warren Commission clearly showed that Lee Harvey Oswald had not only acted alone but was the man who fired the fatal shots which had so tragically brought to an early end the life of the thirty-fifth President .

In retrospect,on the evidence that was available, the Commission could reach no other conclusion ,however its findings were made in the aftermath of a war and a global political earthquake which irrevocably changed the political geography, world order and the Nation's perception of events. The events in Dallas and to a lesser extent in London were cynically viewed by the people of the United States as probably part of a Communist conspiracy but without any absolute factual evidence.

A report of the suicide appeared on the following Tuesday in the local Dallas press and a few days later a short obituary was published but the promised monthly payment of $five thousand never, surprisingly, reached the Post Office Box.

TWENTY-SEVEN

They had avoided detection or any enquiries such was their isolation and caution. The coach, which prominently displayed the title of The Anglo–Italian and West German Film Corporation of Milan, had been deliberately driven into the farm yard from the barn to, if need be, promote the name and the purpose of the temporary residents` use of the property. If they had been observed in the fields,exercising or performing manoeuvres,the purpose would be inscrutable and if, by chance, they had been seen in the barn which dually served as their accommodation and base then the valid explanation of their real life rehearsals would undoubtedly satisfy any enquiries.

It was only on the Sunday afternoon that the elite troops were told that the operation was to be on the following afternoon and that they would be leaving that evening, under cover of darkness, and they were immediately to purge the premises of any evidence that could be used to trace them or even identify them. Once completed, they should again check their Kalashnikov A K 47s,however distribution of other weapons would be made the following day when they would receive their uniforms and be advised of the target though its identity was unimportant, what was the primary objective was surprise and then above any other consideration, the maximum kill ratio. Their commanding officer and the leader of the mission reminded his men that their training had prepared them for a specific operation where their targets would be unarmed but most important of all grouped en masse in one location, and it was essential that they be the focus and the primary target of their action and that once the mission had been accomplished they could then remove any obstacles to their departure.

The leader continued his observations by confirming to the troops that an exit strategy had already been prepared and that before the operation began each man would be handed thirty English pounds, made up of three five pounds notes, eight one pound notes, eight ten shilling notes and the balance in coins.

Also they would be provided with a pouch containing a selection of French, West German and American currency though he did not expect any of his men to end up in New York which was received with an unrehearsed and spontaneous roar of laughter. He was confident that if any of the men were separated from the main body, that their years of training, their initiative and their desire to return home to collect their medals would strengthen their efforts to cross the Channel and to make their way back to a friendly and welcoming Country.

They meticulously cleaned the building that had accommodated them, even wiping down areas where their finger prints could have left incriminating evidence and using lime in the temporary cesspit, to destroy any evidence that could or might be gleaned from their excrement. As darkness descended they boarded the coach placing the two cases in the rear compartment and the commander ,who appeared to know the area well, drove off.

They proceeded in a southerly direction,a fact easily calculated by those troops interested in the journey, since they were, by training and practical experience all able to travel by the stars, though none of them were knowledgeable enough to estimate the direction from various road signs, to Dunstable, Luton and then St. Albans and it was at a roadside public house that they the collected a passenger, who, if they had remembered, was one of the drivers who had ferried them from the docks at Gravesend, and he confidently took over the driving, continuing in a southerly direction before gradually turning, snaking and weaving through numerous built up areas.

His route was through the City, onto the A2, and into Kent, subsequently leaving the main road and he proceeded to journey across country through narrow and seemingly impassable winding lanes reaching and then halting just before an unlit crossroads deep in a wooded area where even now the ghost of Sir John Falstaff would once again be jousting with imaginary foes, however such Shakespearean illusions would not concern, interest or worry the coach's occupants.

Some ten minutes elapsed after which time a vehicle drew up, flashed them and shortly afterwards a knock was heard and another man entered the vehicle, gave a packet to the driver, who vacated the driver's seat which was then occupied by the new arrival as the original occupant then left the coach and walked over to the vehicle which drove off into the darkness. This latest driver was to stay with the group until the operation had been completed and the escape plan had been successfully inaugurated, though in truth it was likely that he was unaware of their intended actions, acting primarily as a guide, but initially as a relief driver, travelling through a succession of minor roads, constantly making changes in direction, passing a public house, with a sign identifying its title as the Globe, until it reached an even more isolated farm in a rural and peaceful village called Kilnbrook.

The farm was reached by a meandering and unlit private road and as the driver adeptly completed the course and turned into the dark yard, the arc of the headlights briefly caught and illuminated four new pristine vehicles that had been delivered only hours before. They were a jeep and three lorries, exact replicas of current British Army vehicles and each bearing military registration plates cloned from vehicles parked either at the Duke of York barracks in the Kings Road, Chelsea or the barracks near the famous Lords cricket ground in Ordnance Hill, St. John's Wood. The tarpaulin covering on each of the three five ton lorries would easily hide the two containers and the camouflage and other identification numbers were so accurate that the only way any of the vehicles could be identified as copies would be, if improbably, they accidentally collided with their originals!

They awoke at first light, watched their final view of an English sunrise, ate their cold military rations and began to prepare for the unknowntask that for two months they had trained for.

Their first task was to check their new method of transport: proceeding through a long list, even changing the immaculate unworn tyres round the two axles as practice, since in the unlikely but always possible event of an emergency change they wished to know that they had the equipment and more important, the expertise. Whilst the fuel gauges confirmed that all four vehicles were virtually full, on enquiry they found that the 'Jerry' cans in each of the three lorries were empty but a decision was made by the commanding officer who did not share his reasoning, that they should not jeopardise their security by buying fuel en route.

At the final briefing the identity of the target was revealed together with the latest intelligence as to the level of security. The troops were amazed to learn not the identity of the target but the ludicrous fact that a single policeman would stand between them and their unwitting victims. The convoy would enter the centre of London via Blackfriars Bridge before turning left onto the Embankment, depositing the troops outside the target at three–thirty p.m. and departing no more than twelve minutes later to begin the dash back towards the Kent coast, though they would *rendez- vous* with the coach at a pre determined point before which the troops would change back into the civilian clothing which they had worn entering the country the previous Tuesday, before catching a ferry across the Channel.

Through a navigational error and an accumulation of traffic, the convoy, on the suggestion of the British navigator (who was in the leading jeep), turned left into Blackfriars Road instead of right but he corrected the error by directing the vanguard into Westminster Bridge Road, across the bridge and then left .

Less than three weeks later, following, in camera, a hastily arranged trial at the 'Old Bailey' (The Central Criminal Court) the man pleaded guilty to a number of charges, including the most damaging, of High Treason, and on the twenty-third of December, that is exactly four weeks to the day after the action, in the most absolute secrecy, he was hung at Pentonville Prison but his body was returned to his family on the understanding and their agreement that his death certificate would show the cause as suicide.

TWENTY-EIGHT

Mandel Goldburgh had resolved that as Monday would be his final full day in London, that after his visit to the British Library he would use the network of public transport to whisk him around London and it would enable him to view the magnificent sites before ending his journey at Victoria Station from where he would walk down Victoria Street to Parliament Square, along Whitehall to Trafalgar Square, up to Leicester Square Underground station and cut around the back (via the British Museum) and towards Kings Cross, reaching the haven of his hotel and a well earned lazy bath.

As he exited the double decker bus at Victoria Station he, undoubtedly, like his fellow passengers and the milling throng of commuters, travellers and visitors, were welcomed by the newspaper vendors announcing their presence and the almost unbelievable news of the incredible murder of the alleged assassin of the President, the previous day, Sunday November the twenty-fourth. Unlike everybody else he wondered with almost academic interest and perhaps with an ominous foreboding, if these two events were part of, or an adaptation of the plans that he had so meticulously prepared and handed to his dear old friend, but such an opening move, if part of a wider vast plan could only herald or portend a most awful, dramatic and frightening future. He put such thoughts as much as possible to the back of his mind and began the interesting journey along Victoria Street towards Parliament Square, passing the Army & Navy Stores, breaking his journey and temporarily escaping the cold and intermittent showers of a typical November London, entering the shop and pursuing the Englishman's right to wander around the store and admire, without any intention of buying from, the various departments and their displays.

He resumed his walk, endeavouring to suppress any thoughts of a possible connection between the recent dramatic events and his plans, concentrating, with an element of nostalgia, on some of the yes, exciting events that had not only shaped his life, but had moulded and defined his values and social and sometimes contradictory political opinions. Such was the intensity of his thoughts and his concentration that both time and distance melted away until suddenly, whilst virtually outside the St. Stephens' entrance to the House Of Commons, he was rudely brought back to reality when, without warning ,he felt a glancing blow and he sprawled across the pavement as he was hit by an athletic looking man ,who in his haste to reach some unknown destination, had misjudged a space between the innocent pedestrian and the edge of the pavement. The man, who was well over six feet in height, towered over the prostrate man, bent down and with sincere regret both apologised and offered his desire to assist the man since he was a qualified doctor, and with the assistance of a number of concerned pedestrians raised the shocked man, who returned to his erect standing position.

Goldburgh was unharmed and began to engage the man in conversation, enquiring first of all on the reason or reasons for his great haste. His reply couched in the most apologetic of terms and tone briefly explained that he was on route to an examination which, if successful, would put him on course to reach his goal of becoming a consultant and specialist surgeon. The doctor then commented that:

"Perhaps it was fate that I was to be late and that we were to meet."

They shook hands and as the doctor departed he was asked, if as an afterthought, for his name to which he quickly replied, to avoid any further delay, that it was:

"Doctor John Wrighton."

Their paths separated. Goldburgh continued his promenade past the St. Stephens' entrance which was guarded by a lone sentinel of the City of London police, whilst a mass of tourists stood behind the railings both in awe of the building and of the policeman's authority. At the junction with Westminster Bridge he turned north towards Whitehall and shortly saw the iconic sight of Admiral Horatio, Viscount Nelson, looking seawards in ever vigilant defence of his country.

He was unable to see the incident behind him when a convoy of military vehicles led by a jeep reached the end of the bridge and turned left towards the Houses of Parliament and stopped outside the St. Stephens' entrance. Within moments an estimated twelve or fourteen troops wearing combat uniforms leaped from the three lorries whilst another four soldiers in the same uniforms also emerged and each positioned themselves adjacent to the four vehicles to protect them from any inquisitive onlookers. According to reports gathered by the police later that same evening the dozen or so troops rushed to the forbidding doors, caught the police officer off guard and unimpeded, entered the building.

TWENTY-NINE

Events are not only made by men themselves, but by the incalculable influence of nature and the whim of the gods, however the intervention of good fortune or adversity,or even serendipity would ultimately be influential factors combining to create the 'End of Democracy'.

It is a tribute to the anonymous reporters and scribes of 'Hansard' that the final debate ever to take place in the Chamber of the House was faithfully and as always accurately and honestly recorded and also witnessed by those unlucky enough to have secured seating in the public gallery or those, whose status secured access to the exclusive and as it happened, dangerously located, V.I.P. seating .

History, or the truth that was allowed to survive, records that under the most difficult of circumstances, that the 'House' soon afterwards resumed its truncated sittings in the great Hall of Westminster but in view of the national and International situation, the sittings only lasted a few days and were seen by its few participants as more symbolic and morale boosting than as a forum for the pursuit of democratic action.

'Hansard' records that the House met at half- past two and after Prayers, commenced with oral answers to questions beginning with the sale of arms to South Africa.

The debate was opened, for Labour, by Christopher Mayhew and was answered by the Secretary of State for Foreign Affairs, 'Rab' Butler (not under any circumstances to be confused or even associated with the Labour and Coop member for Wood Green, Mrs. Joyce Butler). The oral questions and answers continued, raising such diverse subjects as Aircraft Flights (Landing Restrictions), through the Russian – Language Periodical Anglia, the United Nations (involving a spirited enquiry from the Labour member for West Fife, Willy Hamilton), to questions on Indonesia and Berlin, whilst interestingly the matter of ex gratia payments to ex–employees of the Shanghai Municipal Council was raised. Another topic raised, this time by Sir Barnett Janner (Labour – Leicester, North-West) concerned matters relating to Pensions and National Insurance.

Mr. Selwyn Lloyd, The Lord Privy Seal, then announced that:

"In view of the proceedings which are to follow, and which affect the business announced for today, may I inform the House of the rearrangement of business for this week."

After he scheduled the rearrangements, the tributes to President Kennedy began at precisely three thirty-two p.m.

As expected the House was overflowing but there were three major absentees, two in Washington for the funeral of the dead President, the Prime Minister and the leader of the Opposition, Harold Wilson and on the Government back benches a very special place remained empty, for it was the seat of a former Prime Minister, the Father of the House and a man of destiny, Sir Winston Churchill, member for Woodford . The man who had led the House and the nation from the brink of a catastrophic defeat to victory was no longer the energetic and dynamic man of two decades before.

'Rab' Butler opened the tributes and moved a manuscript Motion; at three forty p.m.in response, Patrick Gordon Walker (Smethwick) replied, on behalf of the Leader of the Opposition, followed at three forty-five p.m. by Mr. Donald Wade (Huddersfield, West, Liberal). It was at this moment that two Conservative M.Ps., Mr. William Clark (Nottingham South) and Capt. Richard Pilkington (Poole) by divine coincidence needed to answer a call of nature just as the former Prime minister, Mr. Harold Macmillan (Bromley) rose to speak at three fifty p.m. They jointly decided not to return to the Chamber but to boldly venture to the almost darkened terrace to obtain some fresh air at the moment that the previous P.M. ended his speech (three fifty-six p.m.)

and as Sir Thomas Moore(Ayr, Conservative) rose and began his oration:

"As our revered Father of the House, my Right Hon. Friend the Member for Woodford (Sir W. Churchill), will not be with us today-"

And at that moment the second part of the plan became active and the obituary of freedom and democracy would be written in blood.

THIRTY

The assault was unexpected, audacious ,adroit, swift, and the outcome, horrendous. The elite troops acted without emotion or compassion, only fulfilling the orders and procedures that for some two months they had rehearsed unquestioningly in a hangar under the watchful eyes of their officers and once, unobserved, under their ultimate political master.

Fourteen men in seven pairs literally bounded up the thirty-one steps which led from the door of St. Stephens Gate up to the Central Lobby of the Palace of Westminster. Because their training had been so rigorous they both ignored and did not see, on either side of the passageway, four sets of historical paintings and as they entered the vast imposing lobby, they ignored the eponymous statue of St. Stephen located on their right hand side. They instinctively veered to the left, again ignoring on their left hand side a statue of William Ewart Gladstone and deftly avoided a throng of humanity who would very soon be obliterated. The gaze of a marble statue of John, Earl Russell, strategically placed to watch arrivals entering the lobby was unable to cry out to warn the civilised world of their impending doom. Five of the troops positioned themselves across the first set of double doors which led to the Chamber apparently ignoring the constantly manned reception desk and the imposing Victorian architecture, decorations and artwork.

Nine men went through the double doors, leaving two more on guard at the next set and at the Chamber entrance, facing the Speaker of the House of Commons, five more sentinels stood guard.

Two soldiers, brandishing their Kalashnikov A.K.47s, entered the Chamber both unannounced and unexpected and without further notice they proceeded methodically and without sentiment to walk along the central aisle firing to their left and right both at ground level and at an elevated angle. They continued until they reached the

Speaker`s Chair but he was dead: slumped across his ceremonial and symbolic chair, his face almost peaceful, blood oozing from a bullet hole in his forehead. The two men turned, repeating their simple procedure until they reached the double doors to be replaced by two of their companions, who this time, like a different dance routine proceeded to hurl specially modified hand grenades which landed and exploded between the rows of seats and their lecterns which acted as mirrors, concentrating and focusing the explosions. Once they had completed their task they were finally replaced by the original pair of assassins (having reloaded their weapons) who this time were armed with more powerful grenades which they very expertly hurled, causing additional collateral damage to the walls and the ornate decorations which enhanced the uniqueness and individuality of the room. Reaching the end they turned round, activated their weapons and ended the carnage by again spraying the Chamber with a final burst and flourish of gunfire.

At the same time the Central Lobby had also become a charnel house as a secondary action began, synchronised with the primary action. Three of the elite Spetsnaz troops began to spray the Central Lobby with bursts of gunfire, felling anyone and everyone in sight, then joining the two remaining guards who replaced them and like their compatriots along the corridor ,began to hurl and broadcast the same type of hand grenades to complete their task.

The three original troops, having reloaded, then walked across the Lobby oblivious and uncaring of the dead and dying beneath their feet and took the exit which led to the Members and Members` guests restaurants which they entered and proceeded to rain down another barrage of bullets though their kill ratio this time was not as effective as outside, since a few and a very few number of M.Ps, alerted to the sounds outside had hidden themselves behind the bars, proving the necessity of adequate refreshment and watering holes in the Palace of Westminster. Regrouping in silence, the fourteen assassins exited the building through the passageway leading back to the St. Stephens entrance and the waiting convoy which departed well within the twelve minute time scale and not before some of the bemused members of the general public had finished taking photographs of the convoy and the occupants.

The first brave wave of police officers, ignoring any danger to their health and safety, gingerly entered the Central Lobby to be confronted by a scene and panorama of chaos, death and horror.

The actual number of fatal casualties was not released until seventy two hours later, not solely because of the chaos and mayhem but because of the anticipated shock that would be caused to the nation's morale; the figures for the dead in the Chamber being, in proportion to the total number of M.Ps. so massive, and with the crisis that followed and then the political upheaval, the truth was shrouded and corrupted by the machinations of political intrigue and the sordid manoeuvrings for power and influence.

Shortly afterwards the ever swelling ranks of police officers were joined by the first wave of genuine, bona fide, *BRITISH* troops who at first drew a cautious air of doubt from an increasing mass of spectators outside the general area of the Houses of Parliament as news and rumour spread. The police were accompanied by armed and nervous soldiers from the nearby Duke of York's barracks and as they passed through the first two sets of doors they were confronted with the tragic sight of the first identifiable M.P, the Conservative member for Finchley and the Joint Parliamentary Secretary to the Ministry of Pensions and National Insurance, Mrs. Margaret Thatcher, who less than two hours before had been answering questions on behalf of the Minister. She had been shot at point blank range and may have died an excruciating death but it was the manner of her macabre appearance, for still in the grip of her cold fingers was the leather strap of her handbag as she must have defiantly attempted to attack the assailants, but in vain.

The sight that greeted the first group into the Chamber, after the traumatic shock of the field of death that was the Central Lobby, was of unimaginable and nearly indescribable horror as if the visions of Dante's Inferno or the Book of Revelations had suddenly come to life. There was an explosion of colour, the green leather benches of the Commons stained by the red of the blood which had flowed in profusion. To the left, on the Government's side of the House was an anonymous M.P. who had been hit in the face making identification impossible, whilst a few feet away from him, on the Opposition bench, a member had been hit in the stomach which had effectively exploded and such was the vision that a young police officer later named as John Jeffery had vomited into the lifeless cavity creating both a revolting picture and odour.

There had been little resistance, such was the surprise and speed of the attack, but one M.P. died holding the symbol of British Democracy – The Mace – in perhaps a foolhardy act of defiance or perhaps as an attempt not to defend himself, but the freedom that the House represented. In many cases it was not possible to confirm whether the cause of death was from the initial gunfire or the subsequent use of hand grenades as in many instances the bodies had been ripped apart by the explosions and it is not necessary, in respect of their status and commitment to the community, to list a catalogue of the many various traumas,suffice to state that dismembered bodies and severed limbs gave the room the appearance of an abattoir.

The first official roll call announced by a genuinely grieving Prime Minister after his return to the United Kingdom from Washington, was that five hundred and twenty seven M.Ps. were believed to have been slaughtered, the overwhelming majority being in the Chamber, a few in the Central Lobby and the rest in the two restaurants ,though some actually survived the carnage, probably by good fortune, in the Members only restaurant. Twenty-nine members of the House of Lords also perished, most being caught in the Members and guests dining room socialising with former contemporaries and in excess of two hundred and eighty employees, police officers and visitors caught up in the Central Lobby.

As a post script and in order to close this chapter of events, within forty eight hours the duped English driver had been arrested, though there is some confusion and contradiction as to the actual circumstances as it was claimed by his family and friends that he was literally walking to the nearest police station to surrender himself whilst the police claim that he was caught trying to escape, but since his photograph had been prominently displayed in the national press, his escape would have proved difficult.

Fundamental to his interrogation was the interest shown by the Police and M.I.5 in his recruitment, the identity of his recruiter and what reason had been given for the assassins' presence in the United Kingdom. Since there was already a file on the man, the crucial key fact was the identity of the recruiter and the name given frightened the interrogators and confirmed to the head of M.I.5 that not only buried deep within the British Trade Union movement, but at the highest level, was a subversive clique, with direct access to the Leader of the Opposition, for the name given was that of Jack Jones, the former Liverpool docker, fighter for the Republican cause in the Spanish Civil war and leader of the powerful Transport and General Workers Union. Already suspected of treachery and spying this was the first but uncollaborated evidence of actual treachery but it was his association and closeness to the Liverpool M.P. and Opposition leader which worried and disturbed the Intelligence chiefs.

Whilst the fate of the assassins was never conclusively verified in the turmoil and chaos of the surprise attack which commenced with the assault on West Germany, they apparently completed their vehicle exchange somewhere on the A2 major arterial road that led to the coast, and their coach was believed to have caught a late night ferry to France where all trace was lost in the opening hours of the war and the consequent 'Victory in the West' that their action had precipitated.

THIRTY-ONE

WAR!

Not since the dark days of December nineteen forty-one, when the Teutonic horde stood at the gates of Moscow and catastrophe loomed, or less than fifteen months before, in the autumn of nineteen sixty-two, when the young American President had confronted the Motherland and her husband who had been forced into an inglorious and ignominious retreat from the Island of Cuba, had she sensed and felt such foreboding.

Despite the events of the previous year she was genuinely upset and distressed when she heard the news of the President's death and her thoughts went out to his widow and her pleasant memories of their meeting . She instinctively knew that behind the granite and cold facade of her husband's demeanour, that he was also truly moved at the tragic and callous murder; indeed her opinion was confirmed by his recent admittance, most unusual for a Presidium member and especially for the First Secretary, when he confided in her that on the Saturday morning, following an emergency meeting of the Presidium and with the assistance of the Soviet ambassador to the United States, that he had utilised, for the first time ever, the 'Hot Line' to communicate with the new President. He had wished him well and not only requested that he convey his condolences to Mrs. Kennedy, but reminded him that just as in the Great Patriotic War, the people of the Soviet Union stood side by side with their American friends.

What the First Secretary had omitted to tell his wife, deliberately, was that the real purpose of the call was to gauge the strength and resolve of the Texan, whose accent and style, in the opinion of Khrushchev's analysts, was rough and unsophisticated in comparison to his predecessor, but more important, as expected, the Soviets had detected that the feared and vast Strategic Air Command had become more active and in greater numbers and whilst this level of activity was indeed anticipated in a myriad of scenarios, it concerned the leader of the nation when combined with the impending Warsaw Treaty manoeuvres. Nikita Khrushchev requested, as a sign of friendship and conciliation, that the new President stand down his fleet of bombers whilst in return he confirmed that the Soviet leadership would compel the East Germans and Poles to postpone the imminent manoeuvres.

This offer was of course a well planned and hypocritical bluff, for Khrushchev had, de facto, authorised the assassination and not only that was aware through the designs of his military planners that the

Warsaw Treaty manoeuvres were programmed to begin early on the Tuesday, that is once the second destabilisation operation had been successfully completed. The depth of his perfidiousness was the fact, possibly not yet reported by the American Embassy in Moscow, that the news of the President's murder was still being kept from the Russian people as there was a complete media blackout sanctioned by the Presidium until they considered their posture in the situation.

Monday, the twenty–fifth, saw frenzied and unusual activity in the grounds of the dacha. For the First Secretary's wife the nature of the work, the absence of any prior notification or an explanation as to the purpose of the various operations caused her great concern and worry.

Unbeknownst to her, close to, but not adjacent to the junction of the tributary road that led to the main Moscow road and joining the meandering road that served as the sole access to the estate, engineers were cutting a broad pathway into the forest without any logical or perceived purpose.

Since mid morning a number of convoys had been delivering what she assumed were supplies to the barracks and to confuse or complicate the matter, appeared also to be taking back an equivalent load in terms of the type of goods.

Finally, whilst the normal activity of snow clearance on the perimeter road continued, there seemed to be an excessive urgency and fervour clearing the helicopter pad and also with great vigour, continually keeping clear the broad pathway from the dacha to the landing pad.

Early that evening one of her concerns was answered when she heard the sound of a helicopter, which soon thereafter landed, bringing her husband home. After he had reached the sanctuary of his home she endeavoured to tell him some wonderful ,exciting news that she felt certain would raise his spirits and strengthen him, but his thoughts were concentrated on matters of state and the news that he awaited from London concerning the attack on the centre and symbol of British power and democracy. In the presence of his wife he was able to maintain an air of quiet contentment but this was a facade that hid his feverish preparations and his greatest challenge.

They ate simply and frugally although somewhat embarrassed by the new and unusual experience of being permanently accompanied by two members of a military entourage, both of whom each had in their close presence a metallic briefcase, though each was different in size and dimensions, which they both guarded with intense scrutiny. Only he was privy to knowledge that would surely soon reach Moscow that an unexpected assault had taken place, in London, on the centre of government. This temporary lull in the accelerating path to war gave him the opportunity to explain to his wife that a pathway was being constructed with great urgency to a secret exit from a tunnel that led, at a depth of some seventy or eighty metres, to a subterranean complex underneath the adjacent military barracks and that unknown even to him until earlier in the day, that the complex was constructed with a number of levels up to some one hundred and twenty metres in depth.

Its main purpose was to protect him as the effective leader of the Soviet Union and his family, in the event, and he stressed, the unlikely event that total war (He deliberately did not use the words atomic or thermonuclear in order not to disturb his wife) and that the convoys she had seen had been restocking the complex with food and supplies sufficient for twenty people, deliberately not specifying a period so not to distress her.

It was at this moment that she felt able to tell her husband, what for her was the exciting news, that again all four of the grandchildren would be staying, not only over the New Year but for a whole week thereafter which in truth did raise a smile from her husband but within a few minutes was superseded by an urgent request from the communications room for the First Secretary to go to the first floor as a priority message had just been received and he was followed by the two army officers.

It was the news that he was awaiting and within minutes he was on his way back to Moscow again accompanied by he two men for an urgent meeting of the Presidium.

THIRTY-TWO

FROM A SPEECH BY THE FIRST COMMISSAR FOR WAR,

LEON TROTSKY...

"...wars can be avoided only if we fill the hearts of the imperialists and capitalists with intense fear of our strength of arms..For the attacks of enemy forces to be repelled, we must be armed with all of the latest means of defence which modern war technique can produce. The use of poison gas in the last war requires us to keep even this means of warfare in reserve for the defence of our nation against the enemy."

The history of biological and chemical warfare has a long provenance dating back to the Roman Empire when soldiers would contaminate the water source of the enemy with the carcasses of dead animals and then through medieval times when dead bodies of those contaminated with the plague would be catapulted over the walls of enemy castles. The use of chemical weapons in the arena of warfare had its debut in World War One, when the Germans utilised mustard gas against the French and British.

Chemical weapons were not used on the battleground during World War Two though research and experimentation continued on all sides.

At the end of hostilities ,in May 1945 in Europe, and then three months later in August 1945 following the defeat of Japan, the three victors were able to reward themselves with the fruits and plunder of victory and there was a stampede between the Americans, British and Russians to capture not only examples of the FZG 76 and A4 weapons known commonly and respectively as the V1 and V2 but also to obtain research documentation, and finally, the most important aspect, to recruit the scientists who had created the first generation of a new technology. The post war development of jet powered aeroplanes and the gradual demise of propeller driven planes was again partially due to the 'liberation' of German research, as the Messerschmittt Me 262 fighter, the Arado 234C four engined jet bomber and the innovative Messerschmitt Me 163 Komet, propelled by the Walter HWK 109-509a rocket engine all proved to be a substantial part of the foundations of a new concept in military and civilian aviation and rocket design. But it was in the vile world of chemical and biological weaponry that *ALL* immersed themselves without moral scruples.

In August 1947, Dr. Gerhard Schrader, the chief chemist for Bayer was made a formal offer by the British authorities to come to the United Kingdom and work at Porton Down where chemical weapons were produced. Dr. Schrader had discovered the nerve gas Sarin as a by product of his insecticide research. Sarin ,when inhaled or absorbed through the skin, paralyses the central nervous system resulting in death and later, *YOU* the reader ,will learn more of the proud achievements of our *CIVILISED* society.

In the autumn of 1945 General MacArthur granted immunity to members of the Anti –Epidemic Water Supply and Purification Bureau better known as Unit 731, an undercover medical experimentation unit of the Imperial Japanese Army, in exchange for research data on biological warfare.

It had been set up as a biological warfare unit in 1936 by a physician and army officer, Shiro Ishil at Pingfan near Harbin, a remote, desolate part of the Manchurian Peninsula. What went on there is beyond the bounds of human imagination and gives an insight into the depths that the so called human race can descend. The following is a slightly modified transcription of an extract from a newspaper article that,in hindsight, should have been censored...

Kamada, one of several veterans who felt able to speak out after the death of Emperor Hirohito, remembered extracting the plague-infested organs of a *fully conscious* (Author's specific emphasis) prisoner with a scalpel.

"I inserted the scalpel directly into the prisoner's neck and opened the chest", he said,"at first there was a terrible scream, but the voice soon fell silent." Other experiments involved hanging prisoners upside down to discover how long it took for them to choke to death, and injecting air into their arteries to test for the onset of embolisms."

Whilst primarily the centre had been set up to investigate various elements of biological warfare, experiments were conducted into chemical warfare, for example, Chinese prisoners were exposed to phosgene gas to discover the effect on their lungs and other prisoners were slowly roasted by given electrical charges.

Emperor Hirohito may not have known about Unit 731 but his family did. Hirohito's younger brother toured the Unit and noted in his memoirs that he saw films showing mass poison gas experiments on Chinese prisoners.

To conclude this passing observation on the acts of a supposed civilised nation, one final example was the development of certain biological weapons. Vast quantities of anthrax and bubonic plague bacteria were stored at Unit 731 and thousands of white rats were bred as plague carriers together with fleas to feed on them. The plague fleas were then encased in bombs which were used by Japanese troops to launch against reservoirs, wells and agricultural areas. Infected clothing and food supplies were also dropped and villages and whole towns were afflicted with cholera, anthrax and the plague.

During the Great Patriotic War, the Soviet Union produced, but did not use, a variety of chemical weapons, possibly because on April fifth 1928 they had acceded to the Geneva Protocol (concluded in 1925) that banned the use of chemical and bacteriological weapons. The Soviet leadership adopted a clear policy of the non first use of chemical weapons, however due to reservations made by most States party to the Protocol it virtually became a non first use provision. The reservation made by the USSR went further than most other States:

"The said protocol shall cease to be binding for the government of the Union of Soviet Socialist Republics in regard to all enemy states whose armed forces or allies, de jure or in fact, do not respect the restrictions which are the object of this protocol."

That position was enforced by the pioneering work of the deputy minister (or People`s Commissar) of defence, Marshall Mikhail Tukhachesky (before he was purged in 1937) who devised a new doctrine for mechanised warfare which integrated armoured units together with air power *AND* chemical warfare. Similar developments emerged in Germany under General Heinz Guderian but he foresaw no role for the use of chemical weapons.

I now regret to inform *YOU*, the reader, that following legal advice I have had to delete and expunge outline details of the procedures to manufacture two other nerve gases: Tabun and Soman, however I have been permitted to give some information to substantiate the very grave and powerful consequences of their use. The phosphorous based Tabun, and the even more lethal fluorine based compounds Sarin and Soman came directly from the work and laboratories of the chemist Dr. Gerhard Schrader before and during the Second World War and their arrival heralded and initiated a new more cruel, and in the author`s opinion, inhuman direction.

In the drive westwards, early in 1945, the Red Army captured two factories producing these compounds, both on the Oder river at Falkenhagen near Fuerstenberg and the other at Dyhernfurth near Breslau. Thus the fruits of victory gave them a powerful, potent and highly toxic trio of weapons to add to their armoury. Combined with the colourless liquid Hydrogen Cyanide, the plan devised Mandel Goldburgh using the four diabolical creations would be a lethal first strike weapon in the war that was only hours away.

For those technically minded, details of the four weapons are scheduled:

Hydrogen Cyanide: A very strong and quick acting poison, which effects unprotected humans through the respiratory organs, during the ingestion of food or water or through the skin. Symptoms of intoxication are a bitter, metallic taste in the mouth, sickness, headache, lack of breath and shudders. Death occurs after intoxication as a result of paralysis of the heart.

Sarin: A colourless and practically odourless liquid. Symptoms of intoxication appear quickly without any period of latent effect ,myosis (narrowing of the pupils), photophobia, difficulty in breathing and pain in the chest.

Soman and Tabun: Are both neuro paralytic toxic agents. The former is a transparent, colourless, involatile liquid smelling of camphor and the latter (in its pure form) a colourless liquid. Soman is similar to Sarin in its injurious effect, but more toxic. When it acts on the skin in either droplet or vapour form it causes a general poisoning of the organism. Tabun in its vapour form or after droplets contact the skin is immediately effective, and, subject to the dosage...Fatal.

Tabun was synthesized, by chance, and its molecular formula is...

$C_5H_{11}N_2O_2P$ with a density of1.077g cm-3. A non scientific description of the order of symptoms is as follows:

"First your nose would begin to run, then your chest would feel constricted. Your vision would dim as your pupils contracted into pinpoints. You`d begin to drool and sweat excessively. Then would come nausea and vomiting, intestinal cramps and involuntary urination and defecation. You`d twitch, jerk and stagger as you`re overcome with convulsions and possibly coma. Finally you`re breathing would stop as your diaphragm and the muscles of your chest froze, causing you to die of suffocation."

No doubt some people including YOU, THE READER, would regard the above as a great achievement of our so called *CIVILISED* society.

THIRTY-THREE

The plan that had been refined in the isolated and cocooned redoubt close to the Yamantau mountain complex was composed of three elements:

The first being the secret production of various chemical weapons and nerve gases without prioritising any one particular type, their transportation and temporary storage and the method of delivery which forms the second part of the plan. The subterfuge, like the deception, was to be a massive programme to manufacture organo – phosphates, their distribution and broadcasting by specially, actually slightly modified planes and a 'crash' programme to train pilots, mainly from East Germany, Poland and Czechoslovakia where it was allegedly intended that wheat production was to be increased utilising the chemical fertilisers which were to be broadcast by aeroplane. Finally the coordinated first strike against primarily, West Germany, with the potential 'bonus' of the assault spilling over into the countries bordering the English Channel.

No provision and in consequence no planning had been conceived either by Goldburgh or the elite body of planners in respect of the submarine armada and therefore Goldburgh had not calculated the political consequences and the Presidium's or Khrushchev's options.

The planners were morally cynical and callous about the fate of both the pilots and the tank crews as will shortly be explained, justifying especially the anticipated high loss of pilots(in fact the losses were close to approximately 79%) and for the tank crews who had to traverse the still lingering after effects of the chemical and especially the nerve gas attacks (up to one in three of the crews) as their sacrifice was justified as their contribution to the cause of Socialism and the liberation of the lands under the corrupt control of the Capitalists and the Imperialists. Khrushchev, in order to rationalise the high loss of life reminded the planners, if they had any qualms about the potential high loss of life, that for the Poles it was to be atonement for the humiliation that they had inflicted on the embryonic Soviet nation in 1920 and for the scurrilous falsehood that they had tried to disseminate along with the Nazis that the Leadership of the Soviet Union had been complicit in the so called Katyn massacre and the East Germans could finally, by actions and sacrifice, erase the stain of their parents' support for the perfidious Hitler who had attacked, without warning, the sacred soil of the Motherland and in violation of the Ribbentrop- Molotov agreement of 1939.

From early May 1963, in the USSR, East Germany, Poland and in Czechoslovakia production began of a fleet of primitive, archaic but essentially highly effective Yakovlev Elevens. The original test plane was believed to have first flown in 1946 and was a basic combat trainer with a maximum speed of 286 m.p.h., a dive limit of 368 m.p.h. and a stalling speed of 90 m.p.h., but more importantly it could be configured to have bomb racks under the wings. Not only was the plane suitable for the planned operation but construction costs were relatively low since production techniques and the materials used for the wings and fuselage were cheap, the most expensive element being the engine, however the military had 'factored in' the recovery of crashed aeroplanes and the engines (and possibly other recyclable parts including radios) and the reuse of reconditioned or repaired engines for non military purposes (for example, generating electricity). What was never admitted or most certainly never officially confirmed was that quality control (never a strong aspect of the then East European Socialist philosophy) was disregarded since they knew and calculated the low expectation of the aeroplane's life (and most likely its pilots) even transporting the component parts by road or canal to assembly points safely hidden behind the front lines, fearing an extended long flight might put a strain on the framework.

The cost of the whole operation, borne both by the Soviet Union and her Warsaw Treaty partners, was significantly low in relation and proportion to their overall budgets and would have been exposed within a period, as calculated by Khrushchev, of between fifteen and twenty four months, but he realised that the territorial and political gains would be such that any objections from his opponents could be brushed aside and that they would be ousted from power along with the highly dangerous and scheming Leonid Brezhnev .

The callousness and cynicism both of the planners and Khrushchev was encapsulated in the calculation that the life of each plane and consequently for its pilots could be measured in perhaps only three to five sorties at maximum, or in terms of a time scale, no more than two days! The calculation or assessment was to be proved frighteningly and chillingly (for the pilots) accurate, as delivery of their bomb loads was by gravity only, at low level, and crucially at low speed, to improve accuracy but making them easy targets for any brave soldiers to retaliate and down their enemy. But the contradiction was that a psychology of fear bordering onto hysterical panic was to grip the defenders such was the ferocious onslaught of the 'Angels of Death' as the marauding enemy planes were to become deferentially known.

There is confusion and a disagreement of opinions why the assault was delayed until late November, that is after the onset of winter, making the preparations, the logistics and the attack more difficult and possibly affecting the potency of the four main chemical weapons and nerve gases including Tabun and Soman which had been viciously increased in potency by the application of 'thickening' agents. Military historians now point to the pivotal event – that is the Presidential assassination – as being the foundation upon which *EVERYTHING* depended, however circumstantial evidence and the opinions of defectors from the old Soviet Union confirm that the situation in Dallas, Texas, that is the availability of a suitable assassin, the location of the event and finally the ability to manage and above all conceal the identity of the perpetrators, pointed to Dallas. In conclusion, the fact that approximately four hundred and eighty five further planes were produced between the end of October and the nineteenth of November when production ceased, which might even have swayed the outcome of the battle, is a hefty reason to explain the postponement of the attack.

The Warsaw Treaty Organisation was able to accumulate and muster an airborne force of just over two thousand seven hundred and fifty Yakovlev Eleven planes and to fly them, nearly three thousand three hundred and eighty pilots, part of the elite cream of East German, Polish and Czechoslovakian youth who had hastily been recruited in the short period of February and March of nineteen sixty-three, mainly from Engineering and Technical colleges where they had been studying aeronautics or associated subjects.

They had,in general, been recruited on a wave of patriotism and a naive desire to fulfil their nations` call and demand to increase the national 'breadbasket' since the real reason for their services could not be revealed. Because the *Lingua Franca* of the still secret manoeuvres was German, the Polish and Czechoslovakian contingents had to be conversant in German and for all the potential pilots it was absolutely necessary that they had good three dimensional spatial awareness which could be demonstrated in such sports as gymnastics or the pole vault and that, for reasons not then explained, that they were *NOT* colour blind.

From the original vast reservoir of potential pilots, nearly thirteen hundred were discarded, mainly because they were unable to master the simple flying techniques or if they did not have the physical and mental qualities which were fundamentally necessary, or they were unable to achieve the short but obligatory leap in their ability to master a greater degree of comprehension and oral communication in German and to have the confidence of their instructors that under stress (of course even the instructors were unaware of the real purpose of their students` training so the scenario of battlefield conditions was never raised) they could urgently understand and react to radio orders.

Prior to the Second World War, as part of the economic revitalisation of the German nation, and to create a modern communication system, which incidentally would serve as a vital artery supporting military expansion in the East, a network of 'Autobahns' was constructed which reached westwards into what would become the Federal Republic of Germany. During the period of the Third Reich many military aerodromes were constructed which were upgraded after the war by both NATO and the Warsaw Treaty nations and undoubtedly lengthened and strengthened to cope with a new generation of military technology, but they were vulnerable because of their known existence and locations.

It had therefore been decided, by the planners, that the performance capabilities of the Yakovlev Eleven would lend itself to use the Autobahn network as a takeoff and landing strip. Guided by radio and most important of all assisted by an ultra primitive system of fires built and maintained by agricultural workers and assisted and supported by low grade infantry, the bonfires would be seeded with chemicals normally found in fireworks, for the purpose of colouring. The sophisticated electronic system that Nazi Germany had created for the 'Blitz' over twenty years before on Great Britain had been replaced by a simple fool proof system relying on two colours on either side of the landing strip to locate and identify the landing areas.

It is now important to understand the logistical problems transporting various highly dangerous chemicals (mainly Mustard gas, Hydrogen Cyanide and Phosgene) and nerve gases, some of which were volatile, or corrosive or even unstable, dependant on the ambient temperature or other factors. It had been decided, at the outset, in view of the different types and the very limited number of trained operatives that the production process should include, at the final stage, the filling of different appropriate types of containers, the most abundant being thickened, or the use of slightly toughened glass internally lined with a thin metallic foil. They would then be specially packed in insulated and padded containers and externally marked with instructions.

Significant production only began in April when the different basic raw materials started to be delivered in bulk to the factories, some of which had previously been 'mothballed' since the Great Patriotic War or in the case of three production centres which , during the war, had specialised in the production of Hydrogen Cyanide, and then post war been converted or adapted to operate new non military processes. There was no real competition in the classic Capitalist sense, though in accordance with the Communist economic model unrealistic plans, norms or targets were created, this time supported by the weight of the K G B who were concerned only with security, but not matters of safety. Accidents, leaks or catastrophic errors did take place, as was to be expected.

At three sites where the common denominator was the reopening of plants that, during the Great Patriotic war, had specialised in the production of Hydrogen Cyanide, there were leaks of the gas commonly caused by inadequate maintenance and the cursory supervision of the equipment by poorly trained and motivated staff.

The three plants were the: Asha-Balshevsky lesokhimichesky kombinat, Khimichesky kombinat no. 267 at Asha –Balshev, sixty miles East of Ufa, Khimichesky zavod No.102/15 at Chapaevsk just outside of Ivanovo (approximately one hundred and fifty five miles Northeast of Moscow) and finally (where the largest disaster took place) at an unnamed plant in Karabash, in the Chel`abinsk district in the Urals resulting in the intervention of K G B troops to force the workers back to the production lines. Fatalities at the three works were calculated to be in the total region of four to five hundred but their suffering ultimately ended up as a number of sentences in a report that was probably never reviewed by anyone actually concerned with the tragic fate of the industrial workers and full details of the incidents were deleted from the final version or condensed in a table of statistics completely obliterating the human sacrifice. What actually happened was the classic example of the managements' rush to reopen the special production lines without due regard for its age and condition, grossly inadequate checks of the equipment and finally a disregard for the essential safety of the industrial workers.

In the history of the Soviet Union and during the Great Patriotic War, the glory of the workers' struggle against the barbaric forces of the Teutonic horde was symbolised by the epic stand of the workers and the Red Army at Stalingrad but I can now reveal that part of the stubborn, often suicidal defence, was to protect, in the Bekosovka area of the city, the Khimichesky zavod No. 91 chemical works. It was at this site, after the war, that the Nazi chemical works captured at Dyhenfurth was transferred, and the nerve gas, Tabun, produced.

Hence this factory was the prime source for the processing of Tabun and also for Mustard gas. This site had an exemplary safety record however an early delivery of Tabun in late June ex – factory, by lorry, to the railway marshalling yards , where a special exclusive section had been allocated, out of sight from the general public (the K G B`s concern was *NOT* the safety of the public, but the quick efficient transfer of the containers), as the containers were being removed by labourers from the rear of the lorries,in their haste to complete the task, a box the size of one metre cube was dropped awkwardly, causing the bottles to fracture and...

Within ninety seconds the labourers, supervisors and guards were all dead. The incident had been spotted but not understood, by railway workers some one hundred metres away who, not through knowledge, cautiously approached the location. Four men succumbed to the still lingering gas. Their associates realised that chemicals might be involved and cordoned off the area and contacted the authorities. Within hours the area had been decontaminated and all the witnesses advised not to, under *ANY CIRCUMSTANCES*, discuss the events. But, unfortunately, their associates, train drivers and their crews, had already departed with the knowledge of the incident and like a pebble thrown in a pond, news, which became more corrupted and embellished, spread outwards ultimately reaching the Diplomatic corps in Moscow. It was, of course ,difficult to investigate the incident but by late August the Soviet authorities were aware of gossip and knowledge of an event in Stalingrad which had not even been notified to the Presidium. Following their own enquiries and not being party to the secret plans a statement was issued to representatives of the Diplomatic community in Moscow.

The statement was short, transparent and apparently *SURPRISINGLY* honest. There had been a tragic accident in Stalingrad,which had been correctly 'hushed up' to prevent a diplomatic incident. A cache of German Second World War nerve gas had been located following information gleaned by historians reviewing recently located Nazi records.

It had been intended to use the gas, now identified as the nerve gas tabun, in a final desperate attempt to halt the onward thrust of Soviet troops in their drive West to the old Polish–Russian border but such was the speed of the advance that the German special forces were overwhelmed before they could prepare the operation. The gas had remained hidden and undiscovered until recently located and had been taken, by train, to Stalingrad where a team of scientists were to investigate the containers, neutralise the contents and then appropriately dispose of the cache. No credible reason was given why the scientists did not go to the site of the cache but surprisingly the (Western) diplomats were caught off guard by the apparent honesty of the statement which concluded with the calumny that the Soviet authorities had not wished to publicize the incident which might affect international relations, casting an adverse light both on their ally, the German Democratic Republic and the Federal Republic of Germany and following the very recent Nuclear Test Ban Treaty every attempt was being made to improve international relations.

On the night of November the twenty-fifth, the world was but a few hours from war. A total of only five diesel powered submarines had finally managed to *rendez vous* off the coast of California and were carrying in total thirteen missiles (though the unspoken word was that there was *NO GUARANTEE* that all or most could be *SUCCESSFULLY LAUNCHED*) awaiting final instructions and concurrently a team of N A T O, French and United States military observers, as agreed, dressed in civilian clothes provided by their East German and Polish hosts made their final preparations to be taken early the following day to their various observation points accompanied by their hosts in a genuine sign of friendship and detente.

THIRTY-FOUR

HIRAM JOHNSON, U.S. SENATE,1917:

'The first casualty of war is truth.'

The political assassinations in Dallas and London and then the military assault were based primarily on surprise and the intention to destabilize and delay, for a minimum period of at least twenty–four hours, a N A T O or United States retaliatory non nuclear counter strike in response to the pre -emptive strike.

The initial massive attack was not to be by tanks, but by an unexpected vanguard and spearhead of primitive,nearly archaic propeller powered aircraft broadcasting toxic chemicals and nerve gas not only on the enemy's front line but deep into his rear; the primary targets, which would be attacked by a number of waves, would be offensive air bases, the secondary targets being the tank parks and then finally, thirdly, any troop concentrations.

The anticipated loss of aeroplanes and pilots was, as previously intimated nearly the total force, but the expected gains in territory seized or won made the expenditure and cost, proportionately low. The Federal Republic of Germany would be attacked in three separate regions by, in each, three waves of tank formations at four hourly intervals, supported in their rear by refuelling lorries and mobile arsenals to reload the tanks. Behind the first wave would be replacement crews for the tanks where any of the occupants had succumbed to the chemical weapons or the nerve gas.

In the South, in the Province of Thuringia, the tanks were to be based around Nordhausen and would strike towards and around the old University centre of Gottingen; further North their compatriots in the Province of Saxony – Anhalt, based West of the key communication centre of Magdeburg would strike at the railway complex of Hannover, and in the North, in the Province of Mecklenburg-Western Pomerania in Scherwin, the target was the City and Port of Hamburg together with the vital Elbe-Lubeck canal.

Liberation of Berlin, where it was anticipated that the foe would put up a stout resistance was delegated to Polish tank forces who would initially surround and cordon off the enclave and, if necessary, starve the City into capitulation and surrender.

THIRTY-FIVE

What the eagle–eyed N A T O observer had spotted was the first generation air filtration and sealing devices fitted to the T-55 tanks, the P.A.Z. (Protivo-Atomnaia Zashchita) defence system which, whilst effective against radioactive fallout, gave no protection against toxic agents. Crews, when briefed, were lied to both about the outbreak of hostilities and the protection afforded to them by the PAZ system.

At a tank base East of Gottingen a scenario was to be played out which would be repeated in a number of similar locations:

The telex burst into life announcing an incoming message which the assembled technicians hoped would be 'in clear' such was their concern that the associated enciphering machine had been correctly programmed, however whilst the equipment functioned in excess of the expectations of its designers the message was the absolute opposite to that expected by the crowd of tense East German officers to whom the message was addressed.

It was of the highest priority. All the people in the room expected formal confirmation that the long awaited, overdue and previously postponed manoeuvres could and would now begin and that they would turn North towards the wild bleak barely inhabited countryside that had been specially selected and prepared for the' Kriegspiel'.

Less than an hour before in the crudely erected and temporary building which was to serve as their headquarters and staff canteen they had conjectured when the War Games would actually begin and taking into account any random variations that H.Q. would introduce, the final outcome of the 'shake–out' to test their war preparedness. Also discussed, fleetingly, was the unsubstantiated rumour, but widely repeated story, that within the last four to five months, American and N A T.O officers had been seen and more importantly heard, alongside senior Warsaw Treaty officers discussing the future planned manoeuvres which was in dramatic contradiction to the stunning message that instantaneously demolished any credibility concerning the ludicrous allegations of any relationship between the two power groups.

"*BEGIN*. The German Democratic Republic is under attack by N A T O forces! Warning! Chemical weapons and nerve gas have been used against our front line troops with devastating consequences! Your tanks have been fitted with the P.A.Z. radioactivity (sic) protection system and we believe that the filtration system will give your tank crews some protection. *TOP PRIORITY* (these two words in German were specially emphasised), supplies of chemical warfare suits, masks and the antidote Atrophine are being rushed to the front line.(the message continued and concluded in emphatic capitals) *THIS IS NOT, REPEAT NOT A TEST, BUT URGENT INSTRUCTIONS TO ASSUME A WAR FOOTING! FURTHER INSTRUCTIONS AND INFORMATION TO FOLLOW. END.*"

The officers and the technical staff monitoring the communications equipment were both stunned and elated by the unexpected and dramatic statement. Their emotions were diverse and confused, ranging from euphoric to frightened; any lingering doubts or even reconciliation were dashed a few minutes later when the second message arrived.

"*BEGIN*. Resistance crumbling in Bulgaria. Twenty–four hours ago, presumably knowing that Bulgarian forces were allocated to the now cancelled manoeuvres, Turkish N A T O troops attacked, without provocation, and without a declaration of war, our ally and co – signature to the Warsaw Treaty. Enemy radio ,monitored within the last hour, claims the Capital, Sofia, under attack and that Turkish tank formations have smashed resistance. *END*."

The response and actions of the officers was predictable and honourable, as their training and attention to duty quickly overwhelmed their emotions. An alert was sounded and contact was made with Staff Head Quarters to verify the news and unofficially request instructions.

The web of lies had been concocted and constructed not to validate the moral or ethical right of their cause but to motivate the troops. Conveniently, within an hour or so tank and infantry soldiers were viewing a grainy 16 millimetre film in black and white with a commentary in Russian explaining the dangers of chemical weapons and nerve gas and demonstrating how to don a protective outfit and to apply to oneself or a comrade the antidote, Atrophine. Translation of the Russian commentary was usually given by one of the bilingual officers. Such was the speed of events and the seriousness of the situation that no one actually questioned how the organisers had anticipated the need of a bank of film projectors and film about a form of warfare for which there had been no other preparations. Ahead of them lay an enemy whose land mass stretched some four hundred and fifty miles South from the Baltic, and Westwards towards France in depth varying from two to two hundred and fifty miles.

To defend this land mass were troops of the Federal Republic of Germany supported by various armies from N A T O and the United States, however the successful combination of chemical and nerve gases together with the 'blitzkrieg' of the massive tank assault overshadowed the achievement of those who had planned and had executed the deception of British intelligence and the consequent misrepresentation by the innocent and naive Warsaw Treaty representatives in their relationship with their Western counterparts.

Warsaw Treaty military planners realised that their opposite numbers in N A T O, in their own planning, would calculate that a surprise attack could be concealed under the guise of manoeuvres and that is why so much effort had been put into the deception because also at the root of the planning was a fundamental fault in the preparations of the United States, their neighbour Canada, and most of their allies including the United Kingdom which was simply that their forces were raised by voluntary participation since compulsory service had been abolished. Whilst the' Federal Republic 'still had a form of 'national service' the real 'Achilles heel 'was the time factor and delay not only calling up reservists and auxiliaries but transporting them to the battlefield. Thus the deception ultimately achieved all its objectives .

Preparations had also been in hand for some years (and regularly updated and revised) to psychologically destabilise not only the enemy forces but also their opponents` civilian population. Thus plans had been laid to subject the civilian population to false news broadcasts by announcers specially chosen and trained to imitate their 'Western originals' and to announce that their government(s) had fled (fled being the operative word, implying their cowardice and betrayal of their fellow countrymen, as distinct from the more inscrutable word, relocated) and that the 'Rubicon river' had been crossed and theatre tactical nuclear weapons introduced into the conflict by them. The 'black' propagandists would confirm in the spurious emergency news broadcasts that the United States in a final desperate attempt to halt the ever advancing liberators (readers should note the phraseology), had set off a barrier of nuclear weapons, without regard or consideration for the population, to stem the tide and to avoid the inevitable victory (again readers should note the sole interpretation of that one word) of the liberators.

THIRTY-SIX

On Thursday, February twentieth, nineteen sixty-nine, the United States Government published the long awaited 'Ford' report on the background to the origins and events culminating in the 1963/1964 war, with special reference to the events surrounding the then President's negotiations with the former Soviet leader Nikita Khrushchev, however immediate interest in the publication (fortunately convenient for certain departments of the Administration) was deflected by the cruel,coincidental news and the official announcement by the family,of the tragic death, earlier that morning of the former Attorney General and Presidential candidate Robert 'Bobby 'Kennedy, who succumbed to a massive haemorrhage when, it was believed, a particle from the bullet lodged in his skull 'migrated' causing bleeding. Thus the assassination attempt on his life the previous year, on June fifth, nineteen sixty- eight, by Sirhan Sirhan, a Palestinian (who had recently been identified as a trained agent of organisations, associated or ultimately loyal to Soviet Intelligence)had finally been achieved.

Only some three weeks before, his health appearing to be definitely improving, he had agreed, subject to certain conditions, including the specific requirement that the interview was not recorded, that a new, inexperienced reporter from the Washington Post, Robert 'Bob' Woodward visited the mentally alert but physically stricken politician to gather information and his observations on the Thirty Sixth President's (Lyndon B. Johnson) handling of the crisis. His comments, observations and opinions were damning and not only confirmed persistent but never substantiated rumours, mainly in the American military, but were in absolute contradiction to the overall impression conveyed in the later Ford report. At the personal request and intervention of the publisher, the interview was not published, since the national mood was becoming increasingly isolationist, parochial, definitely anti British and morally and economically self centred. The concept of the United States as the global defender of Democracy and the 'Rights of Man' had been ended by the events leading up to the war and the horrific events themselves. So it was that the 'America First' policy that nearly thirty years before had been expounded by the Country's greatest hero, Charles A. Lindbergh, was now the nation's de facto national philosophy.

It is likely that Gerald Ford compiled his report based on the sanitised, biased and in certain matters, untrue facts that were available to him, however his reputation was substantially enhanced when he took over the Presidency (becoming the Thirty Eighth President) following the incapacity of the previous incumbent(Richard M. Nixon), a man who would be described by Robert Woodward and his fellow journalist Carl Bernstein as a:

"Titan amongst the galaxy of former Presidents, for his commitment to rearm America against its enemies but above all his integrity and single minded defence of the Constitution and the ethical values which flowed from that document and its subsequent amendments."

Visitors to their joint office could not avoid, displayed prominently above their desks, a signed photograph of the three men in the 'Oval Office', following their ground breaking investigations exposing the real conspiracy behind the Presidential assassination in nineteen sixty-three.

The following recounts as faithfully as possible those events which contributed and effected the course of world history and ultimately resulted in the new world order, based on the still unpublished notes of Robert Woodward and with the cooperation of senior members of the Kennedy family and especially the late Edward Kennedy.

THIRTY-SEVEN

He was alone with only his thoughts for company. President Lyndon B. Johnson sat, for the second time in Air Force One as President, considering what was fast becoming the second crisis of his Presidency which had only lasted three days. The first was ongoing: the national crisis of confidence and now the sudden assault on West Germany by the Warsaw Pact.

Events had moved with an ever accelerating pace that Monday, November twenty-fifth, following the hurriedly arranged State funeral for his predecessor, John F. Kennedy. His wife, affectionately known as 'Lady Bird', had consoled the former President's widow with only those words and actions that a mature woman could offer but it was clear that the delayed shock had traumatised Jackie Kennedy. The news of the murder of the prime suspect, Lee Harvey Oswald, did nothing for the confidence of the nation and would clearly terminate the judicial process of a trial and consequently, the ability to investigate and expose the defendant's motives. No one was prepared for the next shock.

The President was in the Oval Office in conversation with the British Prime Minister, Alec Douglas Home and the Leader of the Opposition, Harold Wilson, more as a matter of courtesy than substance, not solely because of the circumstances but because the briefing papers that he had quickly perused filled him with caution and concern. In appearance Home looked cadaverous, but whilst his intellect could not be faulted the President was drawn to his biography and his close association with an earlier British Prime Minister, Neville Chamberlain, and their joint visit in nineteen thirty- eight to Munich, and the notorious piece of paper that Chamberlain brought back, which he had waved to the assembled crowd and then announced: 'Peace in our time'. Johnson then thought how much American blood had been spilt in Europe to secure that statement.

The briefing file in respect of the Leader of the Opposition was even bulkier, but it contained a highlighted section which when absorbed, filled the President with severe doubts regarding the flow of confidential information. In no uncertain terms it referred to Wilson`s close relationship with a British Trade Union leader, one Jack Jones , and the man`s more than tenuous links and ultimate loyalty, not to his Queen, but to 'Moscow', a connection which seemed to have had its roots in the man`s time in Spain fighting for the Republican cause against Franco and his fascist Nationalists.  There were also other hints about Wilson`s loyalties and aberrations concerning his provenance which worried L.B.J.

Their meeting was interrupted by a very emphatic but discreet knock on the door to which the President responded, perhaps too vociferously, but with an assured confidence and the sole word and command ..'Enter'. An aide walked in, acknowledged the two guests and handed to L.B.J. a single sheet of paper which if the visitors could possibly see was brief, comprising no more than six or seven lines. The President excused himself, read the document and instantaneously and visibly paled; then almost immediately, with an emotion of regret, requested the Prime Minister to read the document which had the format of an abrupt, terse telegram. It was from the United States ambassador to the Court of St. James and announced that within the last hour had been what appeared to be a military attack on the House of Congress (sic) and the loss of many members.

From then on events became blurred and confused, the exact sequence ill defined, however what was certain is that the meeting promptly terminated with surprisingly genuine words of friendship and mutual support and his personal wishes for their safe return.

None of the three men knew but this was to be final meeting where there was any semblance, or the foundation, of a reciprocal special relationship.

The next event that the President remembered, with any sense of confidence, was being bundled, yes bundled, like a kidnap victim, into the rear of a civilian estate wagon and proceeding, surrounded by a convoy of aggressive vehicles, South East to the outer edge of the Washington Metropolitan area and finally to Andrews Air Force Base where all sense of respect for his status seemed to be ignored in what was now clearly a well rehearsed scenario.

It was usual for an embarking President to be greeted by the pilot of Air Force One,Col. James Swindal, but such was the urgency, which within about two hours into the flight was proved to be correct, that the colonel with his co–pilot were in the cockpit making the final checks for an emergency departure and significantly awaiting the flight plan, such had been the speed of events .

And in that phrase, still a closely guarded State secret, but confirmed by Robert Kennedy, was possibly the most dramatic revelation, which in context would explain the actions of the President and his closest advisors. The Presidential jet had been allocated the flight plan of its occupant's former status as Vice–President and the two other planes one each containing the Secretary of Defence (Robert S. McNamara) and the Attorney General (Robert F. Kennedy) were diverted from their original destination to accompany the President and instead of them being installed in a subterranean complex hewn from a worked out mine literally deep in the Appalachian Mountains at Latitude and Longitude (it is with regret that following a request from the Government of the United States, despite the incident being over fifty years ago, that I am not permitted to confirm the coordinates) they were individually flown to an anonymous pseudo military landing strip capable of receiving any plane in the civilian or military inventory and was identified on maps as an emergency landing facility, located on the edge of the Mid West and then currently out of range of the latest Soviet Intermediate Range Ballistic Missiles.

It was a safe and secure location but was hopelessly unprepared for its three visitors, the first to arrive being the President following a further car journey which took nearly thirty-five minutes to reach its destination, a mesa adjacent to a dried out river bed, which to the President, thinking nostalgically of his home State, looked like a scene from a John Ford movie with the immortal John Wayne. However he was soon brought back to reality when the Air Force auto left the dirt road and if by a subterfuge entered an underground system that had been originally gorged from the rocks by a long extinct subterranean river aeons ago. Whatever the geological origins, the site was obscure, anonymous and would not attract any interest .

Shortly, the centre would be cut off from the world when the nuclear bomb proof massive steel doors were shut, either securely protecting its important temporary visitors or conversely imprisoning them, however the potential fear of isolation was ignored by the Commander in Chief whose initial impression was that the site was unprepared, that the staff were not yet ready to receive him and that the organisation was in a state of chaos.

Overriding his thoughts and his attention was the news that had been relayed to him from the wireless operator in Air Force One shortly before landing: Warsaw Pact forces had smashed their way into West Germany on two, possibly three fronts, but, and he was filled both with fear and revulsion, it appeared,despite the moral conventions of war (surely a contradiction in terms) that the ever increasing flow of reports from various locations verified the indiscriminate use of chemical weapons and of the widespread use of nerve gases.

He was alone and isolated,and if he could pluck up the courage to admit the truth, frightened.

The three, or was it four?, Secret Service agents who had unceremoniously bundled him into the anonymous station wagon and who had then seemingly pushed him up the gangway to the waiting Presidential jet and who had accompanied him into this chaotic, apparently disjointed subterranean complex were nowhere to be seen and for the first time since he became Vice–President on January twentieth, nineteen sixty–one, he was actually alone in a room, which from his initial impression, was adapted as a conference centre but was cramped and he was the only delegate present .

Soon he would be joined almost simultaneously by his Attorney General and Secretary of Defence who, at that very moment, coincidentally, was being updated on the current global situation but was also, in the most venal and corrupt manner, being briefed by his most senior aide, of the actions that he had unilaterally taken to protect him from any potential charge of negligence and to transfer political blame onto the shoulders of the British Prime Minister and his Intelligence Service. The aide had brought on board the Air Force jet a battered Samsonite tan box briefcase containing the most secret documents of the department but also the Secretary`s file relating to the British Government`s approach and recommendations concerning the Warsaw Pact`s ALLEGED autumn manoeuvres and the offers and subsequent highly unofficial arrangements. Regretfully ,during the flight, one of those unfortunate accidents took place, for which no one could be blamed, necessitating the refiling of all the paperwork. It was during a process of indexing, that two items were misplaced and then accidentally shredded along with various unimportant, superfluous documents.

"Mr. Secretary, I have taken the initiative to bring what I consider to be the most important documents to assist you and the President make the best decisions in perhaps the most crucial meeting of your career and the files include the Joint Chiefs` options and their consequences. No doubt the special advisor that you so wisely, and with great foresight, invited to accompany you on this flight and who probably even masterminded those military options will be pleased to learn of his potential involvement in any decisions that are to be made.

I do have one more matter to discuss with you and to apologise for a grave error in my actions: I took the liberty to also take from your personal safe a particular file which now is highly relevant to the present political and military situation. It is -"

Robert McNamara quickly interrupted before his aide could complete his comments.

"Say as little as possible now and in the future, if there is to be a future for us and civilisation."

Robert S. McNamara smiled. Now no evidence remained and the only witness had been assassinated the previous Friday. He still recalled the slain President's injunction on the short briefing paper which now, as it turned out, had never been indexed or catalogued, that in his own handwriting the President had not only urged caution but to raise the nation's state of readiness before and during the manoeuvres. An accompanying copy document from the Britlsh Prime Minister which Kennedy must have seen, advocating the same or similar caution had now also ceased to exist. He had protected his own position, though his treachery had not only sealed the fate of the 'so called' but now anachronistic, 'Special Relationship' but this sordid and cynical act would ultimately sentence the British people to a totalitarian regime devoid of any moral scruples, whose sole purpose and *raison d`etre* was self survival and the maintenance and continuation of power to the exclusion of the usual and natural responsibilities of democratic government.

THIRTY-EIGHT

The incongruous, irregular shape of the room overwhelmingly dominated by the oval conference table was not conducive to the great, urgent and historic matters of state which were of paramount interest to the six men iterally packed into the room. If it had been designed by an architect it certainly was not for the use of a Vice–President of the United States of America and his obligatory and necessary entourage. At either end of the room were half opened doors: outside of one stood a single, silent, solitary sentinel, his gaze no doubt focused on the lobby and the administrative chaos which was a horde of technicians emptying pristine boxes of electronic equipment that had been shipped from various manufacturers and had lain unopened and untested. At the other end beyond the opposite door was a man's urinal and the cause of the stench that permeated the room and therefore necessitated the half opened door to the central lobby and the frenzied activity of the staff. The plumbing was defective and to compound the situation, the ventilation fan was only working intermittently, not only allowing the sickly sweet and nauseous smell to linger (and accumulate) but also to irritate the participants by the irregular grating of its interlocking gears as it continued to malfunction, unable to perform its task uninterrupted.

Located equidistant between the President and the Attorney General were three telephones, two red and one black, each with a cord which either led to, or from, the latest ,most sophisticated voice scrambler. However it and the three telephones did not work, therefore emasculating the leaders of the United States and rendering them impotent. Every ten minutes, two of the participants, an Army and Air Force intelligence officer would lift each of the three receivers hoping to raise a tone but without success. Patience and consequently tempers were beginning to fray. It was at this moment that the sixth participant caught the attention of a frustrated President and immediately, by his academic and powerful intellect and with a comprehensive grasp of the situation, was able to articulate the suppressed thoughts and fears of all the men in the room. Under normal circumstances three of those present, including this intellectual titan whose I.Q. was reportedly close to or incredibly in excess of two hundred !, by virtue of their status, would not be seated at the table but would have quietly stood at the back, awaiting their acknowledged superiors' permission to be involved, however the shortage of space necessitated them all to be seated at the table with the three most powerful people in the United States. The poorly planned lighting, ill conceived and partially obscured by the seated participants flooded onto the formica topped table creating both shadows and pools of almost magical dancing light beams.

As if symbolically emerging from the shadows, Herman Kahn, author of 'On Thermonuclear War', one of the most powerful intellects in the United States and most likely the inspiration and author of much of his nation's secret defence plans rose, lifting his heavy, perhaps even obese frame, and with his vast presence caught the attention of everyone in the room.

"Mr. President (he did not even bother to address the two cabinet ministers and certainly not the two intelligence officers, who perhaps were unaware not only of his identity but more importantly his contribution to the military ideology of Government thinking and policy), I suspect that at this moment that you consider yourself, and your two cabinet ministers, prisoners in a subterranean vault, but more importantly that you are incommunicado, shut off from the world and above all the instruments of power.

This may be so because your mind and thoughts might have even calculated that the other organs of government, that is the other members of the executive, the legislature, the judiciary in the body of the Supreme Court and Earl Warren himself and especially the Joint Chiefs might have assumed the worst, that this location has been wiped out ,but logic and common sense would dictate that no seismic activity has been recorded to substantiate such a wild and emotional assumption. I am, like you, concerned by our isolation but I believe that in the short time before contact is restored that you will be able to profitably use what we all hope will only be the next few minutes and not hours."

The President signalled one of the intelligence officers to speak and the Air Force officer rose slowly as if suddenly he realised the importance of his contribution, but above all ,what only a week before would have been an incredible dream (or nightmare).

"The following is about two hours old and is already known to us all, though perhaps, for security purposes ,not to the previous speaker. It is the summary of reports from listening stations, diplomatic and military representatives and unconfirmed news agency filings. They all consistently report a rapidly deteriorating political scenario. Worst of all in the Middle East-"

Suddenly the President interrupted the Officer reminding him that:

"Whilst you may be overwhelmed by your involvement in such an important moment and place in the nation's future you should restrict yourself to your duty and not to make any assessments. Continue."

"Israeli Prime Minister Levi Eshkol, in Tel Aviv, has personally announced on radio that in response to the most lurid and inflammatory provocations coming from Cairo and Damascus that the Israeli army has begun to mass tanks and armour on the borders of Egypt and Syria and has both promised and threatened to strike deep into the Sinai Peninsula and into the very heart of Syria, symbolically referring to a new journey on the road to Damascus. Unconfirmed news agency reports speak of the wail of air raid sirens over Tel Aviv and the sighting of vapour trails."

He stopped for a moment to review his notes and audibly to draw a deep breath such was the unfamiliarity of speaking to such an audience but he received a most unexpected fillip of support when the President again spoke to the young man and said:

"Carry on, you're doing fine."

"What the Egyptians and Syrians have been broadcasting, probably for consumption by their own people, and Mr. President, I regret in this instance making a personal observation, is nothing less than outrageous. They demand, what they call a holy Jihad-whatever that is-to rid the world, once and for all, of, and this is verbatim, the Jewish bacillus and the plague carriers of Zionism who have infected the soil of Islam and finally they pledge to create on the purified lands that stretch from the Atlantic Ocean in a great symbolic crescent to the lands of Iraq and the majestic rivers of the Tigris and Euphrates, a new Caliphate, which we believe means an Empire.

They have attacked the Prime Minister Levi Eshkol and his predecessor, who they 'label' as the Yid Pole, David Ben Gurion, describing them together as Satan's representatives on Earth and finally promise to annihilate the antichrist, Joel Ben Yitzhak using a word which we cannot trace and only assume is another word for the antichrist, the Tedesco.

In South Korea, our allies claim that they have monitored a North Korean radio station, which is reporting the call up of reservists, the demand for the liberation of the occupied lands South of the 49TH parallel, in the cause of justice and the expulsion of the Yankee bloodsuckers back to their rat infested sewers.

In India, according to a brief report from our ambassador...

Firebrands and rabble rousers are inciting the population to liberate Kashmir and to crush the growing threat to the Hindu nation from the Islamic nation of Pakistan."

The President courteously cut short the continuing report of an insanity which seemed to have gripped various tinder box areas of the globe and directed his gaze to his two cabinet ministers. Bob McNamara took the opportunity and the initiative to not only comment on the developing and deteriorating global situation but more importantly to clarify the President's ability to influence and control the events.

"Although we are temporarily blinded and incommunicado I am absolutely confident that the systems that have been put in place will give us a breathing space to negotiate a political solution to the various potential explosions of conflict. I regard, after the European theatre, the Middle East as the most important, strategically and militarily. Continued access to fossil fuel energy is critical and to cede control or permit the Soviet Union to influence future events would not be in our long term interests. The Indians and Pakistanis can wage a local non nuclear war for as long as they want and we can, in the future, to the benefit of our armament industry, resupply them; as regards our allies in South Korea we have invested a fortune garrisoning an army who will act and perform to the highest standards and shortly-"

Robert McNamara was undoubtedly about to refer to the European theatre conflict when the Commander in Chief interjected to ascertain not only the military's posture but in his absence, their specific instructions.

The Army intelligence officer rose, but unlike his associate who had spoken earlier, he was calm, confident and assured though it was what he said and the manner of his delivery that strengthened the resolve and the fire within the belly of the Commander in Chief.

"Mr. President, the manuals that I have before me summarise not only the various options of the Joint Chiefs but also their mandatory responsibilities both to you, the Commander in Chief and to the people of the United States of America. I can absolutely assure you that in consequence of the different military incidents that have already taken place, to protect the nation and with its many means to inflict damage to an enemy, that the Strategic Air Command would have automatically been placed on maximum alert, that a substantial amount of the bomber fleet would have been flushed from their hangars and above all a large proportion sent airborne to avoid a 'Pearl Harbour' assault. Across the globe this level of readiness would also apply to our land based forces and our naval fleets, especially in the Mediterranean, the North Atlantic and the Pacific. I am confident that there will be no repetition of December seventh. Until such time as you order otherwise all forces are only permitted to act passively, in self defence, both to protect our own forces and our allies using and I stress the criterion, non nuclear force. This fundamental barrier will not be breached until such time as you and you alone authorise otherwise .

Above all the procedures primarily are designed to give the civilian administration, because we are a democracy, the time and opportunity to resolve matters by diplomacy and negotiation. You Sir have this time. These procedures were drawn up by the best and most patriotic minds in our Country to protect the people and defend the Constitution."

Herman Kahn smiled inwardly, this was the proof to justify his years of erudition, research and academic rigour which had finally resulted not only in the accolade that he had just heard, but in the lectures and guidance which he had given to the decision makers of the American military and various influential politicians and his warnings to them of the horrendous consequences of the descent into an uncontrollable escalation of the use of nuclear and then finally, thermonuclear weapons.

And then, if on cue, the three telephones suddenly burst into life, each emitting their own unique tone but not in unison and certainly not in harmony. As if shaken from a lethargy of sloth, three, four or perhaps even five hands simultaneously reached for the handsets though for the three who succeeded the only sounds were incomprehensible. Realising that the scrambler, like the other equipment was either defective or malfunctioning, a demand to the engineers brought immediate action and if the truth was known, the simple action of moving a switch to the 'on' position; indeed an even more damning truth was diplomatically suppressed which was that outside contact had been cut off solely because an on/off switch had been left in the wrong setting and had been overlooked until someone had made a routine check.

Calls began to arrive, first from the Speaker, then the personal aide to one of the joint Chiefs and then Earl Warren, the Chief Justice, a 'Babel' of conflicting conversations erupted, the common denominator being enquiries concerning the President's health and his knowledge of the apparently ever deteriorating military situation in Germany.

It was promptly decided, until such time as they were confident that the telephone connections would not be terminated, that the three existing lines be kept open.

Yes, the Commander in Chief was in excellent health (though a little irritable such had been his and his associates' frustration being temporarily out of contact) and they urgently required a summary of the current military and political situation.

It was therefore left for the Speaker to summarise what was becoming more and more of a catastrophe,though he ended with the most unexpected and surprising news that a request had just been received from Nikita Khrushchev, utilising the recently installed 'Hot Line', suggesting an emergency telephonic 'link up' through neutral Sweden which might help resolve the situation.

THIRTY NINE

The President pooled the information that had been gleaned from the three telephones and instructed the two intelligence officers to man the phones whilst various matters were discussed. The French were mobilising and President De Gaulle, of course unaware of LBJ's temporary isolation, had notified his allies that he would create a new 'Maginot Line' using tactical nuclear weapons to halt any possible advance of Warsaw Pact troops if, and it was beginning to look likely, that West Germany was to collapse. No doubt this posture was based on an A.F.P.(Agence France Presse) report half an hour old which had been passed to McNamara and was now known throughout the room, repeating an unconfirmed East German broadcast that a major, unnamed American airbase had offered to lay down its arms and surrender but had requested urgent humanitarian aid, such was the terrible medical situation of its officers and men.

It was at this moment that L.B.J. turned to his Secretary of Defence and asked for his comments following the Attorney General's advices that the personal aide to one of the Joint Chiefs had clearly, emphatically and without contradiction advised that some four months before, both the highest echelons of the military and the political hierarchy had been notified of the proposed autumn manoeuvres. It was in response to this simple but devastating enquiry that, and if he had been under oath, that he would have committed perjury the Secretary unequivocally presented the 'facts' that had only recently been manipulated and corrupted. His gaze turned towards the two intelligence officers and he gesticulated in a firm and clear manner that their presence, was, for the moment and certainly in connection with the President's urgent enquiry, unwelcome. As soon as they had left the room he began.

"Shortly after the signing of the Nuclear Test Ban Treaty I had an unscheduled, but more importantly, an unrecorded meeting with the President. Our staff were deliberately requested to 'leak' to the press that the purpose of this meeting was to consider the implications of the financial appropriations for fiscal 64/65, bearing in mind the forthcoming election in November `64, however this was a facade as the real purpose, details of which I know you were made aware of, was the political and consequential military situation in South Vietnam. I argued that Communism had to be confronted and that the expansionism and infiltration into the South halted and repelled and that we should not only bolster and support our allies but more importantly we could give active support using B52s based in Guam at little potential risk, to attack targets in North Vietnam. John argued that this course of action might provoke the Chinese, that Mao Tse Tung was unpredictable and that the Chinese leadership so inscrutable that our analysts and planners could not confidently predict their reactions.

Since the meeting was unrecorded I took the opportunity to raise the matter of certain events which I believed were still not known to the President, which was and I will shortly give you more fuller details, that is a highly unusual approach to our British allies concerning Warsaw Pact autumn manoeuvres. I had incorrectly assumed that John, when he discussed with you our meeting about the Vietnam peninsula, would have also told you about the highly clandestine events in Europe.

You have given me this opportunity to lay before you and the Attorney General the following facts: with commendable initiative, members of my staff, in anticipation perhaps of your interest took from my personal safe, a file whose contents confirm the origins and circumstances regarding the current situation and I insist, if you have the available time, to inform yourself of the history.

Most important of all, unless my memory fails me, initially the C.I.A. were unofficially approached by their British counterparts with the news that a highly placed Government advisor had been contacted by an anonymous (but obviously very senior) Soviet Official and that he had been baited with classified information that had come into the possession of Soviet Intelligence. Who the Soviet source was, and his status, is still not yet known however it is believed to be Khrushchev himself. We agreed to let unofficial contacts proceed. The thrust of the Soviet initiative was that manoeuvres planned for the autumn could be misconstrued as a prelude to a military assault resulting in an unnecessary confrontation. Such was the labyrinthine nature of what is now clearly a highly organised deception which may have further ramifications, that I must, in front of witnesses, inform you that I personally blame the former British Prime Minister Harold MacMillan, his successor, who you met only a few days ago, but above all the British Intelligence Service and finally your predecessor, John Kennedy.

I raised with John the approaches that had been made, terminating in highly unofficial contacts during the negotiations that culminated in the Nuclear Test Ban Treaty. I gave John the file which included the British P.M`s. observations which John concurred with, despite that, on behalf of the military, whilst I welcomed a further cooling of the global confrontation I considered National and International security paramount, but John believed that a further sign of reconciliation could create the foundation of a substantial improvement in American - Soviet relations. John`s attitude was to accept the offer, on face value, which could also, following the probable near humiliation of Khrushchev after 'Cuba' (even though ,as a face saver, we agreed to withdraw certain weapons from Turkey)enhance and raise his position.

With due credit to the Joint Chiefs, they did raise the level of alert and whilst the circumstances on the European mainland must give us all concern, I feel that the precautions our military had put in place give us confidence for the future. British Intelligence and the British Government have a lot to answer for as they appear to have completely misread the situation and have been duped by the Soviets with terrible consequences for us all.

Mr. President I hope that my explanation and this file now in front of you will satisfy your concerns, but we must deal immediately with the deteriorating situation and the approach from the Soviet First Secretary."

Within twenty minutes a Presidential Order, drafted by the Attorney General with some assistance and input by the two intelligence officers, and jointly agreed by the President and the Secretary of Defence had been encrypted and transmitted by the now efficiently functioning redoubt, first to the Pentagon and then to the members of the Supreme Court safely concealed in a facility in South Dakota. The contents were brief but the instructions and exhortation strengthened the will and resolve of the men and few women soldiers on the front and of the Pentagon:

"With immediate effect on land, at sea and in the air, all armed forces of the United States of America are authorised and permitted to use such active force as is deemed expedient and necessary not only to defend themselves but also their fellow combatants in arms including their allies. In the cause of freedom and justice any level of non – nuclear force is permitted in the pursuit of the recovery of lost territory.

The use of nuclear and thermonuclear weapons is *NOT* (the use of capital letters was specifically and especially demanded and inserted on the draft document by Johnson, himself) permitted.

All prisoners must be treated with humanitarian dignity in accordance with the Geneva Convention."

Signed Lyndon Baines Johnson, President, United States of America.

It was noted after the document had been transmitted, that it had not been dated.

There was much more to be done: preparations were put in hand for the President to address the nation, specifically to prepare them for a possible attack on the Continental United States and to bolster their confidence, to advise the active posture to be taken in Western Europe but probably not to give an up to date statement of the latest military situation.

For a few moments, perhaps in resonance, the six men fell silent as if contemplating the future. Even the ventilator fan was quiet and the room was momentarily tranquil. Then, most likely, the accumulation of the pungent odour of the urine and especially of the excreta, combined with semi toxic vapours released from the still not yet dry paint must have united as without warning, suddenly the President was overcome with sickness and deep inside him he sensed that he was about to bring up the contents of his stomach. His head spun and a sharp pain gripped his left arm. He shot upwards, pushed his way forward, ignoring all forms of courtesy, rushed towards the door and relieved himself accidentally upon the solitary sentinel who swore as the vomit covered part of his tunic. Who was the most embarrassed, or humiliated, was unimportant as the soldier recognising the wretched person and endeavoured, mainly through humanitarian reasons, to assist the distressed man.

The medical facilities were located two levels beneath the administration centre, reached by a lift, however on arrival its state of readiness clearly symbolised the original chaotic status of the whole complex. Its facilities were comprehensive, even including an operating suite and other rooms clearly dedicated to various aspects of treatment, but it lacked two vital and crucial elements to function: staff including any doctors and medicine! L.B.J. sat in what was probably an examination room, his shirt smelt of vomit and he was confused, repeatedly apologising to the guard who was not in the room, for his actions.

The call from the First Secretary was imminent and at a time of monumental danger to the future of the United States both the Attorney General and the Secretary of Defence deliberated over the two options that were available, either to postpone the dialogue or for one of them to accept the call on behalf of the President, citing a valid excuse both plausible and diplomatically acceptable to the First Secretary. Even a short delay would give them the opportunity to collate and assess the latest military situation and to give the Commander in Chief time to recover. The chain of communication was instructed, without explanation, to delay the conversation for two hours citing, if pressed, problems involving the official American translator.

The six men sat in the conference room, six pairs of eyes focused almost hypnotically on the black telephone as if it was pregnant and about to deliver. They did not have long to wait as suddenly it burst into life, its tone heralding the First Secretary of the Communist Party of the Union of Soviet Socialist Republics. Johnson slowly lifted the receiver as if the bout of vomiting had drained his strength, expecting the voice of Khrushchev which in any event he would not have recognised and was surprised to hear the cultured voice of what turned out to be Khrushchev`s official translator who identified himself and requested confirmation that his opposite number was now present and also a party to the telephone conversation. At which moment another anonymous voice interrupted and identified himself (even though the person was undoubtedly in yet another subterranean redoubt) in English both by name and position and then for a short time the two men, temporarily oblivious to the epoch making events, engaged in a conversation which frequently changed from Russian to English and then back and forth. Later it transpired, despite the previous protocols and procedures built into the system that the two men had not previously been in communication as the Soviet translator had only just taken over the role.

Contact by the First Secretary was nothing more than part of a deceitful plan to gain time whilst the Warsaw Treaty juggernaut rolled inexorably onwards and indeed the enforced delay caused by the President's temporary incapacity was a welcome bonus. Khrushchev continued to mislead his 'friends' and whilst his tone and delivery would be described as cold as a Siberian winter and inhospitable and unfriendly as the Steppes of Central Asia, the bilingual psychologists employed by the United States government for their expertise in stress analysis, subsequently wrongly concluded that the First Secretary, although cold, devoid of emotion and unfriendly was telling the truth.

"Mr. President, our two nations are in mortal danger. Under the camouflage and the fog of military manoeuvres and war games, which as you must be aware were originally notified to the British Government some time ago, absolutely without the authority of the Soviet Presidium, dissident elements in the armed forces of Poland and the Democratic Republic of Germany, invaded the Federal Republic of Germany and through a pernicious web of intrigue which we are urgently trying to unravel, have incited part of our Pacific fleet to attack your Pacific coast line. I am authorised to give you unconditional permission to take any action which you deem necessary, including the use of tactical nuclear weapons, to destroy the flotilla of, we believe, four submarines, before they are in place to launch their missiles.

Our offer also extends to the destruction of two command and control bunkers situated on the border of the Federal and Democratic Republics of Germany which I am told, can only be taken out by a direct, highly accurate, nuclear strike. Within hours we will have the coordinates and exact locations of the flotilla and the bunkers. I assure you that the Presidium considers a fragile peace more important than a headlong descent into war. In the meantime our civil defence will be readied to give as much medical assistance as is within their power to those who have suffered from the acts of barbarism.

My advisors have recommended that once these two centres have literally been wiped from the face of the Earth then we should jointly be given access in the Soviet press and on radio to explain our actions to protect peace.

Mr. President, I must ask you for one act of good faith. We have detected, not unexpectedly, an increase in the patrols of your bomber fleet close to our border. It is not inconceivable that some if not all are loaded with nuclear and even thermonuclear weapons. This is not only a provocation but potentially could result in a misunderstanding and an attack on the Motherland which would then give us no alternative but to order an all out counter attack.

There is one man in your country whose erudition and analysis of potential thermonuclear war is highly respected in the Soviet Union and whose works are well read by those whose duty is to defend the people and the Motherland. His name, I am told, is Herman Cohen (sic) and he understands the consequences of uncontrolled escalation. I therefore ask that your bomber fleet be withdrawn as a sign of your sincerity.

Within twelve to eighteen hours we will have the coordinates for your planes to destroy the submarines and the bunkers where those who have plotted against you are concealed.

We have differed and quarrelled in the past, now let us go forward together towards the beacon of light which is a world of peaceful co existence based on mutual trust."

What the President and his advisors realised was that those twelve to eighteen hours could allow further swaths of West Germany to be engulfed and the further possibility that those countries bordering the North Sea and the English Channel could also be assaulted and penetrated by the use of chemical and nerve gases .

This was the first time ever that a telephone link had been used either for demonstration purposes or in actual communication between the two leaders and Johnson had been disoriented by an echo which was, in fact, his translator speaking to *HIS* opposite number. He inwardly composed himself, comprehended not only the gravity of the situation but his ability to project, with confidence, his authority and the power of the Presidency to resolve the crisis.

At first his voice audibly quivered, rising and lowering in the style of a classical singer practicing their scales, but within a few moments he had conquered himself and found the strength of his office would enable him to speak with the authority of a President and as Commander in Chief of the most awesome military machine the world had ever known. Such was his confidence and the eloquence of his reply that the First Secretary's staff might have construed his posture as that of a man certain of success and inevitable victory.

"Mr. First Secretary I genuinely believe that your information and offer are not only sincere but also are an honourable attempt to defuse what could be, and I hope will never be, the prelude to an escalation of events culminating in what I understand we both fear, an all out thermonuclear conflagration resulting in a world where the survivors would envy the dead. However my primary responsibility and for which I recently swore an oath ,watched by the widow of my slain predecessor, whose coat was still covered in the blood of her beloved husband, was to uphold and defend the Constitution of the United States of America and to protect her citizens. Actions speak louder than words. The reality is that we suddenly learn that the Continental United States is threatened by an unprovoked naval assault and that an ally, West Germany, where my predecessor spoke to the people of Berlin, and by inference implied my nation's support; 'I am a Berliner', has been assaulted and raped.

At this moment, in self defence, our troops are laying down their lives, sometimes in the most horrendous manner because of the perfidiousness and inhuman, callous actions of your political allies."

For a few moments he halted, sipped a glass of iced Coca-Cola (that was from the one and only machine and the adjacent ice maker which were *GUARANTEED* to operate) and deliberately waited so that his opposite number would recognise his authority.

"No! I cannot and will not order the Strategic Air Command to withdraw its bombers until such time as you compel and order your Warsaw Pact allies to retreat to their original borders and begin an urgent humanitarian aid programme."

As he spoke, a communications officer entered the room and managed, with great gymnastic ability and without the President's knowledge, to pass behind him in the limited space available and hand to the Secretary of Defence a memo, which he perused then reread, exhibiting an emotion of clear concern and then passed the message to Robert Kennedy who could not believe the contents.

"A Voice of America broadcast within the last ten minutes reports an unconfirmed A.F.P. news flash that a further beleaguered United States Air Force base (believed to be Ramstein) had asked for all military action to cease, requesting a local ceasefire and urgent medical aid including drugs to neutralise the horrendous consequences of chemical weapons."

It was now self evident both to the Attorney General and the Secretary of Defence that negotiations or perhaps even the President's conversation could not continue until an assessment of the situation in West Germany was clarified. As McNamara begun to scrawl in bold capital letters on a sheet of handy scrap paper the succinct note...

"URGENT YOU END THIS CONVERSATION! LEAVE YOUR OPTIONS OPEN,"

Another communications officer entered the room and this time handed to the Army intelligence officer a sheet which he perused, then with a pencil appeared to make some alterations and stood up, displaying a clear respect for the rank of Robert McNamara, requested that he read the document, which having done so he then quietly announced its contents even though the President was concluding his discussion with the First Secretary

"The British radio in London (the memo had been incorrectly transcribed and a later version, which by then had become superfluous, correctly confirmed the broadcaster as the British Broadcasting Corporation) has interrupted its main channel (the Light Programme) to announce that British tank formations had successfully halted an incoming East German thrust aimed at Hamburg and was regrouping in preparation for a counter attack."

This corrupted message was, on the limited information available, the first item of positive news that had been received, but the earlier information, which possibly meant the fall of two air force bases (unless the unconfirmed reports referred, in error, to one location) dealt a body blow to the whole infrastructure of power and the ability to coordinate an umbrella of protection for its land forces.

The President ended the call and, as advised, left his options open. The B52s would continue their vigil, their very presence a warning both menacing and threatening.

Most likely the two intelligence officers were the first to comprehend the enormous consequences of the loss of two major air force bases, especially if one was at 'Ramstein' as it formed part of an essential hub integrating strategically located Army camps with air bases. It was conceivable and possible that the precarious infrastructure could collapse and implode permitting the Warsaw Pact blitzkrieg to overwhelm West Germany.

Excluding Herman Kahn's previous, but brief interjection, he had remained calm, silent and passive in his role as an advisor but it had become clear to him, even though he had no permission, mandate or authority, that such was the potential danger of escalation and because above all he could articulate and clarify the possible future scenario that, and with the assuredness of his status as an academic and the supreme expert in his field, that he confidently drew the attention of the five men in the room and delivered his observations which ultimately, and then unbeknownst to his audience, would change the course of history.

"Mr. President (his style was both formal and at that moment also paternal), my chosen area has been both academic and theoretical but I have always hoped that my arguments and conclusions would never be tested in the real world. I have contemplated the consequences of Armageddon and have found, analysing various alternative scenarios, that invariably the only and final conclusion would be the end of civilisation, though sometimes looking at what we call civilisation makes me wonder if we should start all over again. That said, because I do not have the moral right or political mandate to make such a judgement, perhaps it is best, with the help of your two experienced assistants, that when shortly you make a decision so important that if it does not result in a successful outcome, then the lives of, and I do not exaggerate the following numbers, hundreds of millions will end within the next forty eight hours or so. The quantum leap into the arena of even the use of ten kilotonne tactical nuclear weapons invites the enemy to raise the stakes and you would be drawn inexorably into the ultimate and perhaps final game of Poker where without realising until it was too late, your chips would be whole Nations and the pile of chips, the incinerated bodies of anonymous innocent men, women and children of your own Country, its loyal allies, let alone your perceived enemies and even neutral or non aligned States. Can the Soviet leader be trusted and should you discard your intuition and act either passively or actively possibly allowing our Nation`s enemies not only to outwit us but perhaps to deal us a mortal blow ?

Mr. President, I feel that now I must present to you my assessment of the most likely and potential outcome, based on the known current military position. The enemy has not only secured by deception and cunning a surprise advantage, but by the use of weapons banned under International Law and by the Geneva Convention, territorial gains and a momentum which at this moment continues, unabated. Even if the scenario presented to you by the First Secretary is true, including the new dimension of a naval assault on the West Coast, that this complete operation has been organised by dissident and renegade political and military forces, there is now the probability that the leadership in the Kremlin will be swept along by the tide of events, literally inebriated and intoxicated by the scent of victory and will commandeer their allies` advantage for their own ends.

I must, in no uncertain terms, warn you that unless you demonstrate the political will but also your intention to support that posture by military force which I believe the leadership and the military hierarchy of the Soviet Union fear and respect, then they would unilaterally escalate and raise the level of terror and possibly launch a Thermonuclear First Strike against the Continental United States. Even discounting their ability to launch, in response to our retaliatory First Strike, a meaningful Second Strike, I have calculated the most optimistic forecast of our potential losses. I now present to you, the Secretary of Defence and the Attorney General, numbers which may rest on your consciences for the rest of your lives, that within thirty days of the attack ,assuming, and I have no reason to doubt *THE MACABRE INTENTIONS OF OUR ENEMY*, that our losses would be between forty and forty–two and a half percent of our population, that is eighty million people! I suspect that their primary targets will be the air bases from where our strategic bombers would be launched creating a situation whereby returning bombers would have no place to land and would crash land rendering them inoperative. Major civilian airports would be targeted to destroy not only their landing facilities but the accumulation of grounded planes of various Airlines of different Nations. But above all it would be the attack on the centres of population which would utterly destroy not only the fabric and the backbone of the Nation's will but more profoundly its ability to regenerate.

Within five years the Soviet Union will be defended by its first generation of Intercontinental Ballistic Missiles and even if in numbers, their deployment, weapon load or accuracy, are inferior to our first generation systems, their potential kill rate would still make them a credible force.

In the most starkest, but realistic terms, I have to describe a scenario consequent to a successful Soviet assault by their Bear and Bison bombers. Under the weight of the collapse of the emergency services and probably without a rudimentary police or fire brigade, the hospital service, itself decimated and mortally wounded, would be unable to cope and would be ,using a word that I have used before, overwhelmed by the dead and dying, even assuming the living were in a state to or able to transport the injured and dying to the nearest hospital. Water, gas and electricity supplies would be ruptured or impossible to repair.

Food supplies would be finite, with the possibility that the Prairies would have been polluted by the use of Cobalt seeded thermonuclear weapons specially engineered to cause the maximum long term damage.

Above all would be the breakdown of law and order as the survivors realised that Federal, State and local government were unable to carry out its functions and that they were compelled to return to the self reliance of the nineteenth century pioneers and be not only self reliant but also their own administrators of law and order. In the words of the English naturalist and scientific philosopher, Charles Darwin:

"The survival of the fittest."

Johnson signalled to the two intelligence officers to leave the room; decisions of the most profound nature to effect the destiny of his Country had to be made and made shortly. He did not want his associates to be inhibited by their presence or even by the possibility of their passive or active involvement.

According to Robert Kennedy in his meeting with Bob Woodward, Johnson became morose and crestfallen. Whilst for years he had known in the broadest of terms the potential consequences of the 'Unthinkable', to be confronted, as the leader of the Free World, with the imminent reality of all out war was a shock that he had not contemplated and within minutes he was to receive a body blow as if he had been hit by Cassius Clay with an upper cut to his chin. A report had been monitored from Dutch radio which claimed, without confirming a source, that United States resistance was crumbling and that airborne troops were landing on both sides of the Rhine, close to Arnhem, that they had secured the bridge and that tanks and infantry were some twenty kilometres inside Dutch territory, whilst the B.B.C. News in London, again interrupting its scheduled programmes, had within the last fifteen minutes announced, quoting a report from the British Forces radio in Germany, that the Supreme Commander of the United States army had definitely been killed in a helicopter crash en route to Cologne from N A T O Headquarters in Brussels.

Robert Kennedy, an eye witness to the events in what he called, with a tone of dark humour, the mausoleum, had clearly stated, again to Bob Woodward, that the room fell silent, as if a loved one had passed away in front of them and that the President was clearly losing his ability not only to govern, but to make pragmatic and realistic decisions. Kennedy had continued, as if to justify the President's subsequent collapse and the still unconfirmed but whispered hearsay stories of the dispute between him and McNamara, that the mood of the four men left in the room became melancholic when two more reports were brought in, at which moment Johnson requested that the door to the central lobby be opened wide as the stench was ...

"Becoming unbearable and where was the plumber!?"

For a few brief, transient moments, their spirits were raised by an unconfirmed, but normally reliable report from A.F.P. that an assault by Warsaw Pact tanks to relieve their airborne troops at Arnhem had been repelled and that a British Army spokesman was also quoted as stating that the opposition force had been 'wiped out and utterly destroyed' by German and British infantry using anti tank weapons.

This item of positive news was unfortunately balanced by a report from the Pentagon. Its contents, not in its phraseology but in its substance was cold, chilling and ominous. It confirmed in definite unambiguous terms the loss of three air force bases but mitigated the information with confirmation that some, but unspecified numbers of planes had been saved, by flying them West to what was euphemistically called the 'Unoccupied Zone'.

The draft notes of Bob Woodward as to exactly what happened next are no longer extant and the information obtained is somewhat unclear.   What is certain is that Nikita Khrushchev contacted the President using the teleprinter 'Hot Line' with news that the coordinates not only of the two bunkers but of the verified five (not four) submarines were now available and that he was prepared to make unprecedented in the relationship of the two powers which even affected the security of the Motherland.

"It was imperative that the submarine flotilla be taken out, or at least neutralised, because any attack on the mainland of the United States, however insubstantial, might cause such pressure on the Administration that all out war would follow. With the support of the Presidium, the forces of the Soviet Union would cooperate in an American operation to destroy both the flotilla and the two command and control bunkers. The plan was simple but relied on both parties' covert cooperation and adherence to a strict time table and also to the routes to be followed.

They had been aware that U2 reconnaissance flights had been resumed and they regretted to confirm that two planes had crashed (the phraseology was well chosen and masked the truth of the causes. One had suffered engine failure whilst the other had fallen victim to an anti aircraft missile) and the First Secretary was pleased to confirm one pilot had safely returned by parachute and was presently in hospital and would be repatriated through the Red Cross once he had recovered, but that tragically the pilot of the other plane had died it was believed through asphyxiation and his body would also be returned.

The Soviet Union would permit within a specified time scale and a strict flight plan, a U2 flight over the two command and control bunkers, not only to identify them but to take as many photographs as was deemed necessary to be compared with post strike photographs to be taken after the assault by no more than three American planes which again would have to commence and complete their mission within a specified time scale and with an approved flight plan. It was intended, to protect the circumstances of the two missions, that anti aircraft fire would continue, however deviously ,the electronic systems would be turned off and the manual fire directed away from the flight path. The whole operation should take no more than twenty–four hours to coordinate and complete, by which time it was *BELIEVED* supplies of chemical and nerve gases would be exhausted and the momentum of the advance also would come to a halt as Soviet radio intercepts were beginning to record an increasing number of reports confirming mechanical defects and failures in the T54 tanks."

Again, with much intensity, Khrushchev asked, with an eloquent and impassioned fervour, for the bomber fleet to be withdrawn from the Soviet borders.

The offer was attractive and beguiling. It would, at one stroke, partially but not completely, raise the image and reputation of the tarnished and previously highly vaunted American fighting machine and, if the Russians could be trusted, ultimately enable, without an escalation in the fighting, recovery of lost territory. But the Kremlin was still composed of men whose careers had been promoted and overseen by the Man of Steel who had ,at best, misled and in all honesty had duped Roosevelt and Churchill at Yalta and who had swallowed up Eastern Europe and deprived their populations of their democratic liberty. They were men without any moral scruples or ethical values who perhaps had calculated that the humiliation suffered by their enemy had reached breaking point and now was the opportune time to bring them to the negotiating table.

The question was not only could they be trusted but also was there an ulterior motive too labyrinthine for them to unravel?

To which the answer was, of course, yes and would cause a representative of the leader of the United States to take the most drastic and illegal action in its history but what they did not initially know was that the destruction of the two bunkers would wipe out those witnesses, the 'Adventurists' and partners of Khrushchev who had connived and plotted and by an act of irony would be obliterated and unable to bear witness.

The President had made possibly his first major decision:

"Gentlemen, I believe that the time for discussion is nearly over . The situation of our forces in Germany is both critical and dire and we must not tarry. Furthermore immediate action is needed to protect the

Pacific West Coast. I must, first of all ,concede my concern at the train of events, especially following the disclosure and the revelation of Bob (McNamara) that so called manoeuvres had been planned some time ago, and whilst my predecessor had been made aware of the information it is now a lesson to all of us that he apparently did not suggest caution.

It is possible that the offer made by Mr. Khrushchev is absolutely genuine and sincere, however there is a continual, consistent , cautious clarion call to doubt not the offer, but the motive."

L.B.J. stood up, loosened the knot of his tie and also unbuttoned the top two buttons of his shirt asking , as if the great events of State were temporarily of secondary importance:

"Is it hot in here, or is it that stench or the tension?"

He took a long, deep drink of the Coca-Cola ,including the shards of ice which he crunched in his mouth, put the glass to his forehead which he then swiped across as if to cool himself, and then asked, and Bobby Kennedy remembered verbatim what was to be the most profound of questions considering the precarious state of the Nation:

"Do we have the finest drink that ever came from Dallas, any Dr. Pepper?"

He stopped. Put his right hand on the table as if psychologically to give himself support and then continued:

"We will accept the First Secretary`s offer and we will compromise somewhat over the withdrawal of our bomber fleet *ONCE* (he deliberately emphasised that one word) we have verified that the targets have been obliterated ,that the danger to the Pacific Coast has been resolved, that the Warsaw Pact forces have disengaged and are withdrawing and that finally I want you Bob and Bobby to witness and confirm rather unusually, that the decision was mine and mine alone, then the sooner we can save the lives of our boys in Germany.

I'll speak to the Joint Chiefs now with my decision to scale down the number of bombers patrolling the Soviet border and find out how long a rotational system of patrols can be maintained to continue pressure. What about our forces in Turkey and what nuclear and thermonuclear weapons are stored there that we haven`t told them about? We could hit the Ukraine and not only wipe out Kiev but also destroy their inefficiently operated wheat production."

Robert McNamara promptly interrupted him though the information he provided was unhelpful but accurate and factual .

"Following the 'Cuban' deal and the Nuclear Test Ban Treaty, what facilities we had are being dismantled and if there were, there are now no weapons stored inside the Country."

Whilst a draft of the Presidential Order was being prepared, the Commander in Chief spoke to his Joint Chiefs and instructed them that as President he had made a civilian political decision to lower the temperature of the current climate and immediately on receipt of his orders they were to cut down to the barest minimum, the force patrolling the Soviet border and to withdraw the bulk of the fleet to a distance of six hundred and twenty miles or so and the rest of the fleet to be suitably dispersed. The Commander ended his orders to enquire how long a sustained rotational programme could continue supported by in flight refuelling before the operation would fail through fatigue of the crews, ground staff and the bombers themselves.

Shortly after which the response expressed the animosity and perhaps the naked unguarded true sentiments of the military hierarchy when in reply, the President was informed that:

"This was a military matter and not the concern of the President."

L.B.J., controlling his anger, put his hand to the mouthpiece, uttered a string of profanities and then responded that :

"They should get on with the job."

Turning to McNamara ,as Kennedy was absent, he released the pent up tension and stress that had been accumulating and said to the Secretary of Defence that:

"If we get out of this alive and the nation intact, I`m summarily going to call this mother fucker, arsehole and shit bag to the Oval Office and personally dismiss him and tell him that he will have to walk back to the Pentagon to collect his personal effects as he will no longer have use of any military or government vehicles. We are still a democracy and I represent the people, all the people, and I am not a pawn of the military."

Bobby Kennedy returned to the room holding a single sheet of paper and was accompanied by the two intelligence officers who had helped him draft the document. Robert McNamara gesticulated with his thumb and that silent order was understood without query and they exited the room. L.B.J. sank into his chair as if exhausted but emphatically, with assured authority and with that distinctive Texas drawl demanded that:

"Get the First Secretary on the horn, I`m ready to negotiate and deal from strength."

FORTY

Lyndon Baines Johnson, the thirty-sixth President of the United States of America feverishly read the draft Presidential Order and made a number of amendments and notes to the document before he stood up, and in the words of Kennedy, during his meeting with Bob Woodward...

"Tall, proud and free.   He then asked that his conversation be transmitted on a conference call in order that Earl Warren, the Chief Justice and the Members of the Supreme Court and above all the Joint Chiefs and any of their advisors be made immediately aware of the discussion."

"Mr. First Secretary, my advisors have expressed both scepticism and cynicism in response to your offer and whilst I am inclined to orientate myself towards their views and opinions I realise that we have in our joint hands the fate and destiny of not only our two Countries and our allies but of the many non aligned and independent nations. I will, at the end of this crucial conversation, authorise the withdrawal of a major part of our strategic bomber fleet and the remainder to a distance equivalent to about seventy-five minutes flying time from your borders once certain conditions, including the destruction of the two command and control bunkers and the highly dangerous, rogue submarine fleet have been accomplished and the withdrawal of Warsaw Pact forces clearly begins.

A large part will, in accordance with my desire to cool and calm the intense friction that has been generated, return to their various bases awaiting, not only further orders, but, I pray, the instruction to 'stand down'.

The remaining bombers will, I hope, be a warning that the people of the United States will never tolerate an assault either on the Continental United States or on its forces abroad.

The honour, the responsibility and the blow to destroy these 'Adventurists 'must be yours and yours alone as whilst there is a sound moral argument for our own pilots to carry out this mission, the potential problems of crossing unfriendly borders, bearing these

217

terrible weapons, when an unfortunate, unforeseen incident might occur is too much, especially if in error, an accident took place which might be misinterpreted by either side as a deliberate act of aggression resulting in a headlong descent into total war.

We await, without delay, the coordinates for our reconnaissance flights to record the photographic information. It is essential that these matters are swiftly concluded as the American people will not forgive the Communist bloc for an extended delay whilst our casualties and losses increase.

The response was swift.

"Mr. President. These 'Adventurists' are' gangsters' and will as quickly as possible be dealt with, however to keep our side of the agreement we must have adequate time, and in your own words, to avoid any accidents."

"I agree."

In the world of diplomacy and compromise and in this confrontation of power and the wills of two men, the truth and the reality was that the Soviet leader had outsmarted his opponent. Those who knew the truth would be annihilated with the unwitting approval of those who would be astounded to know the real truth. The victorious but physically exhausted Warsaw Treaty troops had virtually overrun vast tracts of territory belonging to the nations bordering the North Sea and the English Channel including parts of France where already a number of' sleepers' had been 'woken'; whilst fifth columnists had been activated and the Communist and extreme left wing trade unions were beginning to cripple not only the railway network but the distribution of fuel by the disruption of the transportation system in a symbolic and actual gesture of opposition to the French President's mobilisation, which in their convoluted logic and argument was a bellicose act of aggression .

Already the apparatus of the totalitarian state was slowly beginning to emerge as East German security police and cadres of political officers made the short journey across the border to begin the dissection and rebirth of a truly democratic state whilst Reinhard Gehlen left ignominiously for the comparative but temporary safety of France. Soon further security officers would arrive from the 'Eastern Bloc' to ply the trade that they had learned less than twenty years before in Poland, Hungary, Czechoslovakia and other, 'free' nations and impose democracy and freedom that had been stifled and corrupted by the American capitalist gangsters.

FORTY-ONE

RETRIBUTION!

December 7th 1963

In the history of the United States of America two iconic dates symbolise it`s turbulent and dramatic past. July fourth is Independence Day, self explanatory, a national holiday and a time for the people to recognise the many great achievements of the pioneers and their heroes.

The other date , December seventh, is celebrated in a sombre mood, for on that Sunday, in nineteen forty-one, without warning, the great naval base at Pearl Harbour on the island of Oahu, in the Pacific Ocean was attacked by planes from a Japanese naval task force and more importantly, without a declaration of war, bringing the United States into the Second World War and thereby creating a truly global conflict. It was this event, defined shortly afterwards by President Roosevelt as a 'Day of infamy' that at the war`s end saw the Country rise to become the world`s most powerful nation but it was left with a trauma that never again would it succumb to another what is now defined as a First Strike and in consequence would remain ever vigilant, the Strategic Air Command being its ever watchful, eternally awake guardian. Until November 1963.

By deception and treachery Nikita Khrushchev had managed to secure a great military advantage and his surrogate Warsaw Treaty forces had conquered vast tracts and were continuing their expansion.

With dramatic irony, its enemy and former ally in the Second World War, the Soviet Union, was now apparently secretly cooperating with its nemesis to undo and correct the events of the previous two weeks.

Soon, two hammer blows would crash down against the aggressor on opposite sides of the globe: on the East German border close to the now 'freed and liberated' West Germany, which had now ceased to have any existence in reality and in the Pacific off of the Western coast of the United States.

In the Pacific, the United States Navy was readying itself, on information to be supplied, to ambush a renegade flotilla of submarines which might be armed with nuclear weapons or even with a combination of chemical or nerve gases which had caused such devastation and terror in West Germany. Literary licence would describe both actions as occurring simultaneously but even taking into account the vastly different time zones the actions took place on that momentous day, Saturday December 7th .

First Secretary Nikita Khrushchev was quietly confident but above all an excited grandfather. He had deceived the President of the United States and his advisors and he expected within a further seven days or so that the Machiavellian plan that he had conceived to protect his faltering career would be completed, his political enemies in the Presidium both routed and ousted from positions of influence and above all the scheming and power hungry President Leonid Brezhnev isolated from his covert supporters (Yes, Khrushchev was no fool, he had learned the craft of power from his former Boss; he had recognised the intended treachery and hunger for power of those around him).

Such was the measure of his quiet confidence that he returned by military helicopter to his dacha and wife, as she had been able to send him a message that late on Friday the sixth, all yes all, his four grandchildren would be able to spend the weekend with their grandparents. He would be able to keep in continuous instant contact with Moscow and the Kremlin as the communication centre on the first floor of the dacha and close to their bedroom was in permanent contact and more than capable of keeping him abreast of developments. At worst , the ever ready helicopter could return him within literally twenty minutes or so.

Late on Tuesday, November 26th, Moscow radio broke into a scheduled programme of the works of Alexander Borodin, to announce that an important statement was to be made. For ten minutes or so, as if to prepare its listeners for a matter of the gravest importance, martial music was played reminiscent of the type played during the darkest days of the Great Patriotic War.

An unfamiliar voice announced that without a declaration of war, the German Democratic Republic had been invaded and that her valiant troops had made a number of tactical withdrawals against an enemy who had clearly planned the assault.

Over the next week or so the news became more and more positive as the G.D.R.,supported by, in the main, Polish columns of tanks, had not only succeeded in repulsing the enemy but had pressed home their superiority and had apparently forced their way deep in to the heartland of the German Federal Republic. Behind them ,according to the newspapers *Pravda* and *Isvestia*, the Soviet army had sealed its border to defend the Motherland.

For the family to be together, complete, was an unusual occurrence, however perhaps his son and three daughters hoped that their step-mother could tell them exactly what was taking place since they knew, from experience, *NEVER* to ask their father about any matters of State and therefore they were normally as well informed as their neighbours and friends. Better informed were the railway workers and those on the Polish border where hundreds of the new generation T62 tanks (fitted with the P.A.Z. system) were being readied and sent West along with their crews and heavily armed infantry troops. Where they were going and their ultimate destination was unknown but experience had told them two things: not to ask questions, especially because the tanks bore the livery, not of what was still sometimes referred to nostalgically as the Red Army, but because the tanks ,partially hidden under tarpaulin were liveried in the colours and identification numbers of the Polish and German Democratic Republic, and that normally weeks before such transportations, the transport officials were notified in order to clear the lines of other less essential traffic.

Whilst all these events were being played out the advance continued, but its momentum was clearly slowing ,giving the French an extended opportunity to ready their tactical nuclear weapons to create a new Maginot Line, and in the Pacific, the five submarine commanders, like their crews, waited for the coded flash message to attack Seattle and the Boeing works with their thirteen missiles and then to return home with their crews for whom the extended and unforeseen delays were beginning to effect their morale and above all their performance. An earlier message timed at 02.17 hours local time December 7th (*NOT* Vladivostok time) had warned them to be on alert for the authority to surface, deploy and fire their missiles and they had, again by a flash coded message, given their acknowledgement and exact location down to the last second). How glorious their return would be, the adulation, the girls, the medals, the leave and the promotions!

But of course they did not know, indeed only the First Secretary knew that they were pawns in a chess game and would be sacrificed and betrayed on the altar of expediency and political power. Even if all the fleet had completed the first part of its mission and safely reached its *rendez-vous* point without loss, an all out assault would have achieved little in terms of damage, and in proportion, the anger and demand for revenge by the American people would have been an overwhelming force for President Johnson not to ignore. Two submarines had already been lost, most likely because of second rate craftsmanship and inferior materials inefficiently welded, causing the hulls to collapse and the rest had ignominiously returned to their ports of departure sharing a common fault being their diesel engines not performing properly under combat conditions. The United States Navy operating out of San Diego and more especially the planners were ecstatic with the golden nuggets of intelligence, not concerning themselves with its provenance, and made arrangements for a force of mixed vessels supporting an aircraft carrier to be dispatched to a site calculated as just over the horizon from the launch area and they awaited only the time when the submarines were to surface, in order that their destruction could be promptly executed and with orders to recover as many prisoners as possible for interrogation.

Half a world away two U2 reconnaissance planes suitably informed of the various coordinates and of the narrow flight paths,made their ascent from bases in the United Kingdom and Italy.

Whilst the pilots were part of an elite group, most experienced and highly competent, they must have begun the operation with some element of trepidation as they had been informed that they had to keep not only within a clearly defined path but any deviation further than fifteen kilometres each side (approximately just under ten miles) would be regarded as an act of deliberate disobedience and consequently they would be liable to attack from ground to air missiles. Since the Americans had realised that one of the two recently downed U2s had undoubtedly been hit by a missile, extreme caution was observed. Though their mission was successfully and safely accomplished, a spectrum of photographs taken, including, since they were under orders, as much as was possible outside of their limited flight path, they did not capture the build up on the Polish–Russian border of troop and tank forces and their transportation West including, at the same time ,the last reserves of Mustard gas and the nerve gases, Tabun and Sarin, which were also being transported on the same line but shrouded under even stricter secrecy to be ultimately delivered to the Belgium and French borders for urgent use.

The two command and control bunkers were embedded in valleys covered by a layer of deep pristine snow further concealing their location. It is then more than remarkable and an accolade to the two anonymous pilots (both believed to hold the rank of Major) that their strikes, using probably 10 kilotonne tactical nuclear weapons were both accurate and totally effective. Since the attacks by the two Tupolev Tu-16 Series G took place within five minute of each other and the devastation total, it is most likely that the occupants were all killed instantaneously and never, using an overused *cliché*, 'knew what hit them'.   Despite the urgency to save as many troops in the now collapsing West Germany (excluding some brave soldiers in isolated pockets who continued to resist) it was decided to allow the iconic mushroom clouds to disperse before taking the next set of photographs which were available mid afternoon on Sunday, December 8th (Washington, E.S.T.).

Dramatically, at about the same time or moment, the United States Navy engaged the unsuspecting and unprepared flotilla of five "Golf" N A T O class designation, diesel powered vessels. They had first been 'spotted 'by carrier based helicopters which were virtually invisible to the surfacing submarines and the attack which followed within no more than four minutes was led by two waves of carrier borne fighter –bombers, the first wave catching the unprepared and therefore defenceless vessels, their direct hits completely disabling them and the second wave administered the *coup de grace* leaving a wing of helicopters to recover the few survivors.

News of the fall of West Germany and of the successful attacks was withheld until the President and his advisors had decided on their next course of action.

The mood in the 'Presidential bunker ('factually the 'Vice–President's bunker') was that of euphoria. It was as if a load had been lifted from their shoulders by divine providence. L.B.J., echoing a still living former British Prime Minister and Statesman, referred to the events as not:

"The beginning of the end, but the end of the beginning."

How wrong he was, for Nikita Khrushchev's plan had still not yet reached its final phase; the First Secretary needed more time for the installation of the fleet of Intercontinental Ballistic Missiles to be completed when he could, as he had always wanted, look face to face with his adversary because once he had sufficient numbers which would then be replaced with the second generation missiles, which were in the testing stage, he would have the facility to launch a credible First Strike or a Counter First Strike either of which would devastate his foe. On *HIS* authority the thirty fifth President had been assassinated and he would humble the thirty–sixth.

On Monday December ninth, the networks ,A.B.C.,C.B.S. and N.B.C. broke into their scheduled morning broadcasts to announce that the President was to make a broadcast later the same day to the Nation , her Allies and armed forces. He was to ask the Nation to commit themselves both to a Day of Prayer and to the values that flowed from the Declaration of Independence and the wisdom of the Founding

Fathers. The Country held its breath, sensing ominous news because since the outbreak of hostilities the flow of news and information had been unusually scarce and vague.

The Pentagon, since the outbreak of war, had arranged and scheduled two news briefings each day at 9 a.m. and 5 p.m., E(astern) S(tandard) T(ime), however the experienced journalists had independently and subsequently concurred that the briefings and information were, at best, parsimonious and superficial and, at worst, evasive, possibly hiding unfortunate news. Their associates, on the news desks, were gleaning more in depth news from the news agencies based in the neutral Countries of Sweden and Switzerland but their reports, though censored, confirmed that the tactical withdrawals spoken of by the Pentagon information officers were more likely to be retreats of ever increasing magnitude. An additional source of news, second hand, were the telephone calls and Telex messages coming from the headquarters, offices and production plants of American companies based in West Germany, Holland and Belgium. They confirmed the onward march of the Warsaw Pact juggernaut and significantly ,as their communications ceased in a westerly pattern, by inference confirmed the catastrophic defeat of the United States and their allies.

At about two sixteen p.m. E.S.T. every radio and television programme was interrupted by announcers to warn the nation that the President was about to:

"Address the Country, her Allies and armed forces throughout the World."

For some thirty seconds or so radios fell silent and the television screens went blank, only displaying static, making the inquisitive wonder what in fact the static was and if it had an origin, whilst the country itself could hear its own heartbeat and deepest thoughts. The networks had cooperated in an unprecedented act of National interest whilst in isolated hamlets, towns and cities throughout the country, virtually every outlet from the barber to the major department stores had set up radios and televisions in preparation for the broadcast and for the American people, as many as possible to hear this momentous broadcast.

After what seemed an age an anonymous voice ,unemotional and cold announced:

"The President and Commander in Chief of the United States of America."

By common consensus the Nation was shocked by his haggard appearance, probably accentuated by the poor lighting in the studio, but more importantly they were impressed and buoyed not only with his news but by the sincerity of his delivery. But the news was not all good.

"I speak to you for the first time as President of the United States of America and Commander in Chief of our forces on land ,at sea and in the air in a solemn hour for our Country, our Allies and above all for the cause of freedom. A tremendous battle has been waging in West Germany. The Warsaw Pact forces, by a combination of the use of weapons banned by International Law and the Geneva Convention, and heavily armoured artillery have succeeded in breaking through the defensive lines of our Allies despite the valiant and brave support of N A T O and American forces and have surged forwards and onwards flooding into Holland and Belgium."

He then stopped, sipped from a glass (which contained his favourite beverage, Dr. Pepper) and clearly prepared himself for further, perhaps even more grim news.

"Fifteen minutes ago, following a telephone conference with the President of France and our Ambassador in Paris, it was agreed, to defend France and to give our forces the time and opportunity to regroup and for our French allies to ready her *'Force De Frappe',* to create a new *'Maginot Line'* to halt the enemy's advance and as I speak to you, from behind the camera, I am being signalled that a defensive line of tactical nuclear weapons has been launched and detonated creating an impenetrable barrier."

Again he interrupted his speech to once more sip from the glass which after putting down, he picked up a small folio of papers, glanced at the top sheet and then put down the thin pile of documents. He looked at the television camera and visibly smiled.

"On Saturday December 7th, two mighty events took place on opposite sides of the globe but each event signified the awesome power and above all the resolve of your government not only to defend the nation but to destroy the enemy."

He paused and then continued but this time did not drink.

"Following intelligence and extended surveillance, a Naval task force intercepted, attacked and decimated an enemy force of submarines heading for the coast of California, armed with nuclear missiles and, we believe, instructed to attack the City of Los Angeles and the densely populated *hinterland*. I must emphasise that we will not tolerate any potential attack on any part of the Continental United States.

Again he halted, deliberately (or possibly)for effect, appeared to make some notes on a page in the folio having first removed some of the top sheets and looked up before continuing...

"My fellow Americans, the use of nuclear weapons for defensive purposes is not only necessary, but in a confrontation against a foe who has descended, without warning, to attack us and our Allies and without a Declaration of War and has used weapons absolutely banned by International Law gives us the moral and legal right to respond, not in kind, but with the full force of the just. I therefore am pleased to tell you that I permitted and approved the use of ten kilotonne tactical nuclear free fall bombs to utterly destroy two command and control bunkers on the East German border thus substantially impeding the enemy`s ability to wage war."

He stopped, this time taking a substantial drink which emptied the glass and in full view of the viewers, an aide walked up to the desk and without regard to any protocol, filled the glass and then went off camera. The President concluded his statement:

"Yesterday I signed a Presidential Order committing the Strategic Air Command to an unprecedented policy of containment and I have spoken on a number of occasions to the First Secretary of the Union of Soviet Socialist Republics, Nikita Khrushchev, and have informed him that the people of the Free World hold him personally responsible for the acts of his surrogate allies and until they withdraw, our fleet of B52 bombers, in rotation, will continue to patrol the borders of the Soviet Union and if necessary, will apply the ultimate sanction against his Country.

Friends, I will keep you informed. May God and the Strategic Air Command protect you."

Television screens and the radio then became blank and silent.

In war the first casualty is truth and had the American people been aware of the true, catastrophic military situation in Germany and the horrendous losses and suffering of their fellow countrymen, the background to the naval success in the Pacific and the actual events on the West and East German border, then the hoped for eruption of national self confidence would not have spontaneously taken place across the Continental United States.

The President had created a scenario in which the truth had not only been distorted but perverted

Throughout the country, a spontaneous show of patriotism and unity expressed itself, wherever there were veteran groups, in the isolated rural enclaves, the towns and in the cities, with impromptu veteran parades proudly displaying 'Old Glory' followed by the youth of the Country and the Churches symbolically opened their doors to Christians, Jews and Moslems where their Priests, Rabbis and Imams actually, in many cases, joined hands to express their belief in one God and the ultimate success of their just cause .

In Dewey Circle, South of San Francisco, the citizens organised an impromptu meal solely for their senior citizens and children; whilst in Harlingen,Texas, the High School band marched to the local airport followed, like the Pied Piper of Hamelin, by a substantial number of its townsfolk who after the event remarked that they had not seen the like since December nineteen-fifty six when they had welcomed home the town's hero, fresh from his meeting with President Eisenhower and his triple gold medal success in Melbourne ,Australia. In the major cities, shops, offices, factories and department stores hung out bunting normally only displayed on Independence Day or, in the case of New York when 'ticker tape' was abundantly broadcast to welcome its heroes, though this time it was to salute the march of various veteran groups as they paraded along Fifth Avenue.

Soon the thirty-sixth President of the United States of America would be confronted with the indisputable evidence that he and his advisors had been duped by the man that the President thought that he might temporarily trust, but not just yet; the deception would continue for a short time longer.

That evening,across America, parents put their children safely to bed, the shadow of war and destruction having seemingly been miraculously lifted. The panorama was reminiscent of those iconic reassuring and homely paintings that featured on the front cover of the Saturday Evening Post. However the real nature of the global situation was different and within four days the nation would be confronted by a nightmare of chilling and horrendous events.

FORTY-TWO

The U2 reconnaissance plane lazily glided, invisible to the human eye, over its first target, an innocuous unimportant site some sixty or so kilometres South East of Moscow; it continued its extended mission (from Greece to the United Kingdom) changing course to overfly the Polish /Soviet border and then, at its maximum cruising height, to follow the route of a railway line from East to West and finally to the safety of home in East Anglia where its precious cargo would be processed and minutely examined .

As the United States bathed in the euphoria and the mythological false sense of peace,so events in the Soviet Union would intentionally not solely raise the temperature but would bring the confrontation of the two superpowers to a head. *De facto* control of the Warsaw Treaty offensive would now come under specialist units of the Soviet army (in truth by those that had, in reality, planned the operation) and the Presidium, though an internal struggle of wills which was about to be played out. The location of this event was to be some four levels or about sixty metres [two hundred feet] below ground in the subterranean bunker complex adjacent to the private dacha of the First Secretary ,where he had superficially invited and lured ,most members of the Presidium including the dangerous, rapacious and predatory President of the Soviet Union, Leonid Brezhnev. Other important participants, including two Presidium members, were scattered across the country in hardened bunkers, East of the Urals but in instant and continuous radio contact .

For Nikita Khrushchev this meeting, this time, was to be the defining moment of his long career and of service both to the Party and then the State. It would be the instance that the hammer of his Machiavellian and labyrinthine plan, conceived less than a year before and less than a hundred and fifty or less metres away, would be fulfilled on the anvil of his opponents probable intended treachery, or ...

In nineteen sixty-seven a document surfaced in the ultra religious Jewish community of New York which permitted, for the first time, 'Kremlinologists' in American intelligence to accurately piece together the political forces, the men and even some of the circumstances that had created the events.

Whilst anti -Semitism was endemic in the Soviet Union, having its roots in the theology of the Russian Orthodox Church, the ruling Presidium was then currently surprisingly lax and tolerant towards the Jews and prepared to accept their quaint rituals and values provided that they did not clash with the true and atheist correct philosophy of Marxist-Leninism. Thus a small number of publications were permitted and published, in the *lingua franca* of the Ashkenazi Jewish people, the anachronistic Yiddish. Although officially scrutinised and censored, an article, highly satirical and for those who were fluent in the tongue, very witty, was published not only identifying the participants (transferring the location to a room adjacent to a synagogue in a shtetl) but also naming other participants as if they were living in nearby Jewish villages.

It can only be assumed that the non Jewish, Swedish businessman in Moscow, who unwittingly was the carrier of the document, inadvertently picked up a copy from a pile of discarded papers to wrap up his wet shoes for his return journey to Stockholm where it was noticed, as it was about to be incinerated, by Jewish friends. Eager to share the pleasure and 'nuchas' of this rare magazine it was sent to relatives in the United States and thence to American intelligence.

Combined with second hand, but not contemporary reports, originating mainly from Swedish, Swiss and Vatican diplomats and more recently from defectors, a picture can constructed along with an interpretation of the magazine article to view the events and draw an understanding not only of the chronology but of the reasons behind the final outcome, though it has been argued that very likely the motives of the witnesses were corrupt or were corrupted or biased for reasons personal to those who made statements or passed on their observations or even relayed certain gossip or hearsay reports.

Above all the one action that changed the course of world history was, without doubt, the concentration, in one site, of Presidium and candidate members together with major political representatives and military officers called by the First Secretary to pursue a successful conclusion to the war. This was in direct contravention to political and military plans which specifically and absolutely recommended that the political and military leadership be evenly diluted and spread out in the many available hardened bunkers to avoid the possibility of a concentrated group being wiped out in an attack. It is certain that there was an element of cynicism amongst those present, crucially the concern that dissident groups had been able to start a military action of such great complexity without both the knowledge of,or more importantly, the approval of the Presidium. Incidentally some informed or knowledgeable readers may wish to enquire why the author has not used the more traditional title, that of the Politburo, however the explanation is simple but the reason behind the explanation is still unknown.

From 1952 to 1966 the ruling body of the Communist Party of the Soviet Union, that is from the tail end of Stalin`s rule to shortly after the accession of Leonid Brezhnev, chose to change its title, again for unknown reasons.

Present in the bunker were the following Members and Candidate (non voting) Members:

MEMBERS:

Anastas Mikoyan-Mikhail Suslov-Leonid Brezhnev-Frol Kozlov-Otto Kuusinen- Nikolay Shvernik-

Aleksey Kosygin-Nikolay Podgorniy-Dmitriy Polyanskiy and Gennadiy Voronov.

Andrey Kirilenko is believed to have been based in a military command bunker (with his two mistresses, South of Kiev, but, of course, in immediate radio contact).

CANDIDATE MEMBERS:

Kirill Mazurov-Vasiliy Mzhavanadze-Viktor Grishin-Sharaf Rashidov-Vladimir Shcherbitskiy and Leonid Yefremov.

Pyotr Shelost (who had only become a Candidate Member on December 1st) was believed to be on a fact finding tour at Arzamas -16 and was 'out of contact'.

Their biographies generally have a common denominator. In their youth they had been the loyal supporters behind the vanguard of the original revolutionaries, they had helped to oust the Mensheviks, had fought in the Civil War against the counter revolutionaries, and then in the fragile peace had begun their climb up the political ladder. They had been sculptured in granite and their hardness and political intransigence could be measured by the coldness of their personalities. For them a smile was anathema.

Most of those present were surprised to see the former Member, Lazar Kaganovich, who along with Malenkov, Molotov and Shepilov had been relieved of their duties in a mini bloodless purge on June

29th1957.Kaganovich was ,of course, Khrushchev`s mentor and a die hard Stalinist .

Approached and questioned by Brezhnev, he apparently admitted, much to the great interest of the inquisitor, according to the satirical article, that indeed he had met the enigmatic, quixotic and mercurial Jew, Joel Ben Yitzhak, the *ALLEGED* controller of the other Jew and the nemesis of Stalin - Leon Trotsky, a man whose very name, even more than thirty years after he had been expelled from the Soviet Union to Turkey, was despised .

Khrushchev, in anticipation of the political defeat of his potential rival or to forestall any action against himself, had skilfully separated the Members and Candidate Members not only from their assistants but from their personal security staff leaving only his trusted and more importantly reliable troops and personal staff.

Khrushchev began with a summary of the military events, facts already known to those present, and he finished by confirming that the highly successful blitzkrieg had stalled on the French border, temporarily halted by the creation of a nuclear barrier but mainly because the force of T54 tanks were breaking down and that the troops were physically exhausted, however on his authority he had released fresh Soviet troops and the latest T62 tanks fitted with the P.A.Z. radioactivity (sic) protection device and that the tanks and infantry had been camouflaged and dressed as Polish and D.D.R. equipment and troops. It was a tribute to his persuasive eloquence and the apparent success of the military action that the doubts and queries that should have been raised were not immediately mentioned.

The reality was the success of the assault; for years his audience had dreamed and schemed to out flank and out manoeuvre the Americans to liberate Western Europe from the yoke of Capitalism and now they were on the brink of success. Doubts and questions concerning the provenance and history of the plan were temporarily set aside *ONLY* whilst success loomed. Failure or treachery would change the attitude of those present. They all stood up in unison, as if the event was choreographed, and politely but with minimum enthusiasm clapped him however he was satisfied with the duration of his appreciation.

Nikita Khrushchev looked round the room primarily concerning himself for signs of any alliances or groupings of the Members present. He was surprised to see his old mentor and dear friend associating himself with his perceived enemy and potential challenger for his position, but for the moment this was unimportant. The venue was convenient for his purposes although stark and basic; there was adequate room for all the delegates and the military who were partially obscured by rows of bunks carefully piled against one wall ,for in fact this level had been allocated, designed and fitted out as the accommodation and recreational area for the personal guard of the First Secretary.

He had brought with him the document that had been carefully and prudently hidden in a long unused recipe book, that had lain unread for an eternity, and had been wisely, vertically cut into three parts to conceal its contents. Suddenly its relevance and importance were brought into perspective as a lone figure rose from his seat, attracting the attention of all those present, and began to speak. It was Viktor Grishin, one of the Candidate Members and in the terminology of Stalinism, an opportunist.

"Mr. First Secretary, whilst our allies have achieved what may be a great victory and more important of all have liberated many millions from the shackles of Imperialism, I am concerned with intelligence reports, not six hours old , which confirm that American bombers have effectively encircled and surrounded our vast and sprawling country and are supported by reserves prowling like hungry wolves at a distance of about a thousand kilometres or, as I am advised, about an hour and fifteen minutes flying time to our borders. Not only that but the British, in contrast to the American brigands, a pin prick, have put their bomber fleet on maximum fifteen minute alert. This situation having been verified by our agents in the last three hours. I believe, as many of those present, that there is more to the events than you have told us and I fear, like Cuba, that its end will be a further humiliation."

The reply was unexpected and not only raised the tension of the situation but began to identify those whose intentions were to topple the First Secretary. All that he had learned at the feet of the 'Boss', the absolute ruthlessness, the cunning and above all the desire for self survival was encapsulated in his reply and in the critical analysis of its reception.

"Comrades, I will deal with the current situation and not dwell on the history of recent events because we are unable to change the past and in any event we are on the verge of a great victory. I have had a number of conversations with the United States President, that is the new incumbent and not his recently deceased predecessor (there was some spontaneous laughter) and he believes that our intentions are honourable and that like our opposite numbers we look for stability and peace.

He is, like many of his countrymen, bold, brash, over confident and aggressive and to bolster internal confidence he has claimed, in a recent speech, that you may have seen in intelligence reports, that he has ordered the encirclement of our Motherland, but in reality I persuaded him to withdraw the vast bulk of his bomber force from our border as I promised to put pressure on our Warsaw Treaty allies to halt their advance. Additionally, he naively believes that our nation is not only encircled but that we dare not try to break this pathetic attempt to strangle us.

Through the foresight, wisdom and planning of our air force high command I agreed some time ago, to authorise the construction of a number of bases which are outside of the cordon and I am pleased to confirm that not only are they fully operational, but they are also supported by refuelling planes and have available, on site, an adequate inventory of nuclear and thermonuclear weapons. The force of Tupolev Tu 16s will, if ultimately necessary, give the Americans a bloody nose, but I do not wish us to attack the mainland of the United States, for I am not a war monger. Soon in the not too distant future when *ALL* (author's emphasis) our Intercontinental Ballistic Missiles are fully operational and as you know their deployment has already begun, then we will brook no nonsense from these bullies.

These plans were laid before our unfortunate withdrawal from Cuba and may I remind you all that the political decision to install missiles on Cuban soil was not my own exclusive decision but was unanimously agreed .

The so called British threat must not be viewed lightly as they suffer from the delusion that they are still a global power and as well the guardians of peace and democracy! [a sarcastic sneer – most unusual for the First Secretary-contorted his face]. Their former Minister of War could not guard a state secret in his bed when the woman opened her legs, much to our advantage as you will no doubt recollect from recent briefing papers.

Earlier today I prepared a draft statement, for your approval, which will be transmitted to the British Government warning them that if they do not stand down their bomber force, then we would have no alternative than to escape their ally's cordon and to attack specified cities and military targets in the United Kingdom. We will then broadcast to the British people direct, with whom we have no quarrel, warning them of our intentions, of the targets and of their government's intended insane aggression in order that they flee from our targets. We, the defenders of the people and the proletarian masses do not want the blood of innocent workers on our hands and consciences. I end this brief statement and ask not only for your approval but support."

He realised that a vote of confidence in his policies might not achieve a majority despite the great military successes and that an eloquent, stirring argument might persuade those present to err on the side of caution and it was then that his old mentor, Kaganovich, rose and requested, with some humility, the right to speak...

"In what I see is a dangerous moment for the safety and security of the Party and the nation."

Whether by design or accident, and this was to be his valedictory speech, what he then said and the manner of his oration was the catalyst that Khrushchev feared .

The speech was brief, ex tempore but hurriedly crafted to express the unspoken, hidden fears of those present and was devastating in its consequences.

"I return to the Presidium, perhaps for the final time in my long career, to meet old and new colleagues to whom the Party has entrusted the solemn role and duty to guide and lead the nation. The responsibilities that you bare and the decisions that you must take are perhaps greater than we took in the dark days of 1942, but our decisions, or leadership, led the Motherland ultimately to victory and free from the dark shadow of fascism. The success of our Warsaw Treaty allies can never be underestimated and the initiative of the First Secretary to authorise the use of our own forces and equipment under the guise of our Polish allies in the short term may be profitable, but if the deceit is exposed then retribution may ensue. Marshall Stalin never underestimated the will of the American people and at this moment they patrol our frontiers perhaps waiting for an excuse to pounce. I urge caution and the guile of leadership to secure the newly liberated territories. I hope that my former *protégé* has these qualities."

The mood of those present changed. Sometimes the wisdom and experience of age, unappreciated by the new generation which took over the torch of duty can only be learned by the experience of errors and mistakes.

Khrushchev looked round the room to gauge the response but only noted one of his personal staff who had tried to catch his attention, cautiously waving a small sheaf of paper which he passed to his master, who read with great relief and pleasure the contents, deciding immediately to announce the contents for his own advantage and in order to mitigate any damage that might have been caused to his reputation and status by his erstwhile friend.

His bold gamble had paid off. Agence France - Presse was reporting, with great confidence, that resistance in Belgium and Holland had completely ceased, that the two joint Royal families, together with their governments, had approached the Red Cross in Geneva, Switzerland, to intercede with the ruling authorities in both the German Democratic Republic and Poland to cease hostilities and to permit, what was left of their medical services, to offer aid and assistance. In a sign of total capitulation and surrender senior members of both families declared that they were prepared, without any preconditions, to be held temporarily hostage, to facilitate help for their fellow countrymen.

The news from France was ambiguous, even contradictory, definitely confusing but above all promising and optimistic. Internally the Communist Trade Unions and left leaning Trade Unions had called a General Strike which was patchy and from press reports only partially effective. Soviet 'Representatives' operating as journalists and trade delegates were reporting that the railway system was completely paralysed and that troop reinforcements for the 'Northern' front were being delayed by heavy local traffic impeded by enthusiastic supporters of the clarion call to halt nuclear escalation.

There was universal laughter at the predicament of the French Government and of President De Gaulle. His nominal ally, the Americans (Winston Churchill described his relationship with Charles De Gaulle, during the Second World War, like bearing the 'Cross of Lorraine' and France was not part of N ATO, most likely because it was dominated by the United States), had readily agreed to the President's decision to cross the Rubicon in a desperate attempt to halt their enemy and authorisation was given to use nuclear weapons delivered by their force of Mirage jets.

In the convoluted world and atmosphere of didactic Marxist-Leninist political and moral philosophy, left wing intellectuals and their camp followers were able to differentiate between the use of nuclear weapons and the heinous and frightening nerve gases to the extent that no element of guilt could or was thrust upon the shoulders of the Warsaw Treaty forces. However the use of nuclear weapons by their own government was considered as a despicable act justifying, even in a time of war and great danger, the call for a National strike.

Agence France Presse also announced unconfirmed reports that the new *'Maginot Line'* had been breached by a widely spread force of Polish tanks which appeared to ignore or be unconcerned with the residue of radioactive fall-out and a force of some four to five hundred tanks (believed to be Soviet made T62s) were beginning to ravage Northern France.

The final item was an unconfirmed ,but from sources that were usually highly connected, report from Stockholm and had its origins in an off the record briefing by Red Cross officials, independent of their associates in Belgium and Holland. It claimed that the East German government was holding in protective custody some twenty or so military personnel from N A T O and American forces who had been caught, at the outbreak of hostilities, in the German Democratic Republic, in civilian outfits which on initial investigation *APPEARED* to have been made in the G.D.R. with maps sewn in the linings and they were clearly spies, the vanguard of an advancing invasion force which in any event had been repulsed .

Contact between the Red Cross and Government officials was, in the words of one Swedish member, 'extremely delicate', claiming that the Government spokesman had also alleged that:

"This was, *de facto* incontrovertible evidence of a plot and conspiracy against the people by power hungry tyrants."

Unexpectedly, Lazar Kaganovich, stood up, walked over to his former *protégé*, shook his hands in a gesture of friendship and brotherhood, and said just two words:

"Dear Comrade."

Khrushchev looked at Leonid Brezhnev and especially at the 'satellites' around him. Soon the political game of chess would end for the final moves were about to be played.

The satirical Yiddish article had a peculiar conclusion couched in the ageless humour of the oppressed Jewish peasants and artisans where the character of Khrushchev is portrayed as a puppet being manipulated by a man whose face is covered by a mask of Khrushchev, and in an accompanying cartoon he is shown as an urbane, sophisticated and scheming Jew and in the corner a coiled predatory snake lurks, whilst the satire ends with the puppeteer cutting the wires of the puppet which collapses on the ground.

In the early hours of Monday June fifth, nineteen sixty- seven, a group of some twenty men gathered in the vaults of the Kremlin to view the latest and definitive, but still not yet released, political epic 'Triumph of the Will'. They were the First Secretary, Chairman and President of the Politburo together with the Members and Candidate Members.

Very few of those present had been in the subterranean redoubt and only knew of the events from the very few who had not been swept aside but had survived and prospered.

The purges had begun soon after the war had ended, possibly more brutal ,callous and inhuman than in the reigns of Yagoda, Yezhov and Beria. The film had been delayed and regularly altered and changed, like the seasons, as leading figures were denounced and purged, finally being permitted to confess their crimes and secret alliances with the enemy including the Jew.

Those present, every one, owed their new status not only to their record as administrators but for their proven, unflinching loyalty and sycophancy to the First Secretary, as they had ,in many cases, literally walked into the shoes of dead men. The historical events, as depicted in the epic, which was for authenticity filmed in monochrome, was a travesty of the facts, however since the national and international atmosphere was one of fear and distrust the nation would receive the film without question .

The first person to fall and a precursor of the new terror was Viktor Grishin, murdered on the authority of Nikita Khrushchev. Khrushchev was not prepared to accept the felicitations of his former mentor, Lazar Kaganovich, but it was temporarily convenient for him to allow the man freedom to communicate with the real enemy, Leonid Brezhnev, when the retribution would be swift and without mercy.

Khrushchev walked up to the Candidate Member, Grishin, put his arm around his shoulders and requested his attention and advices on certain military matters, since the First Secretary was impressed if not by his comments but by the strength of his argument.

"We may need someone from the Presidium at the front in Northern France to supervise political control as I did in Stalingrad all those years ago. Would you accept the position today if I asked the members for their agreement and if I personally recommended you for this task?"

Flattery and power have often seduced the most cautious and prudent of men.

Khrushchev then suggested that perhaps they could share a small evening meal together...

"However first I must go to a higher level to see my private staff."

The two men left as companions, but only one returned to confirm that he had ordered Grishin to the front to take command (already preparing his obituary that he had been killed either in a plane crash or incinerated in a French nuclear strike).

They arrived on the second level by lift which stopped opposite the communications complex and adjacent to a gangway which ultimately and tortuously led to a small office completely obscured and hidden from the rest of the rooms on that level by its poorly designed position They could not avoid hearing the boisterous, intense and loud conversation that was taking place and as they passed through the half opened door, secured by a bucket nearly full of water and littered with cigarette butts, they were confronted by four men sitting around a small square table, shrouded in a haze of smoke and obsessed by a hectic game of Clobyosh. The player opposite the doorway was the first to see the visitors and immediately stood bolt upright, electrified by his master's arrival and the important guest and he was automatically followed by his three associates who turned round towards the entrance. Normally, when in the dacha, the arrival of the First Secretary would only be acknowledged and greeted by a courteous and cursory sign but in public the unwritten rule was always to be formal. Grishin flinched slightly at the men's physical appearance (it was a fact known to those in power, but since a visit either to the subterranean complex was unheard of and an invitation to the dacha virtually unknown, then contact with the men was unexpected).

The visitor, intrigued by the game which he knew well and played occasionally, lifted the hand nearest to him and saw a pair of nines and an Ace, his face was devoid of emotion and he put the cards down, of course, concealing the hand. Khrushchev spoke to the men reminding them of his earlier instructions at which point they deftly flicked their cigarette ends into the bucket of water and drained their glasses of vodka. As they all began to exit the room, the first stopped outside, the second turned round in front of the guest, raising his knee and viciously aimed for his groin and simultaneously his friend caught a flaying arm and commenced to subdue him. Moments later in an act which he had last performed on New Year's Eve, the fourth man, the assassin, produced a garrotte which he threw over the man's head and across his throat. The act of murder took little more than a minute or so; the act of cleaning up the traces of blood, the urine that had spurted from his organ and the more revolting task of clearing up, by hand, the faeces which had been excreted as the man lost control of his functions and which had fallen down his trousers, took somewhat longer as the bucket of water that had been prepared for the task proved inadequate and had to be refilled.

Khrushchev left and returned to join his fellow members of the Presidium. Later that night two of his four staff would successfully fulfil the most difficult part of the operation and remove the body from the complex without being observed and then go, as they had nearly a year before, to the factory outside of Moscow where the furnace remained fully operational and would receive its gift which would be incinerated and consigned as smoke to the heavens.

FORTY-THREE

For the second time in less than a quarter of a century Britain stood alone, but this time there had been no miraculous escape from the beaches of Dunkirk. For the remnants of the British Army of the Rhine, if lucky, they were now prisoners of war, or if they were unlucky, they had suffered the excruciating, horrendous consequences of the chemical weapon and nerve gas assault and died an agonising death, or even worse survived, now experiencing the frightening legacy of the damage caused by these terrible inhuman weapons.

The British Government, literally decimated by the assault on the House of Commons, was secretly in negotiations with the few remaining opposition M.Ps. led by Harold Wilson, to temporarily form a Government of 'National Unity' until a new General Election could be arranged ,however there was a strong conflict of purpose and direction .

The Prime Minister, Home, using the precedent of the Second World War ,wanted hostilities to cease before calling an Election, whilst Wilson ,eager and hungry for power, wanted his opposite number to dissolve Parliament without delay and to let the Electorate cast their vote. What both men feared, was some form of invasion from France, and therefore unknown to only but a handful of the most important national figures, they had jointly agreed to place the 'V Bomber 'force on the highest level of readiness-fifteen minutes-with instructions to hit the major cities of the Soviet Union, West of the Urals, in a counter first strike following an incoming Soviet or Warsaw Pact first strike. The Foreign Office received an urgent request on Tuesday, December 17th at five thirty- nine p.m. for the Soviet Ambassador to be received by the acting Foreign Secretary or his representative on a matter of absolute importance and an appointment was made for eight p.m. that same evening despite the fact that the post was vacant, the Foreign

Secretary," Rab" Butler being one the many casualties on that tragic Monday, the twenty-fifth of November.

Events in Europe and in the Pacific were being carefully monitored by the leaders of the Arab nations and above all by the United States` major ally, Israel.   In Tel Aviv, the Israeli Cabinet, which had previously, perhaps hastily mobilised its forces, was confronted by the realisation that whilst its tanks and air force were poised to attack its enemies in Egypt and Syria, the fragile economy was under intense pressure and even additional aid from their American benefactors might not avoid an economic crisis. The Cabinet agreed, wisely, that the security of the nation could not, under any circumstances, be jeopardised by economic considerations.   The few highly, but strategically placed Mossad agents in the Soviet Union ,under the deepest of cover, were also trying to quantify the Presidium`s intentions since Israeli military and political analysts could not reconcile her benefactor`s claim that they had attacked and destroyed two command and control bunkers on the borders of East and West Germany with nuclear weapons, an incident that would be regarded publicly by Moscow as an unacceptable and intolerable escalation of hostilities.   Mobilisation might have been premature but conversely might just have forestalled an Arab and Egyptian attack, whilst their political masters' eyes were focused exclusively on events in Europe, however if they withdrew their vast fleet of tanks, this very act might even be construed as weakness.

In Cairo, President Gamal Abdel Nasser had also concerned himself with the actions of the two Superpowers, but his motives were more malevolent ,sinister and malignant in intention.

Although the 'Middle East' was considered by outsiders as a single ethnic − Semitic −grouping they were divided by religious (the Sunni and Shi`ite sects) and political differences which resulted in an uneasy coexistence. Nasser wished to grab the absolute leadership of the Arab world and to achieve his aim, he knew instinctively that the destruction of his mortal enemy, the Israelis, would give him both the moral and military authority.   But to achieve his goal he needed not only the support of the Soviet Union, but their actual military assistance and that might mean the deployment of nuclear weapons. Diplomatic feelers had sounded out the reactions of the leaders in Baghdad and Damascus and it was clear that :

"The Zionist bacillus that was infecting the lands of the Arab people could no longer be tolerated and would have to be eradicated, once and for all."

The consensus was followed by a commitment to attack occupied Palestine (as Israel was labelled) and following liberation and the 'cleansing' of the country of its infection, it should be governed by the liberators on behalf of the Palestinians.

Nasser felt confidently emboldened to make the long indirect journey to Moscow via Saudi Arabia and then Pakistan, avoiding India, where his presence, however fleeting, might be observed by his enemy or their friends.

His arrival in Moscow ,incognito, was perhaps also unexpected, for his reception was not by a delegation from the Government or even his own Ambassador, but by an apologetic,almost sycophantic junior official from the Embassy, who had been reduced to chauffeuring his leader, not in the official limousine, but in his own dilapidated vehicle. He did however have important information which was pertinent to the purpose of the visit: an appointment had been made to see a member of the Presidium, in the Kremlin, that same evening at eleven-thirty p.m. local time and possibly the First Secretary...

"Might, just might, be present."

The reception was formal and courteous. He was blunt and direct. He asked a rhetorical question which in itself expressed both his aspirations and the cost of assistance. His hosts were apparently dumbfounded:

"What price would be required by the Soviet Union to destroy the State of Israel in a nuclear holocaust and to impose a benevolent Socialist hegemony in the Middle East which would inter alia deprive the United States access to vital petroleum products?"

His host and advisors, recovering from the shock of the potential consequences of such action were measured and diplomatic in their cautious reply. In essence they had no authority to give a definitive answer since only the Presidium could debate the matter and give a considered response, however as an old and valued friend their personal comment would be that the wrath of the United States, influenced by its strong Jewish lobby ,would make the venture too dangerous even to contemplate. It was then that fate intervened as the First Secretary entered, jubilant and elated. Moscow was two hours ahead of London and he had just heard from his Ambassador. Nasser seized the moment and repeated the question to the First Secretary but slightly changed both the format and emphasis:

"The destruction of the State of Israel possibly following a nuclear assault by our friends would lead to a change in the balance of power in the Middle East allowing the Egyptians to police the region and able to dictate the destination and supply of petroleum products."

The inference was clear but Nikita Khrushchev, despite his mood of jubilation, was guarded in his response. He suggested that, as a sign of friendship, both to the people of Egypt and to a great leader, he should take advantage of the hospitality of the Presidium and stay as their honoured guest for two or three days when a second meeting would be arranged, probably at very short notice, to review the matter. What he did not say was that Nasser's impromptu visit was not the first that he had recently received and indeed the next morning, following an approach from Vatican emissaries he would receive a high level deputation from the Iberian peninsula; representatives of Salazar and Franco wished to put aside ideological differences to agree a new era of, if not open friendship, mutual cooperation and economic and security agreements.

The Ambassador from the Union of Soviet Socialist Republics to the Court of St. James was received with the dignity and respect commensurate with his status, by three 'Mandarins' of the Foreign Office who were well known to him and the most senior sat in the vacant chair of the Foreign Secretary in what was formerly his private office. Officially or unofficially none of the four men knew that the attack on the House of Commons was instigated by Moscow; current common conjecture , still prevalent in the press was that it was part of the overall plot by the Warsaw Pact and independent of Moscow. Both sides were almost apologetic about the recent global events and any damage caused, long term, to their friendship despite political differences. The tone however changed when the Ambassador, with apparent genuine regret, advised that he was compelled to deliver a note and was instructed by his superiors to make absolutely clear that the situation was extremely critical.

He then produced, from an inside pocket of his jacket, an envelope, which in front of the three men he proceeded to open, producing, on A4 paper, a two page document which he passed, with respect and courtesy to the most senior of the three 'Mandarins' who observed that the document had been typewritten, on one side in English, and on the other in Cyrillic. What none of them would EVER know was that the substance of the contents was the latest draft of the many versions that Nikita Khrushchev had worked on over many months.

The document was in two parts, the second being an ultimatum.

The first part, couched in the language of diplomacy, alleged that their Intelligence Services had irrefutable evidence that the British 'V Bomber' force had been placed on the highest level of alert and would soon launch a pre emptive first strike against the Soviet Union. Unconfirmed intelligence led their analysts to believe that 617 squadron (based at Scampton, near Lincoln) and the squadrons based at R.A.F. Waddington and Coningsby had been supplied with 'Yellow Sun' thermonuclear devices and the very fact of these actions led the Presidium to conclude that the British Government was intent on lighting a thermonuclear touch paper to destroy military targets in the Soviet Union and consequently civilisation.

If the British Government did not acquiesce to the ultimatum then the Soviet Union would appeal to, and warn the British people *DIRECT* [author's own emphasis], and would even identify their six intended targets utilising captured radio stations on the French, Belgium and Dutch coasts. The first part concluded with a reminder that in the spirit of cooperation the Presidium had permitted an incursion into the territorial air space of its Warsaw Treaty partner (the German Democratic Republic) by a United States aeroplane armed with nuclear weapons (of course untrue, however the President of the United States had foolishly stated that his own forces had made the attack)and sanctioned an assault on two targets in order to slow down the pace of an unprovoked and unlawful Warsaw Treaty attack on allies of the United Kingdom. Not only that but from the outbreak of the Adventurists' attack, the Soviet Union had been trying to stop the war and to force the gangsters to return to the original borders and reinstate the *status quo*

The Ambassador then appealed personally to the three high ranking civil servants reminding them again that despite their political differences that the Soviet Union had nothing to gain by the Adventurists' insane actions.

The second part, 'the ultimatum', was chilling in its intentions and the Ambassador observed that the intended threats were so frightening in its consequences that refusal would result in war and his own death along with the staff of the Embassy.

The P.M. was immediately contacted and the document, under the highest security, delivered to him for his attention and consideration.

At three seventeen a.m. Sir Ivone Kirkpatrick, the former Foreign Office '*Mandarin*' was woken from sleep by the unexpected demand of the tones of his telephone and agreed that within half an hour or so he would telephone the P.M's switchboard number but would be ready to be collected soon afterwards by a chauffeured limousine which he was told was already on its way to collect him.

The ad hoc meeting ,which began at five fifteen a.m., was attended by the Prime Minister, the leader of the Opposition, Sir Ivone Kirkpatrick, the three most senior officers of the armed forces ,two senior civil servants together with Sir Hugh Stephenson and Sir Kenneth Strong. The purpose and consequences of the ultimatum were frightening, absolutely traumatic and thermonuclear blackmail. The nation would be gripped by a panic that was beyond imagination, the whole infrastructure would collapse and anarchy would reign supreme. Parliamentary democracy and the very foundations of society would, in an instance, be swept aside. The Prime Minister, almost desperate, asked if any one present had any suggestions to resolve an insoluble conundrum.

Harold Wilson slowly, partly to capture his audience's attention and to boost his ego, tapped his pipe on a nearby ledge and began to look at the demoralised and nearly broken leader...

"What is needed is decisive and firm action, unlike the French who have no backbone. Their last desperate gamble, launching a nuclear wall of fire has failed for the Warsaw Pact tanks just temporarily halted before continuing their onslaught. The conduit is the Ambassador who undoubtedly has access to the leadership in Moscow.

In the company of Sir Ivone Kirkpatrick I am prepared to meet and remind him that any attempt by either side to attack the other would be insane and result in mutual destruction. Of course, in reality, we would suffer more than they would but we have to impress them with our pragmatic approach and common sense. Sir Alec, in the privacy of this room, I am going to ask you, in the national interest, to stand down and allow me, with the permission of Her Majesty, to form a Government of 'National Unity'. I pledge that once this affair has been settled then I will dissolve Parliament and call a General Election to ascertain the nation's wishes."

Sir Alec Douglas-Home looked forlorn, wretched and helpless. He was being manipulated and squeezed from office. The 'New Order' was closer than anyone in the room knew and within three years Harold Wilson would be executed and Sir Ivone Kirkpatrick would die by natural causes. But for some of the others fate would cast their futures differently .

Home was left alone in the Cabinet Room for the final time as P.M. and he looked across the room towards the Park (he was unable to see the immaculately maintained garden of 'Number 10' because of the very acute angle and it was still dark) and read the Ultimatum one further and final time:

AN ULTIMATUM TO THE GOVERNMENT AND PEOPLE OF THE

UNITED KINGDOM.

The Presidium of the Communist Party of the Union of Soviet Socialist Republics have become aware that the Government of the United Kingdom of Great Britain and Northern Ireland has authorised and permitted the arming of its Air Force with thermonuclear devices and intends that they launch these weapons onto the soil of the Motherland against the workers and peasants of the nation. This is a provocation and an unacceptable threat, not only to the Soviet Union but to all peoples who value freedom and the right to live their lives free from the acts of warmongers.

Unless by 1200 hours London time,Thursday December 19th you publicly announce that your Air Force, which has been put on a high state of alert, is to stand down, then we will have no alternative but to directly inform the British people that if their Government does not adopt a more peaceful posture, the continued readiness of the Royal Air Force will be regarded as an act of war and that from 0000hours December 21st(G.M.T.), a state of war will exist and that a force of our bombers will attack the following locations with our own thermonuclear weapons:

London

Birmingham

Manchester

Glasgow

Newcastle and Corsham.

Of those present at the meeting, only Sir Hugh Stephenson, Sir Kenneth Strong and the three highest ranking military commanders were aware of, and knew of the secret and vital importance of the Corsham facility. The P.M. was now isolated and whilst he had been informed that the United States had thrown a cordon around the Soviet Union, he realised that her border was so vast that they could certainly breach the tightened noose and attack the British Isles.

He cradled his chin in the half cup created by his two adjoining wrists and began to weep, not for his own failure, but the plight of his beloved Country, not knowing that within twenty-four hours, his ally in Washington would announce a new global policy that would have shielded the United Kingdom from the Soviet threat; thus the fate of the Country would be determined by a breakdown in communication.

FORTY-FOUR

As the front ruptured and the defence of Northern France began to collapse and disintegrate under the weight of new fresh Soviet troops (dressed and masquerading as Polish and East German Warsaw Treaty forces)and supported by T62 tanks (in the livery of Polish camouflage),'Moscow' and the Presidium realised that unexpectedly that they had another stunning victory. Years and decades of subversion by the nefarious covert operation of the Soviet Intelligence Services and their manipulation of the Communist and left leaning Trade Unions had hastened the fall of France by a partially successful General Strike which had crippled and choked the flow of fuel, supplies to the front and above all transportation of troops and their equipment.

The government of President De Gaulle mirrored the military defeat and imploded. Contrary to the hypocritical and biased observation of Harold Wilson, the French leadership had been brave and strong willed in the first use of tactical nuclear weapons to temporarily halt the onward advance of the invaders but they had succumbed to a *fifth column* in their midst. In the vacuum of government, political cadres and security officers arrived from all over Eastern Europe after the initial vanguard of officers from the German Democratic Republic had began to impose their will, the first task being the control of the various branches of the *Gendarmerie* and the supervision of the media, initially radio, television and the national press and magazines.

This then was the situation that the President of the United States saw across the Atlantic on Monday, December the sixteenth, though the ultimatum (Khrushchev had characterised the document as a 'plea' and not a threat) had not yet been 'served 'on the British Government and psychologically the British people, incited and fuelled by the press, prepared themselves for a second 'Battle of Britain' in less than twenty-five years.

But public opinion in the United States was being transformed by a different view of the destiny of the nation and its place in the world as President Johnson, under pressure from his advisors and patiently assessing the recent events ,now was also rapidly changing his own opinions and recalibrating his loyalties.

FORTY-FIVE

Harold Wilson returned to his temporary office to be greeted with an urgent, imperative request to telephone, without delay, an old and trusted political ally and one of the Labour Party`s biggest financial sponsors. Evelyn Jones answered the call and after the usual, but sincere pleasantries, she passed the telephone to her husban, Jack Jones.

As leader of the powerful Transport and General Workers` Union he wielded not only great political power but the moral mantle of an impeccable Communist record for he had fought for the International Brigade in Spain during the Civil War and had been wounded in the shoulder, by shrapnel, during the Battle of Ebro. It was during the subsequent period of hospitalisation-and before he was returned to the United Kingdom - that he met, for the first and only time ever, but did not realise the identity of the man, the International Jew, Joel Ben Yitzhak.

Jack Jones was also a Soviet mole and a well paid informer.

Jones left his council house in Dulwich and met the Leader of the Opposition at Transport House where a 'working men`s' lunch of Ham and Cheese sandwiches was provided along with lukewarm bitter, however the quality of the beer balanced the incorrect temperature.

The Liverpudlian, without finesse, promptly came to the point of his visit. The forthcoming General Election and complications caused by the successful military action of the Warsaw Pact forces.

"Could the date of the Election be brought forward and in view of the current situation could pressure be placed on the Aristocrat Home to call an early Poll?"

He paused for a few moments, then resumed:

"A wave of strikes could easily be arranged, but was not patriotic, so was there any other method to induce the Prime Minister go to the Polls?"

Harold held his pipe in the grip of his clenched fist, assumed the pose of a thinker and after a few calculated moments, to imply that a profound statement was to be made, stated simply and enigmatically that:

"Perhaps the time will be sooner rather than later."

At about the same time, four men were having lunch in a private room of a London Club. Hurriedly arranged by Sir Hugh Stephenson at the request of the P.M., the two men were joined by Sir Kenneth Strong and Sir Ivone Kirkpatrick. Outside of the room, most incongruously, were two Special Branch officers, sitting at a hastily installed table, enjoying the dish of the day - underdone roast rib of Aberdeen beef. They were unable to hear the dramatic conversation and statement of Sir Alec Douglas Home. He was prepared to fight Wilson and outsmart him. During the meal and afterwards, the others individually and collectively conjectured on the impetus that had transformed the man, but that was now no longer important. What was important was that the P.M. was going to stand up to the bullying tactics of the Ambassador and that they would support him later that day in a confrontation at 10 Downing Street.

Coincidentally, at virtually the same time but a Continent away, discussions and above all decisions were being made, like those in London, that would alter the course and the direction of history and the very nature and fabric of the United Kingdom.

The President of the United States of America was barely able to hide his excitement for he was about to leave the claustrophobic and unsuitable subterranean temporary headquarters for a more spacious and suitable base somewhere 'in the direction of the West Coast'. The background, which did not concern him, was an almost paranoid obsession by not only the Secret Service, who were responsible for his personal safety, but also by a number of branches of the Government that in varying degrees and in different respects also could be held to account for his well being, let alone his safety.

It was less than one month since the assassination of John F. Kennedy and any contribution to the safety of the Office of the Presidency was meticulously handled. He would cross the Prairie States to Nevada, where a complex originally authorised by his Republican Presidential predecessor, Eisenhower, with great prescience and foresight had been blasted, hewn and carved beneath a mountain and fortified to such an extent that engineers believed it to be invulnerable to any attack other than a very accurate direct hit by a thermonuclear device.

Thus the transfer not only of the President but also of the Secretary of Defence and the Attorney General, perhaps the three most important members of the Executive, had to be treated with an exceptional duty of care and caution as never before was there such a time of great potential danger to them all.

The plan had taken longer to organise and execute than was at first envisaged since the fear of a rogue Soviet strike was always a possible contingency, though in hindsight a submarine launched missile attack with nuclear tipped weapons could be absorbed though the psychological damage to the nation would be incalculable. The plan had the dubious qualities of a well crafted Hollywood thriller for its central deception was that Air Force One would be liveried in the paintwork of a commercial airliner, in this case as an Pan American World Airways passenger flight and a false flight plan logged though the route tracked by radar would not agree with the flight plan. At a discreet distance the Boeing 707 would be surrounded by a shield of military jets to protect the precious caravan.

As few as possible were to be privy to the true facts and to confuse any potential saboteurs, a United States Air Force Boeing was to act as a decoy, liveried in the paintwork of the Presidential jet and would proceed, at great danger to its volunteer crew, and with some publicity, North up the Atlantic Coast implying its destination as Washington. The Secretary of Defence and the Attorney General were to be separately transported by helicopter to two different airports from whence they would make the same journey to the ultra secret bastion designated rather vaguely as Area Fifty-one.

It was during the four and a half hour flight that details of a new global policy of containment, ordered by Johnson, was laid before the President ,having been already reviewed and approved by a number of high ranking national politicians, the Senate majority and minority leaders and the Speaker making the President`s approval and well being all the more critical.

Johnson was to again speak to the Nation who were still not yet aware of the massive and cruel loss of American lives and the humiliation of the capture and imprisonment of the survivors. Whilst a concerned and traumatised nation suspected, from the highly censored and sometimes deliberately misleading press coverage ,that all was not well, the shock and humiliation would be a blow to the Country as a whole that would have to be repaired by a bold policy and deeds as great as the opening of the second front in June nineteen forty-four.

This was to be a new Monroe Doctrine extending the nineteenth century policy globally and also, with dire consequences to those who would transgress, with malicious intentions, its boundaries. The map that was provided crudely defined the parameters not specifically by exact latitudes and longitudes but by the thick nib of a pen with red ink.

In the Pacific region ,the broad sweep encompassed Japan and its islands, Formosa, South Korea, The Philippines and the islands of Australia and New Zealand. In the Atlantic, the United Kingdom was circled along with Ireland as if the cartographer assumed that politically they were still joined together and finally the Canary Islands, the Azores, and, as if as an afterthought, the enclave of Gibraltar.

The European mainland and the Mediterranean 'basin' were exempt, initially, from the conditions of the new 'Doctrine' however it was clear, in strategic terms, that to contain Communist expansion 'friendly' regimes would have to be maintained or 'installed' in the Iberian Peninsula, Italy and finally in the Balkans.

On the Mediterranean coast, Israel was ominously *NOT* mentioned.

A speech had been crafted for Johnson`s approval which, for the first time, implied the possible perfidiousness of the Soviets and their hypocrisy. He decided that no reference would be made in the speech or during his Presidency to the bad judgement of his predecessor as disclosed by the Secretary of Defence or, until it was convenient, to tell the American people that they had been betrayed by the incompetent misjudgement of the British Government and its so called 'Intelligence Services'. He would delay informing the Prime Minister of the new 'umbrella' which would shield them from a possible invasion, but at the price of making the British Isles a virtual unsinkable aircraft carrier within a new unofficial political union. Communist expansion would have to be confronted ,contained and controlled; there could now be no compromise. Henceforth the exchange of confidential intelligence with the British would cease and until the world order recovered its balance the British were to be treated no better than the other allies of the United States. Not for the first time had American blood been spilled to maintain the illusion of the 'Special Relationship'.

Shortly afterwards, Johnson was handed a report from the communications room which had just received an incoming intelligence resume relaying a news item from the main radio station in Stockholm, neutral Sweden. It confirmed an earlier intercepted report that following the assistance of Vatican diplomats, acting on the express wishes of the Pope, that a delegation from neutral Portugal and Spain representing Antonio Salazar and Francisco Franco had been received by Premier Nikita Khrushchev and President Leonid Brezhnev and a joint statement had been released. It was becoming crystal clear that whilst Khrushchev professed his intention to force his Warsaw Treaty allies to withdraw from their recent military conquests that he was making political capital out of the new enlarged Eastern Bloc.

It was the secular aspect of the agreement that had been reached, as distinct from the religious part that immediately worried the recipients of the communiqué which was publically announced simultaneously in Lisbon, Madrid and Moscow. The three nations agreed, without conditions, to formally accept, de facto, the sovereignty of all three nations, their right to a political and social system which might not be acceptable to the other two and religious freedom .

 Roman Catholicism would now be tolerated in the Soviet Union and its status would be on a par with the Russian Orthodox Church. Roman Catholic prisoners in the Soviet Union, imprisoned for their faith would be immediately released and free to travel to Spain or Portugal, and in return, the few remaining Communist prisoners in Iberian jails including survivors of the Civil War and especially members of P.O.U.M. would be repatriated or permitted to return to the Soviet Union.

Cultural ,economic and sporting links would be developed, especially in the field of football ,and trade between the three nations, encouraged.

In consequence of their joint recognition ,each nation agreed to respect the others` territorial integrity and the right to recover lands that international law accepted had been wrongfully seized. It was therefore agreed that the question of the sovereignty of Gibraltar be urgently resolved if need be by a plebiscite and that Soviet vessels be afforded the right to a permanent docking and berthing facility in the Canary Islands and the Azores.

Even before details of the Americans` new political doctrine had been conveyed to Moscow and then publically announced, the leaders of the

Presidium had taken a bold, aggressive initiative both in their opening attempt to gain control of Gibraltar and 'The Pillars of Hercules', but also by Khrushchev for he now implemented the final part of the plan originally devised , in the United Kingdom, by Mandel Goldburgh. The bombers (which were painted in the colours of the Peoples' Republic of China), based just inside the Chinese border were loaded with their cargoes of deadly nuclear and thermonuclear devices and primed. The targets would be military and civilian centres on the American West Coast and the assault would be a one way mission as the crews were informed that although refuelling planes would be located at various pre determined points en route, the crews should endeavour to penetrate deep into the heartland of the enemy.

Khrushchev, as if as an afterthought also decided, not out of enmity to the State of Israel, that the potential political gains in the Middle East through the destruction of the Zionist state and consequent effective policing and supervision of the oil producing nations through its surrogate, Egypt, was well worth the risk. The imminent attack, in the guise or ruse of Chinese liveried Soviet bombers, would in any event generate an American counter strike, but he was confident that his air force would inflict enough damage on the American West Coast to 'neutralise' the severity of the counter attack and although a number of cities and industrial centres would be destroyed, the United States would suffer more and the shock of the massive damage inflicted by his valiant bombers, publicised by its radio and T.V. services would destroy the resolve and spirit of the American people.

The Presidential jet landed at the military airport and as he exited the plane he was confronted by the bitter, biting early evening cold and as he walked down the gangway, he saw a reception party of four civilians who he could just make out in the dim light but as he approached them he could see that they were all heavily wrapped in coats to protect them from the elements. He shook the hands of the first person in the line up (and didn't quite catch his name), gesticulated and in response to some garbled words (or in fact words drowned by the noise of the engines being shut down) he accepted the gift - or loan - of the man's coat which he very quickly put on to give him some respite from the increasingly bitter cold and rising wind.   Suddenly he heard an unexpected and familiar voice, as a loud almost shriek, which was heard by everyone present.

"Daddy".

It was his daughter, who without concern for protocol or the dignity of her father's new office, broke rank and rushed towards him, finally embracing him. It was this unexpected reuniting of part of his family that strengthened him for the struggle ahead.

They walked, hand in hand to the helicopter that would make the short hop to the redoubt and as they reached their 'ride', which was illuminated by floodlights, she suddenly saw the ravages of her father's incarceration and the consequences of his brief, troubled Presidency. The short period living as a troglodyte, the unhealthy diet (he always, when not under his wife's supervision, drank too much Dr. Pepper and ate steaks without trimming the fat) had helped to bloat his face and his skin was pallid. He was breathing uncomfortably and his eyes lacked any sparkle.

He intended to hold an urgent meeting with not only his closest political colleagues but using the latest technology of a satellite link, a telephone conference including representatives of the National Security Council, Herman Kahn, whose meticulous comprehension of the global military situation might be critically useful and with the Joint Chiefs to plan an urgent military strategy. However on his arrival at the vast subterranean complex he was rushed to the awe inspiring, well appointed medical (this time fully, or apparently over staffed) centre where in any event he had been destined to be brought to, for a comprehensive examination.

He was soon joined by McNamara and Kennedy and there then followed an intensive and comprehensive medical examination of all three of them, conducted by what seemed an abundance of doctors, specialists and technical staff. He was accompanied, except for the most intimate parts of the examination, by his daughter, however even she could see that a great mental and physical strain had been imposed on her father.

When the investigations had been completed the results did not surprise either father or daughter. He was suffering from acute hypertension, vitamin deficiency and two 'Syndromes', 'Raynauds', which was less distressing than the its name implied and 'Stevens Johnson', when he burst into spontaneous laughter, a positive way to reduce his blood pressure, as he wrongly assumed that the health condition was in fact a Democratic Party alliance. The temporary release of pressure was then perhaps cruelly terminated when the chief doctor concluded his diagnosis by informing his patient that the consensus of the medical staff was overwhelmingly that he was suffering from extreme, and he emphasised the degree, stress and that under any other situation, he would not only recommend complete rest, but that he would insist immediately on the cessation of any act resulting in tension and stress.

But he was the President and there was no Vice–President.

Shortly afterwards he went to relieve himself. He was alone but even that situation or subjective observation was an absurd falsehood. As the President of the United States of America and its Commander in Chief he could never be entirely alone.

He sat in the luxurious toilet (in comparison to the unit adjacent to the conference room in the recently vacated complex) and contemplated *HIS* situation and the task that would determine not only the fate and destiny of his fellow countrymen and women but also the lives and well being of his 'neighbours', allies and even the innocent tens of millions who just wanted to live their lives as nationals of his country`s enemies. His mind was full of doubt and fear but he returned to the immediate task which was a simple case of constipation, another of the many minor medical problems that had been diagnosed. He forced himself to move his bowels and as he succeeded as an automatic reaction and not an eruption of jubilation he let out a wordless sigh of relief which created a near immediate call from a Secret Service agent outside of the cubicle:

"Are you all right , Mr. President?"

To which the reply was in the positive. But he knew instinctively that duty and the Oath of Office that he had recently swore overrode any personal considerations.

FORTY-SIX

Harold Wilson was about to leave Transport House and return to his temporary, makeshift office from where he would contact the Soviet Embassy and more important the Ambassador, when the receptionist caught his attention and handed to him two messages originating from his office. The first was from the Prime Minister and requested his absolute urgent attendance at Ten Downing Street, at nine p.m. that evening and the second, more intriguing, was from the Soviet Embassy asking him to contact them on a telephone number that was totally unknown to him.

He would be cautious and very careful in his approach for it had been common gossip, of course prior to the massacre, in the various Commons tea rooms, that the telephone lines connecting the Embassy were monitored and consequently the calls both incoming and outgoing were probably recorded.

Wilson`s intellectual argument was that such an act would be against all the principles of any Embassy`s rights and that if such an act was common knowledge then the Ambassador and his staff would take appropriate evasive action. He decided on caution and used a convenient, local telephone box and with great interest he dialled the number which was answered by a prompt...

"Hallo,"

but with a distinct Russian accent. He identified himself and requested the Ambassador by name and not his status. There appeared to be a definite delay in the transfer of the call and some unusual background noises which irritated and frustrated him.

He was guarded in his comments and remarks and finally agreed to meet the Ambassador in a central London hotel where they could have a private conversation and exchange of views. .

Arriving at the hotel (it was the elegant and discreet Goring) he went to the reception not only to announce himself but to have the Ambassador paged when suddenly he entered the lobby and walked up to the Leader of the Opposition, offering a handshake in friendship.

Wilson did not realise that the events were an elaborate ruse and deception to gain his confidence for two adjoining room had previously been booked and in the other room suitcases had not contained personal effects but eaves dropping equipment to record the meeting. Completely at ease and cunningly led on by the Ambassador, Wilson betrayed his Country for the position of Her Majesty`s First Lord of the Treasury.

Wilson knew, or thought he knew, that the Prime Minister would acquiesce to the Soviet threat of blackmail and stand down the 'V Bomber 'force because logically he had no other alternative and he guessed that the Ambassador suspected that this was the only option.

The Prime Minister and what was left of the Government could announce that under pressure the Soviet Union had been forced to make 'concessions' in response to a British ultimatum which would soon bring certain unspecified benefits and the Conservative Party could possibly reap a political advantage and deprive him of the General Election victory that he believed was his .

He, no the Government, had until midnight to answer the ultimatum and his future could be decided by the outcome of this private meeting. The man opposite him would not know that a meeting was fixed for later that same evening, though he might guess that there would be some activity before he received a reply, but what both men did not know was that Khrushchev had no real intention of attacking the United Kingdom for he had calculated that they would ultimately capitulate once the population had been bombarded with the publicised threat which would then be followed by complete chaos and anarchy, or if that failed (and that was most unlikely) after the successful assault by his bombers on the West Coast of the United States and a devastating attack on Israel.

But then, to further complicate the negotiations, Wilson did not know that the Ambassador had been summonsed to Ten Downing Street to meet the P.M.(who would be supported by the three 'Knights of the Realm' ,Kirkpatrick, Stephenson and Strong) and the outcome of that meeting was unpredictable.

It was then that he sold his soul and his Country.

Time, the purges and the perversion of history has destroyed what independent, objective opinion existed, which was divided on the validity of the recording of the meeting between Wilson and the Ambassador, citing certain inconsistencies and Wilson's admittance of the fact of the meeting and all of the words that were included in the tape recording .

His consistent argument, supported by credible reasoning ,was that the tape was both edited and manipulated, consequently therefore legally inadmissible. But he was appearing before a military tribunal where the only sentence, if found guilty, was death and the judgement had been pre-ordained by the National Council.

Whether or not the Ambassador was a K G B agent is not important, what is pertinent is that he was proficient and adept in the arcane art of prising information from his victim and he was able to lead on the Leader of the Opposition not only to compromise himself but to enter into an agreement that would effectively castrate and emasculate the United Kingdom. Wilson knew, or thought he knew that Home would crumple at the threats and in consequence destroy his Premiership. Wilson was prepared to make an agreement far more craven and damaging to the nation, in fact the offer that he made would in reality destroy the credibility of the Country and leave it defenceless.

His argument was an insight into the philosophy and an analysis and *expose* of Socialism and of the 'Left Wing' of the Labour Party (most of whom had been slaughtered on that fateful Monday) and its attitude towards nuclear weapons enshrined in the policy of nuclear disarmament which was symbolised by the mass movement of the 'Campaign For Nuclear Disarmament' (C.N.D.). He had always privately felt, in the final analysis, that such a policy was unrealistic and unacceptable to the Electorate and would be electoral suicide if it formed the central plank of his Part. Now, even to mention the subject, when the very existence of the United Kingdom was in peril, would be seen as madness and a betrayal of the defence of the Realm.

If Home was going to back down, as was most likely, it would be in a cloud or fog of obfuscation. He had no choice but to offer an agreement that would not only be acceptable to the blackmailers but could be approved by the electorate, who for a short time, that is until they had cast their votes, were influential and then he could gain the political support and confidence of a new generation of politicians who would be elected to Parliament .

Without prompting, he opened his argument with the sensible opinion that the power of the thermonuclear weapon was so tremendous that even taking into account the vastness of the Soviet Union ,an attack on European Russia and the Ukraine would devastate and obliterate the Sindustrial and farming areas of both Republics and that the major cities, including their hinterlands, would cease to exist. For the United Kingdom, so much smaller in area, the consequences would be far more horrendous and probably the nation might cease to exist as a viable entity.

He was prepared to go further than the P.M. He would order the 'V Bomber' fleet and more importantly, all the Nation's tactical and strategic nuclear and thermonuclear weapons to be moved for safety from the United Kingdom, perhaps to South Africa, where they would still pose a threat to the country's enemies.

The very nature of his offer astounded the Ambassador for he realised that his guest had not thought through the consequences, even to the fundamental fact of obtaining agreement from the South African government.

Sensing that Wilson could be manipulated to make an even more massive concession the Ambassador suggested that :

"In the pursuit of global stability and world peace, such an act by the British Government on behalf of the British people would be viewed Internationally as perhaps the most outstanding contribution to the cause of peace and freedom from the devastation of war."

He refrained from using the word pacifism since it had connotations of abject surrender and cowardice,whilst the phraseology that had just been employed was heroic and inferred, in a more peaceful time, the worthless reward of a Nobel Peace prize.

Wilson continued, making a further ill conceived offer which would completely castrate 'GREAT Britain':

"If First Secretary Khrushchev was to make a dramatic offer which was seen to increase world peace and stability and to apply pressure on the renegade elements of the Warsaw Pact to withdraw from the occupied territories of our allies then I believe that as Prime Minister I could persuade a new Parliament and the British people to not only renounce these weapons of Armageddon but to endorse their dismantlement in South Africa ."

The Ambassador had heard enough. The man was pliable and had just sold his soul (a religious concept which had no place in the atheistic beliefs, or absence of beliefs of the Communist Party). The meeting ended with the fraternisation of two men seeking the goal of peace as they embraced.

"I will report to Moscow on this historic meeting and await instructions."

They parted, the Leader of the Opposition euphoric on his statesmanship, but he did not know that the Ambassador was going directly to 'Number Ten' to meet the P. M. to discover or to confirm his anticipated intentions.

FORTY-SEVEN

They met on the first floor of' Number Ten 'in one of the elegant reception rooms that inspired both the appreciation of the master craftsmen`s arts and the continuity of elegance and sophistication.

The P.M. was flanked on either side by the three Knights of the Realm and, as the Ambassador surmised, they had prepared an argument to subdue him and consequently, the Soviet leadership. Home`s argument was simple, honest and originally framed in the language and measured tones of his diplomatic career, however he became overwhelmed by an emotional passion which changed the tone but not the message of the argument.

The Soviet Union was absolutely correct in its intelligence that the United Kingdom bomber force had been and was still on maximum alert and was loaded with an array of nuclear weapons, however this was a prudent course of action calculated by the military planners and approved by the Government. Indeed he would not be surprised if his counterpart in Moscow had not taken the same course of action. He was not prepared to sacrifice the defence of the nation without cast iron guarantees from Mr. Khrushchev beginning with a promise to halt any malicious propaganda broadcasts from occupied Europe designed to destabilise the country and to cause an unwarranted panic. Secondly he was impatient to unfetter the newly enslaved former allies from their occupation which, despite utterances from the First Secretary, appeared no nearer.

He concluded his message to the First Secretary with these exact words:

"Perhaps we should both recognise that we have misunderstood the other's motives and intentions. Our experience of aggression and treachery, personally the deceit of Mr. Hitler when I met the man, in Munich, in nineteen thirty- eight, and you ,close to Marshall Stalin, when in June nineteen forty-one your country was invaded,should teach us both to be able to acknowledge the sincerity of the other. Let us settle this matter amicably."

The Ambassador smiled and confirmed that as an unofficial Anglophile that he would, in everyone's interest, try to resolve this 'misunderstanding'. As he left, he approached Sir Ivone Kirkpatrick and unexpectedly, perhaps even 'to break the ice', asked if:

"Once this matter has, I hope, been satisfactorily settled, could we meet, since I am most intrigued to learn of the wartime meeting that you had with, and the 'interrogation' of, Mr. Rudolf Hess."

Then he concluded with a most enigmatic and cryptic comment which drew a barely suppressed smile from Sir Ivone...

"Perhaps you could even supply a copy of your report."

Sir Ivone commented, after the departure of the Ambassador, that his attitude boded well for the outcome.

259

At nine p.m. that evening, Wilson arrived at Ten Downing Street expecting to be received by a broken Prime Minister who would begin the procedure to hand over the reins of power. However Home, again flanked by his 'Three Knights', buoyantly confirmed details of his earlier meeting and suggested that the 'rump' of the Government be informed the next day at ten a.m. precisely of the secret threat that had been made, his diplomatic reply and what he now suspected was to be a humiliating Soviet change of posture.

Wilson went home deflated, bitter but above all frustrated, for the prize and his dreams of a remodelled society of greater equality, fairness and honesty propelled by the wealth created by the 'white hot furnace' of technology appeared to have been extinguished by the manoeuvres of the P.M.

He was woken at about twelve twenty-five a.m.; he automatically looked at a luminous Smith's watch strategically located by the side of his bed, whilst hounded by the insistent tone of the telephone and immediately worried that it was bad news. Still in that world between sleep and consciousness, he carefully went downstairs, avoiding turning on a light and holding cautiously onto the railing at the side of the stairs and answered the phone. He recognised the voice of the caller who did not apologise for the inconvenience of his unexpected but highly urgent call.

Harold Wilson could not get back to sleep that night and for him time literally 'flew', indeed there was inadequate time to plan not only his tactics but various alternative strategies. It was as if he had been given a narcotic so powerful that it was dictating his actions.

At ten thirty, later that morning, the 'Soviet' government would broadcast to the British people an announcement that they had been in secret discussions with the British Prime Minister and that they were preparing to make a statement that:

"Would affect the lives not only of the people of Great Britain but also of the Soviet Union and Western Europe."

Wilson had until the end ofthe Cabinet meeting to secure the resignation of Home and to inaugurate the process of his summons to Buckingham Palace. Two alternative broadcasts had been prepared, one if Home stayed on (and the consequences were known) and the other, action to resolve the European problem.

FORTY-EIGHT
December 20th1963

Whilst it is important to construct the following narrative in a coherent order, the reader must realise that of the many personalities recorded in this particular part of the investigation, all of the participants present at the Cabinet meeting are now dead, excluding the Permanent Secretary to the Cabinet whose escape to the United States was assisted by the unofficial help of 'neutral' diplomats. His statement, made later to a closed session of a Congressional Enquiry has, no doubt, clarified the real reasons for the behaviour of the Prime Minister and his resignation.

Wilson is claimed to have said later that evening:

"Never did the hands of my watch move so slowly as I furtively snatched *EVERY* opportunity, and the opportunities became more frequent, to check up on the arrival of the hour of ten–thirty and when it came, nothing happened. I had to wait for some fifteen to twenty minutes before a knock on the Cabinet door permitted the P.M`s. Private Secretary to enter and hand him a note, the document that I was expecting, but above all the timing was impeccable for at that same moment those present had commenced the '*coup de grace*'to the Prime Minister`s tenure of power."

It is an error of fact to describe the event as a 'Cabinet Meeting' for only three of those present were members of the now decimated government. Along with the P.M. were only two previously appointed members, the Minister of Housing and Local Government and Minister for Welsh Affairs, The Right Honourable Sir Keith Joseph and Minister without Portfolio, The Right Honourable William Deedes.

The Leader of the Opposition, (James) Harold Wilson sat at the far end of the room with his back to the window so that if he turned round he could view part of the garden and the terrace where a table was surrounded by chairs in anticipation of more pleasant weather. Adjacent to him were two fellow Labour M.Ps., Michael Cliffe (Shoreditch and Finsbury), who had been off ill that fateful Monday and Harold Neal (Bolsover), affectionately referred to both by political allies and opponents as 'The Beast'. From the Conservative back benches were Sir Hendrie Oakshott (Bebington) and Colin Turner (Woolwich, West) whilst finally the Liberal Party was represented by Roderic Bowen (Cardigan).

Those present had no formal authority and had originally been gathered, on the suggestion of one anonymous Permanent Secretary, as a public symbol of the nation's unity, whilst the Prime Minister, *de facto*, made any necessary decisions; endeavouring to persuade the Leader of the Opposition to help him create a Government of National Unity which would rule until the current state of belligerence had been resolved and a General Election could be called.

This was the third meeting of the group, the first had been little more than a public relations exercise to boost the morale of the country and the second ,just over a week before, was to discuss the formation of a Government of 'National Unity' and the calling of a General Election.

Surprisingly, opinions did not veer towards or follow party lines and the general consensus was to create, similar to the Churchill-Attlee alliance of May nineteen forty, a government that represented the whole country and not a particular party. The Prime Minister had not mentioned at the second meeting, although the authority had been given days earlier, that he had secretly authorised the Royal Air Force to be on maximum alert.

The Right Honourable Alexander Frederick Douglas–Home, First Lord of the Treasury, having at some length gone through a number of courtesies came to the only matter of importance which was confirmation that with the agreement of the Leader of the Opposition he had authorised the 'V Bomber' force to be on fifteen minute standby and more importantly that the force be armed with primed nuclear and thermonuclear weapons.

Even before he announced the ultimatum there was a distinct sense both of shock and fear, with those present in an unusual consensus of agreement. There was no moral or military dilemma, no dichotomy, there was no support for the leader and when the P.M. mentioned the ultimatum there was an additional emotion,so palpable that everyone in the room was overcome by a sense of foreboding. Underpinning their emotions was the common thread and shared opinion, as yet unspoken ,that the adventure was foolish and the fact that they had not been consulted, made a mockery of the intentions of the committee and called in question the very competence and suitability of an unelected Prime Minister.

Home had been 'wrong–footed'. He remembered a 'secret' letter that Ivone Kirkpatrick had written on September 10th nineteen fifty–six during the 'Suez Crisis' which now, in perspective, was apparently a less dramatic moment for the Government, and which ended with the resounding objective analysis...

" ...and a country that cannot provide for its defence is finished."

Wilson, with consummate timing, at about ten thirty-six a.m. began to speak calmly but as if he was issuing a death warrant...

He lied, or at best, confronted by the imminent ultimate prize, was 'flexible' with his facts. Just enough to destroy the credibility of the P.M. and to maintain his fellow members' trust and belief in his probity. He admitted, and agreed that Home had both confided and sought his opinion in such a grave matter, however he had strongly urged not only caution but a diplomatic approach to the Soviet leadership to resolve what he saw was fundamentally an unnecessary escalation, however he had not given either his approval or tacit agreement to the P.M.'s intended course of action. Home was livid with anger both at the lie and the betrayal and was about to interrupt and correct the situation when his Private Secretary entered and handed him the note which confirmed details of the radio broadcast. Home was broken. Like an earlier leader, (Robert Anthony) Eden, he had been hammered on the anvil of superpower politics. He interpreted the statement as a prologue to a propaganda assault on the British people which would bring chaos and anarchy. Fate and the malevolence of Wilson had conspired to destroy him. In truth the reality was the opposite and was to be a statement of conciliation.

But within hours Home had been received by the Queen, tendered his resignation and recommended that She call upon Harold Wilson to form a new government and soon afterwards Wilson kissed Her Majesty's hand and returned to 'Number Ten' as its new master. The following day, discreetly, the Soviet Ambassador made a visit to Ten Downing Street and discussed a timetable for the transfer of the 'V Bomber' force and its cargo of death and later that afternoon, Harold Wilson's great friend and trade union leader, Jack Jones led a delegation of trade union leaders but remained after the others had departed. It was while the two men were in conversation that the new P.M. received not only a very brief and cursory telephone call of congratulations from the President of the United States but also prior knowledge of the new 'Monroe' doctrine and the 'umbrella' of American military power, however his 'arrangement' with the Soviet Ambassador was not even mentioned. For reasons that never can be determined, Wilson did not withdraw from the agreement that he had earlier made with the Soviet Ambassador and with Mr. Khrushchev thereby unwittingly setting in motion events that would, for him, end in his execution for High Treason.

Soon Britain would be emasculated and its credibility all but destroyed, creating an environment and breeding ground for forces that would radically and undemocratically forever change the Country. Had the President notified Home twenty–four hours earlier, then the destiny and future of the United Kingdom would have taken an entirely different course.

FORTY NINE

The U2 reconnaissance and spy plane had completed its mission over Northern China and the regions of the Soviet Union bordering the North Pacific, with particular interest in the port of Vladivostok, without mishap, probably because the general area was defended by surface to air missiles unable to reach the cruising height of the U2, but most likely because the operation was carried out at the extreme limit of the plane's capabilities, reaching the maximum altitude permitted by the engineers who had designed the aircraft. Using what was described as 'state of the art' photographic technology, vast swathes had been photographed, but not the hastily built airstrips on the Russian–Chinese border, that actually during the spy plane's flight had seen the departure of the clandestine fleet of some sixty-five fully laden Intercontinental bombers on what had been defined in the final briefing as a one way mission.

The primary targets had been specified and ranked in order of priority with a demand that the crews did not attempt to return to their bases but continue onwards, until their fuel was exhausted, deep into the heartland of the United States, delivering, like the postal service, their cargo of death, destruction and horror.

After the President had made his brief congratulatory telephone call to the new British Prime Minister and in passing, as if as an afterthought, mentioned the updated 'Monroe' Doctrine that would be made internationally and nationally public the following day, he walked to the briefing room where he joined the Director of Central Intelligence (DCI), John Mc Cone and his assistant, Richard M. Helms, a veteran both of the OSS and the CIA, together with his Secretary of Defence and Attorney General. Also at the table were the Senate Majority and Minority leaders, three members of his Cabinet, two members of the Supreme Court, one of whom was Judge Earl Warren and at his personal request, Herman Kahn. Such a concentration of many of the most important men in the nation could only be accommodated at a table and in a room which far exceeded and dwarfed the room and table that Johnson had had to tolerate in the previous temporary redoubt that he had recently left.

Johnson was shocked by the opening report of Helms which confirmed the fall of not only West Germany, but also Belgium, Holland and Denmark. France had capitulated as she had done in nineteen forty but Warsaw Pact troops had not crossed an imaginary line from Bordeaux on the Atlantic coast to Geneva on the Swiss border for reasons that, as yet, no intelligence was available.

Those United States forces that had survived the assault, especially the cocktail of nerve gases, had been imprisoned, apparently in makeshift camps, though the final humiliation was that the infamous concentration camp of Dachau, outside of Munich, was being utilised. United States civilians were literally being rounded up, like cattle, interned in hotels, though not with the accompanying   services normally offered by such premises.

No atrocities had been reported and the Red Cross was passing information, including lists of interned civilians to the U.S. Embassy in Bern, however no information, official or otherwise, regarding U.S. military personnel had been forwarded by their captors but an unconfirmed report via neutral Sweden claimed that a cinema newsreel in the former East Berlin (now reunited with its Western half) had shown captured U.S. troops displayed in such a way as to deliberately humiliate them, combined with a commentary, which sarcastically denigrated the ...

"Capitalist West and their now hollow claims to military superiority."

Those present, including the President, were taken by surprise when the more senior of the two intelligence chiefs then requested that a matter, a purely political subject, and therefore outside of the Agency's Charter not be recorded or ever attributed back to them since their motives, honourable in intention, might be maliciously misinterpreted in the future.

Since the beginning of the crisis, and they now had information identifying the perpetrators, the Agency had detected a growing groundswell of national isolationism which had expressed itself in an article published in an obscure regional newspaper in the 'Mid West', arguing that twice in the first half of the Century that the New World had come to the rescue of the Old World and it was becoming clear that for the third time in less than fifty years, a rescue would have to be repeated and then the thought provoking article culminated in an assessment to determine not only the financial cost but the potential further loss of American life.

The article had been promptly republished in a Houston, Texas, 'daily' and then nationally syndicated resulting in an opinion poll in a New York Sunday paper, based on a survey of five thousand six hundred and forty voters in five North East States, who polled 83 to 9 percent in favour of isolationism as against the projection of American military and economic power globally, summarised by another question expressed in the concept of a 'Pax Americana' which was overwhelmingly rejected with a virtually similar result.

The Agency had discreetly commissioned a new poll using as a 'front', a nationally known food manufacturer and household name to further probe the mind of the nation, this time requesting that the territorial area be based on the 'Mid West' and' Prairie' states with a base of nearly fourteen thousand voters. The result would be published in less than thirty-six hours in Washington and nationally syndicated and its findings gave 'food for thought':

The Country had no stomach for military intervention in Europe, regarded the 'Old World' as a social and political anachronism (a significant number of 'blue collar' workers did not understand this word) and again looked for what was analysed as a policy of isolationism, parochial self interest and increased national but not international defence. A leading journalist (and C.I.A. advisor) whose political analysis was a 'weather vane' of the national mood, was to publish an article tomorrow, Saturday, entitled...

Brave New World?

which in part was an obituary and an appreciation of the author and intellectual, Aldous Huxley, who had died on the same day as the former President, and was to be a prophetic vision of a new 'Pax Americana' where the United States was protected by two vast Oceans and on their rims, by two unsinkable aircraft carriers, the British Isles and Japan, both still nominally independent and, of course, self governing, but in reality colonies of the United States and under the 'umbrella' of the Strategic Air Command for which a price in terms of manufactured goods supplied to the Continental United States at a new adjusted exchange rate would be levied in lieu of a financial contribution for their defence, giving the ILLUSION [Author's emphasis] of independence.

Japan was viewed as the more industrious ,innovative and compliant of the two countries whilst the United Kingdom was seen to be in terminal decline, fundamentally socialist in political orientation, dominated by left wing trade unions which were out of control, and finally permeated by the erroneous sense that their great sacrifices and the bastion of freedom during the dark days of the Second World War had given them an eternal right to the benefits of national wealth, without the commitment of their labour.

Johnson was caught virtually speechless, as if his announcement both to the nation and internationally had been foreseen and anticipated, but he had not judged the nation's mood accurately. Furthermore in less than eleven months there was to be a Presidential Election where domestic issues, national security and above all, most in the mind of the electorate, was and would always be, their standard of living.

In those few precious moments when he could temporarily discard the problems of Europe, of the American civilians and military personnel imprisoned and probably to be used as pawns and the subject of some form of ransom, he had dreamed, yes dreamed of his legacy.

April nineteen sixty-five, only six months after the Election would see the one hundredth anniversary of the end of the Civil War and if he could create a new framework to give true emancipation to the Black community then full equality would result and therefore he could possibly inherit the mantle of successor to Abraham Lincoln.

It was at that moment that the Attorney General, Kennedy, requested that the intelligence chief amplify the comment, which was made in passing, relating to the identity of 'the perpetrators' of the European war. The response was not unexpected and finally destroyed any faith that the President had in the honesty and sincerity of the First Secretary:

"Our sources [the speaker was specific in his use of the plural] close to, but not in the Presidium, have independently confirmed that beyond a shadow of a doubt that Khrushchev himself, was the originator and inspiration behind the plan to attack West Germany; not only that, the destruction of the Command and Control bunkers on the East German border was a cynical exercise to erase all evidence and existence of those senior members of the Warsaw Pact forces who had conspired in the plan. Indeed the cooperation given to locate the Soviet submarines was undoubtedly, like a move in a game of chess, a sacrifice to gain the President's confidence. It is too coincidental, at this stage, to connect the Presidential assassination and the Parliament (sic) massacre with the military events however our field agents are pursuing every line to definitely connect Oswald with Moscow.

267

The identities of our informants is unknown even to us, only to certain operatives placed close to them and working in great danger. I would not stake our two lives on the veracity of their information but since it has come from at least three different unique sources I am confident as to its accuracy."

The President was dealing with a new reality which was about to be tested when those present were connected by a television conference system to another subterranean redoubt, the headquarters of the Strategic Air Command in Omaha, Nebraska. Their spokesman, speaking with the permission of the three star General currently in overall operational command of the complex was sombre in his advices and assessment of the latest report on the cordon and encirclement of the Soviet Union. The strain imposed not only on the flight crews but more so on the ground crews - mainly the mechanics and engineers - had reached such an intensity that it was estimated that the operation, in its present form, could last no longer than a few more days, a week at best, when physical and mental fatigue would drastically effect the standard of work which was already beginning to fray at its edges, to such a degree that the bomber crews and their planes would be dangerously compromised by the literal unravelling of the men`s commitment and more importantly the quality of their labour.

The only option would be to reduce the density of the cordon by reducing the duration of the existing flights thereby making the encirclement more porous. This was to be a Presidential decision that should be taken after much consultation with his senior advisors. The President declined to accept the recommendation citing the current and unpredictable situation but agreed to review the whole programme within seventy two hours .

Those who were closest, both physically and emotionally to the President began to recognise the great strain and stress that he was under, indeed he should have been monitored constantly, on a day to day basis, but the overwhelming bulk of the medical team had returned to their practices and Universities to continue their special disciplines leaving only the President`s temporary personal physician, one other doctor and a limited team of medical technicians, a situation which in hindsight and a later Congressional review was declared grossly inadequate, bordering on negligence.

The Commander in Chief received the greatest psychological support from his daughter as they both awaited the arrival of *his* wife and *her* mother, the formidable Lady Bird Johnson. In the meantime she had taken it upon herself to nurse her father and thought nothing of interrupting matters of state to deliver to him and his associates, without warning or demand, jugs of fragrant smelling coffee (and occasionally she allowed him a Dr. Pepper) and such was the exquisite flavour that her skills were soon in great demand. It was this background combined with the enormous burden on the shoulders of one man, that the final chapter of the conflagration and confrontation were shortly to be played out and the players separated into victors, vanquished and survivors.

The U2 had passed over the coast, performing a great arc and was nearly three hours into its journey home to an isolated and secret base, so secret that no map even showed the very existence of the base somewhere in Nevada, when perhaps forty five thousand feet below, the pilot spotted an armada initially estimated by him as one hundred heavy intercontinental bombers travelling East towards the North American continent. Ignoring, no forgetting his discipline, training and strict instructions, the pilot proceeded to shadow the harbingers of death and destruction slowly mentally adjusting his original estimate of their numbers to approximately seventy five.

They were in three layers, at heights of, he roughly calculated, fifteen, twenty and twenty five thousand feet, each layer grouped in a symmetrical pattern. The pilot admitted to himself that he should have brushed up on his recognition technique but he was 'pretty sure 'they were 'Bears' and 'Bisons' (Tupolev T U 95s and Myasishchev M4s). His neglect of practices that had been instilled into him continued when he broke a cardinal rule, but an act that would save the United States, as he broke radio silence and announced, with unprofessional excitement and informality, not only the exact location of the assembled armada but its direction and approximate composition.

History does not record his identity though his superiors' attitude and response to his behaviour and actions was initially recorded as a clear breach of procedure and in consequence a matter for disciplinary proceedings.

Within fifteen minutes the news was broken to the President and his closest associates. What he had feared most was now both inevitable and imminent. The United States was on the verge of a nuclear and probable thermonuclear attack. It was then, without hesitation, that Herman Kahn took the initiative to express what he considered to be the most prudent option available to the Commander in Chief.

"Mr. President, You have no alternative but to order a counter first strike of every available heavy bomber, holding back some eighty to ninety aircraft for a second strike. I suggest, in accordance with a recent lecture that I gave, that the primary targets should be as many military and civilian airstrips as possible for if they were taken out (and if possible with their bombers and fighters) then the Soviet air force would be unable to function despite its estimated massive inventory.

Their cities and industrial complexes would be defenceless save for their surface to air missiles and at the mercy of a second strike, hostages to a favourable political solution, including liberation of all Europe and not only the recently occupied Western area."

The President turned to his Secretary of Defence, who instantaneously understood that he was the focus of attention of all around him and with the authority of a man who recognised that the mantle of destiny had not only been wrapped around his shoulders but that the security and future wellbeing of every man, woman and child throughout the nation rested upon his judgement and the wise counsel of his associates, began to speak in slow, concise and measured terms...

"Mr. President, immediately order the Joint Chiefs to enforce the plan described by Mr.Kahn, to flush our bomber fleet from their various havens and locations and then to proceed ,en masse, to their fail safe positions, however until you give the Presidential Order, no attack is to begin and certainly the use of nuclear or thermonuclear weapons is absolutely forbidden until you give the order. In the final minutes of peace, a last attempt could be made to negotiate with the First Secretary in an honourable act to avert war and the subsequent loss of perhaps tens, even hundreds of millions of lives on both sides."

The President stood up, stretched his arms to release the physical tension, and everyone in the room, without exception rose, not as a mark of respect, but to enable each and everyone to offer to the Commander in Chief their handshake to express their loyalty and support.

Suddenly, as if as an afterthought, Johnson added what was to be a significant comment and observation, which would change the course of the destiny of the United States, but because of the circumstances surrounding their enactment only a few of those present would know the truth and the sordid allegations of treachery:

"If Khrushchev has betrayed us and this fleet of bombers encroaches upon either our territorial waters or the mainland, I will immediately, without hesitation, authorise and permit the use of nuclear weapons only on military targets in the Soviet homeland."

The Supreme Court judge, Earl Warren, was seen to take Johnson aside and speak extremely quietly to him and what he had to say gave the man both the moral and legal authority to continue.

"Mr. President, no law on Earth or judgement from on High could ever impugn your integrity or commitment to your Oath of Office."

As the President received the support of those present, he suddenly felt his heart pounding and accelerating, beads of sweat seemed to be forming on his brow and were beginning to slide down his face and the pain, vicious, sharp and intense, travelled along his left arm as if barbed wire was being pulled along his flesh. He furtively drew a deep breath, gathered his strength and concentrated on the responsibilities of his Presidential Oath.

He would be in direct communication with the Soviet leader within a few minutes and expected that his motives and intentions would be concealed behind a fog of deceit and a bodyguard of lies, but in the meantime he would join the Secretary of Defence in his conversation with the Joint Chiefs, buried deep in the Pentagon or some other hardened redoubt, and await their confirmation of Kahn's recommendation though he still remembered the snub that had earlier been made to the Representative of the entire nation. It was at this moment that he sensed that something had just occurred which had caught Bob McNamara by surprise and he waited in anticipation of the report.

McNamara had already sensed the Commander's presence and turned to him:

"Mr. President, The U2 pilot has just broken radio silence again and is about to make a report which is being relayed both to the Pentagon and to this control centre."

Unlike his previous message the pilot delivered his report with a cool, calm and comprehensive summary of the current situation. Surprisingly he was unusually apologetic ,referring to his clear breach of protocol and in consequence the potential damage he could cause; not only that, he had decided, on his own initiative, to shadow approximately twenty of the bombers who about twelve minutes before had 'peeled off' from the main body of the armada and had turned South East towards the coast of Washington State and Oregon. Indeed their course would be an excellent marker for his own return journey and he estimated, taking into account their current speed and the fact that he believed that some of the bombers were carrying (air launched) cruise missiles that they would be over Seattle within about two hours.

It was at this moment that an aide to the head of the C.I.A., perhaps through impatience or inexperience, interrupted the broadcast to announce that in his opinion, the cruise missiles were most likely the AS-3 Kangaroo with a range estimated at three hundred and fifty miles, capable of carrying a nuclear weapon - but not a thermonuclear device-at subsonic speeds, mainly due to their size, estimated to be as large as a Sukhoi Su 7 fighter.

The final part of the pilot`s report had temporarily been hidden by the uncalled for interjection of technical information, but the accumulation of intelligence had galvanised and steeled the President in his resolve and intentions .

FIFTY

Tranquillity and solitude. The First Secretary sat at his desk in his private office deep in the bowels of the Kremlin surrounded only by the two companions that mighty leaders constantly seek but rarely achieve. He was alone with only his thoughts for company as a golden silence allowed him to both reflect on the past and project his hopes for the future.

He could have taken Johnson`s call at any time but his experience of human nature, of politicians' impatience, persuaded him to delay his response until such time as he felt able to deal with the man that so far he had successfully deceived.

The time for deception and deceit was nearly over and the two stratagems had served him well. The military campaign in Western Europe had achieved territorial gains beyond his wildest expectations and he already had a cunning plan to retain the conquered lands. The American military and civilian prisoners would first become hostages, carefully located at strategic civilian and especially military locations where their presence, prominently displayed to his opponents would deter them from meaningful military action, that is a bombing campaign and certainly not escalating across the nuclear threshold.

The leadership of the Presidium would not be so grossly stupid and crass to display and exhibit the hostages as hostages but to project their position and situation as an attempt to integrate them into the community and to serve a useful purpose.

The ill conceived and rapidly executed submarine operation in the Pacific had been aborted since an attack on Seattle and the Boeing aircraft works would not have achieved an adequate return, though the sacrifice of the vessels and their crews had yielded a satisfactory investment. The Commander of the Naval Forces had been summarily executed on grounds, some spurious , some Stalinistic for failure, but above all to dispose of an inconvenient witness.

For a moment his mind wandered and he wondered how 'Alexander' had actually conceived such a barbaric but highly effective strategy which had brought such a rich harvest.

Now he was ready. The juggernaut would reach the United States within ninety minutes and broadcast its seeds of destruction. Johnson would not go to war, fearing a second strike on the East Coast and an end to his political career. He would be wiped out in the forthcoming Presidential Election, a procedure of the so called 'democratic' process that he found both inconvenient and foolish, since he did not believe in the proletariat's interest and capability to elect the leadership of the Presidium.

Soon after the conversation ended he would, without hesitation, authorise an attack on the State of Israel by Tupolev Tu-22 bombers supported by TupolevTu-28P fighters specially based south of Yerevan in the Crimea which had been instructed to sweep due South ignoring national boundaries, hit military and civilian targets with nuclear weapons and then to continue towards bases in Egypt where they could be refuelled for the return journey, or more likely, based in Nasser's heartland to police the new Empire.

"Mr. President, my genuine apologies. I have been informed that there was a technical hitch connecting this call to my present location."

His tone hid the real truth of his intentions.

"The brief delay has enabled me to resolve a matter that certainly will help the resolution of the problems created by the criminal gang that plotted and nearly succeeded in redrawing the map of Europe."

With the consummate art of the politician he continued his deception and web of lies.

"At my request and not without some duress Warsaw Treaty troops have halted their advance into France, de facto leaving an unoccupied zone in the South and it is both my desire and intention, initially through negotiations and if need be by pressure, to compel the governments of the German Democratic Republic and Poland to ultimately withdraw their forces to their original borders. Mr. President, I have to confide in you as the leader of a powerful economic and military state to comprehend the fear of those leaders in what you call Eastern Europe following the events of the last four weeks or so. The criminal elements that not only planned the assault, also deceived the political leaders who now fear not only your retribution but the imposition of penal reparations. The cause of peace and peaceful coexistence will be even more dramatically damaged by the temporary, and I hope brief, occupation of certain West European countries."

Johnson listened. The argument was not even plausible. The military assault combined with the impending attack on the United States mainland made a mockery of the First Secretary's alleged intentions. He would warn the man, without anger and if possible without bitterness or rancour, that only a speedy resolution of the crisis and a return to the original status quo would be acceptable not only to the government of the United States but more importantly to the people who, in less than a year, he would have to call upon for their vote of confidence in him and in his administration.

"Mr. First Secretary, all the recent events had compelled me, as the Commander in Chief of our military forces, and on the advice of my military leaders, to raise the readiness of our forces on land, at sea and in the air. Indeed for some days activity in the air has increased exponentially but you must not interpret theses defensive actions as offensive. All that is required is an immediate withdrawal of Warsaw Pact forces and therefore the liberation of what we define as occupied territory.

Tomorrow I will announce both to the people of the United States and internationally, and I am giving you prior notification, that the' Monroe' Doctrine has been updated to include not only our neighbours in Canada but also amongst others, our allies in Japan and England [sic].

The consequences of war between us is too horrendous to contemplate. The loss of life and the suffering..."

Johnson suddenly stopped. Those around him believed it was the magnitude of the warning but he felt unwell. Instinctively he knew something was wrong, dramatically wrong, but he had his duty to perform and the Presidential Oath was not to be taken lightly. He had never experienced such a surge of pain across his chest as if a vice was crushing his chest unmercifully and his head began to spin uncontrollably, as a roulette wheel would perform if powered by a hidden motor.

He sat down, confused and frightened, but some inner strength enabled him to continue.

"Dear Mr. Khrushchev (perhaps it was the excruciating pain that made him so unnecessarily friendly), I am sorry for that short hiatus but there was an accident which distracted me. Time is of the essence and within days I must present to the nation positive evidence of your sincerity in the form of tangible evidence of the voluntary or if need be enforced withdrawal of forces from the occupied territories of my allies."

Nikita Khrushchev smiled inwardly for he knew that shortly after the effective destruction of the American West Coast he would order the asphyxiation of the adolescent State of Israel.

"Mr. President. I have a duty to comply with both your demand and request. I leave you, I hope ,in good health and wish you not only good fortune but the wisdom not to take any foolish action. "

FIFTY-ONE

The new Prime Minister soon recognised not only the responsibilities of his office but more importantly the benefits of his station. He had been a Minister in Clement Attlee's post war government but that was during a time of austerity and shortages; now in the' post Macmillan' era which the former Prime Minister had vividly defined by his slogan:

"You've never had it so good",

He had ordered a small box of his favourite cigars which had been collected by ministerial car and delivered to his official residence. In private, away from the gaze of the media and his supporters, he could indulge himself without fear that his upper class habit would stain his public working class image as a frugal pipe smoker.

He had a promise to fulfil and a decision to make. He had promised the Soviet First Secretary through the Soviet ambassador that to reduce the political temperature he would remove Britain's strike force of nuclear bombers both physically from the United Kingdom and symbolically from the equation of the so called 'balance of terror'. He could easily renege on his promise, made under duress, and seek support from the new President in Washington, but he then asked himself ...

"What would be the economic, military and above all political consequences if he backed away from the ultra secret agreement?"

He was more concerned with the political consequences than the loss of military power which would inevitably leave the United Kingdom impotent in a nuclear confrontation and naked in the conference room. The arrangement would be concealed and hidden by the maximum secrecy possible and knowledge limited to as few as possible but including his associate George Brown who would soon be brought into the Cabinet when he felt strong enough to begin his social and economic reforms. In the meantime he hoped that Brown would remain sober and that the various methods now available would hide from the media, the few remaining M.Ps. and the general public, his decision until he felt the public mood would be more supportive. He made one exception and decided that certain Trade Union leaders be informed of the decision including Frank Cousins and his confidant, Jack Jones, but in return requested their solemn promise not only of silence but of their Unions` loyalty.

Three years later James Harold Wilson was executed for high treason.

The logistics of the move and the immediate political repercussions were kept from the British people by stealth and then, after the press were literally 'tipped off', by the most draconian use of the Statute Book, including the summary arrest, trial in camera, and imprisonment of two national newspaper editors and the cartoonist of the *Daily Mirror* who drew and had published a most unusual cartoon, cryptic and out of keeping with his style, depicting Britannia departing from the shores of England (the white cliffs of Dover) and underneath was the legend and question...

"Will you no come back again?"

The shocked chiefs of the Royal Air Force were presented with a political demand far beyond any rational explanation or justification, a *'fait accompli'*. The new British Prime Minister then made a sordid and ethically hypocritical 'arrangement' with an also shocked and surprised South African ambassador and with the 'white' apartheid government which secured their permanent tenure and the continued oppression of the black ,indigenous majority in exchange for the lease of land where the' V Bomber 'fleet would be based.

Harold Wilson was unreceptive to the desperate pleas to justify his orders and was deaf to the military arguments including the unexpected scenario that they-the R.A.F. chiefs-knew of no runway in Southern Africa that was both long or strong enough to handle the landing of a loaded V bomber and at the least would result in undercarriage damage and might doom the fleet to be permanently trapped as well as rendering them a target for a Soviet sea borne missile strike. All trust was lost.

The bulk of the 'V Bomber' force, loaded with primed nuclear and thermonuclear weapons and an accompanying flight of refuelling aircraft were to be' relocated' in the vast desert regions of Namibia and South Africa. Their very isolation, deep in the obscure desert region, meant that they would be far away from influencing military events therefore committing an act of self – emasculation.

A very limited number of bombers would remain in Great Britain as evidence of their continued presence but soon some of them, accompanied by most of the remaining refuelling aircraft would, once the logistics were resolved, make the gigantic trek to an even more distant home in the Australian outback.

The Prime Minister, a man who usually calculated the consequences of his actions, appeared completely to ignore the potential response from his major ally and partner in the so called 'Special Relationship'.

Not so the incoming air armada of Soviet ' Bear' and 'Bison' bombers that were carrying the ultimate weapon of destruction.

The primitive but effective heater blasted out a continuous stream of hot air which made the cabin tolerable for its occupants who could view from both port and starboard, approximately twenty other heavy bombers on their one way journey of revenge. Above them, at an altitude of five point five kilometres, was a second layer of bombers and as a matter of faith they had been previously informed that there was a third layer of bombers at an altitude of six point five kilometres, making in total some fifty to fifty five planes whose primary purpose was to wreak revenge and havoc on the American West Coast, and, as far as they could penetrate, until their fuel was exhausted .

The pilot allowed himself to remember and reflect on recent events, since his crew and fellow squadron members had been assigned to the isolated, bitterly cold ,windswept and snow bound aerodrome, vaguely defined as close to the Russian-Chinese border though he and his comrades were still not yet sure on which side they had actually been located.

Their superiors must have been wise and prescient in its decision to locate a number of bases on the Russian-Chinese border and to relocate the bombers there, late in October, before the unexpected and unprovoked attack by N A TO. Since their arrival they had been kept in effective isolation, a *purdah* and denied even access to either *Pravda* or *Izvestia* and such was the severity and intensity of their quarantine that the almost daily arrival of lorry convoys delivering supplies including fuel were kept well away from the flight crews whose routine revolved around callisthenics and sport in the morning, board games in the afternoon and card games after dinner but these activities still not alleviate the symptoms of lethargy and boredom.

The engines of the Tu 95s had been permanently turning since any extended period of inaction could possibly allow the equipment to freeze with disastrous consequences, whilst the ground crews had an unending task removing the accumulation of snow, mainly from the wings.

The most repetitive task was the necessity to remove snow from the runway but this was achieved by the use of specially adapted lorries with ploughs which made light work of the task.

Their only contact with the outside world were the previous brief and intermittent notices detailing military events in Europe that were posted on the information board .Dramatically, fifteen hours before, at two thirty in the morning, the squadron had been woken, en masse, to the dramatic news that the Americans had attacked four major cities, West of the Urals, using thermonuclear weapons, destroying the cities, outlying suburbs and industrial areas of Moscow, Stalingrad, Leningrad and Kiev with an estimated immediate loss, provisionally calculated to be in excess of eighteen million lives, ignoring the additional destruction of industrial production facilities.

It was clear that the leadership had truly understood the nature and inherent evil of the Yankee Warlords and by their foresight had created a facility that had been, until a few hours ago their base, and which was to be the springboard for retribution. Even his fellow crews had not anticipated such a vindictive act even though some four weeks before they had all been stunned by the news that without a declaration of war or any act of provocation, West German forces had smashed their way into the German Democratic Republic but they and their N A T O allies had been halted, repelled, forced back and finally routed when Warsaw Treaty troops began the liberation of Western Europe.

They would probably never again see the Steppes of Central Asia, the impressive 'onion' domes of the Kremlin or their families or loved ones, for their orders and instructions were brutal but necessary. Theirs was to be a one way mission, en route they would be refuelled by air borne tankers and that part had been completed in text book fashion. They were to penetrate deep into the heartland of the United States sowing their seeds of death and destruction until their fuel was exhausted and having crashed landed they were to make their way South to neutral Mexico and thence home. Everyone secretly realised that the journey and repatriation from Mexico was unrealistic and a dream since capture and possibly retribution by the American people would result in their deaths but hope and belief in their cause gave them the strength, at least, to attempt the challenge.

They had been handed a set of sealed orders prior to their hurried departure, each identified by a latitude and longitude and the navigator cum bomb aimer was to open the envelope when the plane reached the appropriate point. The instructions were brief and concluded with an exhortation to avenge the dead, defend the Motherland and to inflict the maximum amount of damage on those who knew no compassion or who fought without honour as did the barbaric Nazi warrior knights who had been ultimately defeated by their fathers' generation.

Shortly, they and all the flight on the lowest level were to 'peel off', including bombers carrying short range cruise missiles and to follow a new flight path, essentially South East, where their particular primary target was to be the City of Los Angeles and they were to continue inland, releasing tactical nuclear weapons at previously defined locations until they reached their second target, the sprawling town of Las Vegas after which they were to attempt a landing and travel South to Mexico and finally repatriation.

The armada had been sighted by fishing vessels in the treacherous North Pacific and their approximate course and number estimated by one of the crew, an aviation enthusiast, who had utilised the most powerful binoculars on board the boat to provisionally identify the planes as propeller driven Tu 95s and jet powered M-4s and the ship's captain had promptly radioed the information through to the Coast Guards and within minutes the news had reached Washington and the Pentagon.

Combined with earlier reports from the U2 which was still shadowing the 'break away 'formation the President and his advisors were now confronted with no alternative than to inform the nation and to prepare the Strategic Air Command to be ready to begin a retaliatory counter strike.

Thus the chilling words from the Bhagavad Gita that had been uttered by the creator of the first atomic bomb were on the mind of Herman Kahn:

" I am become death, the destroyer of worlds."

A pre-prepared statement regularly reviewed by a secret sub committee was transmitted from the Pentagon and immediately considered by Robert Mc Namara and Bobby Kennedy, whilst the President discussed with Supreme Court Judge Earl Warren the procedure to temporarily suspend the Constitution and impose Martial Law, as a television staff member attempted to be as unobtrusive as possible, applying some make up to the President. This was the catalyst that within half an hour would fell the Commander in Chief, for the minor act of the assistant's imposition was treated with a reaction of controlled irritation but more importantly the President again felt, but this time more viciously, a sharp rapier like thrust down the length of his left arm, and across his chest, a vice like contraction. He felt short of breath but he had no time and the Country was in dire peril.

He carefully read, then hurriedly reread the statement noting the alterations pencilled in, called over to McNamara to verify where one particular alteration was to be inserted, decided to announce the new' Monroe' Doctrine but in the rush forgot to enter a note to remind him and walked to the studio considering certain improvements to the contents. The lighting was rudimentary and positioned in such a way as to create shadows when there should be a flood of light.

This time the nation was literally caught unaware of the impending and looming catastrophe. Football fans immersed in their pseudo religious act of reverence suddenly saw their television screens turn to a curtain of static and many viewers tried to contact the studios to complain. Radio listeners were no better served or informed.

It was four thirteen p.m. Eastern Standard Time and the Country was on the verge of total war.

Again, like his previous speech to the nation, there was a delay between the interruption of normal services and this, the most frightening programme ever broadcast,since it was most unexpected.

Behind Johnson was the Presidential Seal but it was too late for the technicians to correct the lighting and for the viewers (colour television would not appear for another seven years, delayed by the urgent necessity for military and technological expansion) the appearance of the President was as if he intended to appear half hidden by darkness.

An anonymous announcer, without an apology or explanation for the unscheduled interruption, introduced:

"The President of the United States of America."

A voice, clearly identifiable as that of the new President, appeared to be projected from within a semi darkened figure sparking subsequent comparisons with the actors Lon Chaney Jnr. or Boris Karloff.

"My fellow Americans, I have to report to you that despite ongoing negotiations we are now confronted with the awesome and frightening reality that the Soviet Union - and possibly China-are on the verge of a nuclear attack on the West Coast of the Continental United States ."

The President paused and despite the enormity of his news, strangely smiled. It was only years later that his widow disclosed that she had just entered the studio and had been observed by her husband. He took a sip from the glass that contained his favourite Dr. Pepper and resumed.

"A force of bombers has managed to evade and circumvent the cordon that for some days has surrounded the Soviet Union and is now approaching the coasts of Alaska and California. It is possible, but it is now irrelevant, that this operation and the attack on our allies in Western Europe were also pre planned and part of a wider conspiracy. Perhaps some of my actions have appeared to First Secretary Khrushchev and Chairman Mao and even to my political opponents here at home and to some of you, the acts of weakness but I can assure you all that I have striven always to maintain the peace and above all to defend the nation in accordance with my Presidential Oath."

He paused again, this time because he was short of breath. He knew instinctively that something was wrong and that under any other circumstances he would seek assistance, but this situation was different and on his shoulders rested so much responsibility and duty. He saw his wife again but was unable to acknowledge her. He continued, but the beads of sweat rolling down his forehead were entering his eyes, partially obscuring his vision and he was beginning to have difficulties reading the script.

"As I speak to you our forces at sea, in the air and our army are imminently being prepared to launch a counter attack against those whose motives and actions have betrayed our trust in the false sincerity of their words and promises."

His sweating became uncomfortably profuse and he had extreme difficulty reading the script which resulted in errors and confusion for the viewers and listeners.

"After this news [sic] broadcast is over, a pre recorded statue [sic - he should have said statement] will be played with important instructions and informants [sic – he should have said information]."

He ended the statement with an ad hoc comment:

"I promise you all that I will continue to the last possible moment to peacefully resolve this impending disaster and to defend everything that the American people hold dear. Good luck to us all."

We cannot imagine what strain he was under; he had totally forgotten to mention the new updated global 'Monroe' Doctrine and he was frightened for there was something terribly wrong. Perhaps, in hindsight, omitting mention of the potential horrendous casualties that might be suffered by the American people was not, in itself, an error since it would avoid a panic but all his thoughts, driven by a primitive desire to survive, were to rush to the urinals. He was nauseous, his head..., behind him two secret service men rushed to offer assistance, one hastily spitting his chewing gum into its original wrapping which he then athletically dunked into a peach basket rubbish bin half full of used paper towels.

As they entered the room they heard a thud as the President collapsed inside the cubicle, inconveniently against the door. He had suffered a near fatal, massive coronary thrombosis and for the next few hours would precariously hover on the edge and verge of death. It was only the availability and prompt attention of his personal doctor that would save his life, however he was totally incapacitated and absolutely unable to perform his duties.

The United States of America was essentially leaderless. There was no Vice President and the President, Commander in Chief of all the military forces was, de facto, unable to sign any documentation, either to temporarily suspend the Constitution, declare Martial Law or to authorise the military to use nuclear or thermonuclear weapons. Could the Speaker perform his President's duties?

FIFTY-TWO

In the autumn of two thousand and nine, two officially authorised posthumous biographies were published detailing the lives of two former influential Americans whose careers had effected the history, destiny and the lives of the American people. Both had died earlier in that same year.

Robert McNamara had succumbed to the ravages of time, but survived to the venerable age of ninety three, whilst Edward Kennedy died following an unsuccessful struggle against a malignant brain tumour. He was the youngest brother of two assassinated politicians, President John F. Kennedy and former Attorney General Bobby Kennedy (who had been shot but had survived and though paralysed, unexpectedly died when he seemed to be making a partial recovery).

The economic and military power of the United States protected a commonwealth of independent nations each nominally equal partners but in reality reliant and subservient to the dominant partner since they relied on the United States and her military umbrella for protection and access to her vast consumer market. In exchange for her protection, goods and services flowed to the Continental United States based on an artificial exchange rate since the global turmoil had undermined and destroyed the former economic structure.

Thus from Japan flowed electronic equipment and motor vehicles, from the former United Kingdom, whisky and a wide selection of motor vehicles (especially sports cars from the factories of Jaguar, Lotus and M.G.), from Australia and New Zealand, minerals, cattle and lamb and from South Africa (which seemed to have a special relationship with different Presidents in view of its racial policies which separated the ethnic groups) minerals and cheap labour for the Southern plantations.

The American people, traumatised by the attempted attack on its West Coast had become parochial, inward looking but above all, materialistic, to such a degree that the pursuit of material wealth was ranked as important as conventional religions.

The biography of Edward Kennedy was received with interest by political and military historians, as it gave a second hand account, distilled from conversations with Bobby Kennedy, of his recollections of the events before, during and after the Soviet assault which broadly supported the official report but emphasised Bobby`s demand for military action .

The general public's interest was measured in the poor sales figures and even lower borrowing statistics from the nation's public libraries. Not so the McNamara book whose publication had been widely awaited because an earlier version had been, for all intent and purposes 'banned'. Publication caused a minor sensation because its allegations were in direct contradiction to the official report and if true, cast doubt both on the integrity of the then government and also on the 'Warren'Report into the assassination of President John F. Kennedy which itself had been discredited by the stunning revelations of two intrepid reporters from the Washington Post.

Twenty five years earlier, in April nineteen eighty–four, publication of an authorised version, supported by interviews with the subject and allegedly including documentation and primary source witness statements was halted on the direct intervention of the then Attorney General and it was further claimed, by the demand of the President, Ronald Reagan, on the grounds that certain parts breached national security and that, peculiarly, that intimate views of the events would distress members of the former late Commander in Chief's family. The matter never reached the Supreme Court, however it was never denied that a first edition had been 'pulped' into oblivion.

It therefore seems likely that his observations, which are in absolute conflict with the official report and coincidentally with the President's public appearances, appear tantalisingly correct, and are borne out by the 25th amendment to the Constitution, enacted after all these events allegedly occurred.

The following chapters are thus based on his observations but do not take into account one major aspect which in itself was so minor but its consequences devastating.

Nearly a year before the war, on New Year's Eve, December thirty-first nineteen sixty-two, Nina Khrushchev, in an act of kindness, had offered and taken from a young soldier, sitting at her lunch table, a letter to his girl friend which should have gone through the normal channels including specifically the military censor who would have, without doubt, edited and deleted much of the contents. The naive man had factually stated, without boasting, the approximate location of his posting, the nature of the site but above all the identities of the two main occupants which was the *'raison d'etre'* for his and the other soldiers presence, finally enclosing, as if to substantiate his statement, a photograph of the First Secretary showing also the front of the dacha.

His girl friend had compounded the breach of security by mentioning the information to friends in the presence of a Swedish student whose father was a diplomat in Moscow. Within days the information had been passed, as a deposit on account of a future contra favour, to the diplomat's American opposite number and very shortly afterwards the information was in Washington and Langley, Virginia who it is believed within three months or so had verified the indiscretion.

FIFTY-THREE

He hoped that the hiatus was only temporary. The United States government had unilaterally terminated the previous constant flow of intelligence between the two countries and whilst the various branches of the British Intelligence Services continued their global surveillance the void created by their partner was immediately apparent.

It was too coincidental that the Americans' action had coincided with the exodus of the 'V Bomber' force on their journey to South Africa with their accompanying escort of refuelling aircraft which must have been observed by the United States who would have soon ascertained the purpose, if not the background, to this strategic change in the British Government's deployment of their primary offensive weapon.

Harold Wilson, or more specifically his staff, were unable to contact the American Ambassador to London[sic], the President or, incidentally, the Soviet Ambassador.

Attempts were currently being made via the British Ambassador in Washington.

The Prime Minister, using his initiative and all his devious cunning had decided that a bold plan to set up a three way dialogue and then an urgent conference chaired by him would possibly both reduce the International temperature and ingratiate him with President Johnson.

However, the revelation that the Soviet Union had no respect and regarded as irrelevant any nation that was not armed with nuclear or thermonuclear weapons or countries that had naively surrendered their weapons (in the cause of peace) had yet to confront the Prime Minister.

At the same time the heads of the neutered armed forces had been relocated to the secret redoubt near Corsham in Wiltshire, code name

Burlington, where they embarked upon planning hypothetical future military actions on the European mainland.

But like Adolf Hitler in his bunker in the final days and weeks of the Second World War, in April nineteen forty–five,when he tried to organise a final defence of Berlin using non existent armies or worse still the literally decimated remnants of his defeated armies, so the commanders with their obsequious planning officers, conceived grandiose plans for a new 'D-Day' which would inevitably be destroyed on the beaches by an enemy that would have no qualms using tactical nuclear weapons as they knew there would be no retribution or retaliation.

For Harold Wilson, the reality of the true, dire consequences of his foolish action which would be interpreted by his successors as treason had yet to affect him and his temporary Government of National Unity which was, in fact, currently the previous members of Home's committee. No military pressure had been imposed on the United Kingdom by the Soviet Union so the convenient analysis was that the arrangement would be honoured. Therefore Wilson could at least ,for the moment, ignore his advisors' recommendation to temporarily remove the epicentre of government out of London to the Regional Seat of Government near Brentwood in Essex in the quaintly named site, Kelvedon Hatch.

On the other side of the world in China and in the nation's capital, Peking, life, for the masses and for the leadership continued without interruption or upheaval, for the country was so insulated from the outside world and events it was fundamentally a self contained universe.

Khrushchev had not notified his ally and partner that the air armada had been unleashed and it is not clear if Chairman Mao or Prime Minister Chou had independently been informed by their own Intelligence Services. Perhaps the real truth was that the Chairman had more profound problems to consider, hidden behind and beneath his inscrutable persona.

The ultimate consequence of the arrangement that had been made with First Secretary Khrushchev and the subsequent military encounter between the Soviet Union and the United States was, and there is no definitive proof, that the Chinese nuclear programme was rapidly accelerated and in October 1964, at Lop Nor in Sinkiang province, the first Chinese atomic bomb was successfully detonated.

Although outside the compass of this work, in a brief overview of Chinese history, it is of interest to record that Chairman Mao was planning what was to be called the 'Great Cultural Revolution' which would reinvigorate and purify the nation and then, four years later, in nineteen seventy, the nation was literally, like a pack of wild ravenous dogs, unleashed on its neighbours.

It is conservatively estimated that some seven hundred and fifty million human beings (an unimaginable number), enflamed with almost messianic belief in 'The Thoughts of Chairman Mao' (the 'Red Book' containing philosophical thoughts of the 'Great Helmsman') was the inspiration that saw the greatest movement or migration ever recorded.

Sweeping through the peninsulas of North and South Korea and of Indo China like and the comparison is well chosen, a plague of locusts, the sheer number overwhelmed all military resistance and the indigenous populations and were only halted by the Western Pacific Ocean.

Nearly forty years later, extrapolating from raw basic statistics, in error released by the Chinese authorities, it was calculated that of the approximate seven hundred and fifty million persons who had departed on what was a crusade, about six hundred and ninety million perished, probably most by starvation, or by military action and the remainder in consequence of their untreated injuries and finally by exhaustion.

It was cynically argued by Sinologists that the crusade had resolved the population problem of China though, as an afterthought, it was agreed that the integrity and independence of Formosa under Chiang Kai Shek had been saved making the island a secure base against Chinese aggression.

FIFTY-FOUR

55.500639, 38.515491

He had considered most of the peripheral contingencies and even allowed his thoughts to wander and conceive a post victory strategy but there was one last challenge to overcome and the sequence of events had already commenced.   The strike against Israel was imminent and he expected the Arab states to unite and close in on the carcass of Zionism to claim their own victory and the land of *their* people which would be contaminated with radiation.

His complete family was now safely lodged in the second lowest level of the multi level complex adjacent to the dacha, inside a sanctuary that was self sufficient and above all anonymous for, if need be, a period of some three months and connected to the outside world by the latest, most sophisticated communications system, designed especially for him, the First Secretary.

She had already received the rest of the family including his beloved grand children. Only the eldest, the sixteen year old ,could possibly understand the reason for the incarceration but the others would accept the situation as a game.

There were two absentees, both killed in the Great Patriotic War. Leonid, his son and his daughter Nadia`s husband, a Jewish doctor. But his other son, Sergei, would join Nadia, along with their two sisters, Julia and Rada and their husbands.

The members and candidate members of the Presidium had been dispersed in accordance with plans laid down long ago. A facade, a smoke screen and a deception meant that two members were to remain in Moscow, ostensibly to maintain the levers of power and authority and to promote the image of normality to both the outside world and the foreign community, diplomatic, cultural and commercial. Helicopters were constantly at the ready to ferry the men out of the City to waiting jets, if, and he was very confident that Johnson would not launch a counter retaliatory strike, because ultimately weakness, fear and above all indecision, would overwhelm him.

Despite, and in contradiction to the prudent recommendations of the military planners, a few members and candidate members of the Presidium, including Leonid Brezhnev, were concentrated together, along with the First Secretary, therefore leaving them vulnerable to a possible, but unlikely, direct strike, whilst some individual members or candidate members (mainly Brezhnev supporters)were located at sites South West of Kiev, West of Leningrad, North of Odessa and the elite of the air force based in the bowels of the vast Yamantau complex who had urgently arranged the attack on Israel and who were now supervising the assault on the Continental United States. The First Secretary was in instantaneous contact with all the other redoubts (and, if time allowed, with his wife and family) and was constantly updated and informed of the air armada`s progress.

An unexpected member of the elite group, an old friend of the First Secretary and a political protégé, was Vladimir Semichastny, who owed his position as head of the K G B solely to the influence of Khrushchev whose prescient wisdom appointing his acolyte would soon see the fulfilment of his plans and the political demise of Leonid Brezhnev. On the same level, in the subterranean complex but temporarily separated from the leadership by closed bomb proof doors, was an elite guard of K G B troops totally loyal to Semichastny and by extension, to Khrushchev.

The Presidium would be restructured and revert to its former title of the Politburo, but more important Brezhnev's supporters would be (and there was at least one historical precedent) expelled, allowing him to rebalance the inner and outer cores of the central part of the instrument of authority and power.

He would then use delaying tactics and political and military pressure to force and compel his nemesis in Washington to permanently accept the new order in Western Europe and the Middle East. Subsequently, but not of immediate concern, he would infiltrate, destabilise and finally take over the countries in Southern Europe (Portugal ,Spain, Italy and those primitive, tribal states adjacent and close to Greece which would also fall).

He would leave the details to those who less than twenty years before had liberated Eastern Europe after the Great Patriotic War and had purified those Countries of, what Stalin's agents had called class enemies, 'gangsters' and traitors such as Rudolf Slansky.

He had seen at close hand the manic paranoia and absurd emotional irrationality of Stalin about the 'Jewish Problem'. Stalin's philosophy had changed since the days when the Soviet Union was the first nation to recognize, *de jure*, the state of Israel. In a rare moment of calm, as if his capriciousness, irritability and brutality had finally subsided, Stalin had confided in Khrushchev that at the foundation of his policies was the realisation that his supreme political foe, Leon Trotsky, had been manipulated by a fellow Jew, the dangerous and ethereal Joel Ben Yitzhak, the "Zio",a man who appeared to be eternal and the enemy and symbol that Stalin had fought against throughout his career. As the nineteen-forties merged into nineteen–fifties, the 'Jewish Problem' re-appeared as Zionism and a pro-Western anti Communist conspiracy organised by (using the phraseology, lies and hysteria of the vanquished Nazis including Goebbels, Rosenberg and Streicher) a cabal of 'Jewish Capitalists'.

The final part of his grand design was to completely destabilise the so called but emasculated 'Great Britain' from the influence of the United States and to replace the American military bases with Soviet forces. He would, as had taken place in Eastern Europe after the war, rely on the trade unions, fraternal front organisations, the dissemination of lies about the existing leadership and above all the entrenched existing elite to put such pressure on the Government to destabilise and overthrow them, replacing them with a new acquiescent leadership before finally permanently 'disposing' of the old order.

Within five years, according to his scientists and engineers, the new generation of more accurate Intercontinental Ballistic Missiles would be deployed, armed with substantially more powerful thermonuclear weapons, effectively neutralising any American weaponry.

That would all be in the future, but now time seemed to move at an increasingly slower rate to such a degree that some of those present even checked the second hand of the big clock on one wall against their own Talberg wristwatches but to no avail. The second message was due very soon confirming that the main bulk of the armada was again splitting up and preparing themselves to assault the coasts of Washington State, Oregon and the jewel in the crown of their objective, California, finally turning inland, broadcasting their remaining cargo of destruction before crash landing inland, their fuel exhausted.

The rectangular room was spartan in decoration, in contrast to some of the elaborately decorated rooms in the Baroque style inside the Kremlin, and was dominated entirely along one of the long sides by a table covered by a clean white linen table cloth meticulously pressed on which bestrode a truly magnificent and regal Sturgeon lying on a bed of crushed ice which was surrounded and enhanced by exquisitely constructed wooden casks containing the rarest, most expensive and sublime Beluga and Sevruga caviar. Completing the display was a mountain of succulent, giant blood red lobsters, crabs and crayfish and to compliment this epicurean masterpiece many ethnic Russian dishes were located by the tail including hot and cold borscht, tubs of sour cream, buckwheat pancakes and finally the finest and most sought after vodkas produced by master distillers.

Nikita Khrushchev, surrounded by unashamedly parasitic, sycophantic power hungry and hungry members of the nomenclature waited impatiently for the second telephone call as the ice very slowly began to melt when the debacle ,ignominy and dishonour of Cuba was soon to be revenged.

FIFTY-FIVE

The President would live! Surrounded by his shocked wife and daughter, Lyndon Baines Johnson the thirty-sixth President of the United States drifted in and out of consciousness, but further and further away from the precipice of death, whilst his personal physician assisted by all the available medical staf, fought to stabilise him.

Urgent messages and every available aircraft were put at the disposal of specialists spread throughout the country to bring them, secretly, to the stricken Commander in Chief who was totally unable to fulfil his duties.

The 25th Amendment to the Constitution did not at that time exist and the nation was leaderless and rudderless! There was no Vice–President and the country was imminently under attack.

On the next level above, reminiscent of Tammany Hall, the conference room was heavy with the intermingling aromas and fog of various brands of cigarettes, pipe and cigar smoke(Dominican, not Cuban cigars !) as the nation's leaders argued, without resolution, about the legality of military action without a signed Presidential Order. It was a struggle between the rule of law and utilising again words that have appeared before in this work, pragmatism and also realism. The Attorney General was forceful, but indecisive, 'siding' with Supreme Court Judge Earl Warren that the rule of law was absolute but then contradicting himself that the overriding duty of the state was, and would always be, the defence of the nation. Both the Senate Majority and Minority leaders, again in a rare moment of agreement sided with Bobby Kennedy's second argument, whilst the Secretary for Agriculture expressed, in vague terms, support for the former. Other contributors to the discussion were, as Khrushchev had assessed Johnson, weak and indecisive such that the Speaker who was swayed by every cogent argument, vacillated like a pendulum.

Supreme Court Judge Earl Warren was seen reverentially immersed in the minutia of the Constitution. He appeared to lack any sense of urgency, indeed seemingly he was only concerned with reviewing the Constitution and its amendments at an infuriatingly, leisurely, even funereal pace, oblivious to the impending attack on the Continental United States and imminent potential nuclear catastrophe.

The dispute continued without resolution as the sands of time were literally running out, exposing the whole country, by default, to an undefined attack. The most forceful argument not unexpectedly, came from the Headquarters of the Strategic Air Command and its head, General Thomas Power, whose words and phraseology were so ruthless and extreme that without exception everyone in the conference room was shocked. No transcript or recording exists but according to the 'McNamara' biography he accused the assembled members of the executive, legislature and judiciary of treason by default if they did not at least permit the defence of the country, let alone an attack on the perpetrators of the imminent attack.

It was then that the first news began to come in confirming a nuclear assault on Israel, emanating from British intelligence sources in Cyprus, citing the easily recognisable mushroom clouds rising over more than one site. The next report received some ten minutes later from the same source confirmed that equipment dually used to record nuclear explosions and seismic activity had noted five explosions. Only the blind could not see that the state of Israel was in a desperate state. It was at this moment that McNamara beckoned to Herman Kahn to join him outside and there then began a series of events that would save the United States but would be shrouded in secrecy and a bodyguard of lies.

Kahn's assessment and sense of priorities melded with McNamara`s decisiveness. Kahn gave his considered opinion and reaffirmed his previous, but private, suggestions after which McNamara made the brief short journey downstairs, eschewing the lift, to the President`s suite where he briefly spoke to Ladybird Johnson before, and there are no witnesses now alive to verify what or if any matter was actually discussed, or if indeed the Secretary of Defence wished to confirm to himself that the Commander was indeed still totally and absolutely incapacitated.

He immediately went to the communications room, signed the entry log, and if the witness statement is to be believed and there is no reason to disbelieve the statement of the surviving communications officer, he urgently dictated various instructions to the S.A.C. and Thomas Power.

Having absolved the staff from any contributory responsibility for his actions he returned to the conference room to be shortly confronted by a report coming from Fort Mead the 'home' of the National Security Agency-reporting as yet unconfirmed electronic 'eavesdropping' that some sixteen Tupolev Tu-22 (N.A.T.O. designation 'Blinder') had earlier departed from two bases in the Southern tip of Armenia (South of Yerevan) and had flown South hitting Haifa and Tel Aviv with nuclear devices and then, in a dash to Egypt, had destroyed en route, three Israeli military air bases but losing twelve or thirteen bombers that I.D.F. fighters had shot down, therefore reducing further damage. Shortly afterwards the communications room passed a brief report that Cairo Radio had announced that the nation's army had been secretly mobilised and that a "vast tank formation was bearing down on Israel and soon the defiled land and home of the Arab Palestinian people would be liberated."

FIFTY-SIX

VALLEY FORGE, PENNSYLVANIA
THE WINTER OF 1777-1778

Thomas Paine, The American Crisis,1776.

These are the times that try men's souls: The summer soldier and the sunshine patriot will, in this crisis, shrink from the service of their country; but he that stands it now, deserves the love and thanks of man and woman. Tyranny, like Hell, is not easily conquered; yet we have this consolation with us, that the harder the conflict, the more glorious the triumph. What we obtain too cheap, we esteem too lightly: it is dearness only that gives everything its value. Heaven knows how to put a proper price upon its goods; and it would be strange indeed if so celestial an article as freedom should not be highly rated.

And Henry Armitt Brown, June nineteen, 1878:

"...And here, in this place of sacrifice, in this vale of humiliation, in this valley of the Shadow of Death out of which the Life of America rose, regenerate and free, let us believe with an abiding faith that to them Union will as dear, and Liberty as sweet, and Progress as glorious as they were to our fathers, and are to you and me, and that the institutions which have made us happy, preserved by the virtue of our children, shall bless the remotest generations of the time to come."

In the history of the United States of America, the nation's pride, self esteem and imagination has been fired both by the achievements of various individuals and also by different groups.

The stoicism, fortitude and bravery of the Continental Army under George Washington at Valley Forge still to this day inspires new generations of Americans, whilst less than a century later the struggle between the North and South and the fundamental principles of equality and freedom have been immortalised in the awe inspiring mighty statue of a seated Abraham Lincoln in the Nation's Capital.

Individuals such as the aviator Charles Lindbergh have defined the bravery of the lone adventurer, whilst the Moguls of Hollywood exhibited not only the entrepreneurial spirit but their contribution to a new art form and means of mass communication. The wealth of the country has been enriched and increased by the practical use of new scientific inventions following the work of such pioneers as Alexander Graham Bell and the Wright brothers.

However the defence of the nation has come at a price willingly and freely given by generations of young men (and women) whose bodies lie in many different foreign lands in eternal peace and tranquillity whilst 'Old Glory 'proudly flutters in the wind.

In December nineteen sixty-three a new generation of young men without any thought of their own personal safety or future made the ultimate sacrifice in defence of their fellow Americans and the cause of freedom .

In the history of the Union no individual or group has ever received the accolade and gratitude that was bestowed on a few aviators honoured on behalf of the whole nation by its President during the victory celebrations which deliberately coincided with Thanksgiving Day, November nineteen sixty–four.

The' Few', a characterisation first used by a newspaper journalist, which caught the country's imagination and which became their official title when the President, responding to public feeling, himself used this description on Thanksgiving Day nineteen sixty-four, were the pilots who engaged, incinerated and destroyed the bomber fleet which, if they had only partially achieved their mission and orders, would have dealt such a devastating blow that tens of millions of innocent Americans would have been slaughtered or left terribly wounded and crippled. Even to this day the Country cannot believe how close they came to utter destruction but for the gallantry of the 'Few' and the decisive actions of the President and his advisors.

A dazed sleeping giant had been woken from its stupor and an unimaginable force of Biblical proportion was about to be unleashed in retribution and vengeance on the Soviet Union which could annihilate the country.

In excess of six hundred B52 Stratofortresses ranging from the D to the H variants were in the vanguard of the dual cause of freedom and justice; they were intentionally only armed with nuclear devices despite the availability of thermonuclear weapons (which were primarily the B28 series with yields ranging from seventy kilotonnes, through to one point four and five megatonnes and the awesome B53 series with a weight of 8850lbs.and a yield of nine megatonnes).

The thermonuclear weapons were only to be used in a second strike, their awesome power adequate to end *ALL* opposition but at a terrible price to the innocent civilians of the Soviet Union. With ranges varying from five to nearly ten thousand miles(depending on bomb load and refuelling facilities)the 'B52s'were a formidable force and statistical assessments concluded that if only fifty per cent of the total bomb load was accurately delivered then it would retard the Soviet Union by forty to fifty years, effectively creating such a gulf in her potential military capability that they could be described as being back in the 'Stone Age'. Furthermore within the limitations of this work it is not possible to specify the bomb load of any one B52.

They were either on patrol, held back or mainly located at their home bases including Fairchild in Washington, Minot and Grand Forks in North Dakota, Mather, Castle and March in California and Dyess and Carswell in Texas. Outside of the Continental United States were bases in East Anglia in the United Kingdom and Andersen on Guam in the Pacific.

The primary target was not a city (with its innocent, civilian population), or even a military location or industrial-military complex, but an isolated, anonymous site and the fact of its potential vulnerability and targeting had been ruthlessly (and possibly callously calculated) to destabilise the leader and the members of the Presidium.

More immediately both Alaska and the West coast of the American sub continent were under imminent attack.

The F 106As were each fitted with a single W25Genie (Air 2 Air) unguided strategic air defence air-to-air rocket with a yield of one point five kilotonnes, able to operate at a ceiling of fifty seven thousand feet and at a maximum speed of Mach two point three, however they had a limited operational radius which meant that the fighters dispatched from the base at Elmendorf in Anchorage, Alaska (where they had temporarily been located, with great prescience) were to engage an enemy at the extreme limit of their capability and only allowing a single or possible two fly pasts to deliver their single rockets, after which they would very quickly crash into the icy North Pacific and probably not survive. At the same time waves were launched from Castle and Fresno A.F.B. in California to intercept the other larger incoming attack. The destiny of the nation was in the hands not only of the Gods but of the bravest of the brave.

Critical analysis of the subsequent joyous and exuberant official announcement of the destruction of the incoming two assaults would have exposed certain discrepancies and more importantly the suppression of the tragic losses suffered by the pilots which were only made public some months later. Be as it may in simplistic terms it was a tremendous achievement, but bought at a price of the loss of some of the nation's finest young men.

Immediately after landing back at Fresno A.F.B. and before debriefing one of the lucky pilots, still high on Adrenaline, gave an excited statement to an official Air Force cameraman which was only made public simultaneously with the first official confirmation of the tragic losses:

"It was a Turkey shoot!

We were so excited that most of us did not check our fuel gauges and in consequence did not realise that we had exceeded our safe operational limits. We saw them far below us at about fifteen thousand feet in a tight symmetrical pattern of two layers. They never saw us coming. We bush wacked them!

Three of the (delta winged) planes peeled off so that we could attack from the East and West in two groups of three with five planes holding back to make, if necessary, a second assault on any survivors. We went in virtually simultaneously firing the missiles into various quadrants of the formation, breaking away as quickly as possible to avoid the shock waves. I counted two definite blasts but such was the proximity of the possible six explosions in terms of time and the density of the explosions that it was impossible to make a definite assessment as to the success of the attack.

I have witnessed test detonations but this event was so overwhelming and the cloud like a maelstrom that I would never be able to confirm that all six missiles detonated. The conflagration was enormous!

We immediately began our journey home whilst the second wave circled the corrupted mushroom clouds waiting to see if there were any survivors to deal with. It was this unselfish act of duty which undoubtedly meant that they had inadequate fuel to make the return journey and they may have plunged into the Ocean close to the interception site."

A task force was promptly dispatched including search and rescue helicopters but no trace of the planes or the five pilots was ever discovered.

A similar scenario took place due West of Anchorage but this time there was constant radio contact with the nine planes which attacked their quarry in a copy book manner as their compatriots, however they were aware that they were operating at the extreme limit of their operational capability. Their kill was just as comprehensive but tragic news was soon announced and then repeated eight times as the pilots ditched into the icy cold and inhospitable sea. By the time a search and rescue party had reached the area and joined weather ships and mercantile vessels commandeered to help, darkness and silence had fallen and the following morning only one body was recovered in his Mae West.

FIFTY-SEVEN

The hands of the big clock that had previously seemed to advance so slowly now appeared to march onwards at an ever accelerating pace whilst the crushed ice beneath the regal Sturgeon slowly began to melt and the invisible force of gravity begun to contort the centre piece of the epicurean display which was beginning to lose its magnificent image. The second telephone call was now nearly forty-five minutes overdue and the atmosphere and mood in the subterranean complex was clearly changing from euphoria to deepening concern.

Nikita S. Khrushchev, First Secretary and Premier, sensing the mood of the assembled Presidium and having received an urgent telephone call from his associates in the bunker South West of Kiev, took the initiative to speak to the Supreme High Command based in the Yamantau Mountain redoubt. The response was not what he wished to hear for above all it was both evasive and ominous:

"Mr. First Secretary, all contact with "Attack Forces North and South" have ceased and numerous attempts to make contact have proved futile. We believe that the most likely explanation is that the advanced specialist communication devices installed for this most important of missions have jointly and simultaneously failed."

The answer was in fact imminent and hit the Presidium with a force and power which destabilised and unbalanced their normal cold, cautious, cynical, clinical, unemotional judgement. The recently installed telephonic 'Hot Line' had been activated...

"Robert McNamara, Secretary of Defence, acting on behalf of the President wishes to speak to the First Secretary."

Perhaps it was to be an admittance of defeat and the mighty Bald Eagle was about to sue for peace?

It is important and possibly necessary to remind the reader that the following is still based on the contents of the 'McNamara' biography and the secondary source reports quoted in the book. The official, but probably now discredited and false report of the 'actual' events, are both ambiguous and contradictory. What is clear is that McNamara was not solely a man of single minded action but was totally loyal to his President and Commander in Chief. When he had earlier left the Conference room he had had a clear view of the intentions and will of the Commander in Chief but above all the defence of his homeland. Having unilaterally authorised the Counter Strike he deliberately delayed informing and notifying his fellow Cabinet members and all those who had been involved in the previously unresolved discussions until the military situation was clearer and it was only when he received a private confidential report advising probable success of BOTH attacks on the incoming assaults did he intervene and dramatically end the obsolescent and now irrelevant legal argument.

The message, delivered by an aide, for his eyes only, from the Strategic Air Command H.Qs.in Omaha, Nebraska, confirmed a flash message from the U2 reconnaissance plane that it had witnessed the attack and such was the force of the shock waves that the pilot had temporarily lost control of his aeroplane but subsequently recovered complete manoeuvrability, had flown close to the unimaginable chaos and had not observed any surviving bombers (and that, post haste, he was returning, to the nearest coastal air base, that could accommodate his landing).

The 'Alaskan' encounter had definitely confirmed by radio the complete annihilation of the Soviet bomber force before the tragic messages which reported that the planes were running out of fuel and were crashing into the sea.

His unexpected request to speak to the First Secretary and the shattering contents of his statement and demands must have surprised and dumbfounded not only the Soviet leadership but his own associates.

The recording of the conversation has unfortunately (or conveniently, for some) been 'lost' and we have to rely on a transcript made contemporaneously by one of McNamara's assistants. Secondary recollections are that his tone and attitude were originally courteous, respectful, even deferential and conciliatory but above all friendly and possibly, unknown to him, strengthened the opinion of the Soviet leadership that indeed, their bomber forces had succeeded in their mission. However apparently his tone became perhaps sarcastic but above all threatening and menacing:

(For convenience the opening introductions and subsequent parts have been edited but the full conversation can be found on pages 364 to 371 of the biography).

"Mr. First Secretary...I regret to inform you that in response to an apparent and imminent air attack, detected by our radar facility at Thule, in Alaska, estimated to target Alaska and possibly the coastal States of Washington, Oregon and California, that the President ordered an appropriate response and all the information passed to me in the last few minutes confirms the total destruction of some sixty to sixty–five heavy bombers, mainly Tu 95s, which we conservatively estimate is about forty percent of your total fleet."

Robert McNamara continued, reminding Khrushchev that the loss of life, estimated to be over three hundred souls, was no doubt part of the cream and the bravest of his fellow countrymen.

"Mr. Premier, if my Commander in Chief was here, in person, he would have reminded you of the hospitality given by his predecessor and his wife and would have conveyed his best wishes to your wife, children and above all, your grandchildren. He would most certainly have suggested to the members of the Politburo(sic)and especially to your military advisors, wisdom, prudence and caution at a time in our joint history when, within our hands, is the power to destroy each other, many times over. A short time ago you ended a conversation with my President, by wishing him luck."

(There was a definite pause)

Robert McNamara then took the initiative and what he then said must have dumbfounded everyone in the Conference room and finally shattered and terminated any confidence in the First Secretary by the Presidium.

"Mr.Premier, I regret to inform you and the Politburo (again sic) that a Counter Strike has already been launched comprising over six hundred B52 bombers loaded with nuclear weapons. Despite assumptions made by your planners, I am willing to divulge to you the primary target of our assault. It is not one or any of your great cities populated by millions of innocent civilians, or military concentrations or your industrial-military production complexes but an isolated but not very secret enclave at the following coordinates:

55.500639, 38.515491.

Our foremost military analyst who, I must say, has an arcane strange love for the unimaginable armageddon which awaits you, devised this strategy to save your country from ruin at the cheap price of one insignificant location.

We are prepared to grant you thirty minutes to make an offer that will satisfy not only the President but the people of our nation to whom we are responsible."

FIFTY-EIGHT

The hands of the two clocks advanced in synchronised harmony, the second hands clearly visibly moving, whilst the minute hands seemed tardy in their movement. Though separated by a gulf of thousands of miles, the two protagonists were inexorably joined, their thoughts apparently concentrated on the destiny of their nations as they considered the unthinkable, the outcome of a full scale nuclear attack on the Soviet Union.

In reality the truth could not be more different. If one is prepared to accept the description in the biography of Robert McNamara and again second hand reports appear to verify his observations (Pages 373-379), he was relaxed, drinking coffee and endeavouring to avoid the pungent aroma of the various blends and types of tobacco smoke, but his thoughts were focused and concentrating on the draconian terms that he would force on the prostrate and broken Communist foe, so confident was he of the quantity and quality of the force which at that very moment was imminently beginning to destroy the very fabric of the Soviet Union`s military infrastructure. Around him the members of the legislature, the executive and the Supreme Court were now conjecturing and assessing the theoretical political implications but for all of them, in a strange 'Einsteinian' manner, time seemed to pass more slowly as they waited for the 'Hot Line' to signal an incoming call or Telex and the capitulation of Nikita Khrushchev.

In their subterranean redoubt Khrushchev and members and candidate members of the Presidium watched, with agonising trepidation, the clock hands turn with apparent Olympian speed, as the thirty minute deadline ominously approached.

Nikita Khrushchev was spiritually, physically and mentally shattered and politically isolated, sitting symbolically alone, adjacent to the 'Hot Line', to all intent and purpose deep in thought whilst the room was dotted with small groups which both coalesced and divided and reformed like primitive microscopic life forms. Only the Premier knew what thoughts concentrated his attention and whilst others in the room could make a reasoned guess the truth was more prosaic and personal. He was not weighing the demands and needs of the state but only the potential murder of his beloved wife Nina, his family and above all the future of his adored four grandchildren including his only granddaughter.

During those minutes the 'dark arts' that he had learned at the feet of the malevolent and cunning Georgian deserted him as others plotted and schemed and sought and offered power to others.

Suddenly a telephone burst into life, screamed for attention, and was answered by the automatic reflexes of Robert Kennedy, who grabbed the hand piece and intimately placed the earpiece close to the side of his face. For a few moments his eyes displayed his complete attention when suddenly, for the first time since his brother`s assassination, a broad smile erupted across his face. He turned round to the obese form of Herman Kahn, hijacked his note pad and proceeded to feverishly pen various, different notes terminating the call with a cryptic, succinct enquiry...

"Are they the first?"

For Nikita Khrushchev his greatest failure was not to recognise the increasing support for his great rival and pretender to his position , Leonid Brezhnev, and the dissolving support of his former allies. Under any other circumstance or situation he would have clearly observed and recognised not only the danger which surrounded him but the unscrupulousness of the men who less than two hours before had been his fawning acolytes. Power is a corrupt and venal drug.

Leonid Brezhnev had been circulating quietly and dishonourably, exhibiting the qualities and guile of a potential leader, truly Machiavelli`s Prince, both gauging and gaining support and indicating and noting where power and supreme influence could be given or how cheaply he could buy support and influence. This was a moment in time when for a short period and despite the catastrophic potential outcome, the narcotic drug of power was to prove too addictive to be rejected.

Khrushchev could have been forcibly ejected from the room and shot, quickly and economically with a bullet to the back of the neck but in the new modern Russia, which he had helped to create, he might, just might, still have his uses. His fate was sealed by the almost maternal words of Brezhnev, barely suppressing his loathing and contempt for the fatally wounded First Secretary:

"Nikita, you look unwell. We are all concerned for your health and best interests. We suggest you leave this room and return to your private apartment. We, of course, realise the coordinates given, relate to your dacha where your wife, family and especially your four grand children are safely protected. Let me talk to the American hyenas."

Thus Khrushchev temporarily departed from the world stage but would shortly return though only as a hollow cypher to make a prepared statement.

A new fresh, confident voice resonated on the conference telephone.

"Mr. McNamara, I regret to inform you and Mr. President Johnson (sic) that Premier Khrushchev has suddenly been taken ill and will be indisposed for some time. The responsibilities of state and the most recent events have combined and accumulated so that even we, his closest friends and political allies, did not recognise that the burden and stress that one man alone, even a political giant as great as the First Secretary, could not carry. As a member of the Presidium, I Leonid Brezhnev, along with and assisted by some of my fellow members wish urgently and honestly to resolve what could be the inexorable drift to all out war, the end of civilisation and the human race.

It is therefore regretful that your primary target is, if our calculations are accurate and, your intelligence is correct, the country residence and home of our Premier. Not only that, the tragic loss or possible loss of four young children, deliberately targeted by your bombers seems a callous and vindictive act.

Acting on behalf of the First Secretary of the Communist Party of the Union of Soviet Socialist Republics and of the people of our Motherland I request that you terminate all offensive military action as soon as possible in response to our offer of sincere good faith."

But already, Brezhnev was planning to use American hostages at as many military and civilian targets as possible to thwart any potential new United States' attacks and, more importantly, to delay any substantial concessions until the first generation of SS Intercontinental Ballistic Missiles were operational and then he could threaten the cities on the East and West coasts of the United States.

Robert McNamara rose from his chair, slightly turned his head towards the smiling Herman Kahn(whose 'hard line' posture was clearly justified and vindicated),took a deep-breath, briefly refreshed his memory by perusing his scribbled notes, placed both hands on the table and leaned forward so that when he projected his voice the telephone would receive his words.

"Mr. Brezhnev, I speak not only with the authority of our President but with the agreement, support and absolute confidence of those that act on behalf of the people of our great nation. Already we have received unconfirmed reports that your Pacific naval ports of Vladivostok, Ol`ga and Sovetskaya Gavan all in the Sea of Japan and tragically their associated centres of population have been taken out but you only seem concerned with the fate of four children.

The attacks will continue until the primary target has been obliterated and our secondary targets destroyed. We estimate that you have no more than six hundred and fifty non strategic long range missiles of the SS3,4 and 5 versions but you should know, unless you are unaware of their capabilities, that they pose no threat to the Continental United States not only because of their limited range but because at this moment they are highly vulnerable to our ongoing strike since they are deployed above ground in soft sites with a few, the remainder, only in semi hardened launchers. Our intelligence also indicates that they require, in preparation for launching ,an enormous time and effort, indeed I have just been handed a further (again unconfirmed) report [for a few moments McNamara was silent as he digested the communiqué] that our bombers have successfully hit and taken out SS4 bases at Aluksne (for readers requiring in depth information the coordinates are 57 25N 026 50E), Bataysk (in fact a repair facility 47 08N 039 47E),Gusev(54 44N 022 O3E)and Kolomyya (48 40N 024 48E).

We only have ten minutes to contact and authorise those bombers assigned to take out the primary target and we require from you or the First Secretary your offer of terms and we will not countenance any delaying tactics or procrastination."

For a few moments the line was silent save only for the noises of a telephone being accidentally dropped or deliberately hurled onto a wooden table.

Leonid Brezhnev came back on the line, more humble, contrite and conciliatory, however he was strengthened by his devious long term plans and intentions.

"We must reduce the temperature on the mainland of Europe and I therefore propose, within twenty four hours, to order our Warsaw Treaty partners to begin a phased withdrawal from the occupied territories of France, Belgium, Holland, Denmark and West Germany to be completed within fourteen days. I believe that my offer is more than adequate. "

Robert McNamara`s response was immediate, decisive and blunt.

"If that is your complete offer it is totally unacceptable and does not provide a foundation upon which we can build a mutually acceptable arrangement to resolve this conflict and I see no benefit continuing this conversation. Thank you Mr. President (an incorrect reference to his own President but in fact a correct reference to the then current status of Leonid Brezhnev)."

He placed the receiver in its cradle, turned to his associates and clearly stated, without reference to his notes:

"If that is his only offer, I am prepared to lose up to five hundred B52s and their crews of valiant warriors to smash the Soviet infrastructure and propel the Motherland back to the Stone age.

I want, on behalf of the American people, the following:

The repatriation of all U.S. military and civilians in Europe and the Middle East to commence immediately and where necessary, satisfactory medical assistance to be provided. The same conditions to apply to troops and civilians of our allies .

The immediate release of any persons currently imprisoned by the occupying forces.

Within six hours a global broadcast by the First Secretary denouncing the treachery of the Warsaw Pact.

Medical treatment to a standard approved by the American government to all victims of the aggression for seven years and...

Reparations to be agreed, responding to the military assault from November 25th nineteen sixty- three.

Johnson will not trust Khrushchev after this but we cannot afford to destabilise the Politburo (again sic) and we must try to manipulate them to have a more compliant policy.

We have also to face the formidable Jewish Zionist lobby, rebuild Israel if it can be salvaged, and to recover our influence and access to oil in the Middle East."

Time did not stop still and whether it appeared to accelerate or crawl could only be perceived by its viewer. In strategic terms the longer the assault continued the greater the damage to the Soviet infrastructure and its people who would never know that their leader was in truth more concerned with the fate of his four grandchildren than of his fellow countrymen.

The 'Hot line' announced a call.

"Mr. McNamara, I am authorised not only to increase my offer to you but to ask you ,as a father to a father, to immediately, without hearing details of my proposition to instruct your bombers to terminate their attack on the location South East of Moscow."

It was at this moment that an amicable conflict in tactics took place which would become a portent and symbol of the intellectual dispute between the so called 'Hard liners' led by the Secretary of Defence and the larger group of 'Reconciliationists led by the Attorney General which in practical terms would still be to the 'right' of Edward Kennedy`s later attempts, nearly twenty years in the future, at his own deluded and misconceived policy of friendship.

McNamara correctly sensed that the Presidium would sue for peace at virtually any price and that the subterranean redoubt, South East of Moscow might possibly harbour members of the leadership including Khrushchev himself. On that assumption he was about to reject the new offer out of hand even though he was not yet informed of the details and intended to announce a list of further successful strikes on various military targets, when Kennedy caught his attention and suggested, as a sign of reconciliation that ...

"We should offer to abort the primary strike on humanitarian grounds but subject to an acceptable promise of the Soviet's intentions."

However McNamara was not prepared to exhibit weakness or compromise for he had an objective perception of the nature of his foe but on the other hand he was a part of a democratically appointed government whose members were, unfortunately in this particular situation, allowed to air their opinions and in a moment of compromise, without negotiation, he succumbed to his fellow Cabinet member and sowed the seed of weakness that Brezhnev would ruthlessly exploit when the President returned to lead the country. Thus the Anglo-Saxon Achilles heel of forgiveness and compassion usurped the pitiless posture that would have guaranteed the capitulation of the Soviet Union and in the months and years to come would be seized upon and manipulated by the renamed Politburo.

"Mr. Brezhnev. As a unique sign of good faith, we will arrange to immediately instruct our bombers to abort their primary target but to continue to their secondary targets."

At which stage the President of the Union of Soviet Socialist Republics intervened and began to disclose his hand , slowly and with increasing reticence, listing his suggestions to halt the ever increasing deluge that was raining down throughout the constituent Republics of Russia and the Ukraine.

"We will publicly denounce the unilateral, illegal and criminal attack on Western Europe by renegade politicians in Poland and the German Democratic Republic and will bring them to public trial (at which moment a few, more erudite members of the American elite, including Herman Kahn, remembered, with revulsion, the notorious Slansky trial and conjectured if this travesty of justice was to be repeated)."

 At which point McNamara intervened and stated:

"The bombers will continue to fulfil their allocated tasks until you offer more positive reasons to us to abandon the mission. Do I make myself clear?"

A list of concessions then flowed as presumably Brezhnev plucked them from a previously prepared list, hoping, as each one was offered, that McNamara would signal his acceptance but his acceptance was slow and deliberately intended to extract the maximum sacrifice. When he did signal his acceptance it was vicious in its revenge.

The concessions mainly related to the European mainland and a return to the pre war *status quo*, the withdrawal of occupying troops, assistance to U.S. military and civilians including immediate medical treatment and the release of any imprisoned parties. Part of the agreement was to be supervised by the Red Cross and was extended to the civilians and military personnel of the United States' allies.

The United States were to be given a mandate to maintain the peace and security in the general area of the 'Middle East' and, in return, whilst the U.S. would determine, on behalf of the oil producing nations, the price of a'barrel of crude' an understanding would henceforth take effect that a barter deal between the two nations would begin and in exchange for natural gas, oil and its' by −products the Soviet Union would deliver iron ore, certain rare earths and lumber.

To appease what McNamara correctly recognised would be the wrath of the Jewish lobby who were overwhelmingly Democrat supporters, he 'persuaded' Brezhnev, as a final concession, to allow immediately the emigration of Jews both from the Soviet Union and the Warsaw Pact nations.

It was agreed that the First Secretary, despite his alleged ill health, would make a radio broadcast in which the leadership of the Warsaw Treaty would be held responsible for the premeditated military operation but there was an unspoken understanding that the contents of the speech would be drafted to avoid the humiliation of the Soviet Union.

Nikita Khrushchev made his final public speech within seventy two hours, but it was not the speech that he had mentally drafted a week before and indeed the contents were prepared for him.

Within days rumours circulated in the highest circles outside of the Presidium that he was physically and mentally a broken man, believing that his whole family had been incinerated in a thermonuclear explosion, that politically he had been toppled from power in a coup and that he had only managed to make the broadcast assisted by stimulants administered by a team of physicians.

The speech, carefully prepared, was a victory of misrepresentation and deceit over truth, containing half-truths, fabrications and to use the analogy of the magicians' art, a triumph of illusion and deception. It was preceded by martial music synonymous with the Stalin era and terminated with the 'hymn of Socialism'- the International.

Khrushchev confirmed that the United States had requested a global cease fire and had suggested terms to resolve the conflict which the Presidium were considering.

The might of the Soviet forces, on land, at sea, in the air and their powerful missile force had defended the nation against a foe who knew no moral constraints, were craven in their negotiations but were prepared to atone for the use of nuclear and thermonuclear weapons on the Motherland. With an arrogant bravado Khrushchev announced that in reparation the Americans had agreed to supply natural gas, crude oil and petroleum by products at favourable terms but did not mention, since this important fact was not included in the speech, that it would form part of an agreed 'barter' deal (since he was now excluded from matters of state he was probably unaware of the arrangement). Likewise no mention was made of the political agreement concerning the 'Middle East' and certainly the emigration of Jews from the Soviet Union and the Warsaw Treaty nations, which would deprive them of many of the elite scientists and engineers that they desperately needed.

FIFTY-NINE

No definitive, unbiased or objective history of the conflict exists. Information released by the Soviet Union over a period of years was clearly a long term propaganda exercise mainly for internal consumption but also to mobilise world opinion and the United Nations, not only to condemn the United States (in itself a pointless exercise) but to generate support and therefore internal pressure within the Continental U.S. The discrepancy between the *ALLEGED* number of hits suffered and those claimed by their American aggressors is so vast as to be implausible. It was claimed that the Soviet Union was hit by *OVER FOUR HUNDRED* [author's special emphasis] nuclear or thermonuclear devices whose power ranged from twenty thousand tonnes to two explosions in the six to seven megatonne range, however McNamara's foresight and orders were, prior to the mission, to unload *ALL* thermonuclear devices, therefore nullifying the Kremlin's absurd claims.

Figures quoted by the United States Department of Defence some six months after the short conflict claim just over two hundred 'hits' by nuclear weapons only, implying that thermonuclear devices were *NOT* used.

Analysing Robert McNamara`s observations and comments both in his biography (pages 393-406) and his speech to a representative selection of pilots and crews at S.A.C. H.Qs .some six months after hostilities terminated it is reasonable to assume the integrity and accuracy of the U.S. claims.

Of course from a propaganda aspect it would have assisted the Soviet`s case if the claim and counterclaim was reversed but the credibility of Moscow`s initial statement could hardly be substantially decreased. But graphic (propaganda) film and colour photographs were more searing and traumatic than the black and white photographs of the suffering in Hiroshima and Nagasaki .

From the moment that the Secretary of Defence issued the order to attack (on behalf of his President) it was less than seventy-five minutes before the first B52 crossed the Soviet border and the last bomber departed the Soviet Motherland five hours and forty-two minutes later, but in that relatively short time span more than thirty-eight times the 'T.N.T.' of bombs exploded, than in the whole of the Second World War .Collateral or secondary damage ,incidental to damage directly intended was, in the words of a Red Cross official,' horrendous'. This did not include damage directly caused by devices not wantonly launched but, as you the reader will shortly read, was the result of the bomber crews sacrificing themselves in the face of the brave attempts of the defending fighter pilots.

The primary target, other than the vindictive assault on the bunker complex adjacent to the dacha of the then First Secretary, were the bomber and fighter bases and above all their landing and take off strips since if, and it was correctly argued, they could be eliminated, it would deprive any surviving planes of the facility to take off or land, rendering them inoperable.

The first wave of bombers, flying at or above their normal maximum operational height, were ordered to draw the sting from the anti aircraft missiles – the feared Surface to Air (S.A.M.) that had downed Power`s U2 flight in nineteen sixty. Their E.C.Ms. (Electronic Counter Measures) by modern standards were, even in the convoluted language of the Pentagon and the Secretary of Defence, primitive and barely effective, however it gave the bombers time to draw the sting and eliminate most of the launchers and their accompanying radar and operational facilities.

But the opening confrontation did not go all the own way of the attackers as the missiles appeared to be effective and viciously accurate, resulting in many cases of the pilots, realising that there was no alternative to death in their stricken planes, detonating their most powerful weapons shortly before crashing ,to cause the maximum destruction and havoc. Thus in some tragic cases, civilian centres and areas of agricultural production were hit as was the city of Yerevan in the Crimea when the target was a bomber base (where incidentally some of the Tupolev bombers had been based which attacked the State of Israel) and whilst it was probably the intention of the pilot to aim his stricken B52 on the base some slight deflection turned it off course and onto the city.

War is not glorious or glamorous as portrayed in most of the films that are churned out by the patriotic moguls of Hollywood and whilst national leaders, in apparent humility and sympathy to the bereaved, talk of the ultimate sacrifice and patriotic bravery, it was not them that gave up their lives. War is dirty, callous and does not respect the integrity of the individual or their humanity.

The first wave succeeded by clearing pathways, either eliminating many of the S.A.M. batteries or exhausting their stock of missiles, but at a high price, both in their own losses and the unintended damage caused to civilian sites.

The role of the second wave was the destruction of the runways and as a secondary bonus, the elimination of the bases and any aircraft that had not been scrambled and were caught on the ground, but the bravery and professionalism of the defenders had been underestimated by the American planners as were the capabilities of the aircraft that defended their bases. Powered by one Tumansky single-shaft turbojet with afterburner, the M IG-21s (Mikoyan/Gurevich) had a performance capability that permitted them to intercept and attack the invader using a brace of K13 missiles and a 30 mm N R- 30 cannon estimated to hold from sixty to eighty rounds, creating havoc amongst the bombers.

Not so successful was the Sukhoi Su-9 (Pavel O.Sukhoi) powered by a single Lyulka single-shaft turbojet also with an afterburner and armed with four AA-1 air to air missiles. The phrase 'not so successful' is purely relative and could be put down to the inefficiency or failures of some of the missiles, however within the limitations and purpose of this work only a general description with some specific illustrations can be given to summarise the air combat.

For some years it was rumoured that the bravery and heroism of the defenders was so outstanding and honourable that it contributed to the restricted ability of the attackers to release their weapons. Indeed, in Air Force circles it was claimed that hidden in the depths of the 'Pentagon' was actual combat film of the desperate attempts of the fighter pilots to protect both their bases and the 'Motherland'.

Recently such film emerged, but only available to approved audiences who had been 'cleared' by the C I A, mainly air force combat crews and intelligence and planning staff. I understand that included are shots of two separate group of incidents where the defending aircraft, having exhausted their weapons deliberately rammed B 52s, in one case shearing off a whole wing and in the other, hitting and destroying the cockpit and front nose. In the second example, the bomber recording an exceptional, dramatic incident, immediately veered off but continued taking shots even though the other bomber was out of sight, though about thirty seconds later, the film was seen to violently shake as beneath them a nuclear detonation took place.

Robert McNamara had said that he was prepared to sacrifice five hundred bombers to obliterate the Communists and of the approximately six hundred that were committed about one hundred and sixty- five returned, though some thirty of the total had not entered Soviet air space. The last, or third wave, had an easier task, the hardest part being, in the words of one retired crew member looking back over thirty years later and expressing disdain about the continued demand for secrecy:

"We had to weave between vast plumes of mushroom clouds searching for our designated targets which were tank parks and military establishments only identified by coordinates. I suddenly felt sick and indeed vomited, drenching the co pilot when I thought of the human beings whose incinerated ashes formed part of the swirling clouds that dominated the view beneath, around us and as far as the horizon."

The use of nuclear weapons was not restricted to the United States for, in retaliation to the attack on the Soviet homeland, Warsaw Treaty fighters supplied and equipped by their Soviet masters, launched a retaliatory counter strike against U.S. bases in the United Kingdom including the sites at Bentwaters, Mildenhall and Lakenheath , extensively damaging the runways but causing secondary damage to the surrounding agricultural areas.

Thus victory was achieved and for some of the crews they were able to avenge their comrades who had been murdered by the chemical and nerve gases used against them on the European mainland.

I end the second part of this alternative *TRUE* history with a recollection by an anonymous United States Air Force co-pilot who is now dead. If you have any doubts about the glory of war, please read the following words very carefully and ponder...

"The (B52) bomber flew majestically onwards, weaving its way home through a maze of grey mushroom clouds, some of which, they must have been the earliest hits, were beginning to disperse and dissipate, perhaps accelerated by the now tainted radioactive air currents. If God was looking down on the scene, the returning planes must have appeared as eagles soaring in the deep valleys and riding on hot air thermals whilst beneath them lay vast swathes of the Ukraine, raped, its population traumatised and decimated.

Inside the cockpit an uneasy silence reigned; my own thoughts were concentrated on the loss of my friends who I had seen go down, or in one instance of one pilot, screaming on his radio that his co-pilot had been shot in the stomach which had exploded, broadcasting his intestines and other internal body parts around the cockpit.

My captain turned to me and like an auditor calculated the millions that had been entered in the ledger of death, then speculated on the millions more who would soon join them, their bodies destroyed by heat, blast or the invisible ravages of radiation and then radioactivity.

We both knew but did not dare say the truth.

Falteringly and littered with errors he quietly spoke the Shema. He stopped, looked up at the Heavens and then said Kaddish, not for him but for all those millions. He had half forgotten the words but I helped him as his stuttering rendition became more confident. I, perhaps both of us, had partially redeemed ourselves, or so I thought.

He said nothing and a moment later the sound of gunfire nearly deafened me and looking round I saw the pistol in his mouth and the blood spurting onto his clenched hands.

Thus are the glorious dead."

President Johnson returned to his duties in the Spring.

In October nineteen sixty-four Khrushchev was formally deposed at about the same time as a General Election should have been held in the United Kingdom (but was never held) and when the People's Republic of China announced the first explosion of a nuclear bomb (at Sinkiang in Lop Nor).

In his inaugural speech the new First Secretary and Premier ostentatiously praised his predecessor and acknowledged a "great war leader" whose health had been irrevocably damaged leading his nation to victory against the forces of Capitalism and whose legacy was the reparations that had been forced from their cruel enemy.

Despite wars, changing political alliances and betrayals, the barter deal continued and still continues both to the benefit of the American people, maintaining and constantly improving their standard of living, and the Soviet Union, since the production of the raw materials was based on the exploitation and virtual use of slave labour, the political dissidents and criminal elements .

The United States was not only deaf ,blind and apathetic to the pleas for democratic rights throughout the Middle East but rigorously applied, as originally agreed, the inequitable payment to the autocratic leaders who learned to compromise on their reduced revenues but still seemed, to the detriment of their own people, to live in extreme, opulent luxury.

Khrushchev was allowed to return to his dacha and to be reunited with his wife, family and retinue and to continue his life style (though under guard, including the one conscript whose letter had effectively betrayed him) but he never ate any of the Sturgeon that symbolised the success of his plans.

For the planners of the operation, based in the Yamantau Mountain complex, excluding the hero of the mighty tank battle of Kursk, they were arrested, tried before a military tribunal and executed though they did not suffer the ignominy of the lies and harassment that Slansky had endured at the hands of the Prosecutor Josef Urvelak.

Goldburgh was unaware of the fate of his dear friend (or the influence that his plan had on the destiny of nations), who had saved his life in nineteen forty-four and did not know that events and fate would propel him into the focus of British political power.

Joel Ben Yitzhak, quietly awaited the confusion, convulsions, chaos and collapse of the Old Order that he had orchestrated, for soon a New Order would arise.

THE PREQUEL: IT HAPPENED HERE

AN ALTERNATIVE TRUE HISTORY

THE ORIGINS OF THE CONSPIRACY

(1914-1944)

ONE

The first half of the Twentieth Century was dominated by two 'World Wars' which were, in part, the outcome and result of new national aspirations sometimes of different intentions but also in response to the rise of new international alliances and political objectives. For nearly a century, from 'The Battle of Waterloo', in June eighteen fifteen, which ended French hopes of expansion and European hegemony under Napoleon, to August nineteen fourteen and the beginning of the first 'World War', a 'Pax Britannica' reigned, maintained by a mighty naval force projecting power and influence and creating a global map in which the dominant colour was red.

Great Britain grew wealthy, reaping the benefits of expanding international trade and commerce, fuelled by the import of under priced raw materials for processing from its Empire and unfair low wages paid to the factory workers and those who toiled on the farms, who were defined as 'the proletariat' by a nineteenth century economist and sociologist.

The unfair division of the wealth that was being created resulted in the formation of a new form of the medieval Craft Guilds in which the workers banded together to form 'Trade Unions' developing a technique to force the owners, who were defined as 'Capitalists', to improve the terms of employment, specifically wages, working conditions and hours of employment using both the threat and the actual use of the withdrawal of their labour, en masse, 'the strike'.

Internationally and nationally, the increasing conflict between the 'Workers' and the 'Capitalists' was developing in various directions but was symbolised by the rise of new political parties (some of which were declared illegal and banned) so that like boiling water in a kettle which had been constructed to ventilate steam to relieve the pressure, so certain countries adapted their various forms of government and systems and were able not only to control and integrate these new forces but enabled all the parties to benefit from an evolving new social order.

In certain other countries the conflict between the workers, the employers and society in general was not satisfactorily resolved and resulted in internal conflict and civil war with different outcomes.

In nineteen forty-nine, in China, the Communists under Mao Tse Tung and Chou En Lai finally succeeded in ousting the Nationalists under Chiang Kai Shek who were expelled to the Island of Formosa.

Ten years earlier, in nineteen thirty- nine, in an even bloodier civil war, the Fascist Nationalists in Spain under General Franco defeated the legitimately elected Socialist government and nearly twenty years before, in what would become the Union of Soviet Socialist Republics, there ended a vicious civil war between the Communist Bolsheviks under Lenin, who had seized power in nineteen seventeen, and counter revolutionaries, representing the deposed autocratic and discredited monarchy.

There is one thread that binds these three events in the journey towards the new World Order and that is the involvement of a Jew, Joel Ben Yitzhak, who had mentored Chou En Lai during the latter's sojourn in France many years before. He had also manipulated the various left wing organisations in Spain, especially P.O.U.M. in their internecine struggles (fatally weakening them and accelerating the ultimate victory of the Nationalists) and finally he had also personally supported his fellow Jew, the ultra revolutionary Lev Bronstein(Leon Trotsky) in the creation of the Red Army. But Ben Yitzhak's perfidiousness and deviousness became apparent on January the eighteenth, nineteen twenty- nine, when in Alma Ata in the Crimea, he was present and incited the local chief of the O G P U (The Joint State Political Directorate and a forerunner of the N K V D) to hold a special session resulting in the expulsion order of Leon Trotsky (to Turkey and permanent exile)under article 58 clause 10 of the criminal code which accused him of:

" counter revolutionary activities expressed in the organisation of an illegal anti-Soviet party whose recent activities have been aimed at provoking anti–Soviet speeches and the preparation of armed struggle against Soviet power..."

...and on January the twentieth the document was validated by the chief of the Alma–Ata Section of the O G P U.

The struggle between two ideologies, that is Capitalism and Socialism would henceforth dominate national and international relations and would create new derivatives of social and political creeds such as National Socialism and Fascism in Germany and Italy respectively and less aggressive forms of Socialism in Sweden and France. But it was in the Soviet Union that from an early date after victory in the civil war, that plans for the struggle against and the downfall of Capitalism were being conceived and promoted.

In the vanguard was the Communist International which would promote the demise of their enemies by subversion in different forms and ultimate revolution. We will never know by whom or exactly when the plan was conceived that involved Goldburgh but it may well go as far back as Felix Dzerzhinsky, the first head of the Cheka (the secret political police),but what is beyond dispute is that the official approval was given by Lavrenti Beria, head of the N K V D, probably early in nineteen forty-two, when around the same time plans were laid to penetrate the most secret activity in America, code name The Manhattan Project, the development of an Atomic bomb.

The object was to metamorphose, to completely change and induct select groups of young Soviet citizens into Americans and to infiltrate them into the United States where they would settle anonymously, blending into their local communities, completely cut off from their roots or any association with their past lives until, one day, they would be activated for a purpose or purposes that currently could not be conjectured. Each group and each member would be independent of the others and would be supervised, even unknown to them, by a leader who would also be a 'Sleeper'.

Early in nineteen forty-two the European map had been radically altered by the military successes of Germany who had first defeated Poland, in the autumn of nineteen thirty-nine, which was then 'carved up' between the victor and their then new ally, the Soviet Union, following a peace treaty which had stunned both Europe and the United States because of the wide gulf and contradictory nature of their social and political ideologies and philosophies.

317

In the spring of nineteen-forty, Germany, in a lightning assault, had expelled British forces from the mainland after overrunning France, Belgium, Holland and Denmark and, before turning on their former ally, the Soviet Union, had threatened unsuccessfully to invade the United Kingdom. In the summer of nineteen forty-one (to be exact, June the twenty second) Germany invaded its former ally, reaching the outskirts of Moscow before being halted, not by military might, but by the harsh winter conditions.

It was into this background that Mandel Goldburgh had been born and raised.

TWO

Perhaps it was providential that the location of the camp site to house the indoctrination programme was chosen to be in an area of the Ukraine that was never over run by their erstwhile ally, the Nazis, in nineteen forty -three or forty-four, permitting a programme to produce its first and what turned out to be its only team of 'sleepers'. There was a substantial pool of American citizens to fill the camp which for reasons shortly to be explained and disclosed was always, in the presence of its American occupants, described as a rehabilitation and education centre.

The pool of residents, or the ones that had survived or more importantly were in a physical condition to recuperate and be useful, were languishing in the prison and labour camps of the Gulag, their crimes or usually their only crime was that they were American citizens and in the eyes of Stalin, untrustworthy.

The Great Depression, which finally created thirteen million unemployed citizens in the Continental United States, was the catalyst that propelled an estimated fifteen thousand U.S. pilgrims to travel East to the new Promised Land and Socialist Utopia of the U S S R where, under Stalin, the country was in its latest Five Year economic plan. At first there were jobs and possibly for some, the realisation of their dreams, however, they were later caught up in the Great Terror and since viewed first as Americans, many in consequence were arrested as potential spies and dispatched to some of the camps that comprised 'The Gulag'.

Their release, along with their families, must have appeared miraculous, together with the reason for their rescue. The official explanation was highly plausible and was that since the United States was now allied to the Soviet Union and that the government accepted that they had mistakenly been processed into the prison system , the country wished to make amends on behalf of First Secretary Stalin and to that end a rehabilitation and education centre was to be built (West of the Urals) with their help where they could recover their health, help to train young Soviet emissaries who would join them if they wished to return to their former homeland (though it was hoped that they would stay and join in the rebuilding of their new adopted country). Whether the excuse was accepted at its face value would depend on the response of the imprisoned individual pilgrims but any reason to escape the cruel and normally fatal environment of the Siberian climate and the prison system was reason enough.

The first groups were specifically chosen for their general better health and also for their qualifications and former trades. They arrived in early spring nineteen forty-three via a newly constructed road (which unknown to them had been built by criminal slave labour) besides which lay a parallel chain of telephone wires and poles and an invisible subterranean electricity cable which connected the camp to the outside world. So isolated was the camp that the road meandered for some twenty or so miles into the anonymity of unexplored virgin territory. When the first occupants arrived they were greeted by the outlines of a nascent town, its concrete roads defining its geography but with little else visible as the underground sewage system and water supply had been built waiting to be connected.

In preparation for the opening of the centre, the N K V D had been active, purchasing equipment and goods to support the town which they hoped to have operating in the early autumn of nineteen forty-three. It was financed by hard American currency earned by the sale of artefacts plundered after the Revolution, or works of art, jewellery and antique furniture expropriated from the victims of The Terror and sold through special shops or exported to the United States and sold by 'specialist' antique dealers with' connections'. Waiting to be installed and operating was a drug store together a soda fountain, a doctor's and dentist's surgery (but not an opticians), a substantial hardware store which conveniently stocked all the necessary equipment to construct ninety or so single storey homes to accommodate the new arrivals, a barber's shop and finally a local civic centre (also single storey to minimise building costs and labour) which incorporated adequate facilities to accommodate students from the ages of five to seventeen, the regulatory textbooks and finally, in the same complex a cinema and 'ten pin' bowling alley.

Thus the whole operation had been carefully and meticulously planned and adequately financed, the latter by the 'Plutocrats' who Lavrenti Beria described as drawing up their own death warrants. The attention to detail was such that even though the Soviet Union entered the war on June the twenty second nineteen forty-one (initially suffering tremendous military losses and the seizure of much land to the Nazis) and the Americans being 'dragged in' less than six months later following a catastrophic attack on their Pacific fleet based at Pearl Harbour in the Pacific, the flow of what was luxurious staple food continued via neutral Sweden, being delivered to its final destination by refrigerated lorries so that the inmates (or as they were known, the residents) were not only isolated from the traumas of war and the suffering of the combatants and the civilian population but lived a life detached from the realities of the global situation.

By the early autumn of nineteen forty-three the complex had not only been built but was operational, filled with its American families who unknowingly awaited both its administrators and the dozen candidates for induction.

THREE

During a tutorial, in the presence of some of his fellow undergraduates, and in response to his tutor's request, Goldburgh made both an unexpected and candid announcement, without shame or embarrassment, that the definition 'bastard' was a factual description of his true status and was really the result or the consequence of his parents making the deliberate decision not to marry. It was completely out of context with the subject that their tutor had requested they discuss ('Should modern warfare be subject to ethical and moral constraints - with specific reference to the current struggle in the ongoing Spanish Civil War?').

Goldburgh continued, and explained, that:

"It is only the antiquated and anachronistic values of society that decree a child, born out of wedlock ,was a bastard and subsequently had no rights, including the right of inheritance.

" To the surprise of his fellow students and to satisfy the voracious intellectual hunger and demands of his tutor he then argued convincingly that :

"Any leadership, constrained by ethical and moral values deserved to be defeated and subjugated by its victorious enemy and that [the following statement absolutely shocked those assembled] Leon Trotsky, founder of the Red Army and first Soviet Commissar for War, who his parents had known well, had answered the tutor's question in a speech which he had given in the early nineteen twenties.

For the attacks of enemy forces to be repelled, we must be armed with all the latest means of defence which modern war technique can produce. The use of poison gas in the last war requires us to keep even this means of warfare in reserve for the defence of our nation against the enemy."

Apparently, according to folklore, Goldburgh stopped for effect and then added, as if finishing a letter with a postscript, that:

"My parents regularly allowed me to sit on his lap and that once I wetted him, much to everyone's embarrassment and good humour."

It is now unimportant to learn the outcome of the tutorial .

Mandel Goldburgh retained his mother's family name in preference to his father's patronym of Kaganovich. She was the scion of a Russian Jewish family who were amongst the first to emigrate from what was known as 'The Pale' and settled, not in the United States, which was hungry for immigrants to populate vast new territories, but in England where the Victorians, in pursuit of power and trade, had created a vast empire of political domination and economic wealth. She was born in about eighteen ninety-five (which was coincidentally when her future partner was also born) when her family had grown substantial roots in the more Anglican suburbs of North London and not in the artificial ghetto, which was not forcibly imposed on the Jewish community, in what was known, with great affection, as the 'East End'; however this geographical diversion was only to emphasise the family's assimilation into the wider society.

The family, by sacrifice, diligence and basic hard work were financially successful as merchants, using the family roots in what they nostalgically referred to as 'The Old Country ' to trade in furs and semi precious stones from the Baltic in exchange for specified manufactured goods which they bought in bulk, in London, or by special negotiation. Thus she was bilingual or in fact trilingual, since English had become her first language, followed by Yiddish which was still her mother's primary means of communication with her family and friends and lastly Russian which the whole family viewed as antiquated and only useful for the purpose of trade and commerce.

Her father, personally deprived of an education, took advantage of the educational facilities in London to give his daughter the best possible start in life and had not fate, or destiny, imposed its mark she might have pursued a university career. However in June of nineteen-fourteen she journeyed to Moscow to meet her family for the summer holidays and then found herself marooned in an island of upper middle class luxury and security, temporarily unable to return to England because of the outbreak of war and the uncertainty of sea travel. At first the inconvenience was seen as a temporary hiatus but as the intensity and breadth of the conflagration expanded it became proportionately more hazardous to return to her homeland. It was decided that she would continue her education in Moscow until such time as it was deemed safe to return. Her private education allowed her to perfect her Russian, to take advantage of access to the Conservatoires where she found great pleasure in music but not the ability to play an instrument or to dance or sing, but to meet the sons and daughters of the minor aristocracy and of the families of wealthy foreign business people.

It was shortly after the tumultuous, almost volcanic eruptions that saw the overthrow of the Tsar and the autocratic monarchy ,that fate began to weave a pattern of events that would unite her with the man that she would share her life (and death).

He came from a shtetl in the vast rural and undeveloped countryside of the Ukraine, close to the village of Kabany, Radomyshluyezd in the Kiev Governorate and left home in the autumn of nine teen sixteen with very little money, a letter of introduction written in Yiddish by his Rabbi (since for all intent and purpose he and his family were illiterate) and the name and *POSSIBLE* contact address in Moscow of a family member, Lazar Kaganovich, who might be able to help him find employment.

Early in nineteen seventeen Moscow was in turmoil, a new Socialist government under Kerensky was in power, the Tsar and his family apparently under arrest and rumours that Vladimir Lenin might return from Switzerland and with him a more left wing type of government.

Lazar Kaganovich was chairman of the Tanners Union (he had been in nineteen fifteen a Communist organiser for a shoe factory where he worked) and it may never be known when the two close relatives first met, however Joel was placed in employment, under the wings of his cousin whose career and reputation flourished. In hindsight Lazar's greatest gift was to insist that his cousin 'better' himself and in consequence Joel embarked on an ever increasingly intensive course of education, first learning to read and write both in Cyrillic and in Yiddish (which was frowned upon by his cousin) and then in various disciplines which he absorbed with ease, including, as a compulsory requirement, the theory and philosophy of Marxist- Leninism, which secretly he rejected, since he believed that the ideologywas not only in contradiction with his values but appeared realistically unattainable in view of human nature.

The young, beautiful Leah Goldburgh was introduced to the world and environment of the Soviet revolutionaries by a school friend who regarded the experience of associating with perhaps the future rulers as yet another experience, whilst for Leah Goldburgh it was an entry into a new world of vibrant intellectualism and adventure.

For Joel, the place where they first met had provided, for some months, three fundamental essentials, heating ,cheap wholesome food and light so that he could read and study.

It was a cafe, frequented by students and factory workers mainly politically active in left wing causes and including members of the Communist party whose main topic of conversation was the possible return of Vladimir Lenin and the creation of a truly Socialist– Communist society. It was here that one of the threads that would change global history was drawn, a catalyst that created a chemistry that can never be defined, quantified or scientifically measured and annotated, they were instantaneously drawn to one another, despite the differences in their upbringing, though they were both still to continue, throughout their joint lives, the traditions of their Jewish upbringing.

As he continued to pursue his education, she began to neglect hers, preferring to be at his side and it was possibly in April nineteen eighteen that she was first introduced to Lazar Kaganovich who, at that time, was the Commissar of the Red Army propaganda department and was, as such, in contact with another Jew, Leon Trotsky, the founder of the Red Army.

According to reports, Lazar was overwhelmed, enthralled and captivated by Leah Goldburgh, not solely by her classic semitic beauty, but by her cosmopolitan nature and her ability to blend in and mix with various disparate groups and with his increasing influence and above all his growing connections, Lazar was able to support Joel in his budding academic career and her support for Joel. Fearing her family's potential objection to her new relationship and the reaction of her parents in London she conspired to keep the liaison secret for as long as possible, even secretly accumulating assets to support the two when and if the situation altered.

By the autumn of nineteen nineteen she found that she was pregnant and she could no longer hide the real reason why she had declined a number of offers to finance her return to England and her parents. She was given as much capital as possible when her relatives left Moscow and Russia to join her family in London with hopes and aspirations to maintain the family trading company.

Joel and Leah continued their lives together, if not directly financially supported by Lazar, since she was prudent in the disposal of monies that she had previously saved but by the benefit of an apartment conveniently allocated to them and most treasured of all, a Party food ration card, even though neither were members of the Communist Party. It was during this time, when Lazar Kaganovich's star was dramatically rising, mainly because of his loyalty and support of Stalin and Stalin's appreciation of Kaganovich's administrative abilities, that the couple and the young Mandel were guests at Party functions and hosted, on behalf of their close relative, receptions for leading members of the Party, including Stalin, Trotsky ,Bukharin, Kamenev, Zinoviev and Kviring though the pair were extremely cautious not to involve themselves in the higher matters of Party ideology and above all the clearly developing struggle for ultimate power itself.

Joel was able to continue his academic career and research whilst Mandel was placed in schools attended by the sons and daughters of the main Party functionaries but the child, displaying an incisive depth of common sense well above his age had that single minded independence and ability to think for himself and not to accept the tenets and mantras of the Party line.

In nineteen thirty-four, Stalin allowed academic and artistic representatives to travel abroad and to promote the image of Soviet Russia and its growing achievements and peaceful intentions. The flow was to be two ways, as Russia, for example, had previously received the British author and socialist, H.G. Wells, and was very soon to receive the noted American singer and actor Paul Robeson, so the great film director Sergei Eisenstein went to America and Joel, Leah and Mandel were permitted to go to Western Europe to promote his unpublished work on the early history of the Russian people and their origins in the Viking explorers and traders .

324

One possible additional reason that facilitated their extended overseas journey was, at this late stage, their sudden and unexpected membership of the Communist Party and Mandel's late admission to the Young Communist league. They left Moscow in a private carriage of a locomotive train, used normally by the upper strata of the Party, Joel holding documents so powerful that the authorities at the station had to check their validity and then be castigated for their apparent impertinent enquiries concerning unimpeachable travel documents signed by the First Secretary Stalin, the People's Commissar for Internal Affairs, the recently promoted Genrikh Yagoda and Secretary of the Central Committee of the Communist Party, Lazar Kaganovich.

The first part of the journey was in unadulterated luxury as the three were waited upon as the Romanovs must have been before the revolution. Ahead of them was an unknown future in an England that Leah had last experienced twenty years before.

FOUR

As he opened his eyes, his mind was confused by the changed appearance of the carriage, still opulent but not as luxurious as before and decorated in an entirely different style. Even the rhythmic sound of the wheels had changed and finally something most unusual, even rare was taking place. His parents were speaking in English, his mother fluent and eloquent, his father, slow, unsure and halting, displaying a strong Russian accent. His mother, aware that her son was now awake turned to him and confirmed that they were now in Poland and that whilst he was still asleep they had transferred to a new train.

They were unable to travel due West effectively through Germany because of the current political situation:

"With Soviet documents they risked immediate arrest and in view of the signatures authorising the various papers further difficulties might arise, combined with the fact that they were Jewish, was a risk far too dangerous to be undertaken. They were to take a circuitous and tortuous route via Switzerland to France where they would spend three or four days visiting the famous sights and various sites before the final part of their journey to England and her family.

"

This was the first time in his life that his parents had ever mentioned that their Jewish origins would subject them to potential danger.

Possibly to divert their son's attention from this new potentially dangerous situation, his father speaking in Yiddish, told the story of how he was given the name Mandel (pronounced Mundel).

אויך זײן ברית זענען געװען פופצן ייִדן –צװישן זיי לייזער קאַגאַנאָװיטש (װאָס האָט אומגעריכט,
ניט געקוקט אויף דעם גרויסן דוחק נאָך דער מפלה פֿון דער װײַסער אַרמיי אינעם בירגערקריג,
געברענגט מיט זיך פֿרישע, זיסע מאַנדלען פֿון די װעלדלעך פֿון גאָרגיע) און דער אַטעיסט לעאָן
טראָצקי (בשעת זייער אַ שיכּורער סטאַלין איז אָנגעקומען שפּעטער, פּונקט װען מע האָט
דערלאַנגט די װאָדקע מיט אַ ברייטער האַנט). אָן קװענקלעניש און פֿון דער העלער הויט האָט ער
דערקענט דעם פֿאַרכּישופֿטן און מיסטישן נומער פופצן, די העברעישע אותיות „יוד" – „הא",
מיט װאָס מע לייגט אויס דעם שם-המפורש. דאָס איז באַשײַמפּערלעך געװען אַ סימן צו געבן זײן
זון דעם שטאָלצן נאָמען מאַנדל.

Af zayn bris zenen geven fuftsn yidn – tsvishn zey Leyzer Kaganovitsh (vos hot
umgerikht, nit gekukt af dem groysn doykhek nokh der mapole fun der vayser
armey inem birgerkrig, gebrengt mit zikh frishe, zise mandlen fun di veldlekh
fun Georgye) un der ateist Leon Trotski (beshas zeyer a shikerer Stalin iz
ongekumen shpeter, punkt ven me hot derlangt di vodke mit der breyter hant).
On kvenklenish un fun der heler hoyt hot er derkent dem farkisheftn un mistishn
numer fuftsn, di hebreishe oysyes "yud" – "hey", mit vos me leygt oys dem
Shem-hamefoyresh. Dos iz bashaymperlekh geven a simen tsu gebn zayn zun
dem shtoltsn nomen Mandl.

" At his ritual circumcision (Briss) there were fifteen Jewish males present, including Lazar Kaganovich (who had unexpectedly brought with him, despite the many shortages following the defeat of the White forces in the civil war, fresh, sweet almonds from the groves of Georgia) and the atheist Leon Trotsky (whilst a heavily drunk Stalin would arrive later, just as the vodka was being liberally served). Without hesitation and on the spur of the moment he recognised the magical and mystical number of fifteen, the Hebrew letters yud – hay spelling the name of G-d. It was clearly a sign to give his son the proud name of Mandel".

The journey exhausted him and his waking hours were spent practising his English, outshining his father, and repeating by rote, the names of his mother's parents and other close relatives who he had never met and whose particulars were listed by his mother as old faded and dog eared photographs were taken from her handbag and shown to him. He was, of course, unaware that like him, his father had also not met his partner's family and in that brief phrase was a matter that had caused and would cause certain friction.

"The Eiffel Tower was exhilarating but very windy; part of the journey , up the staircase, exhausting.   Sacre Coeur boring, the Arc De Triomphe frightening, because of the cars careering round the building and the Mona Lisa just another painting. "

He, and his parents, were visibly proud and excited to see a parade of workers preceded by two flag bearers, one displaying the French national flag, the other, the Hammer and Sickle, but they were all upset to hear some onlookers jeering at the parade of some three hundred men. His father commented, rather aggressively that:

"This type of behaviour would not be tolerated by his fellow Muscovites in the Soviet Union."

Sometime later Mandel mused that:

"The vanilla ice cream wrapped inside a warm pancake, now where was it, in Montparnasse, La Coupole?, was the best thing that he had ever tasted,"

As he wondered what life and for the first time ever, what food would be served in his new home.

The boat train whisked them quickly to London and they partially 'doubled back' on themselves as another train took them in a North

Easterly direction to the Norfolk coast and the provincial town of Southwold.

FIVE

Mandel was fourteen and his intelligence far exceeded his age but like most children he also had an innate ability to sense the atmosphere around him, much as a radio could be tuned to receive different stations.

The taxi drew up outside of a bungalow that obviously needed repair and attention but the front garden was excellently maintained, the lawn immaculately mowed and the flower beds rich in vibrant colours. Leah walked hand in hand with her son to the front door whilst Joel paid off the driver who was lifting the suitcases from the boot of the vehicle. The front door of their new home needed to be painted, flakes were peeling off and the wood base was clearly visible. As she lifted her hand to the knocker, the door was opened and she was confronted by her father and without any words of communication or signs she knew the awful truth. Father and daughter embraced, then he attempted ,as any grandfather would try, to lift his grandson but he was too big and his grandfather was no longer the man he used to be. When she looked at him she instantaneously realised that in the two decades since they had been last together, time and events had eroded his strength and prematurely aged him.

Her father put out his hand to Joel and the two men shook in acknowledgement but Leah sensed a reticence and a formality in her father's reception of her partner. She learned that her mother had died some three months before and that her father's correspondence must have missed their departure such were the vagaries of the postal service. Her hopes and expectations had been dashed by fate and she could see in her son's face his unhappiness and disappointment.

They were to eat that evening at the family home of the relatives with whom she had originally stayed in Moscow all those years ago and she could not suppress her excitement and eager anticipation.

In accordance with Jewish tradition, as it was a Friday, she suggested to her father that as Shabbat was approaching, that she would 'bench' candles as her mother had done and was astounded when her father, in response, stated that the tradition had lapsed and that not only was he no longer observant but had embraced the Protestant faith! Leah stopped and promptly changed the subject, telling her father how excited her son was to meet his grandfather and was also looking forward to meeting other members of the family.

The journey was brief and they received a profuse and sincere welcome punctuated by the offer of sherry for the women and gin and tonics for the men. Mandel was offered and received locally brewed ginger beer which was to become a staple pleasure, when available, in his diet throughout his life.

The menu was conservative, abundant and typically reflected the whole family's embrace of everything British. The usual Jewish Shabbat meal which focused around chicken or carp was replaced by English roast beef, a dish which her partner later admitted to her was:

"Excellent and explained the strength and fortitude of the British people and their army."

It was after the meal when perhaps their hosts felt more relaxed that Leah and Joel began to learn of the reasons and reasoning which had changed the family's attitude to their values and religious and political loyalties. It was clear that the whole family had been in financial decline for some years. The World War had reduced the demand for the goods that they sold and then the Revolution in Russia and the subsequent Civil War had substantially reduced the supply of furs, though Lenin's later economic policies had increased the supply, but it was when Stalin finally crippled the former lucrative trade (at this stage, as if by telepathy, both Leah and Joel decided that it would be unwise to mention their close association and Lazar's intimate professional relationship with the First Secretary) that business dramatically declined. It was at this juncture that her father argued with fervour that he had been deserted by God despite his hard work and sacrifice and that he had found solace in the English Church.

In the Soviet Union the Russian Orthodox Church had been effectively suppressed and was barely tolerated, indeed ,and Leah deliberately did not announce the fact, that her partner's relative ,Lazar Kaganovich, had recently organised and contributed greatly to the building of the first Soviet underground rapid transport system, the Moscow Metro, and at the same time he had also supervised the destruction of many of the city's oldest monuments including the Cathedral of Christ the Saviour. It was at this point that Mandel, previously a silent participant, asked his grandfather a rhetorical question so simple, yet profound, that he was received by a deafening silence that was only broken by a joint resolution to move to the lounge which was...

"More comfortable and where the men could have whiskies and soda."

"Grandfather, if there is only one God but who is revered and worshipped differently by various religions why was it necessary to desert your Jewish roots?"

He did not realise, but from that moment onwards and for the rest of his life, he would face evermore complex dilemmas concerning his ethical, moral and philosophical values that would create an insecurity, indecision and lack of loyalty to any one nation or cause.

Life soon took on a structured ,organised plan which conveniently suited the young boy. He had missed the beginning of the summer term and one of the local and highly regarded private schools suggested and recommended that he continue his studies at home supplying a list of books and a summary of subject matter to prepare him for the autumn term. He was diligent in his pursuit of knowledge and success, assisted by his parents, whilst his father literally eked out a living giving Russian lessons locally, but in a town the size of Southwold and with a limited demand, income was scarce. Unknown to Mandel, and there was no reason whatsoever that he should be informed, his mother received, via a discreet firm of Zurich lawyers and paid by an associate firm of solicitors in London, a monthly salary emanating from the Soviet Union which permitted the family independence and allowed them to contribute towards the household budget, a fact that was conveniently accepted by her father though it was only years later, with the maturity of age and experience, that Mandel could understand his grandfather's disapproval of the irreconcilable clash of two different cultures, of nineteenth century Victorian values and customs confronting the cohabitation of unmarried adults and the more liberal disregard for the values of the Bible, combined paradoxically with an adherence to a religion based on ancient traditions.

September saw his arrival at the new school, daunting and unfamiliar; with customs, traditions and procedures alien to his experience. Tragically he was the butt of his contemporaries' bullying for though he was fluent ,and in comparison to some of his fellow classmates, more eloquent, they noted a slight accent and mercilessly taunted him, for children sometimes do not comprehend the inhumanity of their venomous cruelty, and his protestations in fluent Russian were ignored and ridiculed and he was ultimately rescued by his English teacher , Mr. Michael Riddle, which began a life long association.

He was introduced to English literature including the socialist works and exciting science fiction novels of Herbert George Wells and the works of Shakespeare to which he became addicted and he spent many hours analysing and comprehending the subtle and diverse interpretations of his works and learning how his teacher had enjoyed his three years study at Cambridge and how it had helped him in his journey, so far, in life.

He had little interest in his mother's regular and frequent journeys to London (ostensibly to visit the many sites of culture) or his father's frequent visits to the post box and his eager anticipation of the post) for he immersed himself in a world of literature and contemplation whilst the taunts and bullying slowly decreased and petered out.

It was in April, nineteen thirty-five that at dinner, his father, with his partner excitedly smiling and his grandfather showing contradictory emotions of pride and disappointment (for he was about to lose a regular and sizeable income) announced with emotion, which brought out his strong Slav accent that:

"Next month we are to leave for the United States and the Mid West for I have secured work assisting a Professor of Russian and Slav studies and whilst the position is unofficial there will be undoubtedly a steady flow of students."

No mention was made of the College or University and Mandel was too disappointed to ask where they were to live. As a matter of course he commenced, with great enthusiasm, the summer term, allowing himself more time to study and absorb knowledge of English literature which he would take with him to his new school.

They left on Saturday, May the twenty-fifth, nineteen thirty -five and he would never see his grandfather again. The family returned to London, where they spent a week sightseeing, before travelling up to Liverpool to embark on a trans Atlantic liner bound for New York where they would spend a further two weeks before travelling to Chicago and thence to Nebraska and the State Capitol, Lincoln .

He was overwhelmed by the panorama and sounds of New York. Like many before him and even more after him he was captivated and enraptured by the 'skyscrapers', the traffic and above all the vitality and the diversity of its population expressed in a myriad of different tongues and accents, indeed in certain parts he heard Russian being spoken as the speakers' first language and he couldn't help listening to their complaints and their bartering. He also heard another familiar language and he noted with interest how his mother, like him, monitored the conversations, visibly smiling and silently moving her lips as if she was joining in the conversation.

Time flew by. Never had he enjoyed himself so much. One morning, as the heat and humidity of early summer was slowly becoming potentially oppressive, his parents suggested that they enjoy the sunshine and walk from their hotel to Central Park which they shortly reached and then they wandered aimlessly around until nearly exhausted they sat down on a park bench next to a man and women conversing in Yiddish.

It was at this moment that his mother engaged them in conversation and after a time introduced them to her son, explaining that he was unable to speak Yiddish fluently as intentionally they had concentrated on teaching him English whilst living in Moscow which they had left the previous year. Such were their mutual interests that they exchanged not only their names but also their addresses -Jack and Myra (Soble)- Mandel observed, as they left ,that the woman took his father`s copy of the morning paper which he had hoped shortly to briefly read but especially to enjoy the cartoons. He mentioned his observation during their walk back and was most surprised at his mother`s very sharp response that he must be mistaken.

The incident was promptly forgotten as they departed for Chicago and after a few days vacation and rest they concluded the last part of their epic journey deep into the heartland of the United States, passing many seemingly isolated railway stations, finally reaching Lincoln, Nebraska on Thursday July fourth, nineteen thirty-five, Independence Day.

Accommodation had already been arranged and the taxi driver had great pleasure, even though he had not been requested, to give a running commentary and description of the city and its many outstanding buildings including the fact that a major sporting event was currently taking place in the University`s stadium.

SIX

There then began, for the growing boy, perhaps the happiest period in his life, when the embers of intellectual discovery and erudition, first ignited by his English teacher in Southwold, were recognised and promoted by his new English teacher, Mr. Barnes. At the same time he was also to make a discovery and begin a lifelong obsession with the cinema.

The family's accommodation was, in size, even larger than the apartment in Moscow, but was more modern, and where he was to learn ,with pleasure, that the premises had central heating, a blessing that he was to enjoy in the bitter winter months, and his own personal shower room! It was conveniently central and close by the university campus and became, for his father's financial benefit, a magnet and a recognised location for the teaching of Russian.

For the whole family the next ten weeks were to be a period of exploration and discovery since both the university and high school did not commence their autumn terms till mid September. Late in August, his father met for the first time the professor who he only knew by a personal introduction and with whom he had been conducting a relationship by correspondence.

Like a contrived plot in a poorly crafted novel, he was on good terms with Mandel's future high school principal who it turned out was just as interested in meeting his first ever student from Moscow as was Mandel keen to begin the new semester. Joel's potential success was secured when his wife was introduced to the professor who was immediately captivated by her as Kaganovich had been nearly twenty years before though at that early stage in their friendship no mention was made of the family's association with the leadership in Moscow.

The high school had strong connections with the university and certain of the latter's facilities were sometimes available to the students including access to an unofficial and unregistered cinema club which obtained ,through one of its prominent members, whose family owned a chain of cinemas in Nebraska and the 'Dakotas', European films that would not command the support of the local communities whose primary interest was the entertainment produced in Hollywood that was seen by many, as an escape from the worries of the Depression.

The family had had little if any contact with the awful reality that was still casting its shadow over Europe and the United States. Unknowingly the only direct contact had been the demonstration that they had witnessed in Paris which they had wrongly interpreted as a march in support of the Soviet Union when in reality it had been a procession to awaken the people of Paris to the plight of the unemployed. Their visits to London, New York and briefly to Chicago had been to areas shielded from the worst blasts of the storm that had begun in the autumn of nineteen twenty- nine and the collapse of the New York stock market on October the twenty-ninth.   Coverage in

Pravda and *Izvestia* had been reporting events in the United States, Great Britain and especially Germany, focusing on the desperate plight of the workers, but both Joel and his partner knew that not only was the press and radio state controlled in the Soviet Union but they were biased and did not permit an open forum for discussion or argument.

It was only when the university and the local schools commenced their new terms that the tragic damage that had been caused to peoples` lives became apparent.

The teenager immersed himself in his new environment but was not swept along with the herd in their hysterical obsession with their high school football team and basketball squad, both of whom were even revered by the principal and teaching staff. His English teacher, Mr. Barnes, had been forewarned about his new student and an association began which was to last nearly three years. The embers that had glowed in Southwold were fanned and burst out in Lincoln, Nebraska.

Towards the end of his first year at high school, in the early summer of nineteen thirty-six, he was informed by a fellow high school student of the existence of an unofficial film club at the university which welcomed interested high school students and that shortly they were to show a silent Russian epic that he might wish to view, and two days later, together with some forty enthusiasts he sat down to watch the titanic epic, The Battleship Potemkin. One of the university students was translating the sub titles but became irritated when Mandel began to laugh at the many errors and mistranslations and in response to the challenge...

"You then try to do a better job,"

he suggested that the film be rewound and that he correctly translate from the beginning.

At the end the audience stood and applauded, rushing up to the young man to congratulate him for the excellence of his work. His place was assured and his reputation confirmed.

Before his return to Europe in the summer of nineteen thirty-eight the association would meet another twelve times showing works including Robert Flahery`s Nanook of the North, London Film`s The Man Who Could Work Miracles and then their vision of the future, Things To Come ,based on the novel by H.G. Wells, the score by Arthur Bliss being specially enjoyed by him and finally towering above all of the

335

other works Leni Riefenstahl`s superb, but fatally flawed (and sycophantic homage to her mentor Adolf Hitler), Triumph of the Will.

In the autumn of nineteen thirty-seven he was called into the principal`s office, to be received by his English teacher, Mr. Barnes and surprisingly his father, to be informed that they were considering his future. The principal was most helpful reminding everyone present that he had excellent connections on the 'West Coast' and was prepared to recommend him for places at Stanford, if he wanted to become a Cardinal, or the University of Southern California (and become a Trojan) or still in Los Angeles, the University of California (and become a Bruin) and finally he believed each college would grant him a generous financial sponsorship . Rather confusingly, and neither father nor son understood either the meaning or relevance, the Principal added with a flush of pride that he personally knew the father of Earle Meadows, one half of the 'Heavenly Twins' from 'U.S.C,' and it was unfortunate that he was not more sports orientated.

Had he decided to accept his principal`s suggestions and offer or even tried to obtain a place at one of the prestigious universities on the 'East Coast' instead of making what was perhaps a wiser choice, then the lives of the whole family would not have been so tumultuously changed.

The family had deliberately embraced the American way of life and its traditions, indeed they had informally agreed to apply for American citizenship but since ...

"Procrastination is the thief of time",

so their application was delayed.

SEVEN

Their apparent interest in Soviet politics was restricted to information published in the morning Lincoln Daily Star, whose main focus on events in Europe centred on the developing and increasingly vicious Civil War in Spain, Hitler`s continuing and increasing militarism and the consequences of his anti–Semitic policies together with perfunctory and scant coverage of a number of trials in Moscow where former members of the government and in many cases founders of the revolution were on trial for treason and surprisingly in many cases had admitted their guilt.

Mandel announced over dinner some three weeks later that he would prefer, subject to his parents' approval and acceptance, if possible to go to Cambridge University, in England, as he was attracted to its outstanding academic record and reputation and it was that one decision that would dramatically influence the future of the family. His high school principal was surprised at the decision but believed it would be an accolade in the school's record if one of its alumni studied at such a prestigious centre. There then followed a tortuous and lengthy chain of correspondence involving the high school, the university and his former school in Southwold and Mr. Riddle acting on behalf of his headmaster who coordinated the enquiry and application.

One day, whilst their son was at high school, his mother received a telephone call (Joel was giving a Russian lesson) to hear a man announcing his status as an officer of the Federal Bureau of Investigation who wished to interview them about certain specific matters arising, following receipt of information, and wished as a matter of urgency to clarify the facts.

It was early February nineteen thirty-eight and the height of winter. The appointment had been mutually made seven days from the initial telephone call and Joel and Leah agreed that the matter could not be critical if the meeting had been delayed for a week, however the very fact of the visit and above all the unknown reasons weighed on their minds and was noted by their son who seemed satisfied with their comments.

Two men arrived promptly on time, initially offering their badges as identity and then absolutely insisting on wiping their shoes before entering the apartment. The senior of the two was in his late twenties and well dressed, whilst the other, in his early forties, was wearing a crumpled suit and a cheap pair of glasses with thick lenses.

They jointly accepted the offer of coffee and the younger man explained that the Bureau had been alerted by their associates in London to their son's application for a place at Cambridge, which in itself was not a crime, and from his point of view was very commendable since he had finished his own education at high school level, but because the British authorities could not trace from their records exactly what documentation or passports had been produced on their arrival and departure to and from the United Kingdom;and that likewise no evidence concerning the documentation could be obtained about the family's entry into the United States through New York.

Very simply all they required was sight of their three passports, or if they had been deposited with the bank, for safe keeping, permission to check the documents.   Joel explained that they had been given a special document procured by a close relative, which they had used on their journey, adding that they had avoided Germany because of the political situation and because they were Jewish .

At that point the second man asked if he could see the document but Leah interrupted him and commented that:

"The document was in Cyrillic with a French translation however she or her partner would be more than pleased to translate the form if they did not understand Russian. "

When in fluent and impeccable Russian he responded that:

"It would be his professional duty to read the document and his personal pleasure to conduct a conversation with them in Russian, however his associate could only speak English and he would insist on being an active party to their discussion."

Leah took the opportunity not only to leave the room and gather her thoughts, since she had been unexpectedly surprised by the announcement, but also to take out the document from its secure hiding place.

It was contained in a plain and unmarked sealskin folder, the very appearance and construction marked itself out as of the finest quality.

The man took off his glasses, put them down and carefully, almost reverentially, took out the document which he unfolded and then raised to the electric light, observing first a water mark and then an embossed stamp.

Whether it was his poor eyesight or his professional scrutiny, his eyes were only inches from the document which he intimately examined, occasionally uttering incoherent sounds of amazement as if his continued investigation raised further and additional gems of discovery. He replaced his glasses, looked again at the document, which he had partially refolded, clearly spent some moments considering the situation and then asked Joel :

"If he had been present when the document had been signed (and then, if as an afterthought), if the document was a forgery?"

Joel sat silently, unable to formulate an answer which allowed Leah confidently to look at the younger man and assuredly state that:

"Joel did state earlier that the document had been delivered to them."

There was, for a few moments, what is sometimes called a pregnant silence, when the older man asked in the most naive way, without malice:

"If they knew any of the three signatures?"

Joel, in hindsight, rather foolishly, answered immediately and briefly:

"Yes, of course."

The young man rose, thanked them for their hospitality and the honesty of their answers, signalled to his associate and then asked if:

"He could return the following day with his associate and possibly his superior, who he felt certain had never seen such a document and Stalin's signature."

It was not until the two men had departed that they suddenly realised that at no time had the scrutineer mentioned the identity of any of the three signatures.

That evening no mention was made to their son of the afternoon's events though he noted and commented that they both seemed' on edge' to which they responded that:

"They were waiting for the response to his application for a place at Cambridge and irrespective of the reply they were very proud of him."

EIGHT

The following morning Leah received a most profuse and apologetic telephone call from the younger F.B.I. officer, explaining that they should not be concerned or worried but the matter had been reported to his superiors and in consequence a senior officer had been delegated to resolve the situation and would shortly arrive from Washington to meet them.

For Joel and Leah time dragged slowly as they awaited the telephone call that would herald the resolution of their worries and the week's hiatus seemed to them to last a month in duration.

When the two original officers returned they were accompanied by a third man whose very appearance and personality marked him out from the two officers, indeed their very relationship was both deferential and courteous as if his status in the hierarchy was some levels above them. After the three men left and the couple had digested the immensity of the situation they concurred that the new man was clearly and without doubt a person of supreme influence and power. In his thirties, and they judged nearly a decade younger than them, by the very manner in which he carried himself, he projected an image of breeding, education and erudition .

Undoubtedly he had been born and raised in an environment and life style of wealth and influence, he was immaculately dressed, conservative and elegant, well groomed (as she handed to him a cup of coffee she had noticed his finely manicured nails), his hair very recently cut, for some peculiar reason she sensed that this was a regular procedure and habit, and finally whilst it was not in her nature to observe such things he must have been shaved earlier that day, as distinct from having shaved himself and there was a subtle and discreet hint of rose water applied to his skin. Towering above his appearance was his strong, assured, courteous and diplomatic approach.

There was not even the hint or an undertone of menace for:

"There was a problem that like any other difficulty could be readily resolved."

The difficulty referred to their statehood and nationality. They did not possess any passports (they were confused how she originally entered Russia without such a document), though she might be able to claim British nationality because of her birth, which undoubtedly could be confirmed in London, but as regards her partner and son that might be more problematical .

He had been informed that under International law they were possibly stateless, however these were mere technicalities and in any case unimportant and superfluous, as was the probability that on their entry into the United States it had been granted for tourism purposes and not for the purpose of teaching or *de facto* for their son`s education.

She then remembered, verbatim, his surprise announcement and statement as if there was some secret organisation that controlled events and manipulated society:

"I can resolve these technicalities especially as I am pleased to inform you that your son has been accepted at Magdalene College, Cambridge, and that his high school principal should receive the formal offer within a few days. The document signed by the First Secretary, Stalin, will permit you all to exit from the United States and enter into the United Kingdom but no more. To resolve the matter I am able to grant you all immediate United States citizenship or if you wish, assistance obtaining citizenship of the United Kingdom though you would have to travel via Washington to complete the legal formalities, or you may make your own arrangements especially if your hearts and principles demand that you confirm your Soviet citizenship."

They had a week to consider their options by which time Mandel would be formally notified of the college`s offer. The most senior of the three men could only be contacted in New York where they could meet en route to Europe if they decided on American citizenship or even in Washington at the British embassy.

Two days after the meeting , an excited high school student was called to the principal`s office and given the news, therefore promptly ending his parents` ordeal though it was decided not to reveal the fact of their two meetings and above all, prior knowledge of his acceptance.

They diplomatically raised the family`s future and the resolution of their nationalities which his father claimed had been mentioned, in passing, some months before by the university`s Professor of Law.

The whole subject weighed heavily on the three, the deadline coinciding with the imminent end of term at the high school and his father terminating his Russian lessons to the dismay of his students and those students about to start the following semester. Then, suddenly, in a burst of activity and decision, their son announced that he wished to take British citizenship, his father, American citizenship leaving Leah alone and undecided; finally as if as an anticlimax and to dispose of the problem, she confirmed with little enthusiasm, that she would confirm her citizenship of the United Kingdom.

It was agreed, for convenience, that the procedures all be arranged in Washington, preceded by the necessary visit to a photographer for the required passport photographs to be taken.

Thus ended for the family a stay of just under three years in Nebraska and for Mandel, the foundations of his future life. The rail journey to Washington passed without any excitement or incident other than a collective agreement that a most pleasant and happy period in the life of the family had ended .

Events then moved with urgency and speed. They received preferential attention whilst in the British embassy, never wondering how much influence had been applied or if there was to be a *'quid pro quo'* and then transferred to an innocuous and unassuming government building where again their reception and attention were dealt with courteously and quickly. The man who had orchestrated the documentation discreetly stood in the background, unobserved by Mandel, and only made himself public after the young man`s departure as Mandel had decided unilaterally to visit the site of the Capitol building, leaving his parents who embarked on a celebratory lunch hosted by their benefactor.

He had never formally introduced himself until they entered the restaurant of the private members' club that he had recommended. It was apparently frequented by members of the government and politicians, not solely because of its reputation for outstanding cuisine but because it was discreet and was able to keep out the rapacious press, and in Mr. Lennox`s own words:

"Their running mates, the radio reporters, at arms' length."

Mr. Lennox was able to conduct a conversation which was friendly and above all interesting, without actually saying or committing himself to any facts or ideas that might identify and expose his own personal opinions and views, indeed in truth they were unaware that he was slowly and inexorably, with great finesse, manoeuvering the direction of the dialogue to the matter that had been his purpose all along .

The menu was limited and their choices, recommended by him, superb. For the two men, prime rib of beef and for her, wild duck enhanced by a sauce of cherries and brandy. The service was as good as they had received on their journey from Moscow and better than the functions they had organised for Joel`s cousin Lazar Kaganovich and it was on the mention of one of the Politburo`s members that the conversation changed direction.

The conversation had previously meandered and wandered from trivia to irrelevancies until the subject of Lazar Kaganovich was mentioned . In fact the catalyst had been Joel`s comparison between the restaurant`s excellent service and the superb service in the private carriage arranged by his cousin, Lazar. From then on the discussion was in realms and matters that they could not have previously anticipated.

He was then more forthcoming and informative than his partner, drawing on their personal reminiscences of the political leadership in

Moscow, and drew unrestrained laughter from their host when the incident of Mandel pisching on Leon Trotsky was mentioned (she intervened to explain the meaning of the Yiddish word which he had already deduced). His attention concentrated on the personalities that they knew including Zinoviev, Bukharin and Yagoda, Joel remembering to comment on the fact that he had briefly read that Yagoda had been replaced by Yezhov, who he caricatured as the 'dwarf' and assessed as more ruthless than his predecessor who, he thought, had been dismissed by the' Man of Steel 'for his inability to resolve, to Stalin`s satisfaction, blame for the assassination of Kirov though they knew the real truth.

This observation allowed Mr. Lennox to broach the subject, which was the real purpose of his original approach to the family, and what followed was a convincing and persuasive request that was cogent and both morally ethical and honourable.

"I wondered, (he said inquisitively) if you could help me and my associates?"

He continued, testing the water and their reactions, daring every moment to expand on his requirements and imposing on their good nature and presumably on their gratitude.

"As you must realise I have certain connections with the Administration and with a number of leading figures in major corporations including General Motors and I.B.M. (he briefly paused); F D R and a body of his cabinet, despite the fundamental and vast gulf between Capitalism and Communism, and because they genuinely wish to develop a better understanding between the two nations ,have asked and entrusted me to seek ways of building an association independent of normal diplomatic channels.

The government believes that the worst of the terrible Depression has past and has noted with a little envy, the success of Stalin`s five year plans. Certain major corporations would be interested in creating partnerships, offering their technical skills and commercial expertise with State run organisations in exchange for raw materials and access to their markets.

Furthermore the government believes that the biggest barrier between the two nations is a lack of insight into the way the leadership`s policies are conceived and above all their attitude to the 'outside world'.

I believe that you are uniquely placed to help both nations draw closer together in friendship and harmony.

It is absolutely essential that you make clear to your friends in Moscow that I am acting in a personal capacity and *NOT* as a representative of the Administration and that any information that you are able to pass on or suggestions about future cooperation reflect my ideas and not the government's intended policy. I am, of course, not interested in trivia or gossip, though such tittle tattle is, to a limited point, interesting, but to understand the motives and intentions of the Politburo.

You would undoubtedly incur travelling costs and expenses and I would not wish you to defer or postpone any journeys to the Soviet Union for lack of funds and therefore, if you agree to be an intermediary, I could arrange for payment of four hundred and fifty U.S. Dollars each month to be paid to you and I would insist that again such payments were disclosed because it is my intention that our association be seen as an act of friendship between American Industry and their Soviet counterparts.

I would ask that before you give an answer you jointly consider the task that I wish you to undertake, for by virtue of your unofficial status and the discreet nature of your work, both the United States Government and the Soviet authorities could at any time deny knowledge of the whole matter and (chillingly)treat you as an enemy of the state despite the fact that you are only acting as messengers and would never be expected to carry out any clandestine acts. However, having warned you, I believe that provided you act in good faith then you would be contributing not only to an improvement in relations between the two countries but it would directly help the living standards of both nations."

There was a brief silence as the magnitude of the request began to dawn on them. Joel responded, holding out his hand and fingers to touch Leah's extended arm and the palm of her hand as if to reassure her.

"I never contemplated that such a demand or request would be imposed on us and any decision would have to be jointly agreed between us; perhaps you would allow us a few minutes of privacy on the terrace outside, which appears now empty of diners. We will speak quietly in Russian and return shortly. "

Shortly became twenty minutes or so; later Mr.Lennox, who had been most patient, graciously accepted their apologies. The reply was inconclusive and naive, indeed his initial reaction was that they were wavering.

"We thank you for your offer and request for us to serve our new homeland but we require some little more time to consider the situation since we were hoping to move to Paris until the summer of nineteen forty-one when our son would have finished at university after which we would settle permanently in the United States. The money (he quizzically asked and was about to say that it was such a large amount) and our duties, we wouldn't be spies?"

Mr. Lennox looked at them both, smiled as if he was talking to his own children and with a tone of integrity reminded them that:

"It was important to tell their friends in the Soviet Union of all the events that preceded his approach and above all his recommendation that they disclose everything that he had told them."

His assurance appeared to resolve their concerns and doubts and it was agreed that they would return later that day with a definitive and final answer.

At six o`clock that summer`s evening they arrived by taxi to learn that their host had been unfortunately delayed but that they should enjoy the pleasant weather and have a cocktail on the terrace. They rather enjoyed the bar tender`s suggestion and were imbibing their second drink when their host entered followed by a man of clear Semitic origins who shook Mr. Lennox`s hand and left his company. Their answer was brief, succinct and affirmative. In summary they would be proud to help their new homeland.

Since they would be based in Paris, the journey to and from the Soviet Union (by-passing Germany) could easily be accomplished and he would make arrangements the following morning to have paid into their account the agreed monthly stipend together with, payable quarterly an additional amount of six hundred U.S. Dollars to cover their travelling and hotel costs. Finally he confirmed that in future they should contact him via the Paris office of a leading international firm of travel agents (or if urgent, through any branch of the firm) marking their correspondence not only for his personal attention but as deputy head of international currency facilities. Handshakes confirmed the arrangement and ended the brief meeting.

NINE

It was their final night in New York and though they did not know, for it is impossible to peer into the future, it would also be the last night that Joel and Leah would ever spend in the United States. They had previously agreed not to, indeed ever, disclose to their son the task that had been entrusted to them and in consequence they were also unable to inform him of the origin of their additional income. They would enjoy the transatlantic voyage together as a family, then a few days in London when Mandel would travel to Southwold and meet Mr. Riddle who had kindly agreed to take him in his nineteen twenty- nine Bentley (his pride and joy) to Cambridge, like a pilgrim, visit his old college and at the same time assist him settle in at Magdalene college. His parents would continue on to Paris where Joel was to do research for a new academic work drawing on the historical experiences of members of the expatriate Russian aristocracy now domiciled in France.

For some years Joel, and with the help of Leah, had derived great pleasure, enjoyment and intellectual satisfaction entering the challenge of crossword puzzles, in fact he had historically found and still continued to find that they were a great help in the expansion of his vocabulary and his general knowledge.

He had found the *New York Herald Tribune* both informative and its daily cross-word enjoyable, but he was sometimes frustrated as he wrestled with the clues.

That day, Friday August twelve nineteen thirty- eight, two headlines on the front page especially caught his attention:

BERLIN TO NEW YORK IN

24 HOURS 56 MINS 12 SECS

"...the four-motored condor-type monoplane Brandenburg, arrived at Floyd Bennett Field" (and)

"... which was kept secret until the flight was more than half over."

And then, before reading the whole article his attention was distracted by the headline in the first column:

"3000 BRITISH FIGHT ARABS

IN MAJOR BATTLE IN PALESTINE"

He read on and although he was not a Zionist he feared for the future both for the Jews and their Arab brothers. Then on page six was a further article which he could only interpret as heralding yet another nail in the coffin of the Republican cause in Spain...

"REBELS POUND WAY TO

SPANISH MERCURY MINES"

"... reach last loyalist guard for rich deposits, government thrusts relieve pressure on Valencia"

He thought silently to himself that perhaps the work that Lennox had entrusted to them might somehow help in the cause of peace and understanding.

They decided to go to a movie and on page eight was a large enticing advert for...

IRVING BERLIN`S

ALEXANDER`S RAGTIME BAND

starring Tyrone Power, Alice Faye and Don Ameche, playing at the Roxy on 7th Avenue and 50th. At a total cost of 75 cents an exceptional bargain for the three of them but Mandel was not enthusiastic and then noted an advert for the Cameo on 42nd Street...

THE DEFENSE OF VOLOCHAYEVSKY

the rout of the Japanese from Soviet Siberia 1918-1921.

It was hurriedly agreed that they would go their separate ways but meet up afterwards for a final celebratory dinner. Leah had to make an urgent call to confirm the booking for the following day and Joel sat down to finish the puzzle.

Twenty five across. Female character in Hawthorne's 'The Marble Faun' - four letters.

He could not answer the question and resolved to buy the paper the following morning to satisfy his frustration and curiosity [incidentally the answer is Sans-author].

The film was outstanding and most entertaining though some twenty minutes before the end Leah had to go outside and accidentally took the newspaper with her. On her return she furtively passed the paper to a lone man sitting at the end of row thirteen, by the aisle. It was the man that they had met in Central Park three years before. Jack Soble read a note that she had quickly penned and which he would pass on to their joint masters...

"The angler has caught a big fish."

Joel was, and would never be aware of his partner's perfidiousness and true loyalty and in the haste and excitement leaving the hotel to travel to the docks forgot to purchase the *Herald Tribune* and resolve his frustration.

Within twenty four hours the cryptic message had been enciphered by use of a 'one time' pad and the encoded message sent with others by cable to Moscow. The Venona Project had not yet begun and the encrypted message would never be subject to the cryptanalysts' scrutiny, but even if they had perused the document and even if they had magically unbuttoned its secret they would have learned nothing for 'Angler' would be based in France and the only two messages that she would send would be to an American intelligence officer, 'in clear'.

TEN

The family would be together only one further, final time the following August when Joel and Leah briefly returned from Paris to London to meet their son and be confronted by his desperate pleas and request for them to stay in England because of the ominous approach of an inevitable war and the recent announcement of the so called Ribbentrop-Molotov Pact that shocked Europe and the United States and which had united two apparently implacable foes. It was at that final meeting that his parents bequeathed to their son information that would ultimately save his life.

His father confided in the most discreet terms and tone that:

"If he was in dire difficulties he should contact a Mr. Lennox , a friend that they had made in Paris, and if he was in the Soviet Union, his father's cousin, Lazar Kaganovich and he was provided with a special telephone number in Moscow. With great solemnity his mother confirmed that whilst Lazar still possessed a sense of humour, absolutely no reference, even indirectly, should be made to Leon Trotsky, even to that 'special incident'.

Since they were last together, his parents had twice secretly been to Moscow, secretly because many of the people that they mixed with in Paris were *émigrés* who had fled after the Revolution and were helping his father in his research for a new academic work and might misinterpret the reasons for their visits. Indeed they had found the political temperature cooler as the worst excesses of 'The Terror' appeared on the wane and the nation's prime motivation was to meet and even exceed the targets of the latest five year plan.

However all those events were to be in the immediate future and for their son, the only subject that concerned him and on which he focused, was his imminent journey to Southwold and then shortly afterwards his journey across East Anglia to Cambridge and his new life.

Cambridge in late August was besieged by tourists and day trippers and the colleges were defended like medieval castles. Michael Riddle went to his old college and was fortunately recognised by one ancient servant who granted them sanctuary from the invading hordes.

" It would be virtually impossible for his young friend to gain access to his new college .as he knew that the staff were themselves on vacation and that the list of the new students and the allocation of their accommodation had not yet been circulated."

It was suggested that he seek temporary accommodation somewhere in Thompsons Lane until the college was open.

For the first three days he would make the short journey along Thompsons Lane and then turn right into Bridge Street passing Matthews the grocers, then Bacons the tobacconists and finally the bicycle shop before crossing over the bridge into Magdalene Street and into the college grounds but not the still deserted college buildings.

On the fourth day his efforts were rewarded when his hopeful, plaintive knocking was answered by a helpful porter who confirmed that he would contact a 'Bedder' and would arrange, in view of his enthusiasm, to give him a room whenever it was required. He knew that Ivor Richards, his future English teacher was abroad, either in China or more likely in the United States but he had a long standing arrangement with Tommy Henn, a Fellow at St. Catherines who could help and would look after his friend`s students. Conveniently Mr. Henn would be at his own college the following morning and directions were given to Queens Lane where the college was situated.

Mr. Henn was fascinated by the young man`s experiences in Nebraska and deeply interested in his earlier life in Moscow but would have been absolutely astounded if the young man had been more forthcoming about his family`s connection with the political hierarchy. The future undergraduate was disappointed to learn that French was the main and virtually only modern language taught at Magdalene but Tommy Henn would urgently contact a Fellow who could help.

It was not the first time that he had been inside an English pub but the room in which he sat awaiting the associate of Tommy Henn was depressingly dark and could have been a medieval dungeon had it not been scantily illuminated by a narrow beam of light entering via the space above the curtains that covered the windows. The pint of ginger beer sat on the table awaiting his pleasure, which suddenly shuddered and the mug lost part of its contents when the table lurched away from him as an old man manoeuvred the table to find a space.

He confronted the young man and asked in Russian if he was the potential student and receiving a positive response began a conversation in Russian which was to last until the man, outshone by Mandel, perhaps in frustration and in a desire to illuminate his nemesis drew the curtains to allow the light to clearly expose him.

"My young sir, it is I who should be the pupil and you the tutor. I look forward to meeting you again in order to expand and improve my understanding and command of this wonderful language. Use your three years to expand your horizons. May I suggest that you speak to Tommy and Ivor with a view to increasing your knowledge and that you consider, in addition to studying English, that you take History. Ivor is due back next Monday and I feel confident that once the two of you meet that he will be as interested in your potential and future as much as I was impressed by your natural command of your mother tongue."

Soon he was established in his room in the college and was meeting his fellow undergraduates, who would be his contemporaries for the next three years. Sometimes first and initial impressions are the most accurate and when he received his degree and looked back he knew,

350

without doubt, that his assessment three years before was accurate and correct. Overwhelmingly they all came from London and the South East of England, had been educated at some of the most famous public schools and by upbringing assumed their place was in the highest levels of society. Indeed he found it difficult to accept the structured organisation of the college, a situation that his associates appeared to regard as the natural order, as their rooms were maintained by'Bedders', their requirements by the 'Porters' and very importantly their dining requirements by the 'Butlers'. It was, as if, the pre revolutionary life of the aristocracy had survived in this isolated backwater .

He was, by his own admission, not gregarious, though he was not a solitary and lonely individual in a sea of young men slowly evolving into manhood. His own analysis was that simply not only by upbringing but by his own unique interests and outlook on life, he had little in common with his fellows.

ELEVEN

The formidable, extensively well travelled and above all erudite Ivor Richards sat facing him (the undergraduate realised that his tutor had spent so much time travelling that he had profitably used the periods for study and reading). As they talked he also realised that the description garrulous should have been incorporated in his assessment but the two were instantaneously drawn to one another, the senior of the two had never been to the Mid West and was intrigued by all aspects of the diverse American ways of life and had been forewarned by his dear friend Tommy Henn of the new student's origins in the Soviet Union and asked early in their first meeting a question which was as unexpected as it was simply penetrating in its enquiry.

"How and when did you manage to leave Russia?"

He could only answer in the most simplest terms possible that:

"As he was only fourteen at the time in nineteen thirty-four and without experience in these matters that he had assumed it was a natural right to travel.

" It was agreed that he could and should additionally take the course in History but not to the detriment of his studies in English which for the first year would be more intense and rigorous than probably he had anticipated. Ivor Richards had been informed of his meeting with the irascible and pugnacious Russian tutor who had great respect and admiration for the boy`s command and knowledge of his mother tongue. Ominously Ivor Richards concluded the conversation, as they shook hands, by reminding his future pupil that:

"He would have to earn *HIS* respect. "

Whilst he did involve himself in the social side of the college and university, watching inter college rugby, and during the Summer, cricket matches, his heart was never drawn to these or other sports, an attitude noted by his associates who, in attempts to draw him into the fraternity of university life, encouraged him to indulge in the obligatory drinking bouts but he found this wasteful, preferring to spend his leisure time in solitary contemplation, especially during the Spring and Summer terms, sitting by the edge of the River Cam accompanied by a good book and he had taken the advice of his tutor and found great satisfaction and pleasure in the English translation of the epic Persian work, the Ruba`iyat of Omar Khayyam. That first year saw him only twice indulge himself in his other great passion, visiting two cinemas in the town but he promised himself that when, or if his studies allowed, he would find the time to make regular visits to London.

His tutor's warning was correct, for the course was unexpectedly difficult, but rewarding. Ivor Richards was also shrewd and uncompromising, to which should be added pedantic for he immediately detected in the student`s written work a lax attention to the formal rules of grammar, syntax and sometimes punctuation, which had been tolerated not only by Mr. Riddle at Southwold but also by his teacher in the Lincoln High School as they both appeared to encourage not only his creative imagination but the fluency and style of his ideas over the ingrained imperfections of the formal grammatical construction of English. Such was the resonance between the pupil and the tutor that the pupil, in one essay, cleverly and cunningly, which in this particular instance, was the correct description ,expressed his position thus ...

"The glowing, white hot metal being shaped between the anvil and the blacksmith`s hammer or the clay being turned on the wheel by the potter into something more useful than a lump of imperfection.

Suddenly he was thrust into a new world of experiences and events that had changed the course both of national destinies and the intellectual concepts of civilisations, when he begun the course on History, drawing pleasure in the extensive list of works that he had to read, but not the practical work preparing and submitting essays; however he made a profound fundamental private observation that the theoretical utopian description of the morality and ethical values of human nature conflicted with the reality of the acts and deeds of so called civilised man.

Once, in his History tutor's rooms during a discussion, Mandel astounded not only his tutor but his fellow undergraduates, when requested to comment on the question that:

"Should civilisation be subject to ethical and moral constraints when it was necessary to wage a just war with specific reference to the current struggle in the ongoing Spanish Civil War and the medieval codes of Chivalry?"

It was January nineteen thirty-nine and by then it was tragically clear that Franco and his Nationalists were on the verge of victory and that the Socialist Republic was doomed.

He argued convincingly that:

"Any leadership, constrained by ethical and moral values, deserved to be defeated and subjugated by its victorious enemy and that Leon Trotsky, founder of the Red Army, and first Soviet Commissar for War, who his parents had closely known, had answered the tutor's question in a speech which he had given in the early nineteen twenties...

...For the attacks of enemy forces to be repelled, we must be armed with all the latest means of defence which modern war technique can produce. The use of poison gas in the last war requires us to keep even this means of warfare in reserve for the defence of our nation against the enemy."

He paused for a moment remembering *THAT* event and continued...

"My parents regularly entertained Leon Trotsky, Comrade Bukharin, who had a special place in their hearts, and other members of the Politburo including First Secretary and the Man of Steel, Comrade Stalin and I am reminded by my parents that on one occasion I pisched on Commissar Trotsky, much to everyone's good humour and apparently Lev Bronstein, after an initial explosion of anger, burst into a rare uncontrolled bout of laughter."

The room fell silent, the four undergraduates and the tutor apparently looked at the orator both in amazement at the power, if not the immorality of his argument and the surprising announcement of his family's connections in the Soviet Union. His tutor ended the discussion with a question which remained unanswered:

"If we have to fight Herr Hitler and his gang of thugs will we be bound by the laws of Chivalry and have one arm tied behind our backs?"

TWELVE

The Lent (Spring) and Easter (Summer) terms were a period of intensive study, interspersed by the enjoyment of literature in the tranquillity of the University grounds, but he was concerned for his parents' security, regularly writing to them in the ninth Arrondisement of Paris where they lived, warning them, in Churchill's words of ...

"The gathering storm",

and suggesting that they return to what he called...

"This island fortress".

Replies were both brief and intermittent and it was only in the middle of August that they arrived in Cambridge, only preceded by a telephone call the previous day. He suggested that war was imminent and that they would be safer in England but they were adamant and confident that even if war came, France was prepared and could rely upon the impregnable Maginot Line behind which they could assemble a vast army.

"In any event we have made Paris our home and we have certain responsibilities".

They had secretly been to Moscow on two occasions and had met Lazar Kaganovich. Secretly, because they had many new friends and academic associates in France and they might misconstrue their visits. Then, as if it was a prescient gift, they informed him of a connection with a Mr. Lennox (in the most vaguest terms) and suggested that if he was in the most gravest of difficulties how to contact him, along with a telephone number in Moscow to speak directly to 'Uncle'Lazar. They had grown apart, or he was maturing into someone that they were beginning not to recognise or understand or alternatively they were more interested in their new lives and also were blind to the now inevitable conflagration and likely violent eruption of hostilities.

He was in his room at eleven o`clock on the first Sunday in September and for the first time since he was a child he could not suppress a brief gentle flow of tears as he tried to peer into the impenetrable fog of an unknown future.

Nearly three weeks later a humble porter brought him a summons to appear before Tommy Henn and Ivor Richards who had just returned from his most recent trip to America. They could see the concern and worry etched on his Semitic features but surprised him with both an unexpected and to the three of them, a priceless gift.

Ivor Richards handed to him a book which was no longer in immaculate or pristine condition; no doubt he had used the opportunity to read and, in hindsight digest, the moral message of the work. The surprised student opened the book, noted the title and author and expressed his great pleasure and excited anticipation. Then he noted the familiar handwriting of his tutor...

"In anticipation of your twenty first birthday, may you have many years of happy days and everything you wish your dear self."

It was signed by Ivor and he thought immediately that the words, but not the sentiment, were far too personal and emotional. Then he noticed on the opposite page beneath the title...

The Grapes of Wrath by John Steinbeck, a further annotation in black ink, broad, masculine and confident:

"Good luck Mandel"-signed by the author and dated some three weeks earlier.

The two older men detected tears in the young man`s eyes. For them it was reward and appreciation enough.

War!

His second year at college can be historically described as from the rape of Poland to the miracle of Dunkirk.

Slowly and visibly, the image and environment of university life began not only to unravel but to peel away, like layers of an onion, as his contemporaries and other university undergraduates, many, as he found out ,who had trained in their public school Officer Cadet Forces were either persuaded or volunteered for active service. He found even greater solace in two Renaissance works that were important to his course, More's Utopia and Machiavelli's The Prince but it was the tragedy that was exposed in The Grapes of Wrath that allowed him to understand the poverty that he had seen but not understood during his time in Nebraska.

He received regular but brief letters from his parents complaining of the inconveniences of war-time existence but assured him that his father's academic work was proceeding with a sense of urgency. Strangely they confirmed that they had made a journey to Moscow, but the route, however indirect, was not mentioned or discussed. Their last letter to him was dated May the second nineteen forty and was forwarded via the United States Embassy in Paris, on the day before the Barbarian hordes began their devastating assault and offensive. The subsequent silence and uncertainty tore through him and he decided that he would submit his name to the government, offering his assistance and reminding them of his loyalty and more importantly, his ability in Russian.

The Summer break was overshadowed by the developing titanic struggle in the skies above South East England and the nation's realisation that they were alone and that invasion might be imminent, especially if their pilots could not gain mastery of the air, but it was the uncertainty of his parents' fate or whereabouts that focused his attention.

The Michaelmas (Autumn) Term which heralded his third and final year saw a dramatic reduction in the intake of new undergraduates and in consequence a wider availability of accommodation in the college but he decided to return to Thompsons Lane, indeed to the house and rooms where he had originally lodged, in his own mind 'in a different world'. Whether or not the rigour or the standards had been deliberately reduced or he was better able to cope with both courses, he found the work less arduous as if he was now descending a mountain that he had previously found beyond his capability to scale. In January nineteen forty -one shortly before the Lent Term was due to commence he received a note, via the college porter to attend Mr. Richard's rooms the following Friday and he was at a loss as to the reason and purpose.

THIRTEEN

He instantly recognised three of the four men in the room. Ivor Richards sat in his usual chair flanked by Tommy Henn and on the other side by the man who had interrogated him and conceded the young man's superior ability in Russian. But it was the fourth man who both concerned and caught his attention. He wore a pin stripe suit and next to him on an umbrella stand was a bowler hat and an umbrella, disconcertingly Mandel sensed that the man was analysing and weighing him as much as he was forming an opinion of his opposite number.

Surprisingly Tommy Henn spoke first and indeed, whilst his friend also spoke, it was Henn who was the dominant orator in the ensuing discussion. He introduced the anonymous man as a senior civil servant from the Foreign Office to whom his letter had finally reached and the contents, and offer, had been under review for some months. Tommy Henn allowed the man to introduce himself and then made an observation that surprised him and like a gust of wind unbalanced and even for a moment disorientated him.

"The University and its constituent colleges, like our old nemesis, Oxford, have unique connections with the organs of government, partially because so many of our leading politicians and administrators have been to our colleges and understand the connection between patriotic loyalty and loyalty to the student's place of study.

We would consider it inconceivable, even abhorrent, that any graduate would betray their loyalty to His Majesty the King or to the organs of government. We therefore wondered why you did not approach us before writing, since much time was wasted dealing with the application through the laborious systems of the civil service."

And then, quite unexpectedly, Tommy Henn announced that their guest had news of his parents.

The man's tone and delivery was unemotional, formal and objective, indeed he spoke in a monotone and would never have succeeded as a public orator but it was his news and the nature of his questions that caught Mandel's and the tutors' attention. He answered the questions honestly but later, on reflection, decided that there must be more beneath the veneer and superficiality of the enquiries.

"Through the Swiss Red Cross we understand that shortly after the fall of Paris and France that your parents were arrested by the Gestapo but were released following the intervention of the United States embassy in Paris and, most unusually, a direct approach by the government in Moscow to Berlin. "

He displayed no emotion, but inside of him he was both excited and exuberant to learn that his parents were still alive.

"Mr.Goldburgh, whilst we can appreciate your emotional state following my news which you should not divulge, I have been instructed to ask a number of questions and I hope that you will give me your candid, honest answers. We are aware that your parents, since they settled in Paris, made three journeys to Moscow via Turkey and it is of great interest to us to learn for what purpose; how was it financed, bearing in mind that they opened a special account in Paris and received monthly a substantial payment in U.S.Dollars and that finally and we are most concerned, that your mother, a Hebrew, is actively associating herself with the French Gendarmerie, acting in conjunction with the occupying German forces and has been denouncing Russian *emigres* to the Germans?"

He was both shocked and surprised by the questions and the information. He looked to his tutors for support and guidance.

Ivor Richards looked back at him and responded supportingly:

"We believe that you have nothing to hide and certainly nothing to be ashamed of."

His response appeared to satisfy not only his interrogator but the men who were currently responsible for his education.

"I know of only one visit to Moscow which I was informed of in a letter sent in the spring of nineteen forty and the only reason for their visits to the Soviet Union were to further my father's academic research and my parents never mentioned their finances or income. Before we left in nineteen thirty-four I know that my parents joined the Party, but in general they were apolitical preferring to listen to the observations and comments of some members of the Politburo, for as you know and I have never hidden the truth from you, my father's cousin is Lazar Kaganovich, who is closely associated with the First Secretary, a man who I have met and who knew me well when I was younger."

At which moment had he been looking directly at the civil servant from the Foreign Office he would have seen an emotion of surprise and shock which in itself was surprising since he had been previously made aware of these facts and was the very reason and the crucial purpose for the visit and meeting which ended with courteous handshakes and an unspoken and unasked question.

A week later Sir Ivone Kirkpatrick, specially delegated to evaluate the whole subject, read the civil servant's report before questioning him, deciding to speak personally to the Foreign Secretary, Anthony Eden, before submitting his recommendation, but his razor sharp intellect had made a decision which would change the young man's life and career.

The day after he completed his finals he received a note to urgently attend the rooms of Tommy Henn.

"Congratulations! No, we have not yet marked your papers, but Ivor has received a telephone call from the civil servant who came to see you, requesting your urgent presence at the Foreign Office. I have had some little experience in these matters and I can assure you that invariably for months they take no action and suddenly, without reason, the matter becomes absolutely vital."

His appointment had been confirmed for Friday, June the twentieth, nineteen forty-one at precisely two p.m. and he was to take the correspondence that was received shortly after the telephone call as an introduction to the Foreign Office. He would be provided with two travel warrants (the return journey being open for five days) and the appointment diary allowed two hours for the meeting.

A double double first! Never did he hope, or expect, such a reward for his intense labour and application over the last three years and most unusually his mind turned to his many contemporaries who had withdrawn from their courses to answer the nation's and His Majesty 's call to arms. He knew, from reports, that some had already made the ultimate sacrifice, whilst the fate of many of the others was unknown. This year, presentation of the degrees and awards was to be kept as simple as possible since the exigences of war clearly superseded the social event. And by a logical sequence his mind turned to the current fate, whereabouts and safety of his parents and he hoped that perhaps some light could be shone or even information provided at the meeting.

He took an early train from Cambridge to London, then the underground from Kings Cross to Leicester Square, arriving a good three hours early so he decided to visit the second hand book shops in Charing Cross Road en route to Trafalgar Square and his destination in Whitehall. Such was his avid interest and concentration that he did not observe the drabness of central London or the many buildings whose entrances were protected by neat piles of sandbags or as he walked closer to the cockpit of government and the administration, the armed guards and an atmosphere of defiant resolution.

The room was functional and sparse, the walls painted in camouflage green, a well used oak table that had seen better days but was still brilliantly polished, was surrounded by four identical chairs which even with his inexperienced eye he could see formed part of a set and three of the chairs were positioned opposite the single fourth seat. He had been ushered into the room and been offered the solitary chair and waited for his host who very shortly afterwards entered by himself, this time offering his hand as he laid on the table a thin manila file, acting in a more friendly manner than in their only previous encounter. He offered tea and apologised that the consequences and economies of war precluded coffee and also enquired if his guest wanted one or two sugars, a previous essential that:

"...was becoming a luxury."

He did not 'beat about the bush' and was forthcoming in his offer and reasons though this time and continuing the more friendly tone gained the young man`s confidence.

"We would like to send you to Moscow, initially to act not only as a translator, but also to help the diplomatic staff to translate, analyse and report on various documentation such as newspapers and journals.

You would not have any diplomatic status but to set your mind at rest you would be protected by diplomatic immunity and your salary would be equivalent to that of a... (he briefly stopped, perused the manila folder and apologetically continued) ,I have mislaid the note but I believe that your salary would be equivalent to that of a second secretary and would be subject to an additional local allowance. Unofficially the main purpose of your posting is to make contact with any senior members of the government and introduce them to the ambassador and to act as his personal interpreter. No one, even the ambassador, will be made aware of your connections and it is vitally important that we learn of Stalin`s intentions in view of his Pact with Nazi Germany which completely surprised us. You should be prepared to work closely with the Soviets to cement any relationships that can be created.

Mr. Goldburgh, I have been instructed to ask you a very personal question because there are people in Moscow who could use a human failing against you. You seem never to have had a girl friend. I must ask you, are you a homosexual?"

360

He was dumbfounded both by the nature of the enquiry and above all its very personal and intimate investigation.

"No, these last few years I have concentrated on my education and have had very little contact with any young ladies but being bold and seizing the nettle perhaps you could introduce me to some intelligent, sensitive and eligible companions?"

The man was about to warn him of the potential dangers that might be placed in his path but was satisfied with the response.

The future was then mapped out for him: he would be contacted in about three weeks time and sent on a one month course that was usually three months in duration, to prepare him for his posting, but in view of the priority had been 'concertinaed' because of the importance of despatching him to Moscow. His salary would commence on Monday, June the twenty third and arrangements would be made to send him to Moscow by the safest means possible which probably meant an extended journey via South Africa and then via the Suez canal, Palestine, Iraq, neutral Turkey and finally Russia. Strangely the man apologised and admitted that he had worked in the Foreign Office for nearly thirty five years and could not yet reconcile himself to call Russia by its current correct title of the Union of Soviet Socialist Republics. There was one final procedure to be fulfilled before they could shake hands and he could leave. He would have to sign The Official Secrets Act."

The physical act of signature and the procedure was brief, though he foolishly, in hindsight, did not read the document, only being warned that in view of his special status, the Foreign Secretary had personally ordered that the normally simple procedure be witnessed by two junior officials who were summonsed and sat in the vacant two seats.

The signed document was witnessed, good lucks were exchanged and he departed, satisfied and euphoric. It was only shortly afterwards that he remembered, with regret, that he had not used the opportunity to ask for any up to date news about his parents though he justified the omission by assuring himself that if there had been any news then the Foreign Office representative would have raised the subject. He threw caution to the wind and decided to stay in the Strand Palace Hotel for three nights and rekindle his love of the cinema, seeing on three consecutive afternoons films all in Leicester Square, first at the Empire, Jimmy Stewart and Hedy Lamarr in 'Come Live With Me' ,then at the Odeon, 'Nice Girl?' with Deanna Durbin and then on the last night the best of a disappointing trio, at the Warner, Michael Redgrave and Valerie Hobson in 'Atlantic Ferry'. Suffice to say one of the films had a

Donald Duck short 'Timber 'which he thoroughly enjoyed but he thought that the three films were typical wartime entertainment to raise morale.

Nearly three weeks later he received a telephone call from a Mr. Maddox who wished to meet him about a private matter. A day and time was set for the end of the week and the location was the elite Savoy Hotel. Goldburgh was most surprised by the unusual approach of a Foreign Office representative, especially one with a distinct American accent, however the man's request for his discretion seemed to be in harmony with the nature of his future work.

Shortly after he left his rooms in Cambridge to go to London, the postman delivered a plain envelope from the Foreign Office with comprehensive instructions, including, initially, the address he was to attend the following Monday to begin his work and details of his accommodation at twenty six Portobello Road, London West, which, of course had been paid for on his behalf.

FOURTEEN

"Mr. Goldburgh, I assume."

He rose from the well used, comfortable black leather chair to see in front of him an immaculately dressed man in his mid to late thirties. He had never before judged a person by their attire but his suit was both elegant and conservative and without doubt came from Saville Row. It was not in his nature to observe an individual as he was now assessing Mr. Maddox but he was extremely well groomed with finely manicured nails and must have just been shaven earlier in the day and he could fleetingly smell a pleasant and tantalisingly elusive odour that he could not identify. As the conversation and meeting progressed his opinion hardened for this was a man who was strong, confident, assured, and by breeding inherently courteous and diplomatic.

The young man had been made known to him by friends at Cambridge but he never elaborated on their identities and Goldburgh was never able to confirm the identity or identities of the parties involved. Mr. Maddox was closely connected with the United States Government and the Administration but currently was acting on behalf of two International corporations, General Motors and International Business Machines and, (and he specially noted the exclamation) thank God, he

362

was still able to visit the neutral nations of Portugal, Spain ,Switzerland and Sweden (at which moment he realised that this man might, just might, be a conduit to his parents), but the purpose of this meeting was to introduce himself and possibly explore an arrangement (he noted the phrase, but was both intrigued and confused by its implications).

"Mr. Goldburgh, may I not only congratulate you on your superb 'double first 'but also on the mark that you have left at Magdalene. I have found that honesty and good faith are far superior to subterfuge and dishonesty and can I explain that ever since your stay in Lincoln, Nebraska, when you were first drawn to my attention, I have been waiting to meet you and ask for your help, not now, or even tomorrow but in the future.

If my motives and intentions were dishonourable I would feign ignorance and await your confirmation that you had been appointed to serve the ambassador in Moscow but I thought it best to disclose my knowledge .

I am shortly travelling to Lisbon and would like you to consider, certainly not now, and whilst you have a patriotic responsibility to His Majesty and His Government, but in the future, because none of us can foretell where they will be and in what situation and whilst our loyalties will, we both hope, remain steadfast neither of us can be assured of our status."

"I have, at this time, a desperate concern for the situation and fate of my parents; my father, Joel Kaganovich holds a United States passport and my mother, Leah Goldburgh, a British document, both supplied, in my presence in Washington. It is a fact, known to friends and family, that by mutual agreement, for a reason or reasons that even I do not know ,that they never married. They were living in the ninth Arrondisement from where they travelled to the Soviet Union a number of times though since the attack by the Nazis on Russia that course of escape is now closed. I would be grateful for your help or assistance."

Mr. Maddox was, of course, also Mr. Lennox and would become, or use other names as aliases and when the circumstances necessitated the use, of at least two *nom de guerre*. He already knew the fate and of the execution of the pair in Lyons but they had served their purpose passing him two messages in the spring of nineteen thirty- nine and the autumn of nineteen forty, prepared, of course, unknown to him, with the approval of the N K V D with the sole purpose of duping their American counterparts before feeding them with false information concerning certain Communist agents at the heart of the United States

Administration, but events on June the twenty-second had irrevocably changed their plans.

He was correct about the future but not exactly in the way that events actually took place. The two messages that he received were initially ridiculed and threatened his career but were proved true and enabled him to become, if unheralded ,as powerful as a chess grand master manipulating through his pawns the policies of his own nation, their allies and foes. Indeed though not verified by documentary evidence, whilst he colluded with Reinhard Gehlen and directly negotiated with Markus Wolf it was claimed that during the Cuban crisis of nineteen sixty-two, on his instigation, the three men met and in direct consequence gave the U.S. President a strategy that allowed his Soviet opposite number to withdraw with the minimum of humiliation.

It was agreed that Mr.Maddox would try to find out the whereabouts and fate of his parents and would make contact as early as possible, but in the meantime Goldburgh was informed how contact could always be made through a leading chain of international travel agents.

Mr.Maddox was as true to his word as he wished to be. On his return to England he endeavoured to contact Goldburgh via his flat in Cambridge and Magdalene college by which time he was involved in his course and when it was completed he immediately embarked on a military transport (with the status of a senior officer) for Cape Town and then the Suez Canal not even having time to thank his former tutors in Cambridge.

The man known as Lennox, Maddox, Menzies or at least two other flights of imagination and deceit died in nineteen eighty-seven soon after which his archives were examined and certain of the records released to a select few. The first message was totally true and was in two parts, the latter absolutely incredible; the former stated that assassination teams had been authorised to kill Leon Trotsky and that (and this was why the intelligence was ridiculed) Stalin had put out tentative probes to the German government to arrange a non aggression pact in order to secure his Western borders and to destroy and occupy part of Poland as he had not forgotten the humiliation that the Poles had inflicted on the nascent Red Army in nineteen twenty.

The second message was yet again true but was fabricated with the sole intention of preparing American Intelligence to be mislead by future messages, however the arrest and execution of Joel Kaganovich and the agent Leah Goldburgh ended the operation. Soviet Intelligence was already aware that the British code breakers were breaking into the German machine code known as Enigma and that, in the higher levels of the Roosevelt Administration, there were 'fellow travellers' who had begun to supply the beleaguered Soviet Union with sensitive information.

This was of course true but the long term objective was to deflect enquiries and interest away from their sources and onto loyal Americans.

He reached the border of the Soviet Union in the spring of nineteen forty-two via Turkey and made the difficult and hazardous journey north through the Crimea, then the Ukraine to Russia and finally Moscow by train in a carriage not as luxurious as the one that he and his parents had shared when they left the Soviet Union but far superior to the ones used by the ordinary travellers who had to suffer the inconveniences and the shortages of war as the train trundled along through unending forests where once or twice were eerily illuminated at night by cascades of tracer bullets close to the horizon as the Motherland suffered the continued pain of invasion and occupation.

He was met at the station by a chauffeur driven car and a second secretary who intimated that the driver was in fact part of the embassy`s security service and, as standard procedure, there was a pistol in the glove compartment but he had never known a situation when the weapon was needed. He was very pleased to meet a' new face 'since there was only a limited diplomatic community and the claustrophobic surveillance by the authorities gradually eroded the community`s feeling of freedom.

He was introduced to the ambassador who was only aware of the new member`s linguistic qualifications and not his potential connections, or his mandate to strengthen the embassy`s association with members of the Politburo.

Work was mundane and repetitive. Entertainment sparse, though the junior members looked forward to visits to the United States embassy where the quality of the food was far superior to the embassy cuisine and above all, the regular showing of recent Hollywood productions. Goldburgh used his leisure time to explore the excellent embassy library but became bored and like his associates he looked forward to the potential, possible freedom of exploring the city and visiting the sites and locations of his childhood.

Early summer, nineteen forty-three. Muscovites and the Moscow embassies of those nations that formed the major part of the 'United Nations' were in a state of great excitement. Moscow radio had announced, that under the personal direction of Marshall Stalin, the Nazi barbarians had been defeated at Kursk and that Russian forces were sweeping westwards. For possibly the first time since the invasion of the Soviet Union the people began to again smile and enjoy the warmth of the Sun. Goldburgh received an urgent summons to the ambassador's office and advised that the following evening he was to join a diplomatic party from the embassy to a reception which Stalin was scheduled to attend along with members of the Presidium (he was not certain of its current title which might have reverted back to that of the Politburo such was the confusion and inconsistencies of the press coverage) and he wished him to be prepared for the event. The ambassador sensed his reticence and confirmed that he should wear, like the others, a lounge suit though Stalin, if he attended, would no doubt wear his customary tunic.

The British party was made up of some seven members and gravitated to the United States contingency of a similar number. Goldburgh fell into conversation with the recently installed new American ambassador, Averell Harriman who was more, through inquisitiveness than courtesy, interested in the young man's experience in Lincoln so much so that he did not find the time to enquire his status and responsibilities in the embassy.

The British ambassador, Archibald Clark Kerr, joined the pair and the junior of the three was about to give his excuses to leave the two senior members when he saw his 'uncle' enter the room along with Vyacheslav Molotov and join the First Secretary together with Lavrenti Beria and Nikita Khrushchev. This was the opportunity that he had been waiting for, though when the moment came, which was then, he felt strangely weak and doubtful of his reception. He excused himself and confidently walked across the room, which for a moment felt vast and forbidding and went up to Lazar Kaganovich, in full view of the surprised ambassadors.

Age and maturity had changed him and it was necessary for him to announce not only his identity but his relationship.

Moments later, to the shock of the two ambassadors and the visitors, Goldburgh was smothered in a dramatic embrace by the Politburo member who in his excitement subjected the young man to a stream of questions about his recent life but more importantly the whereabouts of his parents, concluding the friendly interrogation by asking if his mother was as beautiful as ever. The dialogue continued for some minutes when the First Secretary, stood up, gently puffing on his pipe, asked to be introduced to him and then surprisingly, as he embraced the now embarrassed young man, also enquired about his mother and shedding the armour of the 'Man of Steel' actually asked when he could again meet his parents and especially his mother in Moscow.

Goldburgh had never met Beria or Khrushchev and only occasionally Molotov, who were dragged from their conversations by Stalin and hastily introduced.

Lavrenti Beria asked his parents' names but did not immediately know or realise who his mother was. It was at that moment Goldburgh took the initiative to mention his responsibility to the British ambassador and finding Stalin receptive and unusually amicable, returned to the incredulous pair of ambassadors, confirmed that he had made arrangements for an immediate meeting and escorted the 'shell shocked 'British ambassador to meet the man who had until then been so elusive and ethereal .

Stalin reminded the British ambassador that Averell Harriman had been a friend to the...

"Workers and peasants in nineteen forty one when he had travelled to Moscow and negotiated the terms of a Lend–Lease agreement."

Thirty minutes later Stalin insisted on an arrangement for the two ambassadors to meet him in a more formal meeting, attended only by their closest advisors and, without fail, to the initial confusion of the two men, to bring as their joint official translator...

"The man who had pisched on the counter revolutionary and the Party's and the Peoples' enemy."

The following morning, not unexpectedly, he was called to the ambassador's office and asked to explain his behaviour and the meaning of the events that had taken place. It took some little time to give the complete background and a translation of the Yiddish but he concluded his answer with a tactful warning that even for him mention of Leon Trotsky's name or even his original name of Lev Bronstein was dangerously antagonistic and best avoided.

No documentary evidence of the ensuing meeting exists and requests by the two ambassadors for a joint group photograph were rebuffed by the First Secretary who acted as the 'Man of Steel'. Gone was the bonhomie and the friendship of two nights before; this was the leader of a nation that had been invaded and raped and was desperately fighting to oust its bitter enemy. The representatives of the 'Atlantic Alliance' were subjected to a tirade of invectives, personal insults and slurs on the manhood of their two leaders. Goldburgh struggled to keep up with the translation and later admitted in a meeting with the American ambassador, the following day, that he had toned down the vehemence of the translation and had moderated Stalin`s personal insult of the United States` President.

"A fucking cripple who probably couldn`t get an erection and who has allowed the blood of the workers to bleed on the soil of the Motherland."

Ad nauseum he had demanded that Churchill and Roosevelt open a 'Second Front' and not only relieve pressure on his valiant fighters but...

 "Commit their eloquent words of freedom and justice to the real task of destroying the nests of the Nazi rats and vipers."

The two ambassadors later concurred that Stalin was a storm that literally blew itself out, for as abruptly as he commenced the apparent hysterical tirade, he ended the verbal assault and suddenly, with great friendship, suggested that the three leaders meet by the end of the year to discuss a global strategy.

Within hours a long enciphered message (on a modified typex machine) was on route to London confirming not only the meeting and Stalin`s request for a tri party conference of the leaders of the 'United Nations' but in a postscript, which was more a limp appendage, formal confirmation, in response to a joint request by both Stalin and Beria (who the ambassador analysed as more abnoxious than his reputation), that Goldburgh be permitted to act as a liaison officer with, and based with the Soviet authorities.

Churchill personally congratulated Sir Ivone Kirkpatrick, in the presence of his Foreign Secretary, Anthony Eden, for his inspired initiative and before continuing on matters of state including ideas for a convenient venue , hoped the young man would fulfil Kirkpatrick`s hopes.

Lavrenti Beria now knew not only the identities of Goldburgh`s parents, but of his mother`s allegiance to the N K V D and finally, tragically, of their executions in Lyons after they had been tortured by Klaus Barbie and that their son was clearly unaware of their fate. He intended to use the young man for an operation that was about to begin in the Ukraine, if possible subvert him and turn him against Britain.

To mask his true task, the N K V D planners hurriedly, without considering the full consequences, devised a plan that would effectively render him incommunicado, thereby concealing his whereabouts and more importantly his real work; to this end they informed the British embassy some three months later that on entering liberated territory he had contracted dysentery and typhus which explained why he had not contacted the authorities with his reports. The British embassy, despite the many problems of war, were scrupulous in their concern for their absent translator but found that their enquiries were either ignored or rebuffed by a wall of silence and when they were able to raise the matter with members of the Politburo the reply was off hand.

Both Kaganovich and Molotov, no doubt in fear of the 'Boss' replied that:

"Allies should trust each other",

and that:

"Why are you troubled by the fate of one man when we are concerned with the fate of whole armies and the salvation and purification of our defiled soil?"

In the meantime Goldburgh was unaware of the subterfuge and bodyguard of lies that surrounded him.

FIFTEEN

This was to be the second and final time he was to meet Lavrenti Beria. The first was at the reception and the second, in the private office of the head of the N K VD.

"You have been chosen, with the knowledge and approval of your ambassador, Sir Archibald Clark Kerr, and with the tacit understanding of the United States ambassador, to jointly lead an operation to further cooperation and friendship between the 'United Nations'.

Shortly you will be sent on a mission with two English speaking assistants and it is expected that your work will take anything from twelve to eighteen months. On completion you will be allowed and assisted to return either to the British embassy or directly to London;

however you may find the joy of living in the land of your birth so strong that you may wish to make the Motherland your permanent home (he paused, giving the man an opportunity to consider prematurely the offer and suggestion before continuing with a well conceived lie).

On humanitarian grounds, I urgently instigated enquiries which have confirmed that your parents are now based in an internment camp, supervised by the Swiss Red Cross in France, close to the Swiss border but your mother is not in good health. If I was not honest I would certainly mislead you but these are the facts that we were able to verify. It seems that your mother is suffering from a stomach infection which is nonlife threatening and the Boss has been informed and wishes you luck and your mother, Leah, may I be permitted to call this loyal friend of the Soviet Union by her first name, a prompt return to health?

My assistant, who is in overall charge of your mission, will now introduce the young N K V D lady officer who by rank is your superior but for the purposes of this very important operation will be your equal. Good luck!"

He was led through a labyrinth and maze of reception and ante rooms, offices and depressingly gloomy rooms containing wooden filing cabinets, weaving past anonymous bland officials seemingly addicted to their tasks, finally ending up in a reception room not unlike the one where he had met the First Secretary less than a week before. Sitting elegantly, as if she had been trained in the almost magical world of Hollywood, especially for a glamorous Fred Astaire movie, was the young lady who was to be his associate in the still secret operation. Before she even spoke he was overwhelmed by her beauty and radiance; never before had a woman so affected him. He intensely scrutinised her and in response she smiled at him and introduced herself in faultless English though he detected a clear but very mild accent which after some time he determined to be from the 'West Coast'. They spoke for half an hour or so, rarely mentioning, conjecturing or even discussing the unknown task that lay ahead of them, switching constantly from their mother tongue to their second language but neither could determine which was the other's first and natural tongue .He was captivated and intrigued by her natural beauty, her Slav and dominant Semitic features as if the humorous request that he had made to the Foreign Office official had been answered in an unusual way. Of the future and the task ahead of them, all she knew was that they would shortly meet a man who had recently fought at the Front and that very soon afterwards they would leave, by train, to a secret destination .

SIXTEEN

The luxurious, impeccable service and surroundings had ameliorated the slow and indolent journey, and their arrival at an anonymous and unsigned destination, was greeted with regret.   For three of the travellers they had profitably used the time to introduce themselves and learn something of the other two.   The fourth member, and *de facto* leader of the group and indeed the whole operation, appeared more interested in the copious amounts of alcohol and delicacies that until now had only appeared in dreams but was readily available on demand.

The only female in the group was nineteen, named Natalia and spoke English immaculately with a slight American accent which she put down to the fact that she had lived in San Francisco for some seven years where her father had been an assistant to the Consul and they had travelled extensively, when and where permitted by the authorities. As to her father's responsibilities and actual status she was reserved in her comments since, by nature and inclination, work was not discussed, however the other two, by inference, correlated the family's unusual foreign sojourn with the daughter's membership of the Communist party and above all her rank in the N K V D.

Of the trio, the army officer had the poorest command of the English language, having learned the subject at staff college in order to follow his intended chosen career as a military attaché but the war had intervened and he had distinguished himself on the battle front. Whilst he was proficient and understood the more subtle aspects of grammar and syntax he still had a strong Russian accent which became exaggerated when he was emotional, for example when he spoke of the great tank battle of Kursk, confusing his listeners ,but he was assured and confident in his communication with others.

Surprisingly, when he controlled his emotions and concentrated on his diction he spoke, much to the enjoyment of his two companions, with a 'Western 'accent, as he admitted that his position at the staff college had given him access to Hollywood Westerns, his favourite film being 'Stagecoach' starring John Wayne .

The third member was Goldburgh, who spoke with a refined accent and intrigued and captivated his two new associates with vague memories of his upbringing in Moscow and his life in the United Kingdom and the American Mid West.

Natural caution, especially in view of the girl's status and rank, was quickly dissolved and the three not only enjoyed the others' company, but later acknowledged how each felt comfortable in the others' presence. They all had a common love of the Motherland and its' people, combined with a determination not only to rid the country of its Invader but to destroy Fascism and National Socialism. She was a dedicated Communist but paradoxically loved the United States and the American people though she could not reconcile their genuine easy going ways with their apparent hatred of communism and socialism which conveniently exposed their reticence to mention or more especially to discuss the political leadership and the First Secretary (jovially nicknamed), Uncle Joe.

They were met by two N K V D black limousines which took them to the outer perimeter of the camp at the beginning of the newly built road. Dusk had fallen and as they transferred to two functional and basic lorries they did not see a very recently erected sign which declared the nature of the camp:

'Danger! Entry forbidden. State property. Leper colony .'

Those last two words were more than enough, not only to ward off any further interest, but to answer the inquisitiveness of the local community who in the last year or so had seen much unexplained activity. The curtain of darkness also hid many clumsily and hastily constructed stone mounds and tumuli which rose on either side of the road and were illuminated by the headlights of the two lorries which trundled along towards the camp and signified the human sacrifice made during the road building.

Less than forty eight hours after their arrival, ten young men and two teenage girls arrived ,ignorant of their fate and the reason for their surprise release from military service. The two girls were housed in the N K V D block and adjacent to Natalia ,not specifically for maternal reasons but for purposes that would soon unfold, whilst the ten young men were domiciled in the main residential area in what was known as 'The Motel' but under the ever vigilant watch of the benign N K V D guards. The first meal was attended by all sixteen and was lunch and certainly surprised the twelve novices as undoubtedly it was the most gargantuan and luxurious repast that they had ever eaten, however it was after lunch when they were addressed by the camp commander that the contents of his news and the reason for their residence suddenly and dramatically shocked them and spoiled the pleasure of the meal. He read from a statement typed in Cyrillic and drafted by the N K V D in Moscow some weeks before and included in the file that the commander had been perusing that first day when alone in the railway carriage.

The following, for brevity, is not only a summary and a resume but in parts a verbatim transcription of that statement.

We can only wonder and conjecture how some of the twelve young men and women received the news and information.

It began with the usual Socialist exhortations of brotherhood and of the workers' struggle against the oppressors and the Capitalists' betrayal of the dignity of man. It continued with an announcement that the group, or the ones that completed the course ,would have in their possession the ability and power to strike a blow against the Motherland's enemies but those who did not complete the course would, without due process of law, be sent to labour camps in Siberia where, undoubtedly, only one outcome would terminate their sojourn .

The camp commander continued, without emotion, to inform them :

"That from this moment onwards they were forbidden to speak in Russian or in any regional language, including, for the three Yids (Jews), the guttural Yiddish and that they would all begin that same afternoon to speak American English. Uttering even one word in Russian would be punished and they risked the potential wrath of their fellows if they spoke deliberately in the language of their birth which was to be forgotten."

When they left the dining room, each one was photographed then informed of their new identity that had been allocated to them and their new dates of birth (which for logical reasons would be similar but not the same as the true date). Their re-education and first English lesson would then begin.

The camp commander had concluded his statement with a warning, repeating and emphasising his earlier remark, that they would be punished for speaking Russian.

No details were given as to their future once they had successfully completed the course or the penalties that were to be imposed for the error or crime speaking in their mother tongue.

It is important to remember that the N K V D were in possession of a vast haul of passports issued by many countries including the United States, most of those having been 'requisitioned' or confiscated from the 'pilgrims' who had settled in the early thirties, as well as passports 'lifted' from volunteers who had travelled to Spain to fight against Fascism in the civil war.

SEVENTEEN

Natalia and the Englishman Goldburgh were ordered to organise a session to complete the record files of the twelve trainees, the actual files being held personally by the camp commander and under lock and key at all times. Neither of the two supervisors, speaking in English, could discern or identify any factor that could have marked out any of the twelve as potential long term agents and since currently they were unable and forbidden to examine the record files, no considered opinion could be reached. She, however, was strangely drawn to one youth, barely a man but of similar age to her. He was not particularly handsome, nor was his physique athletic (two factors that were, she remembered as a teenager in California, the closer you reached the magical and surreal town of Hollywood, pre requisites for one's status and reputation). He carried himself with a quiet dignity and acted as if he was a hunted beast in the forest - ever alert and aware of his surroundings. When his old and new name was called and his new date of birth notified, she inwardly smiled as it meant that he was figuratively exactly a month older than her.

The trainees were confronted by a regime that none of them could ever have conceived and the absolute conditions that had been imposed upon them. Their introduction to English was initially chaotic, the few instructions being given in the simplest of English supported by hand signals. Shortly afterwards Natalia and Goldburgh requested, again in the most basic and simple English, supplemented once more by hand signals, that the twelve follow them into a room which was fitted with a black board and desks.

The army officer replaced Goldburgh and the two tutors spoke slowly and clearly in English when a ripple of laughter spread through the room in response to his strange accent. That first session was to teach them the numbers from one to ten, then eleven to twenty and finally in sets of ten up to one hundred .

How long the lesson lasted is unimportant, the tutors had caught the full attention of the class who enjoyed reciting the numbers by rote. That evening, before dinner, a second lesson was held but this time the blackboard was covered by twenty six symbols, some of which appeared similar or recognisable when compared to the Cyrillic alphabet. For an hour or so, again by rote, they constantly repeated the letters, sometimes dwelling on an individual letter, repeating it a number of times until it was spoken to the satisfaction of their teachers.

They then ate their first meal of the new regime, for all of them a strange new experience, creamy, rich milk poured from a jug, a luxurious white fluffy paste which they recognised, on tasting, as potatoes liberally mixed with butter together with corn, off the husk, and finally something that they all knew, chicken, but fried in a batter. During the meal Goldburgh would come up to a small group and begin reading out loud from a book, slowly and precisely, but no one understood what he said except, possibly, for two words which were occasionally repeated.

The four officials ate in the same room, at a separate table enjoying identical food, carefully speaking only in English and like an examination hall at intervals, one of the four would circulate in the room navigating three rows of tables perhaps listening for an errant illegal whisper in Russian but the trainees were at that time too frightened and also ignorant of the dire consequences if they uttered, even accidentally, a word in their banned mother tongue.

By the end of the sixth week, by a combination of rote and attention to specific individual items, they understood how the sequence of numbers was constructed and expressed, the alphabet, the days of the week, months of the year, how to tell the time and the States of the Union including the major cities of each of the States, but they were unable to communicate, even in the most infantile way. Since the three tutors were satisfied that the students had a foundation upon which the English language could now be taught, the twelve were passed to (under constant supervision) a first grade teacher in the 'rehabilitation' centre and joined the small class of five year olds much to everyone's good humour. Parallel to this, the community had two remedial teachers specially trained (and clearly targeted for their inclusion in the camp) to teach immigrants to the United States the language, and every hour, two of the group were taken out and given intensive one to one tuition.

By the end of the ninth week they were beginning to speak to each other in English but for some it was tarnished by a strong Slav accent, though Yuri (for that was the new given birth name of the young man who had caught the eye of Natalia and who still seemed to capture her waking thoughts) appeared to have totally mastered an acceptable accent though it was rootless and could not be recognised as coming from any particular region. For the group in general the pace rapidly accelerated, Goldburgh regularly read to the students who now recognised that he was reading from Romeo and Juliet and they were beginning not only to understand the dialogue but looked forward to the daily reading. Their tutors then decided they should be introduced to the wider community though one important test was to be applied that night.

The camp had no walls or barbed wire fences to imprison any of the residents though the artificial town was surrounded by dense forest only pierced by the scar of the road that had been created to connect the community to the outside world and was protected by the presence of N K V D troops whose disposition and nature was passive and friendly clearly giving the American residents and the twelve trainees the impression and the confidence that there was no malevolent intentions in their presence and the purpose of the camp which was commonly referred to as' the town' was not a bizarre facade for a prison.

It was about three or half past three in the morning, a time when the ten young men were deep in sleep (a fact well known to the inquisitors of the N K V D for the purpose of interrogation) that they were rudely roused by the urgent entreaty of voices warning of fire and for the residents to leave the building !

Overwhelmingly most rushed out to be confronted by a line of guards and two of the tutors.

The warning had been given in Russian!

For three hours the nine men stood in a line naked and to emphasise their mistake, their humiliation was forcibly witnessed by the two girls and the only man who, either by good fortune or having realised the ploy, escaped the punishment. Yuri smiled at Natalia as he watched the fate suffered by his associates but inwardly sympathised with their predicament.

Over breakfast the twelve were told the consequences of any potential error. The second time they were caught, the penalty would be six hours in the open irrespective of the season, the third ,nine hours, the fourth, twelve hours and on the fifth occasion, twenty four hours. The last three periods would also include a dowsing of cold water by hose pipe! From now on they must be prepared for tricks to make them speak or to be observed understanding Russian.

Contact with the wider community had been minimal, primarily because of the language barrier, but it was now agreed that the group be introduced to the community and each one lodged with a family (specially chosen for their regional accents and under strict instructions to report any violation, however minor, of the language embargo). Surprisingly the arrangement was dealt with on trust, no devious or sinister methods were applied, for example the use of hidden microphones. The three tutors agreed and it was endorsed by the camp commander, following suggestions from Moscow, that mistakes be punished in the presence of the rest of the group and was the best deterrent and warning.

By the end of the fifth month the group had made a dramatic leap in their communication skills and under questioning (but not in the crude sense of the worst aspects of Beria's henchmen) they begun to appear convincingly as American born nationals. There had been three cases of mistakes or lapses, two involving one member who had been part of the group caught by the original fire ruse.

He was being watched and assessed very carefully as were all the others and the three tutors had been obliged to submit, individually every week, reports on all the trainees for the commander and they concurred that there must be twelve very large, fat files in the locked cabinet.

She noticed that Yuri frequently disappeared into the forest, always in the area opposite the road entrance and returned some two hours later, but never worried the guards who were used to his frequent excursions. She made it her business to mention this fact In her reports as also she commented upon the behaviour of most of the men who seemed to have totally accepted what was to be the first stage in an unknown journey.

Integration into the community had proved most successful so much so that the twelve, on their instructors' recommendation, had been promoted to the second, then third and fourth grades and were currently based in the fifth grade where their fellow American students (mainly ten year olds) were teaching them the rules of baseball and football. Within a further two months, miraculously, despite the privations and inconveniences of war, various books (and equipment) about the history and rules of the two sports were obtained and became both unofficial and obligatory reading.

It was suggested that a baseball game be arranged between the residents and their lodgers and on the field that separated the administration block and the town, a diamond was marked out and an impromptu game organised.

Yuri joined the boisterous, enthusiastic and partisan crowd, appearing to both enjoy and involve himself in the excitement and competition of the occasion, however Natalia noticed that he furtively left the event and she saw him speak to one of the guards before walking into the forest directly opposite the road entrance. She determined to pursue him and having made her intentions clear to the same guard she entered the forbidding and immense forest of pine and birch trees. Her task was hopeless as her quarry was so far ahead of her that she lost his trail, aimlessly wandering in increasingly random directions foolishly believing that she would stumble across him. She realised that she was hopelessly lost and sat at the base of a full grown birch tree and inwardly began to cry. She had no pistol to fire one shot which she felt certain would warn and draw attention to her position and she had no compass to guide her. The sun was setting lower in the sky, indeed the density and height of the trees hid the sun from her but she remembered that she had warned the guard of her intentions.

How long she slept for she did not know but it was still light and not cold. Suddenly she felt the gentle, reassuring pressure of a man`s hand on her shoulder and a kind, concerned voice in English enquired if:

"All was well and if you were lost?"

She turned round and saw the strong confident face of Yuri smiling benignly. For a moment, a minute, the gulf between teacher and pupil, N K V D officer and civilian disappeared. She was a woman and he the gallant protector of her feminine weakness. When she answered that she was able to return unaided to the camp they both knew instinctively that her answer was untrue.

In order to bolster her confidence he then pointed in a specific direction, mentioning that:

"You then know that we are only about a hundred and fifty metres from the edge of the forest and the outer limit of the town."

She then looked at him in a way that not only betrayed her vulnerability, her inability to extricate herself from her predicament but something very personal and emotional. Then suddenly, simultaneously, even telepathically, they both announced with only thought and consideration for the other that:

"We had better not return from the forest together as the commander might incorrectly suspect something. "

At that moment any inhibitions that separated the two evaporated and they both burst out in a contagious bout of laughter. He gently took her hand, felt the softness of her arm as she deliberately walked close to him because inside of her she felt an emotion, a sensation that she had never previously experienced and it was growing ever larger and more powerful and she realised that she could not challenge its inevitability which she knew would overwhelm her thoughts, her commitment to her duty but above all her ability to think rationally.

Guided by him she returned to the camp's perimeter and he entered some fifteen minutes later from a different part.

EIGHTEEN

For Goldburgh and his associate, the army officer Viktor, the friendship that had begun in the railway carriage on its journey through the Ukraine,was cemented and strengthened by their companionship and the shared values that they mutually discovered during the many conversations and discussions that took place in walks that they jointly took around the camp and when they discovered the corrupting and decadent pleasures of the ice cream parlour inside the pharmacy, where they joined in the conversations of some of the trainees and the younger residents of the town.

Viktor was fascinated by Goldburgh's experiences at Cambridge and in Nebraska, frequently and persistently enquiring if he had seen any cowboys, or if they had been armed with pistols, or if they wore leather belts lined with bullets and attached holsters, but he was always disappointed as his friend explained that those days and events had ended half a century before. Viktor, like a schoolboy, was ecstatic when Goldburgh remembered that at parades (such as on Thanksgiving Day-he had to explain the reason for this important anniversary) some of the residents and especially members of the equine clubs would don replica clothing or possibly original clothes deliberately or unintentionally preserved from that historical period in a tribute to their heritage. At first Viktor could not comprehend or even grasp the concept that the government and leadership of the United Kingdom or the United States was subject to the whim of the people expressed through the electoral voting system and that the leadership and ruling party could be legally ousted from power and legitimately replaced by other politicians .

He had been born just before the glorious Revolution and had only known the leadership of the Bolshevik Communist Party under Comrades Lenin and Stalin though he admitted that he was really too young to remember life under Lenin but he did remember the excitement and joy of his family when they read that the counter revolutionary and enemy of the state, Leon Trotsky, had been found guilty under the criminal code and expelled from the Motherland .

Goldburgh spent considerable time explaining the British political system that was composed of three major parties and that there were others, even a Communist party, as well as an extreme right wing group (which did not have any elected Members of Parliament) though its leader, Oswald Mosley, had been imprisoned at the beginning of the war. Such was the strength of democracy in the United Kingdom that in the national interest, with the country in dire peril in nineteen forty, a government of national unity was formed, combining members of the three parties who temporarily put aside internecine disputes to support the overriding important national interest.

Viktor was amazed to learn that although Parliament had to be re elected every five years, the Prime Minister had the right and the prerogative to dissolve Parliament at any time and seek a new mandate (a concept alien and surprising to Viktor) through what was known as a 'General Election' and that the strategy could 'backfire' (a phrase that he found strange since he was used to the propaganda that the Communist Party and its leader were infallible) and that the leader and his party could lose.

He was even more interested in the United States system, for as they both knew, the twelve trainees would have to be intensely indoctrinated in many areas of life in the United States before each was given a drab, vague background and then inserted into America. Failure would result in only one other journey and every trainee was aware of the ultimate, alternative destination.

For the American residents of 'the town', they had been informed on their arrival that they could soon return either to the wider Soviet Union as respected members of the community and help in the rebuilding and development of the nation once the Fascist invaders had been expelled and destroyed in the hell of Berlin from where the evil of National Socialism had sprung or they could return to the United States.

They both understood that a new group of former Americans would replace the original group and a replacement team of trainees would arrive to repeat the operation.

NINETEEN

Goldburgh grappled with, and was becoming tormented by, three problems and he was unable to confide his concerns with anyone around him. He felt, despite the promises given to him in Moscow, that he would be returned to the British authorities once his mission had been accomplished ,that his knowledge of the purpose of the camp could never, realistically, be permitted to be divulged, even by accident, thus exposing the whole operation and the information would guarantee that the American government would be generous for such a prized gem of knowledge .

The N K V D were the same people who had personally promised him, when he was assigned by the British Embassy in Moscow to the Soviet authorities in a liaison position, that they would deal with the regular monthly reports that he was due to submit, but he had never been able to submit a single document.

The other matter was an intellectual problem which was currently insoluble and concerned the nature of power and government, for he had observed the actions and deeds of politicians and governments in three countries and on two continents. In essence, though he had fortunately been absent from the Soviet Union during the worst period of excesses that were graphically described as 'The Great Terror', between nineteen thirty-six and nineteen thirty-eight, and through his family he had met and even sat on the knees of many of the 'Old Guard', he believed that because the Communist Party was not elected by the people, and more importantly was not accountable to the nation, only to the ruling elite in the secrecy and privacy of the Politburo or whatever title or designation currently was in force, it was a form of government that was inherently unfair. However the systems which operated in the United Kingdom and United States incorporated that crucial element of accountability and the regular necessity for the politicians and government to appeal to the people in their capacity as the electorate for a continued or new mandate to represent the nation.

Whilst Viktor found this most commendable and the better of the two alternatives it relied on the common sense and wisdom of the people.

The fundamental problem was that both the electorate and the politicians were sometimes motivated by short term personal considerations which superseded the long term interests of the many.

Goldburgh was confronted by a dilemma that he could not trust the electorate and that the alternative was the self interest of the unelected elite and the few.

The day began as normal without the hint or an indication that a major change was to take place. They awaited the delivery of supplies, but additionally certain equipment that had to be specially imported and was immediately requisitioned on delivery and installed in the permanent classroom inside the administration building.

When the twelve entered, they were surprised to see sitting on each desk, new typewriters, together with an abundant supply of coarse paper and carbon paper. They were invited to use the machines and the majority watched the minority who had previously seen or used similar but cumbersome machines constructed to print out the Cyrillic script. Shortly afterwards the sound of hammer on ribbon was to be heard as the group began to explore and use the devices manufactured to produce the twenty six letter Roman alphabet.

Before the three tutors, assisted by one of the American teachers could begin their lesson, they unexpectedly received an urgent message to immediately go to the administrative office, an event that had no precedent since all the previous meetings had been held in the early evening and were usually rather informal .They were confronted by the presence of an anonymous N.K.V.D. officer in the commander's chair and the commander standing by the door in a state of shock and distress.

TWENTY

Mandel's first reaction was an ominous concern for the future; the N K -V D officer's physical appearance was the embodiment and personification of everything that he feared about the darker side of power in the Soviet Union and for Viktor, similarly, the man was the epitome of power without humanity or accountability. His face was drawn and sunken, his skin pallid, his body thin and his fingers unnaturally long and boney. His jaw emphasised the overall appearance of his body protruding in an almost skeletal manner. His uniform and epaulettes identified his rank and N.K.V.D. membership.

He looked at the four as though he was reviewing a line of soldiers, perhaps even searching for a weakness that he could exploit for his benefit and impose his will. He spoke in Russian, rough and earthily, immediately betraying his origins and antecedents...

"I have been appointed to replace your commander (a situation that in reality had also been thrust on the three and had been borne with sufferance) who will be escorted back to Moscow and reassigned to new duties that he is more capable of administering. I have absolutely no knowledge of the English language and my instructions from the head of the N K V D (he meant Lavrenti Beria) is for you to continue your work, however whilst you are to maintain your weekly reports on the twelve candidates, they are to be submitted, typed in Cyrillic.

Circumstances and recent events mean that you have twenty-two weeks from today to prepare the twelve. Any that are found wanting from now onwards will be superfluous and will be immediately dismissed . Personally I want to see evidence that not only have you been able to rebuild them but that no vestiges of their past remains, indeed I also want to see proof that they have mastered their new identities. That will be all. Natalia, will you please stay for a moment (which struck Goldburgh either that the man had some human emotions or that he was going to confide in his fellow N K V D officer)."

The two men exited the room, undoubtedly concerned why they had been excluded from the further briefing.

"Natalia, I have a brief message from your father, who I saw some four days ago and is in excellent health, the General has confided in me certain matters that should be outside of my knowledge, that you are both to be assigned to the North American continent but in different actions. You must not try to contact your parents or if your paths accidentally cross you must not communicate with them, however they will make every effort to meet you when it is safe and secure for both missions.

Natalia, a personal word from me. You have been seen close to one of the candidates; do not ruin your career for someone who is expendable."

Despite his concern for the future and his intellectual and ethical dilemmas about the nature of power and the fallibility of the democratic system, Goldburgh looked back with great affection and nostalgia at his time in what he euphemistically called 'the town'. The arrival and new demands imposed by the authoritarian commander, in reality, did not alter the tempo and procedures of the candidates` induction to their new life.

The three teachers agreed that whilst no reference be made to the deadline that had been imposed, they would warn the twelve that the arrival of a new camp commander coincided with an important warning that they were immediately under greater scrutiny and that they should be prepared and be more vigilant for any attempts to betray their true origins. It was suggested that whenever they were in conversation or under pressure that they think and talk slowly and carefully as it was in moments of anger or stress that they might accidentally speak out or even expose their knowledge of Russian. Furthermore they were reminded that the camp was alcohol free (save for a very diluted lager that was only available to the 'townsfolk') and that foolish drinking of spirits, especially vodka, might in a moment undo all the training and the hard work that both the teachers and the trainees had put in. As a final warning they were told that an innocuous or even seemingly harmless mistake could irreversibly damage their facade and that they should be ever on their guard.

The first change was literally cosmetic for, with immediate effect, every fortnight for the men ,and weekly for the two girls, they had to attend the barbers and hairdressers so that they might develop a style of grooming which was natural and typical of an American.

Then three of the male candidates were called into the administrative offices amidst fear for their future since none of the twelve had ever previously been even close to the department but their concerns were satisfied when an optician, specially brought in from Moscow, gave the three, the only ones who wore glasses, a thorough examination, and some ten weeks later they received three pairs of glasses manufactured in the United States.

Thirdly, an unanswered question was answered ,when the twelve were called, one at a time, to the medical department and examined by a dentist and for each one he confirmed that their teeth continued to be in perfect condition. They had each been originally selected partially on the condition of their teeth and had dental work been performed in the Soviet Union then this act COULD have exposed their TRUE origins.

Within two weeks they had all mastered the typewriter and not only received further, more concentrated personal tuition to improve their language skills, but once or twice a week each made an appearance before the three teachers and the formidable commander when they were interrogated and any potential defects exposed.

It had been decided, in Moscow, that the successful candidates be spread out over the United States and that shortly before leaving the camp they would be told where ultimately they were to settle and where and when they were to register for their Social Security number as there were just over one thousand main post offices able to process applications and they did not want any of the twelve registering at the same post office .

To obfuscate and hide their origins it had also been decided that for all the group they could share a typical common history and since they were dispersed, such similar backgrounds would not appear to be too coincidental, indeed the circumstances must have occurred on many occasions . Each believed that their parents entered the United States, some of them illegally, in the early nineteen twenties after the end of the great wave of immigration that terminated at the beginning of the First World War, some via the ports on the East Coast, others via San Francisco and the remainder via Canada or Mexico, having, they understood ,travelled from ports in Central America or Japan.

In any case they had grown up in orphanages as their parents had either deserted them or told the authorities that they were temporarily unable to cope or provide for the child. Unhappy memories, frequent changes in their residence and illnesses blighted their childhood and made recollections and memories distorted and crucially difficult to trace even for the most persistent of investigators. For all of them their lives would really begin when, to obtain employment, they applied for their Social Security document and on the instructions of the N K V D, in some cases, to take courses at night school.

What the two men would not know and Natalia would only find out after her two friends left the camp ,was that the new names allocated to the twelve would be changed, deliberately, at the last moment, as would their dates of birth so that Goldburgh and Viktor could not identify them, other than by a description.

Four months later, the three tutors were confident that the group could be sent on their mission, though three had reached the stage where they had not only suffered the humiliation of being punished for accidentally speaking in Russian, but by being hosed with cold water and kept in the open for twelve hours and one of the two girls had reached the six hour penalty and, despite her supplications for leniency in a 'New York' accent, she was also doused in cold water.

At the next regular weekly meeting, when the three presented their typewritten reports, Viktor unilaterally, without the formal approval of the other two, suggested they believed that the group, despite rare slips, was ready or as ready as they were ever going to be and could now be sent abroad, to which the commander responded with an unusual and strange smile and suggested that he now be involved in the group's final test in accordance with instructions clearly specified by Beria on his appointment, and before his departure from Moscow.

The initial analyses and opinions of both Goldburgh and Viktor Kashkarov were to be proved quite tragically correct and accurate.

For the camp commander, the art and act of subtle trickery was not his strength or forte, only the violence of the bully and the arrogance of power without accountability.   For some, adept, competent and capable ,trickery can expose the deception and facade , for the sadist, only the cudgel will uncover the truth and then there is always the probability that a statement made under duress was only made to avoid potential or actual physical violence.

The two girls were first, brought into a makeshift interrogation room. He expected that one would betray the other. The N K V D guards, formerly passive and friendly, suddenly imitated and acted in the callous, vicious manner of their commanding officer. In two groups of three they forcibly and sadistically restrained the two surprised and shocked girls whilst the commander began to tear at their clothes with the apparent intention that he was to rape them but he then permitted another soldier to violently hit the girls in the stomach and, whilst short of breath, they were partially immersed, head first, into an overflow barrel as he shouted in Russian and then surprisingly in passable English that both would immediately be released if they would admit, in Russian, that they were Soviet infiltrators to the United States. Whether they had learned from their period of induction never to use the Russian language or more likely since they both fainted, they were thrown on the floor and allowed to recover. Still semi conscious they possibly heard him methodically announce and pronounce the single word statement:

"Passed."

The fate that would greet the ten men was intended to be both more sadistic and degrading and would expose the unnatural inclinations of the commander.

For all the candidates, they had lived for nearly the past year in an unreal, unnatural world, detached ,isolated and cocooned from the of excrement, because of the presence of human faeces lying storms of uncertainty, upheaval and of a titanic war that was raging outside and was sometimes so close as to be heard had it been ever so slightly closer or if the wind was in a favourable direction. The life of relative tranquillity and personal security was instantaneously overturned by the sudden and horrendous act that had been planned and authorised in Moscow.

The three tutors were alerted to the fate of the two girls and the imminent test or interrogation of the first of the ten men by a sympathetic N K V D soldier, incidentally the same person that Natalia had approached and notified of her intention to pursue Yuri in the forest and who had deemed it prudent to inform his superiors of the incident. They rushed to the officer's toilet where 'the test ' (for in the eyes of the N K V D this was nothing more than a stringent imitation of methods that their opposite numbers would use in the event that any of the twelve were arrested) to be confronted by the first male candidate, his face covered with human faeces pleading in English that he could not understand why they were demanding a confession that he spoke Russian. One of the soldiers, inconveniently suffering from diarrhoea again excreted into the toilet bowl after which, in front of the three tutors, the youth's head was again thrust into the bottom of the bowl and he was then pulled out crying and whimpering, in English like a child, that he wished he could speak Russian to end the humiliation and degradation, hoping that his torturers would teach him some words in the Russian language to speak.

It was now self evident that the camp commander had been specially chosen for this assignment, partially for his ability to speak at least some English, for despite his initial denial and his previous apparent ignorance of the language which the three had spoken in his presence, he began to shout at the distraught youth in English slang using a vernacular of swear words and unbridled threats.

Like the two girls before him he had passed the test and a bowl of water was thrown over his face to wash away some of the excreta. As he walked away the commander again spoke to him, but this time in a pleasant friendly voice, congratulating him on his performance but with his guard down and disoriented he replied in Russian to the compliment which was also in Russian , thanking him!, to which the commander replied in English:

"Failed."

Another of the candidates was brought in, just as the floor ,smelling revoltingly in small dung heaps, was being cleared away on the initiative of the soldiers, who were throwing buckets of water and using brooms to sweep away the foul detritus.

The commander spoke to the young man courteously in English assuring him that he had no reason to distrust him and that he wished to converse in Russian to verify that he had not forgotten his mother tongue, but the boy, although confused by the surroundings and nauseous at the overwhelming stench convincingly denied any knowledge of the language other than one word:

"niet"

that he had heard in a film. The commander continued, clearly losing self control as he became ever more frustrated and exasperated, finally reverting into Russian and uttering a threat that compelled Natalia to rush from the room and immediately vomit .Even the concept or very idea of the threat was beyond the pale of decency or natural behaviour.

The boy, of course, understood the threat but like Natalia and the others believed it so perverted and unnatural as to be ignored and continued his denial .

Three of the guards then held him down, supine, whilst a fourth forced his mouth open and inserted a piece of wood to keep his jaw firmly open and then proceeded to unbutton his coarse trousers, expose his genital organs and excrete urine into the partially exposed mouth of the now frightened and hysterical youth. As he finished, another guard began to unbutton his trousers whilst the first guard, without regard for any hygiene, took out the piece of wood to be greeted by noises and sounds that were incomprehensible but as the fluid was either spat out or was imbibed was clearly Russian.

Without emotion, the camp commander repeated an earlier statement:

"Failed."

The subsequent and later events are disputed, however what is not in question are the core facts of the matter: Natalia returned to the room propelled by an incandescent anger. She was driven by rage, a profound sense of injustice, compassion and the realisation that the insane actions ordered by her superiors and most likely by the head of the N K V D were about to destroy what they had all striven to create. As she purposely walked towards the commander she must have clearly seen the shock etched on the faces of her two comrades and to everyone`s surprise stood face to face to her superior officer.

Whether she had previously considered her proposed actions and weighed up the possible consequences is now unimportant for the man might have taken out his pistol and shot her without regard for the consequences.

She spoke in Russian, clearly and precisely ,though her two associates later told her that the cadence of her delivery was much faster that her usual pace of conversation.

"The consequences of your actions are in distinct contradiction to the task that Moscow must have ordered you to carry out."

Then she uttered a statement that must have been heard but ignored a thousand times before in the Lefortovo and Lubyanka prisons in Moscow, the Shpalerny prison in Leningrad and in the political isolators in Alexandrovsk, Yaroslavl and Verkhne-Uralsk.

"They are patriots and not Trotskyite enemies of the State!"

For an instant, time must have seemed to be suspended and for everyone in the room they were momentarily frozen with surprise. She would threaten him with the wrath of her father, for his influence and connections with the Presidium were clearly known to the camp commander . And if he shot her and her two companions dead it would be an act of suicide once her father pieced together the events, but she was not a child at her father`s knees, she was an officer dedicated to her duty and..suddenly she also realised that she was a woman and she thought of Yuri. She was confused as duty and human emotion clouded her judgement.

"Natalia", he spoke to her not in anger but as if *HE* had been struck by a Christian revelation (a description factually inapplicable in an atheist state and for a member of a violent group of thugs).

"These actions are necessary to determine if the indoctrination has been successful."

She sensed that, at last, she could actually reason with him and communicate a logical resolution of the problem.

" Viktor told you only yesterday that we believed that all the group was as ready as they would ever be and I stand by that judgement. We previously warned them that alcohol would loosen their tongues, a far more likely possibility than the perverted methods that you have just employed. I suggest a compromise, a test, in the best traditions of Soviet manhood.

All the twelve will now be aware of the possible physical consequences of any interrogation by the Americans and we will back you up in any report to our superiors, confirming that it was a warning to them all of the nature of our enemy. Let them celebrate the conclusion of their course, let them have access to alcohol and especially vodka. Any that succumb and speak Russian will fail."

She looked round for support and agreement for her proposition. The emotion of surprise etched on her compatriots` faces had been replaced by smiles and as she turned to face her nemesis, he thrust out not a pistol, but his hand and sealed the bond.

"One day you should be a politician, but remember that if any speak in our mother tongue that they fail!"

She had won a battle but not yet the war and he was not to be trusted.

TWENTY-ONE

Information gleaned from the penetration of the Manhattan Project, despite the extraordinary security surrounding the work, was beginning to reach Moscow and an inner clique close to Stalin had reached the conclusion that their ally was well on their way to building a device ,indeed the top American scientists had voiced their opinion that a weapon could be detonated in the summer of nineteen forty-five, less than a year ahead, whilst an enormous investment, mainly financial, in valuable American Dollars continued to flow, supporting the operation in the Ukraine and no foreseeable return could be gained for some years.

It was imperative that the Soviet Union take every possible action to ascertain the technological secrets and to develop their own programme. As far back as the autumn of nineteen forty -one when the subject had been discussed between Stalin and Beria the former had dismissed the potential creation of a weapon as:

"Propaganda."

It was only later when Kurchatov who was to become, in nineteen forty-nine, the 'father' of the Soviet A bomb, at the express request of Beria, gave to Stalin a clear description of the weapon`s potential, but more importantly the necessity to commence the first technological steps, after which the First Secretary wisely approved the momentous journey of discovery and ultimate technological success.

Later, by the summer of nineteen forty-four, another decision had to be made and without hesitation, Beria confirmed cancellation of the operation in the Ukraine, indeed had the inaugural group of trainees been in the preliminary stages of their training they would have been immediately deported to a labour camp and ultimate liquidation, however General Koenigsberg`s support and his daughter`s presence in the camp allowed the first and consequently only group to be finally inserted into America, to complete their training .

The preliminary notice reached the commander some two weeks after his confrontation with Natalia and strengthened his resolve to avenge his humiliation. There had never been a safe in his office and in accordance with the brief notification, he destroyed the document and awaited full details of the procedure which was to be brought by courier who he would meet outside of the camp, which incidentally meant that for the first time he would actually venture into the 'outside world'. In the meantime he was instructed to continue normally and not to impart the news to anyone, but it was anticipated that the whole camp (he was pleased to read this comment since it might appear that the complete operation was to be shut down permanently)would cease operating within six weeks.

The girl was untouchable. Unless her father had fallen into disfavour with either Stalin or Beria he could not satiate his anger on her. The army officer Viktor Kashkarov had been specially chosen by Beria and was probably immune but that left the Jew, Mandel Goldburgh. Individually he was vulnerable if separated from his two associates but in a group ,no doubt, he would be protected by them.

He would plan his revenge when he received his instructions from Moscow.

The relationship between the three teachers and their twelve students became closer and more friendly as the trio were recognised not only as their saviours but as a group who could be trusted. The format of their education changed as they regularly held what would be seen in a university such as Cambridge as 'tutorials' where various aspects of life in America were discussed and analysed and finally each student was asked to write(or type) a brief argument which in itself was a test of their command and understanding of the written English language.

It was at one of these intimate 'seminars', when the subject under discussion was the inequality of the 'blacks' in the Southern states, that

Natalia foolishly allowed her emotions to overcome her professionalism and responsibility to her duty. Yuri was typing his argument in response to a matter that he found in direct contradiction to the Declaration of Independence, submitting the proposition that:

"In the land of the free, that the individual could only be free if he had been born with a white skin."

As she passed his desk and looked at his typed critique she allowed her hand to touch his and without thought of the consequences whispered to him to meet her in the woods urgently that same day at around four o`clock.

TWENTY-TWO

She was consumed and obsessed by a fire that had suddenly ignited and was burning fiercely within her. It was impossible to douse ,even if she wanted to end the symbol of her yearning. She wanted to be with him, to touch and know him, to understand him and to smell the very essence of the man.

She also wanted to warn him of the danger to come and to protect him. She had never felt like this before. The fervour that she had witnessed at the political rallies was false and shallow in comparison with the feelings that had just erupted within her and were uncontrollable. Then she was gripped by a new emotion, one that she had experienced before but not in this situation. Panic. What if he decided not to come, what if he thought that this was part of a labyrinthine trap, a bait to betray him. How could he be so foolish?

Her mind and body were focused on one thing only and that was an overwhelming desire to be with him. Him alone, without the interference or supervision of an individual or the state. The new camp commander`s warning was of no concern to him for she was the mistress of her own destiny and the judge of her own hopes and aspirations.

Suddenly, from where the idea sprung she did not know, she had the wish to be dressed like a woman and not like a political officer, but she only possessed clothes suitable for her work and an outfit for more ceremonial occasions and this meeting was in no way ceremonial. Her mind concentrated on solving an impossible conundrum.

She washed as best she could using the coarse soap which was bland and without perfume. She hoped that her femininity would shine through the austerity and drabness of her costume and that he would see within her the woman and her emotions. Then she rationalised the situation for if she did possess such clothing and if she was seen in public adorned in such bourgeois finery then not only would she draw attention to herself but would generate an enquiry as to her reasons and motive.

She incessantly looked at her wristwatch but time itself seemed to have conspired against her as the minute hand appeared to move ever more slowly and then as she repeated her observation, then not at all. Viktor, without question, had provided her with a compass, but apologised as it formed an integral part of a hunting knife that he had 'rescued' from a German tank crew member who was slumped across the front of his chariot, profusely bleeding ,surrounded by his dead crew members and awaiting treatment. Viktor mentioned to Natalia as he handed over the knife that:

"He put the man out of his misery with one shot between the eyes that had looked at him with a desperate hope of compassion, but two years earlier he, or his friends, had cut through the Motherland like a scythe destroying ,without pity, the very foundation of the Soviet state."

Thus was the value of human life so defined.

She located an entry point into the forest that appeared not to be under observation by the guards and she cautiously walked towards her target whilst at the same time she furtively looked for the man she had come to hate, both as an individual and as a symbol of the vilest aspect of the state, the camp commander, but he could not be seen and she entered the gates of hope.

She was slow and deliberate, carefully referring to the compass for the general directions of her journey which she would reverse on her return, whilst at the same time making notches in the bark of the trees as an added precaution.

Shortly she decided to stop and wait. She had been walking and meandering off course for some fifteen to twenty minutes. It was pleasantly warm and she could hear the birds singing and, yes she was certain, there were animals scurrying to and forth in the undergrowth. She sat down to wait for him and she hoped that he would respond to her invitation.

Almost instantaneously she heard behind her the unmistakeable sound of the snapping of dead branches and as she automatically looked round she saw him coming towards her bearing the beautiful gift of a smile. She got up and lifted her hand and arm in acknowledgement. Deep within her she felt not only an excitement but more, a hope and anticipation of things to come.

"You were so easy to find, it was not necessary for you to make marks on the trees for I had been watching out for you since you left your quarters."

She felt a glow of happiness, a feeling that she had not experienced since her parents had showered her with love and attention as a small child.

And then rather guardedly and with caution he asked her:

"Why are we here?"

She was confused and answered him in the only way she knew:

"Because we wanted to meet each other and I am so thrilled."

He looked at her, put his right index finger gently across her two lips, smiled almost paternally and quietly but emphatically responded:

"No, I meant what are we doing in this camp, isolated from the war and the outside world since I should be at the front defending the Motherland from the Barbarian hordes as I was previously, before unexpectedly I was pulled from my brigade and sent here without instructions."

She looked at him. He was so strong but vulnerable, she could protect him and he could provide for her. She answered him, not with candour but to protect him from the test that was to come shortly.

"You have been chosen by the Party to represent the people of our Motherland in a greater war than if you had remained at the front. But I must warn you that soon, and even I do not know when, you will be tested. We, your three tutors, have warned you of the dangers of alcohol. Soon you be allowed access to drink. Be careful, it is a test and if you fail, if you speak in our beloved mother tongue then you will be lost both to yourself and (then she said what she had wanted to say but felt inhibited but now suddenly free)...to me."

He held out his hand which she clasped without hesitation as if it was a natural, normal response and as if they had been partners for a thousand years.

"I would like to show you my discovery; it is not far from here but be silent for it is some one hundred metres from the road and sometimes the guards wander away from the camp along the road and might just hear us if we are too loud."

He moved with a confidence born of experience and guile as if he was carefully assessing the possibility that there were others close by and in order to avoid detection. Eventually, she didn't time the journey as she was so content being with him and holding his strong but gentle hand, they reached a glade, so tranquil and cool that she felt that she reached Paradise, and he then pointed to a cairn of stones clearly hurriedly assembled.

"It's a Jewish grave (he spoke with pride as if his reasoning had been made with great intellectual investigation, gently taking her round to the other side). Can you see (he continued enthusiastically) you can just make out that formation, it is a Hebrew star."

Then something caught her eye, perhaps he was about to draw her attention to the other item. She bent down, reverently pulled at the cloth and saw something that she had not seen since her father used to wear a similar item in the privacy of their home in San Francisco but she now realised, never in the Soviet Union. It was damp, slightly mouldy but still retained a distinct blue thread and tassels. She could not hold back a tear which he gallantly wiped off with the tip of his index finger.

"Yuri, you are right and this is, or was, his prayer shawl."

And then, without hesitation,he held her close to him as if to protect her from the unspoken forces and events that had caused the anonymous Jew to lie in peace and at rest in this isolated and tranquil site.

TWENTY-THREE

They walked to another spot, deeper in the forest ,which was cooler and more isolated from the world outside. The ground beneath them was dry as without either's request they lay down together, her head cradled in his strong right arm. Then, as their two faces drew closer together they instinctively kissed, briefly and tentatively. Their faces temporarily pulled away from the other and he smiled at her and they again drew close to each other and their tongues physically and perhaps literally intertwined as they became united .

She felt a hand gently caressing her right breast as if investigating her reaction and she placed her own right hand on his, guiding him towards her firm erect nipple. His hand was unusually soft and smooth like silk and she felt so satisfied that she could not express her joy. He withdrew his hand and proceeded to unbutton, with a little difficulty, her blouse, coarse and hard in comparison with his hands and fingers. Then he repositioned himself without disturbing her and commenced to caress her breast and nipple with his tongue. Her head fell back as she luxuriated in the pleasure of his appreciation of her body.

Her excitement and joy suddenly increased as she felt his left hand begin to explore her lower body. Soon he would enter her.

Like a vine they wrapped around each other, his hand feeling her thigh and gradually drawing closer to the sacred home of her femininity and the very foundation of her feelings for him.

As his fingers reached her vagina she felt the mass of his organ, firm, erect and potential. How she communicated her desire they both would never know but as she sucked him, his tongue was inside her vagina, lubricating her in anticipation of their future unity. In harmony and unison their two bodies changed position and as they curled around each other they must have had the appearance of an ancient ammonite such was their youthful ability and flexibility.

She suddenly drew a deep breath: He was inside her. He began to slowly and intentionally raise and lower his groin as he partially withdrew from the gates of paradise and then re entered. He continued. Then the pace began to accelerate and she was in ecstasy. He still continued as the blood rushed to her vagina.

And then the fountain erupted showering the inside of the most private place of her existence with his gift of love. And then twice more he repeated his silent ,wordless expression of his feelings for her.

She wished that they could be joined for a thousand years but life and fate can be cruel.

She had savoured the scintillating, soft, sensuous, silkiness of their joint sexuality.

They lay together silently, listening to the birds and the invisible animals living their lives in the undergrowth hoping that the moment would last forever when he turned to her and asked:

"Will we be together, like this, after we leave the camp for I could not live without your companionship?"

Then, without answering him,she realised that they might never see each other again.

TWENTY-FOUR

She returned the hunting knife to Viktor who made no enquiry as to its use. The following day began and continued as normal but she did not see Yuri since he was being tutored by Goldburgh who tended to substantially increase the duration of his lessons, always testing the students' understanding of the subject matter.

In the middle of her lesson, she received an urgent demand from one of the guards to terminate forthwith the lesson and go straight to the office of the commander. She was overwhelmed by fear. Had she and Yuri been seen in the most intimate and private moments of their lives and what were the consequences?

She was going to be exposed in front of her two friends and humiliated. As she entered the office Viktor and Mandel were already standing just inside and appeared shocked. He had already told them!

Fearing the worst and calculating (and dreading) the consequences, she avoided the faces of her two friends and looked directly towards the commander whose tone was surprisingly friendly and triumphal.

"I have informed your associates that Moscow has confirmed approval of your joint assessment and that the training is to be wound down pending deployment of the twelve trainees or pupils whatever you would like to call them (he stopped for a moment or so before continuing). They have also agreed to my recommendation that a final test be used to weed out any of those that might succumb to alcohol.

Moscow has made an arrangement through the American embassy that those pioneers who wish to return to America can leave via neutral Turkey. We are close to the border of the Russian Republic and whilst the journey may be arduous they will be taken to the Turkish border via the Georgian Republic and handed over to representatives of the American Red Cross at which time their passports will be returned to them (he again stopped as if he wished to make a personal point). It will be your responsibility to inform our American residents of our intentions but I expect and hope that most of them will decide to stay here, in the Soviet Union, and join with the workers and peasants to create the Utopia that was nearly destroyed by the Fascist warmongers.

Our forces are steadily moving Westwards through Poland towards the border of Germany where the rats nest and their women folk and bastard children will soon know the wrath of the Red Army.

Those of our American friends who wish to stay are to be sent to Kiev to help in its rebuilding, but will be given priority housing and special rations. Once we have weeded out the failures, you two men are to return to Moscow, Goldburgh to be handed over to the British embassy and comrade brother Kashkarov reassigned to a front line tank corps leading the assault on the fleeing barbarian criminals.

Natalia Koenigsberg, I am proud to confirm your promotion within the N K V D and you are henceforth my equal and I salute you. You are to remain with me here, to organise the departure of the successful students and then you are to return to Moscow while I accompany the students who will soon be injected into the North American continent."

At which point or moment as an automatic reflex Goldburgh tendered a question which clearly antagonised the commander:

"Once we leave here what is to happen to the camp?"

"That is of no concern to you or even to any of us in the room, however since you all have been loyal servants of the Party and this cause I wish to confirm that I understand we will all be replaced and the camp will continue and maintain its original purpose."

He dismissed the three with a characteristic (and perhaps patronising movement of his hand) but then ominously called out to Natalia to once again remain behind.

"My dear (this time she detected a tone of sarcasm tempered by caution in contradiction to his previous manner), your father's star is in the ascendancy in Moscow, especially with our ultimate boss (she did not know if he meant Lavrenti Beria, head of the N K V D, or more importantly the First Secretary, Joseph Stalin) and therefore I am cautious in what I have to say to you .

I warned you before about being too close to our trainees. Yesterday, despite your poor attempt to enter into the forest unseen you were observed and I am not a fool and can work out why you took a compass. A candidate was also seen entering the forest at a different point and the two of you may have spent some time together. I do not wish to incur the disfavour of your father. Beware anything foolish that could prejudice your future career. Shortly our two paths will separate and our careers take on new challenges. Do not fail yourself."

The announcement spread like an uncontrollable forest fire both amongst the twelve trainees and the American residents of the town. Within days more than half of them had signalled their desire and intention to return to the United States confirming, en masse that:

"They wished to spread the message of socialism and the achievements of the Soviet people in their titanic struggle against the forces of National Socialism."

Which generated an observation from the (perhaps cynical) camp commander that:

"Their loyalty to socialism and the Soviet cause, in his opinion, was only transitory."

Members of the American community announced that to celebrate what was...

"No doubt, a successful conclusion of the education of our [sic] ambassadors of peace and cooperation, that they would organise , for the whole community, a festival taking the best of Independence and Thanksgiving Days, since the event would take place between the two holidays."

 The camp commander – unlike the trainees – did not understand the significance of the two days but when informed, spontaneously agreed to offer every assistance, including alcohol, provided that everyone drank in moderation.

He would make certain that for the trainees this condition would be ignored since he still had every reason to obtain revenge for his humiliation.

The town resembled Main street, U.S.A. How the townsfolk were able to make the banners, impedimenta ,flags and other paraphernalia to recreate the atmosphere still remains an unresolved mystery, but in part, it reflects the substantial investment that had been made and the initiative and ability of the excited residents and was a fitting climax to their stay .

In an ocean of turbulence and suffering, they feasted on the dishes of *THEIR* homeland including turkey and cranberry sauce, hams and ribs of beef, a feast that even corrupted the commander and his Socialist epicurean diet.

But for the commander, the highlight of his sadistic pleasure was the failure of three of the trainees to control themselves, once they had thrown caution to the wind and imbibed excessively. One was the girl who had previously reached the 'six hour' penalty and the other two, who had previously likewise been in the highest penalised group ,all had caroused in Russian and when admonished by their friends and warned, had persisted in arguing in their old mother tongue.

TWENTY-FIVE

The reality of the situation was somewhat different, dark and ominous. The motives and methods of the only two men who had any real influence and who controlled the destiny of everyone in the camp was callous and indifferent; for the head of the N K V D, Lavrenti Beria, and the First Secretary of the Communist Party, Joseph Stalin, they were all insignificant pawns, dispensable and superfluous to their plans.

There are two anecdotes that summarise the nature and mind of Stalin. When advised of the influence and power of the Pope, he enquired how many divisions were at his disposal and on the nature of human life he answered:

"The death of one man is a tragedy, the death of a million is a statistic."

The repatriation of over one hundred and fifty Americans via Turkey was a complete fabrication, but plausible. It was obvious that their experiences in the Siberian labour camps, if publicised in 'The West', might influence Churchill and Roosevelt in their negotiations over the structure of Europe after the war, but transcending that disclosure was the realisation that the purpose of the camp would be deduced and counter action taken. For those who wished to remain in the Motherland there were also millions of Russians to whom the scarce resources could be given and the logistics of transporting the immigrant pioneers to Kiev would tie up precious rolling stock when the first priority was the transportation of troops and equipment West. The

Russian Jew Goldburgh could never be allowed out of the country with the knowledge that he possessed and although he had connections with Lev Kaganovich, it would be impossible to hand him over since his complete disappearance and the government's reticence to give details of his whereabouts would be explained by a most illuminating *expose* of the Soviet's true intentions.

With unusual secrecy Viktor was summonsed, late one evening, to the office of the camp commander and when he entered the office he noted that the commander's desk was unusually barren, except for an unopened bottle of vodka, two short glasses, two thin files and an envelope all neatly arranged, as if in anticipation of his visit .Boris Ribak, for that was the name of the camp commander, but he always insisted on being addressed as commander, was unusually amicable, as if he looked forward to vacating the camp and returning to other, more interesting duties. He beckoned Viktor not only to sit down but first to close the door.

"At long last your task has been completed and I am pleased to hand to you the contents of these two files. You must pass one set to Goldburgh and give to him, on my behalf, thanks for the work that both you and he have contributed to the success of this venture. Inside are permits and travel documentation operative for twenty one days from the date I countersign the forms, valid throughout the Soviet Union and any foreign territory under the Motherland's control which should give you both adequate time to report back to the headquarters of the N K V D. I am instructed to inform you that you have been made personally responsible to deliver your associate and that you are to be reminded that you are still under the jurisdiction of the N K V D which continues to supersede your rank and responsibility to the army."

It was at that moment that Viktor suddenly recognised the reality of the situation: that one word, deliver, had been used to confirm that his associate and friend was to be arrested on his arrival in Moscow and that he was to be the man who would hand him over to the scaffold.

It was clear that the commander's instructions and his motives-going back to the recent event when he was torturing the two girls - was an obvious sign of his true nature, sinister ,menacing but above all corrupted by evil. Had not his friend realised that the information that he possessed would make it impossible for him to be allowed to return to England or the United States?

Viktor's appearance must have alerted the commander to the fact that Kashkarov realised either the truth or that the future was not as he had foreseen.

"You will have at your disposal two guards and this, though I doubt if it will be necessary (at which moment he opened the draw of his desk and produced a pistol). Your duties will cease on your arrival in Moscow and then, I assume you will be free to return to your unit and, we both hope, the final push on Berlin and the rats' nest of our enemy."

He pushed the revolver and an adequate supply of bullets across the desk and then surprised him with a statement and comments which he found both distasteful and an insight into the man and his values.

"I am surprised that even after my short stay here you have still not yet recognised me. I can only assume that when you went to Army Headquarters and were confronted by the panel of high ranking officers you were both shocked and surprised at your appointment. I was one of the officers present at your induction (without pausing he immediately went onto the other reason for the meeting). I want you to accept this envelope, it is partially a gift and you are to act as a courier. Moscow, in its haste to complete the operation, delivered funds of three hundred U.S. Dollars for each of the twelve trainees but as you are aware, three have failed and I intend to return the overpayment to correct the error. There is, therefore, if my calculations are correct, an amount of nine hundred U.S. Dollars to return, which I would ask that you deliver to my home as, since you know, I am responsible to accompany the nine agents (it took a moment for him to comprehend the meaning of the word agents). You seem unsure of my instructions. As a gift I intend for you to have an amount of one hundred U.S. Dollars for your inconvenience."

Kashkarov was being dragged into the quagmire and corruption of an organisation that was not accountable to the laws of the Soviet Union and if he was found with foreign currency it might well be punishable by death such was the severity of the law. But could he refuse the man's request?

He had within him the germ of an idea to save Goldburgh, at great personal cost, and without a guarantee of success. He therefore took the envelope, without even checking or counting the contents such was his naivety and ignorance of such matters but remembered to ask his superior's address and telephone number in Moscow, which he wrote down on a piece of paper. They shook hands and agreed to meet or for him to deliver the envelope in six weeks time or earlier, depending on what happened after he reported to his unit's H.Q. in Moscow.

For the Americans a more callous end had been planned and would be executed with the later intention of creating political capital. Both Beria and Stalin were antagonised and stung by the Nazi propaganda coup exposing the Soviet Union as the real culprits behind the Katyn Forest massacre of the Polish military elite, though rumours had recently surfaced that the Nazis had left evidence of a series of massacres in a ravine known as Babi Yar near Kiev. Careful planning could create a propaganda coup for Stalin and divert interest from the Katyn Forest incident.

The three failed trainees were dispatched within days by the tortuous railway system, ultimately East and past the Urals to a labour camp but not before they had been humiliated before their former comrades who were reminded of the warning that had immediately preceded their training programme.

The repatriation of the one hundred and fifty one adults and children began with a great show of comradeship as those who were to shortly leave for Kiev gave letters and even photographs which they expected to be delivered to their friends and families 'back home'. In many ways that first group appeared as if they were departing on a picnic, as they were laden with baskets and trays of food which had to suffice for the next forty-eight hours, when they would reach the food depot that had been their supply store. Accompanied by five N K V D guards, they were greeted, as they had been informed, at the end of the long tortuous road that joined the local highway, by a troop of elite troops that had been specially dispatched from Moscow to protect them. They arrived at the railway station that they had not seen for a year and within an hour were travelling not South, but North West on a journey towards, but not close to the front and an ever retreating enemy.

About forty eight hours later the exhausted party disembarked at a station whose identity and location had been obscured and hidden. They were then taken in a fleet of lorries, singing and laughing, to a deserted farm where the elite troops armed with captured German semi automatic weapons and loaded with enemy bullets shot the incredulous party, then using a tractor, bulldozed them into a convenient cesspit which they hurriedly, effectively and crudely, filled in.

A similar fate, but at a different location, awaited their friends within a few days.

TWENTY-SIX

The coat was modern, elegant and sophisticated, well made from expensive materials and exquisitely lined, but unfortunately showed the signs of careless use. Quietly she realised that such bourgeois thoughts would not be tolerated in the Soviet Union or that she yearned to be seen attired in the coat by Yuri but that was impossible. She looked up at the commander and asked about the history of the coat and the large selection of menswear that almost completely filled the room. His reply was part conjecture and part a cynical analysis.

"There are a number of organisations in the United States promoting support amongst the American people for their allies in the Soviet Union in their struggle against Fascism and donations of clothing and food are sent by well meaning friends to our country. Because of the current military situation the appropriate authorities in Moscow have found it difficult to distribute the clothing and have taken the opportunity to supply certain groups in the Moscow area. As regards the food, most of which is tinned, I heard that on medical grounds it was decided not to make available the limited supply because the rich quality of the food might be dangerous and unhealthy for those whose diet for the last three years was based on simple, plain food. Indeed and I must apologise for the following example, I ate something called 'baked beans' which caused a most embarrassing outcome."

She knew exactly what he meant and deliberately changed the direction and tack of the conversation by unexpectedly tearing along the edge of the lining allowing the material to flap uncontrollably. She then announced that she was going to show him a trick that her father had learned from Felix Dzerzhinsky, the almost legendary founder of the Cheka (a forerunner of the N K V D) at which moment and as if by magic she completely captured his attention.

She explained that her father had joined the Cheka during the Civil War and was, by luck, attached to Dzerzhinsky and helped to arrest fleeing White officers and members of the aristocracy. They would sew into the lining of their heavy clothes an item of value, such as a high denomination U. S. Dollar note and nearby or sometimes adjacent, two torn pieces of newspaper between which was more money which they pretended should not be discovered. These discoveries normally would placate the investigators who usually left the item of clothing with the person however, more subtlety hidden

404

away, would be an item or items of great value and Dzerzhinsky showed him examples of collections of diamonds that were also found.

With some personal reticence and great emotion she told him that her father had first seen her mother, his wife, during the final days of the Civil War when the counter revolutionaries were in full flight. Whilst he instinctively knew that she was not an enemy of the state he arrested her on the spurious grounds that she appeared to be similar to a wanted fleeing aristocrat and was then able to introduce himself. Sometime later they married and although it was in a Jewish Temple, Dzerzhinsky insisted on being present, so struck was he on the young man's initiative; and that one event was the catalyst that accelerated his career.

Now the commander knew how she would import into America the lists that they were soon to prepare concerning the nine trainees.

Earlier that day, and she was using the enjoyment of choosing some clothes to blot out the painful memory of the experience, she bade farewell to her two friends and comrades. She did not realise how close they had become until the moment of their departure when each said to the other that they hoped to meet again, but she knew and intuitively felt that they also knew that their paths would never again cross. Then, like a child, she suddenly hoped, soon, to be reunited with her parents.

But she did manage, when the commander was out of earshot, to warn Mandel that her intuition felt that he was not safe and to beware the authorities.

Late that afternoon, as dusk was beginning to fall, the nine trainees were asked to assemble in one of the rooms and then to be confronted by Natalia and most unusually, sitting close to her, the camp commander. As she spoke to them an audible ripple of excitement could be detected.

"Three of your friends have failed the course and may I remind you that nearly a year ago you were all warned of the consequences of failure. They have been sent to labour camps each for a period of six years. Within a week or so you will all be sent to the Pacific coast and infiltrated into either the United States or Canada.

Before you leave here your final act will be to join the N K V D as serving officers and immediately, and for the rest of your lives, you will be subject to their authority. Whilst you are on duty you will accrue a salary which can be drawn in the Motherland when you are able to return, but no earlier than nineteen seventy-four, for your task ,once you have settled in America, is to remain undetected and to lead a normal life until such time as a superior officer makes contact.

For security purposes and at this late stage, each of you has been allocated by Moscow a new name and you will revert to your true dates of birth (she did not know the rationale behind this change but it was realised that Kashkarov and Goldburgh could identify the agents if they had noted their dates of birth or names). After this meeting ends each one of you will individually meet the two of us to confirm the information and in the next few days you will each be rigorously tested and you are to practice your new signature which you will first officially use when you sign the membership document for the N K V D.

You are not to discuss your new identity with any of the others and rather confusingly you may, when in conversation with your associates, use your current names.

Any breach will result in immediate transportation to join your three friends and may I remind you that any error, however insignificant, a lapse if you speak Russian will even at this late stage again result in your transportation to the camps.

A new life is to begin for you all. You will bear a secret that can never be disclosed ,be it to a doctor or if you marry, your partner. It will not be a burden but a memory that will dim with time. Before you leave you will be supplied with new clothing and symbolically just as you discard your current clothing so you will sever any connection with this place forever.

You have been repeatedly trained and drilled in the procedures to be followed on your arrival in America (and those of you who are to be infiltrated via Canada). Each one, prior to departure will be provided with two hundred and seventy-five U.S. Dollars in small notes which you must prudently use.

You will all be given an ultimate destination where you will settle down and create roots for yourself and probably your families; it is important that you blend in with the community but do not stand for public office since it will be unwise for you to be subject to public scrutiny.

It is important to obtain American citizenship and as we have clearly explained to you this must be completed before you reach your ultimate destination and in order for you to register as a voter but do not become active or passionate about politics in general, indeed the values and principles of Socialism that are ingrained within you should create a feeling of disgust when you see the American pursuit of materialism and greed. Within a month of your arrival in your new homeland you should first obtain a Social Security number and for each of you we will again give you each a different town or city where to register and it is important that you register *SEPARATELY* [author's emphasis]. Once you have obtained your Social Security number and when you apply for American citizenship, be careful, disclose as little of your background as possible and as we have prepared you and I must repeat myself, do not apply in the city or town where you are finally to settle down.

Our agents will not contact you until the earliest, nineteen fifty-three, or even for some years but you must be ready to perform any act that your superiors order.

During the last few months we have thoroughly gone over many different aspects but I will end this very important talk to remind you that once you disembark you must cease all contact forever with your friends. Good luck!"

TWENTY-SEVEN

It was decided that Natalia would prepare for each trainee, in duplicate, hand written by her, in Cyrillic, the original birth name and true date of birth, followed, in Roman script by the trainee's temporary name and date of birth and finally the name that the person would be known by in the United States. An adequate space was then left in order to insert their ultimate destination.

Immediately after their birth details had been confirmed and their new names advised they were given time to practice typing and writing their new names and also their signature.

That last week passed with unusual speed as the intensity of their one to one tutorials and group lessons filled the days and early evenings. Sometimes the students confided both in the commander and Natalia their fears and concerns for their new lives. The commander was unsympathetic and formal, desensitised of emotion; his mantra, his *raison d'etre* was loyalty to the Party and the State; the titanic struggle that was raging now close to the border of Nazi Germany was the Party's battle to prove by military victory the supremacy of Marxist – Leninism over the pseudo intellectualism of ill conceived and discredited National Socialism and they were to be soldiers in the vanguard of the next and perhaps final confrontation of Socialism and Capitalism. He therefore could not comprehend that any of the nine should have any doubts concerning the task and the great responsibility that the Party had bestowed upon them. For Natalia her emotions and response were more human especially as she had lived and was soon to return to the country that in truth she had found not only hospitable but deep down as friendly and as concerned for their neighbour as the people of Russia were, and more so, since the shadow of the state and its intrusive nature in her homeland was unlike the fervent expression of freedom that the American people drew from the country's Declaration of Independence. That last and final day saw a flurry of activity and a different routine that confused and excited everyone. Their old clothes and their old lives were discarded, new sets of photographs taken, currency distributed and finally each one signed the articles in their new names and swore an oath of allegiance to the N K V D.

She had to return to Moscow and that final parting clearly expressed the bonds that had been created between the two sides. She desperately tried to talk privately to Yuri as even she was not permitted to publically declare his new name and, of course, she feared even at this late stage that she might be observed . She smiled at him and silently opened her mouth and said something that was intimate and deeply personal.

On the commander's instructions the kitchen was denuded of its stock of food which they all hoped could be eked out during the long train journey to the Pacific coast. Within a month, engineers emptied the buildings of any usable materials including the kitchen fixtures and equipment and from the pharmacy and drug store the unique soda fountain which was all transported back to the headquarters of the NKVD and an unknown fate.

For Kashkarov, Goldburgh and for two of the nine agents, for the latter were now officially junior officers of the N K V D, fate would intervene. The ten, of course including the commander, managed to complete the arduous journey isolated from the other passengers, by cautiously rationing the food which was supplemented by supplies generously given by N K V D officers travelling on the same train but in a separate compartment. Within days of their arrival in Vladivostok the nine agents were secreted in three different boats going to Vancouver and San Francisco but in that short hiatus, whilst they were based in the local naval headquarters, one of the men suffered food poisoning, the first symptoms only becoming apparent just after the vessel set sail.

The only other member aboard was the man formerly known as Yuri and to him fell the first test of his initiative. There was no doctor on board the freighter, and the officers and crew had little basic medical knowledge or by their lack of interest, any concern for the future or fate of the two young men who had arbitrarily been embarked at the last possible moment before departure with a sinister request for their safe but illegal disembarkation in America. Yuri was guided by common sense and trial and error, finally discovering that once the vomiting had ceased that starvation and a liberal supply of fluid, which was the unpleasant tasting water, would gradually clear his friend`s stomach of any infection. They were illegally disembarked shortly before dawn on a November day - the beginning of their new lives. The sailors who actually facilitated the act of their clandestine disembarkation hurriedly deserted them, only supplying the address of a local boarding house that they had been previously told offered room and if requested, board at economic rates.

It was Monday morning of a brave new world and Yuri had the self imposed responsibility to help his friend, not only to recuperate, but to assist him walk, such was his enfeebled condition. They wandered aimlessly without a definite destination or purpose until they reached an open space, with benches, where a number of people were sitting reading newspapers or strolling in the cool late autumn morning .It must have been a major achievement for Yuri, as they both sat on a bench adjacent to an elderly couple, when he tentatively and above all cautiously engaged them in a conversation but as the communication continued and his confidence grew he found them as normal and as natural as the people that he had known in his past life. They were most helpful (and kind) directing them to a fast food diner which served an excellent, cheap breakfast, especially to the military as they presumably assumed that the two young men were members.

The barrier had been broken. They could meet and mingle with Americans without fear of rousing any suspicions. They could blend in and above all remain anonymous.

The boarding house was cheap, but clean and comfortable and included in the cost was access to a bath which could be used every day. Never in their lives had they known such luxury. It was agreed that they would only have breakfast and would eat out, using diners that were recommended by the owners .

After a few days Yuri`s friend had nearly fully recovered both his strength and some of his lost weight. Then the inevitable day arrived; despite the instructions how and where to obtain their Social Security numbers they queued together and made consecutive applications for the documentation. Later that day, having paid their bill at the boarding house, they emotionally said their farewells including, unexpectedly, profuse gratitude to Yuri for his support which his friend would never forget.

They would not meet for...

TWENTY-EIGHT

He quietly suggested to Goldburgh, who he still thought was ignorant or unaware of his potential fate, shortly before entering the lorry with the two guards, that in order to confirm that they did not understand the English language, that the two men would endeavour to surpass each other in insults and invectives directed at the two guards who, when the time came, clearly did not understand one word of English and would therefore make implementation of his plan simple to enact. Viktor was surprised when his friend admitted a long held fear of his potential fate but they were buoyed by the possession of travel permits, foreign currency (if it was used cautiously) and a pistol, in the event of an emergency. Viktor outlined his plan which involved great personal risk to him, and to his friend no guarantee of a successful escape, though with luck and initiative Mandel could be over the border (he did not specify the destination and therefore a route because if the authorities did not accept his convincing story, they might extricate the truth by other means).

Shortly before they left the isolated road that led them from the camp and which would soon join the main road and finally the railway station, and in accordance with Viktor's plan, they signalled to the driver to pull over so that each member could relieve themselves; in the dusk, five men stood with their backs to the lorry and proceeded to answer a call of nature and then there was an exchange of cigarettes as the men relaxed in the dying embers of daytime.

Slowly, but methodically, Viktor drew the concealed pistol from the space between his leather belt and trousers and immediately shot the two shocked guards and the driver, administering to each a definitive *coup de grace* as they lay in mortal pain. Then he committed the act that his friend had pleaded him not to take. Quickly reloading the pistol and continuing the carnage of violence he shot himself in the thigh, the shock of which caused him to involuntarily drop the gun which

Goldburgh automatically picked up, possibly to return to his friend who called out, in excruciating pain, to shoot him again thereby giving an authenticity to his story that Goldburgh had overpowered him and committed mayhem before his escape. Perhaps Goldburgh shut his eyes and pulled the trigger randomly, aiming the weapon directly at his friend, however the bullet hit Kashkarov`s shoulder blade causing him to spin round and collapse. Mandel was committed ,taking the envelope and the spare shells before commandeering the lorry which he drove with great difficulty towards the station but which he abandoned before completing his journey, walking to the station unobserved in the dark, guided by the lights of the station and the noise of soldiers waiting to embark on the next available transport.

Less than six days later he was arrested outside of Yerevan in the Armenian Soviet Socialist Republic attempting to reach the Turkish border. He realised that he was a hunted man, aware that once the bodies of the three soldiers were found and possibly that of his dear friend, then the alarm would be raised and a coordinated 'hue and cry' begun. He was relieved of the dangerous, incriminating pistol and the envelope containing nine hundred U.S. Dollars and had voluntarily handed over his travel permit bearing two signatures.

The money was laboriously counted and then twice recounted by the local most senior N K V D officer who had formally requested his prisoner to witness the accounting along with two other officers such was the senior officer`s fear of possessing foreign currency which strangely totalled one thousand and fifty U.S. Dollars! The successful apprehension and arrest had been reported to 'Yerevan', together with confirmation that photographs of the man would shortly follow and they awaited a response from 'Moscow' with instructions. In the meantime fatally using their initiative with damning consequences, the three officers began their own interrogation, presumably hoping that their initiative would be recognised by their superiors.

They first concentrated on the address and telephone number written on the piece of paper inside the envelope, and in response the prisoner dishonestly answered that he was not aware of the identity, but when they confronted him with another number, in his own handwriting, which was neatly printed on the travel permit, surrounded by a doodle that he had subconsciously drawn, he refused to confirm any knowledge, but deliberately, accidentally mentioned that it was an unlisted telephone number in Moscow which was private.

His intention was obvious.   The senior officer left the room accompanied by one of his junior officers leaving the prisoner with the other officer and two guards. Time seemed to crawl as he awaited the inevitable return of the two officers who came back some three hours later clearly showing signs of frustration and anger, confirming that the resident was, in fact, the counter signature of the travel permit and that the first signature was clearly a forgery, purporting to be that of Commissar Beria. The interrogation became more intense and bitter as the senior officer demanded the identity of the other number's user. Goldburgh decided to tell the truth which he knew they would not believe.

"It is the unlisted number of a member of the Politburo, a family member, and a personal friend of Lavrenti Beria."

The force of the blow across his cheek and chin was violent, vindictive, vicious and vengeful. He found himself prostrate on the cold concrete floor and then, just as he was orientating himself he felt a tremendous sharp blow to his genitalia as he witnessed the leader kick him. Time ceased to exist. When he regained consciousness he felt an excruciating pain in his left hand and looking, though his eyesight was blurred, he realised that his hand had been crushed by a boot. He cried out but his words were in English.

Events were confused and he was in physical agony, all he remembered was a shouted exclamation...

"A spy."

More excruciating pain and then oblivion.

There was no clock in the room and his wristwatch was missing along with his belt and shoes. He sensed that darkness had descended and he saw towering above him a solitary guard; he tried to talk to the man who clearly had instructions to ignore him. His thoughts concentrated on what he believed to be the unavoidable and inevitable only outcome; at best a trial and his subsequent 'dIsposal'.

TWENTY-NINE

The woman doctor was gentle and kind, concentrating on his crushed hand and then his face, finally on an area so personal and intimate to him that at first he instinctively shielded his body, by moving his uninjured hand, from the gaze and healing hands of the old but experienced woman. Whether he had been given morphine or the doctor`s compassionate care had begun, or accelerated the healing process, he did not know or care only that his gonads felt so tender that any slight movement ignited a pain so sharp as to be unimaginable.

"Comrade Goldburgh."

He heard a voice behind him but could not, would not move for fear of the consequent pain. The man continued:

 "I am the head of the N K V D in Yerevan and up to five hours ago I had been previously instructed to arrest you and personally escort you to Moscow, however you will be pleased to learn that your three interrogators have themselves been arrested following a telephone call from Comrade Kaganovich and I am awaiting a personal call from Comrade Beria with any additional orders. I have never spoken to the head of the N K V D though Comrade Kaganovich states that you know them both well."

Goldstein uttered an ursine grunt which must have impressed his saviour who continued with further good news:

"The local N K V D chief clearly exceeded his responsibilities and I have ordered his execution since I know that no one in Moscow will be interested in his fate, only that an exhibition be made of him since he wilfully disobeyed a document personally signed by Commissar Beria."

Goldburgh`s response was totally unpredictable:

"Please can I have a sip of water?"

Shortly afterwards he slipped into a deep refreshing sleep and was not disturbed by the noise of a fusillade of rifle fire.

The events of the previous evening, including its termination, were as brief as his recollections. The following morning he awoke consumed only by the physical feeling of stiffness and the dull throbbing pain of soreness in his hand and the most personal part of his anatomy. His bed, he found out later, with little interest, had previously been occupied by his chief interrogator. Later that day the doctor persuaded and assisted him to walk, but with extreme trepidation. That evening, he met face to face the man who he had instinctively called his saviour. He had exciting news:

"Comrade Kaganovich (he visibly smiled, possibly because he had never and would probably never meet or speak to such a high ranking official again) has rung not only to ask about your condition but to give me instructions. May I ask you a very personal question: who is the Boss, is it who I think it is?"

The reply was honest but said with an unaccustomed authority and ruthlessness so that it achieved the desired intention and result:

"Comrade Stalin knows my parents and perhaps the last person I met before leaving Moscow over a year ago was his associate Lavrenti Beria."

The borsch was cold and refreshing, amply mixed with boiled potatoes and sour cream. As he savoured the simple food and the slightly stale black bread he considered his future position.

Lavrenti Beria would not be concerned ,or even interested, in the circumstances or death of three inconsequential guards and driver , or even of his friend, Kashkarov, if he had died from his wounds, however he would at sometime, if not now, but in the near future, worry that knowledge of the secret plan to infiltrate agents into the bosom of their then current ally be allowed to leave the Soviet Union. He also had a responsibility and moral duty to his 'uncle 'who was certainly unaware of what he had been doing for the past year and he wanted to protect the man from any consequences. He had only one viable option and a single course of action: to protect his 'uncle'. He would leave the Soviet Union and ultimately return to the United Kingdom, however he would suppress any information about his duties, the camp and its purpose from the British authorities and would endeavour, by stealth, to find out what the Soviet authorities had told the embassy about his duties as a liaison officer.

He would prepare a letter, to be delivered to Beria by the helpful and most likely obliging N K V D officer and he would ask for the assistance of the same man, to help him to the Turkish border and into Turkey.

No doubt the thought of an official journey to Moscow, combined with a possible meeting with the legendary head of the N K V D, on a matter of secret state business, would seduce and corrupt the man and influence any objective judgement.

He composed a simple letter to be personally delivered to Lavrenti Beria and if that was not possible it was to handed to Lazar Kaganovich for his assistance. No one, but Beria, was to read the contents.

The letter, on coarse headed N K V D notepaper, was brief and its contents succinct, but above all it was unambiguous:

"Comrade Beria,

I pledge my loyalty to the First Secretary, the Party and the N K V D. I am returning to England and when you need me no doubt your agents will contact me with your (he underlined the single word your, for emphasis) orders. On my return to Landon [sic] I will, if necessary, give a cover story to conceal any information from being divulged about the events of the last twelve months. I also hope to trace and meet my parents. Mandel Goldburgh."

THIRTY

He was deemed fit to travel,although his left hand was still heavily bruised, seven days after the incident which, unknown to him, was recorded as an accident when he fell down a staircase, whilst at the same time of his departure, the N K V D chief began his journey to Moscow accompanied not only by six unnecessary guards but by the most impressive brief case that he could procure which contained only the private correspondence and some food that had been prepared for him .

Goldburgh`s travel arrangements were less spectacular but effectively resolved his urgent, immediate needs. The envelope, containing the U.S. Dollar currency was returned to him and a lorry was placed at his disposal, along with a driver, two guards for his protection and ,until he could make contact with the British authorities or any reliable English speaking organisations, a guide who had intimate knowledge of the border region (he decided not to enquire into the circumstances). The man was fluent in the regional dialects for it was not intended that he legitimately pass through the border check point as, other than the still valid travel permit, he possessed no other documents and they did not wish to provide him with a Soviet passport.

It was clear that the guide was experienced and well used to what was become for him an arduous adventure and explained the necessary period of recuperation. The lorry was well provisioned, including a number of fuel cans which took up a disproportionate part of the available capacity as did a number of jugs containing drinking water; not unexpectedly, the food was simple, nutritious and plentiful. A large packing case was covered by a sheet of material that appeared, on inspection, to be waterproof and of nautical origin and was protected and guarded with even greater attention than him.

The first part of his journey took just over four days from his departure until the guide finally passed him to a trusted friend. He was disoriented, not having a wristwatch or a compass and having to solely rely on rough observations of the Sun and stars which exposed his inadequate knowledge and reliance on his guide and the driver .

They seemed generally to be travelling West, however the lorry regularly veered off the dirt tracks taking routes that seemed in contradiction to the Westerly direction and after they had been travelling for some ten days he was informed that they had entered Turkey some three or four days before and that they would make their *rendez –vous* within about six hours when the lorry would return to Yerevan and the Armenian Soviet Socialist Republic.

He remembered an earlier journey, travelling through seemingly unending forests but this journey was mentally boring and physically exhausting since the geography was arid and featureless, dominantly grey in colour and the ride rough but above all, and it only occurred to him at a late stage, devoid of any significant signs of habitation, indeed only twice had they come across solitary shepherds herding their flocks, one of whom appeared angered at the interruption to his work. He had taken the opportunity to resolve two potential problems. The first was an explanation for his absence for the past year and the second , how to hide what was a large sum of foreign currency which had been returned to him with obsequious apologies and no questions as to its origin.

He would use, as the foundation of his explanation, the fact that after some delay he had been sent to an isolated region of the Southern Ukraine, well away from the fighting, though on three occasions he had heard the sound of gunfire in the distance, to a former, almost derelict military barracks which had been requisitioned and used by the N K V D as a school to teach the basics of English to a number of officers. Why this centre had been chosen, when facilities nearer and within the 'Moscow 'area could have been used, he did not know and found it prudent not to enquire. There had been two commanders and conveniently only ten officers, most of whom had previously suffered various injuries on' the front' but had subsequently recovered before being assigned to the mini camp.

He decided that, for convenience, he would name them after twelve famous Russians including some authors and composers and that if he was intensely quizzed about the men he would have, for each, a brief resume that he memorised during the boring and uneventful journey, including anecdotes about incidents at the camp.

There was no plausible explanation for the large amount of money that he was carrying, and if discovered, would undoubtedly cast a shadow of doubt on the story that he had created. For some time he was at a loss to resolve this problem, when in a moment of inspiration, he noticed the majestic and beautiful sunset and the glint of sunlight on the horizon. He could not remember the logical sequence that followed but he finally calculated that diamonds could be more readily secreted on or in his body rather than a thick wad of American Dollars of low denomination.

He even remembered a prayer that was recited on the holiest day of the Hebrew calendar, Yom Kippur, The Day of Atonement, when the congregation thanked G-d for the human body that contained many tubes and orifices, without any one of which they could not live, but this then raised two new questions. Who could he trust to give him a fair and honest deal and how could he actually secrete them?

He had not been forewarned of another changeover. As the lorry disappeared beyond the horizon, leaving a trail of dust and the sound of grating gears, the guide stoically sat on the large case which had been so carefully guarded and handed a portion of the food that had also been left by the returning guards, before propping himself against the case which gave him some shade from the sun which was at its zenith. Goldburgh inferred from the man's actions that there was to be a long wait, using the time profitably to consider his situation and his future actions.

He had effectively been held incommunicado since being seconded to the authorities in Moscow, on the understanding that he was to act as a liaison officer and he had not attempted to contact the embassy or, indeed , had he heard from them.

He had sworn the Official Secrets Act but did not believe that the intentions of the Soviet authorities concerned the British government since this was purely a matter that should be disclosed to the United States authorities and he had an ideal contact that would be interested in his experiences. He then confronted himself with the realisation that his intentions could be misconstrued or misunderstood, should the ever more complicated strands become unravelled. And then he considered his own position and the ultimate question that he could not answer.

"Where did his loyalties lie?"

It must have been some five hours later, as the Sun began to set ,that the two men were alerted to the imminent arrival of another lorry, which came from the general direction in which their previous conveyance had been last seen on the horizon. It had seen better days and the bodywork was dented and rust was clearly evident like an eruption of eczema, but the engine sounded sweet and smooth. The driver embraced the guide and then began, feverishly, to open the large case and to lift out the contents which were initially packs of Philip Morris cigarettes and then other brands of well known U.S. cigarettes, finally, by tearing the side of the case, removing small boxes and opening one, no doubt as a test, to unveil a pair of ladies nylons, making a strange noise to show his pleasure or satisfaction. The two men then began to earnestly talk in some local patois, the intensity and fervour being undoubtedly the method of negotiation or barter when suddenly they shook hands, embraced each other and walked to the lorry, emerging with a bottle of some unknown drink, which after having imbibed was then offered to Goldburgh for his pleasure.

They both laughed when they saw him reel from the strength of the alcohol.

While he recovered, they continued to speak in a tongue that was as alien to him as perhaps English was to the local man who proceeded to walk up to him and, in a strange heavily accented and disjointed English and waving a single nylon, introduced himself with the statement:

"I help you get to Istanbul and you get the girls with this,"

laughing both at Goldburgh and at his own joke.

This was the site where his loyal guide was to leave and presumably begin his long journey back. He hugged his charge and confirmed that the new guide would take him as far as Istanbul, mainly by road and that the consignment of tobacco included a fee to transport him. He was utterly reliable and any demands or orders should be obeyed without question.

The three spent the night camped by the lorry and Goldburgh was woken shortly after dawn by the sound of another lorry which collected the guide and proceeded to move off Eastwards. Within minutes he realised that he had not asked his original guide two important questions, the first, his exact current location and the second, since it was now self evident that both his guides were experienced smugglers, where he could purchase a diamond or diamonds but above all ,since he knew little of these matters, a trustworthy vendor.

Conversation between the two men was scant as the driver seemed concerned only to concentrate on the barely defined dusty road and also on the changing terrain of ridges and hills which were becoming a normal part of the route, however once, unexpectedly, without reason, he mentioned that:

"Bandits. Very bad and dangerous, but I know them."

Suddenly bending down and hunting around, he lifted a rug from which dropped two pistols.

He laughed as if the journey was a game and adventure when Goldburgh then produced his own pistol and was surprised when the man began to call out, in a raised, but not loud voice...

"Bang, bang ,bang. Like the cowboys and Indians."

He allowed his new guide to continue the journey uninterrupted, succumbing to the tedium of the journey, falling asleep until he was woken by a sense of inertia and the pleasant,sweet smell and aroma of cooking. He found the guide tending a pile of stones which he had just excavated, opening a bundle of leaves from where the sweet smell originated and as he looked he saw a large piece of meat, the appearance and texture which seduced him, and requested a piece which was readily given, lying on a large leaf. Never before had he eaten so well by such a simple method.

After five days of monotonous travel and adequate but very simple food , when his only contribution had been to carefully pour petrol into the tank , the driver announced that they would soon reach the port of Amasra where he had business that might take...

"One or two days or a few hours but he would send him to an hotel to rest and clean himself up. "He continued with a warning...

"Girls are very, very naughty in the hotel and the men outside, criminals. Stay in your room. I get food sent up. Don`t give the girls these nylons."

At which point he handed over a fistful of nylons as if they were the local currency.

It was now or never. He had to take a chance and he made an indirect reference to the purchase of some diamonds, receiving an unexpected reply from a man who he had come to regard both as uneducated and lacking in erudition but wise in the ways of the world and probably human nature.

"You Russians are clever (Mandel was surprised and pleased that he was perceived and treated as Russian and not English). I take you to Istanbul to a man – he is not a cousin - my cousin is a very dishonest man, he is one of you, a Jew, but he is clean and washes regularly. I soon sell some of the cigarettes for English and American money and the rest in Istanbul. I give you a present because you work on the ferry looking after the cigarettes and the nylons."

He saw little of Amasra and even less of the hotel that had seen better days. The room possessed one attribute that was worth the cost which he did not bear as this was presumably paid by his host.

The bedroom contained, on the ceiling, a fan that actually and effectively worked so he lay down naked and unwashed and savoured the pleasure of the cool room as he frequently heard outside the laughter and voices of young women as they were possibly plying their age old profession. The water was hot and the bath overly large, as if it had been designed either for someone of excessive size or, he conjectured, for two people. He felt clean for the first time in many months since he had only been able to shower in the camp, though some of the accommodation constructed by and for the American residents did incorporate a small bathroom. He wondered where they were. Then he thought fondly of Natalia and wondered where she was at that very moment in time. He had suppressed his emotions and his physical desires and felt drawn suddenly to his own physical needs. He would take up his new friend`s suggestion but first he would sleep on the bed even though it did not give the most relaxing experience.

He was abruptly woken by the noise of a fist hammering emphatically and thoughtlessly on his door. In a dazed state between consciousness and slumber he opened the door to be told by his excited guide that he had completed his business and obtained ferry tickets to Istanbul and departure was imminent and he did not wish to miss the ferry. He hurriedly dressed, collected his few personal effects including ,especially, the wad of Dollar bills and the pistol with the accompanying supply of bullets and followed his guide and host through a maze of streets and alleyways and then saw ahead of him the magnificent sight of the Black Sea, the first time he had seen a large body of water since he had crossed the Atlantic .

He was to be responsible for the case and his guide confirmed that much of the contents had already been sold in exchange for American Dollars and British Sterling which were now in great demand and commanded a premium (actually the man's words were somewhat less eloquent and related to men's urges and the beauty and desirability of a virgin's breasts). He further commented, again in his broken English, this time alluding to worn out women, that German currency was being sold off and that he should not be enticed into buying any Reich Marks as they were going or would go 'Kaput 'and that remark reminded him that this was the first news he had heard about the war for some time and raised his hopes and his expectations of a swift reconciliation with his parents. The lorry had also been sold and he was flushed with money that he would use to buy a newer, better and bigger vehicle in Istanbul for the very long return journey home and the next deal.

THIRTY-ONE

Istanbul. They arrived on a Friday afternoon and the guide used the convenience and pleasure of a taxi, after much negotiation and argument over cost, to an hotel which unlike the previous hostelry appeared decent and luxurious. En route the taxi diverted and passed what he was informed was the British embassy though the building was small and unimpressive and which had all the appearances of being shut for the weekend ,and then made a second diversion to an area which the guide said housed the diamond dealers. The man who he was to recommend was not available, having left his premises early for the Jewish Sabbath, but having approached a nearby shop, he was informed that it was usual for him to open on a Sunday morning, for a few hours.

In comparison with the previous hotel, the new one had some of the trappings of luxury and elegance, but lacked the element of excitement that he had sensed when he heard the occupants – and their guests – outside of his previous room. He resolved that the following day he would go to a synagogue to celebrate the Sabbath and calculated , with a little guilt, that he had not been to a synagogue since before his family's departure from Moscow, a decade before.

He breakfasted frugally and followed the concierge's directions to the nearest place of worship and was welcomed with great hospitality as he was informed that visitors on the Sabbath were a rare occurrence.

He actually enjoyed the service though whether he gained any spiritual enhancement , he found doubtful. What he had not realised was that the community was of Sephardi origin and he was of Ashkenazi descent which made the service superficially different and he lost his concentration and found himself dozing off much to the irritation and humour of his fellow congregants during a sermon given in Turkish.

Afterwards he was surrounded by offers of hospitality but decided to return to the hotel and he was accompanied by two families, both intent on guiding him, especially as the route was on their way home.

That afternoon - he realised that he was a liberal and flexible Jew-he tried, as a matter of procedure to telephone the embassy on a number efficiently supplied to him by the hotel, but received the expected lack of a response.

His guide arrived late that afternoon to confirm that he had successfully completed his business dealings and would arrange to take him the following morning to the diamond dealer before beginning his long journey home. He would pay the hotel account with one of the new five pound Sterling notes that he had been paid to him and unexpectedly announced that he wished to buy from Goldburgh, his pistol and the bullets. There was very little haggling and a deal was struck and confirmed by a handshake though it was agreed that the vendor retain, for sentimental reasons, four of the bullets.

THIRTY-TWO

Outside of the shop, drinking the local coffee, was a large, fearsome man and adjacent to the cup was a large plate filled with the local exquisite and fattening pastries and a pistol close to the man`s left hand cocked for immediate use. The two men entered the shop and the guide requested the personal attention of the owner who he identified by his name. They would have to wait. He was in the rear working and would be available shortly.

Goldburgh examined the jewellery that was on display inside the large glass cabinets and had his back to the rear of the shop as the proprietor entered the room. The guide must have introduced himself for they spoke in Turkish and as Goldburgh turned round, as if fate had intervened, he instantaneously recognised the man as not only a fellow congregant but a member of one of the families that had offered him his hospitality and had accompanied him back to the hotel.

The two visitors were ushered into the rear of the shop and requested to sit at a small table covered in baize and brilliantly illuminated by a strong light directly over the table. The owner began to open two paper bags, each containing about ten or twelve diamonds of various sizes and shapes, meticulously and with almost religious intensity, dividing each diamond with the aid of a pair of tweezers and also keeping the two contents separate from the other, beginning his negotiations by asking the rhetorical and perhaps superfluous question:

"I understand that you wish to purchase some diamonds?"

Continuing his opening gambit with his first relevant question...

"Are they ultimately for a young woman or for investment?"

Goldburgh immediately responded, confirming the second option.

The merchant used the tweezers to hold a diamond to the artificial light and then asked the question which would ascertain the potential buyer`s knowledge of the subject and would, of course, partially expose and undermine his bargaining position...

"Do you know much about diamonds and how both to evaluate and value them?"

He would have confessed his ignorance and exposed his complete inexperience negotiating a deal, when his guide, who had been originally introduced to him as being utterly reliable, interrupted the shop proprietor and in Turkish, to the shock of the jeweller stated that he would have to deal with him if an unfair deal was completed.

The conversation had been conducted in Russian and in response the man looked at Goldburgh, put his hands on Goldburgh`s hands and stated that:

"I have many customers, some of them like us are of the Hebrew faith, and they all mistakenly believe that because they are Jewish that they will get a better deal. That is never so. I have a reputation and I make a reasonable, but never excessive profit on my trading. You have to trust me or leave. There are a number of dealers in this little area who may or may not give you a deal which is fair or reasonable. You will only find out how fair they have been, or I have been ,when you come to trade on the diamonds. I will not be offended if you both get up and leave."

It would be some years before Goldburgh was justified and proved right in his next decision as he firmly sat in his place.

"Good (the man continued). Do you know what is known as, in English, the four 'Cs'? They are known as the Cut, the Clarity, the Colour and finally the Carat Weight. These are the four factors that determine the price or when I worked in the special area of London, that like this little enclave housed the diamond dealers, there were two other 'Cs' - Competition and Cost. If we complete a deal, how will you pay me ?, I will take any currency, especially American Dollars but not German Reich Marks, not because I am a Jew and they hate the Hebrews, but they will soon lose the war and their currency, like in nineteen twenty-three, will be worthless."

He was slow in his reply, not realising that his response would draw out the vendor...

"I could possibly pay in Sterling or Dollars but need first to ascertain your sale price on, for example, the diamond that you are currently displaying."

A price was mentioned and then the guide pointed to a rather beautiful rectangular stone that was smaller than most of the others, but even for the layman had an indefinable quality.

"You either have exquisite taste or knowledge that you are hiding from me."

It was becoming clear that the prices being quoted might permit him to purchase five of the best stones that were available, which led him to enquire, without considering the consequences of his interest, if...

"There were any other stones he could view (now disclosing his hand) at a similar price to the stone that his friend had observed?"

The diamond merchant called and his assistant promptly rushed in and was instructed to collect two further packets from his employer's home and to return within an hour but first to order on his way out, coffees and pastries which arrived within ten or fifteen minutes.

During the hiatus the three men discussed the war and Goldburgh was scrupulously careful only to divulge the absolute minimum of information, stating that he would, tomorrow, visit the British embassy and expected to be repatriated to the United Kingdom when transit could be arranged.

He listened to the other two men discuss the war and was able to construct a comprehensive picture of events and it was clear that the Germans were now being squeezed on two fronts in Europe and that the Americans were pushing forward across the Pacific despite stubborn Japanese resistance.

The diamond merchant opened the first new package as if he were a magician unveiling the surprise that his audience had not anticipated and he was right in his judgement as both Goldburgh and the smuggler were visibly excited by the superior quality and brilliant colours that perhaps even dazzled their eyes; when the second packet was displayed it utterly eclipsed the contents of the first. Using the tweezers Goldburgh selected four diamonds and figuratively laid his cards honestly on the table...

"I wish to purchase, if possible, these four diamonds but whilst price is, without doubt, an important consideration I want to be reasonably confident that these diamonds are of the highest standard."

He then indicated one particular stone whose size, colour and clarity were so self evidently magnificent that it made its desirability inevitable It was by the very description ,outstanding.

"My friend (the jeweller, with finesse, effortlessly began the REAL negotiations), you have selected the most expensive stone that I have available and shows that you have a keen eye. For this stone my best price is (he mentioned a figure in U.S. Dollars looking all the time at the potential purchaser's face in order to gauge his reaction), however the stone comes with a story, a story that I must recount to you because it symbolises the age old struggle of our people and both the tragedy and hope that is our lot.

I bought the stone late last year from a Hungarian Jew, a newspaper publisher and a man of renown in his own country to men of all faiths. His family had been attacked by either the Nazis or their Hungarian fascist thugs, anyway the family managed to escape, assisted by many members of the community and reached Turkey and this magnificent city via a tortuous journey travelling through Romania and then Bulgaria. They were a tragic sight but the father had qualities that like a warning beacon made him shine through the ordeal. His strength and determination and the stone, which represented the total sum of his worldly possessions, symbolised his strong personality. With the money he received and utilising certain connections that I only have a peripheral knowledge, the family was able to indirectly and circuitously travel and illegally enter Palestine where I heard some months ago they had started a new life on a farming community. "

Goldstein listened with pride and humility, saw the vendor isolate the stone and then bluntly made a statement and enquiry...

"I would want over one thousand U.S. Dollars. What price would you make (he didn`t say offer) including these two other stones (pointing the tweezers at two of the three stones that had previously interested the potential purchaser)?"

However Goldburgh was still concerned that he was being offered a fair deal and that he needed some money to tide him over if there was any problem with the embassy. For a moment he hesitated, a reaction noted by the jeweller who now was caught between the loss of a potential, lucrative sale, and indecision on the part of the buyer.

"Mr. Goldburgh what is delaying your decision?"

The reply was most unusual and confused the seller forcing him to compromise.

"I am concerned how I am to carry these three diamonds without discovery and still I am unsure that the diamonds are as valuable as they have been offered to me."

The jeweller must have been in this situation many times before and made a final offer both in terms of price but more so to confirm his integrity...

"Your friend threatened me with retribution if I struck a dishonest deal and I believe that although the threat was made in a moment of passion, was still meant, however it does not change the sincerity and good faith of my offer."

Within minutes they shook hands and the vendor received the reduced negotiated price of nine hundred and sixty -five U.S.Dollars, a deal which was sealed by the age old phrase,'Mazal'.

"There is no way that you can deceive an expert looking for hidden goods on your body, only never give a reason for others to suspect that you are carrying something that is of value to them. Here is some Vaseline and some cotton wool. Place the diamonds within a little cotton wool and then wedge the ball between your toes, two on one foot and one on the other. Always wear socks, never wash in a bath and again always leave the diamonds in a receptacle whilst you clean between the toes. Do not carry the Vaseline around with you as this could be seen as unusual, use yoghurt ."

THIRTY-THREE

He would not know the true value of the deal that had been struck until a few days after an economically catastrophic day for the British people. Neither would the paths of the three men ever cross again.

The following morning, his guide performed one final task as he led his charge to what was, in fact, a consulate, and not the British embassy, which was situated in Ankara. Goldburgh had earlier exchanged his pistol along with all but four of the bullets to the man in exchange for ten pounds of English currency. He waited at a cafe opposite the three storey building until the office was clearly open and then walked across the street, in one pocket two five pound notes and the balance of his once large amount of Dollars and in another, the expired travel visa and bullets. He had no other personal effects and completely obliterated from his thoughts any knowledge of the three diamonds which might give a tell tale hint to a persistent and inquisitive investigator, indeed he concentrated on his story and the intention to be both consistent and to convey the minimum of information.

The front door led directly into a rectangular hall in which there were five rows, each of five chairs, all of which were unoccupied and facing them a solitary desk at which sat a lonely individual and behind him, hanging on the wall, a black and white framed picture of His Majesty, King George .

The man was clearly wasting time by moving a set of blue files from one pile to another and occasionally opened a file and typed something that he would insert into the file. The official pretended not to see the lone visitor who sat in the front row waiting for an acknowledgement when after an appreciable time, he called out:

"Next,"

and Goldburgh rose from his chair and walked the very short distance to the desk and a seat opposite the official. The clerk's tone became more civil and amicable.

"How can I assist you?"

At which moment he commenced the pre prepared statement or mini speech being careful to be vague whenever a situation was mentioned that might have to be explained in greater detail at a later stage. He was most surprised at the response of the official who clearly expressed his confusion as he suddenly realised, to his horror, that he was so used to thinking and speaking in Russian that he had mentally prepared his statement in that tongue. He swiftly apologised and repeated the statement in English.

"My name is Mandel Goldburgh and just over a year ago I was seconded from the British embassy in Moscow, where I was a translator, to the Soviet government and some time later I was sent to the South of the Ukraine to teach English to a number of N K V D officers. About six weeks ago, I was provided with a special travel visa which has now expired and is still in my possession and I have been travelling almost constantly, except for one stop of a week, and I now know that I entered Turkey illegally since I had no other documents. My passport is still, presumably, being held by the embassy. I wish to return to the United Kingdom as soon as reasonably possible."

The official's response was both prompt and positive: he was to wait whilst he referred the whole matter to his superior who, no doubt, would personally wish to deal with him and that he was welcome, in the meantime, to read his own personal copy of 'The Times' which was the latest available to the consulate.

He was so immersed in the newspaper that he did not concern himself with the passage of time, which turned out to be some forty minutes or so, before a more mature official entered the room from a side door and introduced himself as the local consul and wished to assist him, however he requested that:

"He recount his experiences and could he perhaps amplify details of some of the more recent events."

The story was recounted, but he intentionally did not amplify, as requested, any of the basic facts, deliberately putting the onus on the consul. After which the consul responded with an acknowledgement and a number of unexpected questions.

"Thank you for your story. A report will be sent today to Ankara for their instructions and in the meantime may I ask if you have any accommodation?; if not, we are able to assist you even though you are not a diplomat. We can be flexible about any financial subsidy. Do you have any funds to make a contribution?

Goldstein took from his pocket the Sterling and the Dollars which the man promptly counted and returned to him but did not query their provenance.

"My assistant you take you to a local hotel where we have an account and will introduce you to a few restaurants where, again, the bills will be paid by us. Unfortunately, as a formality I must ask that you return tomorrow at ten a.m. and remain in this office all day, every day – other than at meal times – to await our further instructions.

Also would you remember not to abuse our hospitality as it is wartime and our masters in London at the Foreign Office are entitled and may pursue reimbursement from you of our outlay. Be a good chap and take things easy. He will also show you an excellent cafe which serves the best coffee and superb pastries."

The demand and requirement that he effectively remain in the building each day was more honoured in the breach than the observance ,even to the extent that the consul would join him in the highly recommended cafe for coffee and a chat – never about his situation- usually to fill him in about the general military position and his frustration that he was unable to follow his passion for fishing and that he hoped, following the successful ending of the war , he could retire to Hampshire, obtain a Knighthood and enjoy himself pursuing his sport.

Tuesday, Wednesday and Thursday all slowly passed as did the Friday until the afternoon when he returned from a pleasant light lunch and a short sleep to be amicably greeted by the underworked and probably inefficient but friendly clerk to be informed that, unofficially and off the record, there had been a development and that the consul, who was out on other important matters, wished to see him as soon as he returned, but he should not indicate his prior knowledge.

"I have some excellent news for you. Let us go into my own office, where I feel comfortable conducting my affairs and let me tell you what Ankara has cabled me (Goldburgh followed the consul through a side door, incidentally noting a trait that he had never observed before, as the man actually skipped, as if the excitement of a real act of work had woken him from a stupor). You are to be sent to Cairo via Haifa and ultimately, subject to the military situation, home to England. Officially or even unofficially I am unaware how this will be accomplished, since I read that the Mediterranean is still plagued by some enemy vessels.

A local photographer will arrive shortly and he will take a number of photographs that will be sent onto Cairo who have promised to issue a new passport which will take about three weeks, when we will be able to make the travel arrangements. In the meantime we have been requested to obtain a standard application form for your completion. Please use my fountain pen."

Under a question relating to 'previous passports held?', he answered evasively...

'In the possession of the ambassador in Moscow.'

After the consulate had officially closed the photographer arrived and was ushered into the consul's office and proceeded to set up what appeared to be an antique camera taking a number of pictures, some rather ominously profiles of the subject, as if he had just been sent to prison.

THIRTY-FOUR

On the following Monday afternoon he was summonsed to the consul's office where he was examining the various photographs and a limited number that were suitable for a passport. He handed Goldburgh two large photographs and requested amicably, but officially, that:

" He verify that both photographs were of him and on the reverse of each, testify to the fact and sign and date both statements - only a formality, you know, old chap."

Once this procedure had been accomplished the consul confirmed that the photographs would be forwarded to Cairo who had just contacted the consulate with a not too unusual request that the man, either in his own handwriting or typewritten, supply a comprehensive report of his activities after he had left the British embassy in Moscow and been seconded to the Soviet authorities.

"Dates might be helpful, but names and locations were of greater interest since obtaining any information from inside the Soviet Union had been and continued to be difficult, even though they were ostensibly our ally."

Thus began the interest that he had feared and for the rest of the day and the whole of the next day and again the following day as he repeatedly pondered on his situation, he realised that if and when the authorities in London investigated his story and compared it to any information that the Soviets might have or would supply, then his integrity and the story would cease to be credible. They would certainly not admit the real truth and might concoct a fabrication, indeed he was unaware that they had already supplied a cover story. He resolved to stand by his story for at worst he would suffer the consequences in England which would be far more lenient than any punishment in the Soviet Union. Suddenly, as if he had deliberately suppressed all memory of the act, he remembered the letter to Beria. In some malevolent manner they could use his declaration of loyalty against him. He made a decision. He would prepare a statement and let the British authorities challenge his account. Didn't the consul state just a few days before that..

"...obtaining any information from inside the Soviet Union had been and continued to be difficult."

No one had commented on his left hand which still displayed signs of an injury or had even commented on its restricted movement and he decided to attribute the injury to an accident in a lorry when his hand was crushed. Great emphasis would be placed on the assistance of the N K V D in Yerevan because of the identity of the first signature.

He obtained paper and carbon paper from the clerk and the consul allocated space in an empty downstairs office and the use of an Underwood typewriter. He initially mentally prepared and drafted the statement and when he completed each page he would impose upon the consul to review the document and make any suggestions or comments, thus the final definitive document (with a carbon copy for his records) went through a number of drafts .

It was during this period that an incident took place that made him suspicious that the building housed not only two inconspicuous officials but others performing work that was shrouded in secrecy and subterfuge. One day whilst he was ensconced in the room and discussing a draft with the consul, the conversation was interrupted by a knock on the door and without confirmation a man totally unknown to him entered ,holding a sheet of paper and who immediately addressed the consul requesting ...

"His presence upstairs as an important document had been received and demanded his attention."

The consul in an obsequious and dutiful tone apologised for the interruption and left with the man, leaving the door open and subconsciously inviting him to satisfy his curiosity. He ventured out to the bottom of the stairs and whilst he could hear more than two voices talking he could also hear, distinctively, the chatter and pounding of at least two rapidly operating typewriters. He returned to his own office and continued typing the report, making it mandatory, every day, to read his copy of the statement and draw mental pictures of the ten students and the two commanders.

Then one morning the consul approached him and announced that:

"All the preparations had been finalised and that on the following day he would be handed his new passport and would then be driven by car to the capital, Ankara, which would take two days after which he would be flown by military transport to Cyprus and then either by ferry or again by military transport to Cairo."

The whole journey took just under four days, a surprisingly quick period, being the outcome of a fortuitous combination of events but was balanced by the funereal pace of procedures in Cairo.

THIRTY-FIVE

The following morning he arrived at the consulate to see a pre war American Sedan parked outside the building and the consul engaged in conversation with, presumably, the driver and a third man who he recognised as the official who had interrupted his earlier meeting. He was younger than him and was informally introduced as...

"The man that you fleetingly met, Mr. Andrew Duggan."

His final act was to genuinely and richly thank the consul for his help and remembered to remark that he hoped that he could pursue his hobby, sooner rather than later, and that perhaps they could meet ,in London, after the war.

They arrived in Ankara, late the following afternoon, after a journey that was above all uncomfortable but also monotonous and consequently boring as the terrain was devoid of any interesting or significant features and his attempts to engage his fellow traveller in conversation, however shallow, superficial or just to pass the time was rejected or even rebuffed, as Duggan seemed intent in existing in his own solitary world.

The road had been built to the most primitive and basic standard, most likely over and following an ancient caravan route, riddled and punctuated with pot holes and it was this hazard that compelled the driver to maintain a low cruising speed. It was only after the driver mistimed evading a particularly deceptive hole, causing the vehicle to lurch, then temporarily lose control, that Duggan withdrew from his self imposed isolation and cursed the road and its builders, a theme endorsed by his fellow passenge, both because he agreed with the opinion and because it gave him the opportunity to talk with his travelling companion.

Duggan was taciturn and reticent admitting that he regularly made this ...

"Journey every couple of months or so and found no pleasure either in the conservative nature of Ankara or the wearisome, exhausting challenge of the road."

There was little else that he discussed as if, Goldburgh concluded, the man had an aversion to him or for other deeper reasons wished to retain his privacy.

The first and only night of their journey was spent in a village that was located just off the route and must have been bypassed by both civilisation and the twentieth century, containing only one house of any substance, and it appeared, because of the fraternisation between the driver and the owner, that they were well acquainted.

A simple meal and accommodation was provided, bare rooms lit by rudimentary oil lamps and beds that were essentially wide boards covered by thick coarse rugs permitted an uncomfortable sleep. It was only in the morning just before they thankfully departed that Goldburgh noticed that a briefcase Duggan was carrying and possibly had been concealed in a well in the Sedan, was literally chained to his left wrist.

THIRTY-SIX

They arrived at the British embassy late in the afternoon, the vehicle`s speed having increased following access to some of the few , but more modern roads that the capital city boasted. The party was met by a second secretary and Goldburgh specifically noticed that his travelling companion had swiftly entered the building and disappeared from his life. He was sent to an hotel, more opulent than the one that he had been staying in Istanbul and advised that he was due to meet the ambassador late the following morning .

He had bathed and dried himself when yet again his privacy and pleasure were interrupted by a repeated knocking on the door which this time he resolved to ignore but shortly afterwards, the telephone in the room came to life and he answered the call: it was the second secretary.

"Events had moved more quickly than planned and a seat had been obtained on a flight leaving in three hours time, that is at nine p.m. He was to be ready to leave in ninety minutes which would give him time not only to wash but to eat in the hotel's restaurant.

At seven thirty he was collected by the second secretary in his own car which he drove with great pride, pleasure and panache.

"It's a nineteen twenty-eight Bentley four and a half litre open four seater which I picked up recently from some wealthy refugees who needed some Sterling urgently. When, hopefully, this bloody mess with Hitler is finished I'm going to ship the vehicle back home to my parents' estate and use the vehicle in Devon. There is an unofficial and unscheduled civil flight organised by our friends in the American embassy going at least to Cyprus. Once on board, use your initiative to finally reach Cairo, where you should report to the embassy. Your exploits had become widely known in the community so it shouldn't be too difficult to get there."

The primitive airport was subject to the obligatory 'Black Out' and he was unconcerned about the aircraft which had the minimum of identification and, if he had any interest in the matter, he would have learned, was owned and operated by the United States government for the benefit and use of its diplomats and businessmen working in neutral Turkey and probably the oil wells of Persia. His primary consideration, indeed his only concern, was his repatriation. Once the plane had left the neutral airspace of Turkey it was accompanied by Royal Air Force planes to its first destination, Cyprus. It landed at a British air force base where he made his presence known to some American officers who verified that the plane was due to go on to Palestine but they also were aware of a military transport leaving early in the morning and with that positive approach to the resolution of problems ,they offered, there and then, to fix up his passage and he was introduced to an officer who confirmed his place but also offered accommodation, if only for a few hours, whilst he waited. He ate well but very late (It was about four a.m.), the menu being similar to food that he had enjoyed at the camp but he realised that any memory should be erased, lest he inadvertently make a public reference.

By late morning he had arrived at the military airport just outside Cairo and made his presence, and needs, known to some helpful officers who insisted on their assistance. They commandeered a Jeep which one of the three officers recklessly drove, without regard to his own or his passengers' safety, but they reached their destination and he was left at the embassy gates thankful for his deliverance, shortly before closing time which gave him little, but enough time, to contact an official who was aware of his planned arrival but...

"Not for at least two to three days and that his unexpected arrival had thrown their arrangements, or plans, into confusion."

The embassy official urgently arranged hotel accommodation for him on the same basis as had been previously provided in Istanbul and Ankara and also recommended certain restaurants where the embassy maintained accounts.

"Daily attendance was not required but you should telephone each day to inform the officials of your where-abouts and to confirm when you were to attend the embassy."

He had begun to follow a regular pattern of activity after nearly three weeks of inertia, as Christmas and the New Year loomed. Daily walks enabled him to grasp the geography of the ancient city and he learned how to navigate, not by the Sun or stars but by the great monuments of antiquity allowing him to calculate his bearings. He had managed to save the two five pound notes and had only spent three one dollar bills that were in so much demand that he had an abundance of the local currency as change.

It was on or about the twentieth of December that his daily telephone call was this time answered by the demand for his attendance that same afternoon and that, worryingly, he was told to bring the Sterling and Dollar currency that he had declared to the consul in Istanbul.

Goldburgh sat in a sombre room, poorly lit and windowless, painted in a dark 'Sherwood Forest' green and opposite him, at a long table, sat three men including Duggan and to their side sat a male stenographer who scrupulously took notes of the meeting. The first meeting was superficially friendly but he sensed an undercurrent of not only coldness but also of a pre conceived doubt and perhaps even cynicism concerning the veracity of his statement. In front of Duggan was a thick manila file which, when opened, included as part of the contents,some of his portrait photographs.

Duggan was the youngest and as it turned out the most junior in status of the three tribunal members, but was permitted, under supervision, to at times lead the investigation but also, whilst tempered by British courtesy, to attempt to discredit his statement. He began by formally introducing himself and the other two members and described them as intelligence officers from London who had...

"Kindly offered to assist him, but were primarily involved in other, more major work, and that he should not infer by their presence any degree of importance to his case."

Duggan then made a brief statement outlining the agenda of the meeting and by disclosing its requirements allowed Goldburgh to defend his position. Initially they wanted to clarify the origins of the currency that he had declared in Istanbul and secondly, and this was where Duggan made a strategic error, that Goldburgh reconsider or withdraw his statement.

He reminded the three men that his statement included the specific information that the two five pound notes had been given to him by the final guide, in exchange for the pistol and all but four of the bullets which the head of the camp (he deliberately,at that stage, did not identify him) had given to him and also the dollars to fund his journey from the Ukraine. The man's motive to give him the dollars was probably motivated by friendship and the fact that most likely under Soviet law it was an offence to be in possession of foreign currency and his gift served a dual purpose.

It was then that Duggan announced that whilst he was not confiscating the Sterling and Dollars, for he had no current legal authority, he was asking him to hand over the money which would be retained as evidence but he would be promptly reimbursed at the exchange rate operating at the embassy's bank in Cairo. Goldburgh immediately offered the currency as a sign of good faith and at the request of one of the two officers signed and dated the two five pound notes which, other than being folded and refolded, were in excellent condition.

Duggan then asked him to read a copy of his statement in the presence of the three members whilst at the same time, they would also read their copies, the original now being held in London together with his passport application.Goldburgh used a pencil to highlight certain errors and the omission of various items that he knew, instinctively, were in the original document. They proceeded at the pace of the slowest reader and some eighty minutes later Duggan asked if the document was...

"A true and accurate transcription on which they could discuss the contents ?"

Goldburgh had no other option but to explain that excluding many errors of spelling and punctuation the document contained, no...

"Did not include various matters and, for example, he clearly remembered that he had described travelling South by train along with the camp's commander through beautiful forests of silver -birch and there was no reference at all in the document that he had just read .

Furthermore a most memorable long paragraph was glaringly absent, when he recounted certain anecdotes about life at the camp and how two or three of the officers acquired the reputation as scavengers as they would appropriate a lorry and disappear for the best part of a day when they would return laden with produce and once with a wild boar which was roasted on a make shift spit and a liberal basting of vodka. I would have remembered not only the incident but more importantly, mention of this happy occasion."

Duggan responded by asking if his fellow members wished to make any observations or ask any questions and the visibly oldest of the three, named Goodacre, most memorable because of his appearance and diction, since he had a thyroid condition which meant that his eyes bulged, a pronounced lisp and a noticeable stammer, with difficulty , asked point blank...

"If he was prepared to withdraw the statement, whether it was the disputed version or his original which was lodged in London and own up to a fabrication, for reasons that he could explain and at this early stage dig himself out of the hole that he was digging himself into?"

Goldburgh patiently sat silent, obviously mentally preparing his answer. He was, of course, unaware that the Soviet authorities had spent the previous year or so deliberately stalling the many enquiries raised by the British embassy in Moscow concerning his safety and where-abouts and they had clearly been evasive and uncooperative.

"I have nothing to hide and would gain no advantage by concocting a false statement of my time serving the Soviet government as a British representative."

Duggan then announced, with a tinge of frustration and irritation, that there was no point continuing the meeting because of his apparent intransigence.

With the spectre of the ongoing war still casting a shadow upon the lives of the diplomatic staff, their families and the local expatriate community, Christmas and the New Year were celebrated with muted enthusiasm, their thoughts and best wishes directed to families and friends back home especially as a second "Blitz" was still taking place with V 1s and V2s raining down on the South East of England and troops fighting a determined German offensive in the Ardennes.

December merged into January then as February loomed he became lethargic and bored following the absence of any developments ,however he was shaken from his inertia, when he received a request to appear and, this time he was more concerned, since the summons worryingly referred to a formal tribunal hearing. Fearing, or anticipating the worst, he decided to hide the three diamonds and urgently procured some water proof cloth in which he wrapped a chamois cloth concealing the treasure. He found a loose floorboard in the bathroom and with an expertise that he did not know he possessed, he first removed the floorboard and concealed and wedged the packet as to be unobservable to anyone who might notice a peculiarly loose replaced floorboard.

THIRTY-SEVEN

The interview took place in the same dreary, sombre, poorly lit room and again there were three members, Duggan, Goodacre and a new third member whose appearance so shocked him that he only just managed to conceal his emotion. Probably the man was suffering from some local water–borne disease as he appeared literally close to death, cadaverous and craggy browed, with ashen skin and deep-sunk eyes and who was introduced as another intelligence officer. In anticipation of an in depth enquiry he took the opportunity to have available the carbon copy of his original statement and declared its existence when he had the first opportunity, a fact that was noted by the same male stenographer.

Duggan was blunt and asked if Goldburgh, having had several weeks to consider his situation, was prepared not only to retract his statement but to give an explanation of his perfidiousness and to tell the tribunal the truth about his time in the Soviet Union. Before he had the opportunity to reply and indeed he was given further time to consider his answer, the newest member of the Board asked sarcastically if he was being...

"Both disingenuous and not candid since the travel permit had been examined and the signature of Lavrenti Beria declared a forgery, leaving him, as an expert on Soviet Intelligence, with the opinion that the loyalty of the accused..."

At which moment Goldburgh rose, looked at the triumvirate and stated, with calmness, confidence and not only with great authority but with the support of the invisible force of law that...

"He was not aware that he had been charged with any offence, that he was not a traitor and that he felt not only an affinity with Galileo Galelei but could now, in the middle of a war against a totalitarian regime understand how Galileo felt when he stood before the Holy Roman and Universal Inquisition after he had written 'The Dialogue'."

An ominous and eerie cold silence permeated the room. Sensing he had seized the initiative, he made what was to be the final observation on what had been intended, but was about to be abruptly terminated, as a possibly lengthy investigation.

" May I remind you of the alleged purpose of the camp and my private thoughts about its isolated location?"

Duggan looked at his two associates and then at Goldburgh. Perhaps he could not comprehend the intellectual concept, but in fact it was the argument of a man of deep intelligence and flowering wisdom.

"It is clear that without further evidence we are unable to shake you from your statement, despite our joint opinion to the contrary. Arrangements will soon be made to confirm your passage home."

As Goldburgh left the room he noted not only the rage on Duggan`s face but a strange malevolent appearance as if the true inner man was being exposed.

THIRTY-EIGHT

His humble accommodation on the troopship clearly implied the worth and valuation that had been placed on him by the authorities, or likely as not a final assault by Duggan, however the camaraderie and excitement of the returning troops made up for the inconveniences that he easily learned to endure. He had adequate time to plan his most urgent tasks once he reached England but pondered on his financial position. The derisory exchange rate converting the local Egyptian currency back to Sterling had left him impecunious, however he remembered the bank clerk's parting words of wisdom that if he was endeavouring to convert German Reich Marks he would find an exchange rate comparable to the days of nineteen twenty-three and the hyper inflation which had been a contributory factor in the social and political unrest which had culminated in the rise of Adolf Hitler.

London was drab and colourless, except for the many black American soldiers on leave, strolling around the West End which was still subject to the 'Black Out'. The newspaper vendors called out the latest headlines and, without exception, the nation and the many troops and civilians of the United Nations could see the end of the war in sight, at least in Europe, as Marshall Zhukov's Red Army was bearing down on Berlin from the East and Eisenhower's forces marched onwards from the West.

He had decided to spend a couple of days in the capital, before travelling to Southwold, hopefully to meet his old friend and teacher before going up to Cambridge, for he had had an idea which necessitated his return to the University. As he walked from Piccadilly Circus towards Leicester Square, such was his deep contemplation and concern for his future, that he completely ignored and forgot to look at the various cinemas advertising and promoting numerous frivolous works as 'Keep Your Powder Dry' with Lana Turner at the Empire,' Here Come The Co-Eds' with Abbott and Costello at the Leicester Square Theatre and the more cerebral Noel Coward production of his' Blithe Spirit' at the Odeon .

He continued his walk, turning right into Charing Cross Road and then into Trafalgar Square where he was assailed on all sides by the many and varied different uniforms and languages that were being spoken and, strangely, his own English tongue spoken not only in its many regional dialects but also in a myriad of different foreign accents.

It was good to be home, if in fact this was his home but he had no real roots, or was he stateless?

He had not forewarned his good friend of his intended visit to Southwold and therefore his unexpected arrival, literally, 'on the doorstep' was even more surprising for his host. That evening the two enjoyed the simple pleasure of a walk along the sea front where the anti invasion defences had recently been dismantled, signifying not only to the local community, but also to the nation at large ,that finally the threat of invasion by the Barbarian horde was ended and that life could partially return to normal.

He did not confide his innermost secrets, only repeating the story contained in his statement and no mention was made of his meetings with the leadership of the Soviet Union and more importantly his direct involvement in the discussions that had culminated in the talks at Tehran. Such was his intense, vigorous description and eloquent story of his journey that it was recommended that he begin a new career as a writer but he knew that potentially a far greater challenge could lie before him and on their return home he discreetly, in an envelope that was provided for him, secreted the diamonds and noted where his friend placed the envelope without him even asking about the nature of the contents or unquestioningly agreeing to deny any knowledge of the envelope's existence.

Two days later they travelled to Cambridge by train and bus, the beloved and well maintained nineteen twenty-nine Bentley being currently 'on blocks' because of petrol rationing. His friend again did not question either his reasons or actions, assuming that they were only as they appeared and that there were no ulterior motives, consequently he joined his former pupil when he visited the bank to confirm the status of his account, taking with him his passport as evidence of identity but the clerk responded with confirmation that his word was adequate and that he would only need his last address which was given as Portobello Road, West London.   The clerk disappeared to shortly return holding a bundle of envelopes marked:

'Gone away. No forwarding address.'

The account was in credit in an amount of one thousand two hundred and ninety six pounds, thirteen shillings and eight pence, a sum that he had not anticipated and far exceeded his expectations and would provide for his needs for some time. He would peruse the statements that evening to ascertain how the balance had been made up. They then took a leisurely walk to the college of the Russian tutor who had been such an indirect influence on his life, to be informed by the college 's staff of his absence, but anticipated return ...

"The day after tomorrow ."

It was agreed that his friend return to Southwold and he would remain in Cambridge in anticipation of the man's arrival which, with the accuracy of a pre war railway time table, indeed took place on the mid afternoon of his estimated arrival.

"My dear boy, what a most exciting and pleasant surprise to meet you again, especially as you were the subject of a most interesting conversation with my Soviet friends, for as you may know I am a member, no not of the Communist Party of Great Britain, but of an Anglo-Russian friendship society determined to raise the awareness of cultural and social links between our two nations.

Through the embassy, information reached London concerning your help bringing together the United Nations in that historic conference at Tehran which was viewed by my friends as the supreme example of friendship and harmony between our two nations that they could ever believe possible and the ambassador himself, normally a dour and enigmatic figure, actually shook my hand when I told him, not that we were friends, but that I had helped, in my own little way, to assist you in your journey through university. And the rumours: it was whispered that you had been spirited away and were doing secret work for both the British and the Soviets. It all sounded too exciting for me and my dickey ticker."

Goldburgh was at the same time both proud and troubled by the man's remarks and he conjectured that somehow possible knowledge of his activities had seeped out. If only he could talk to the embassy as they might act as a conduit between him and those in Moscow who could help him protect the secret of the camp by supporting his statement, but would there be a price to pay?

He also realised that his knowledge could be shared with the suave American Mr. Maddox and the information could command not only a substantial reward but the security of the American's protection.

"Could you arrange a discreet private meeting with the ambassador or his representative as there were certain matters that had not been finalised when he left the Soviet Union and he wondered if the embassy could assist him resolve these minor but irritating matters ?"

He returned to Southwold and took up residence in his friend's home paying a contribution towards the expenses of the property and also found part time work, like his father before him, teaching Russian to a few enthusiasts which also gave him the opportunity to write to the International Red Cross to ascertain either the where-abouts of his parents or, and he thought the unthinkable, their fate.

By early September he had all but forgotten his request and enquiry and also assumed that any interest by the British authorities of his time in the Soviet Union had been exhausted and his records filed, most likely misfiled. Then one morning he received a letter postmarked Cambridge that he opened and devoured with almost excessive ravenous haste.

"An apology. Whilst he had promptly attended to the matter, he had mistakenly put away the letter, but from the time he corrected his oversight and urgently sent out his missive, within two weeks the embassy confirmed their interest and that he should urgently (that word had been written in capitals and was also underlined for emphasis) telephone the embassy to arrange an appointment."

Signed, your dear friend.

Events progressed with a speed and a priority that raised his spirits and It was agreed that he should meet the First Secretary on Tuesday September eighteenth at Lyons Corner House, Maison Lyons, Marble Arch, at the junction of Oxford Street and Great Cumberland Place at noon and he should bring with him a copy of the statement that he had prudently retained. It did not take long for Goldburgh to ask himself how the Soviets knew about the document, or what else they knew – and how-and why they possibly still had an interest in his life.

He arrived early and saw that Laurence Olivier`s 'Henry V' was playing at the 'Pavilion' and he immediately booked a seat for the two thirty performance, which was an excellent excuse if he wanted to terminate his meeting and on the stroke of twelve he was seated by a 'nippy', but before he could take off his coat he was accosted by the representative from the embassy who introduced himself in Russian and suggested, unless Goldburgh had any objections, to conduct their discussion in Russian, but would acquiesce to any request .

The ice was broken over a pot of tea and toast accompanied by butter and jam and their joint love of Moscow, especially at that time of year but Goldburgh was determined to discuss his situation without stressing his concerns. He realised that those in Moscow aware of his actions would provide to their representatives in London the minimum of information upon which they were able to conduct discussions. He was therefore circumspect and vague in the information and the requests that followed beginning his statement with an enquiry if the man wished to take notes, but the reply was that it was unnecessary, provided that he speak clearly and be prepared to be interrupted if and only if, he did not understand any part of the information that was provided.

"With the approval and cooperation of the British embassy in Moscow, I was seconded to the Soviet authorities at the specific request of Comrade Commissar Beria and First Secretary Stalin (he closely observed the Soviet diplomat for any special reaction and was pleased to note that the man visibly appeared impressed) which I did so for about a year. The nature of my work should not concern you but was rather boring , teaching N K V D officers English and a typed statement to this effect was given to the British authorities on my arrival in Istanbul. I retained a carbon copy and was able recently to have a copy taken by an obliging printer in Southwold which is in this envelope. You will note that it is addressed to Commissar Beria, a man that I personally know (at that moment he noticed a sense of awe across the man's face). It is essential that he and he alone opens and reads my statement for he will know what action to take. Also, before my departure from Yerevan the local head of the N K V D was entrusted with a letter to be delivered personally, again to Lavrenti Beria or if he was unable to complete the mission, to be passed to my uncle Lazar Kaganovich who would forward the document to the head of the N K V D. "

The man took the envelope and promised to contact him in Southwold when a reply was received from Moscow but as the matter would be dealt with at the highest level and as he was ...

"Only a diplomat, it was impossible to judge how long the matter would take."

The meeting was concluded with a request to the Soviet authorities to assist him trace his parents and a brief list of facts were handed to the diplomat to assist him.

The diplomat's statement was not exactly true since he was an officer in the N K V D and whilst he was unaware of the real events in the Ukraine it was imperative that he discover what Goldburgh had disclosed. Sight of, and a copy of his statement meant that the Soviets could completely cover their tracks and protect their loyal agent.

In the spring of nineteen forty-six the whole affair was revived when, 'out of the blue', he received a semi official invitation to Magdalene college which was ostensibly a reunion of former students arranged by the dons themselves and not the college. He arrived with great eagerness and hope that many of his contemporaries and students of earlier and later periods would be present but a tragic inventory was calculated of friends that had not survived the six years of war. He did meet certain of his fellow students but realised that like the different periods of their courses he still had little in common. He was 'rescued' from his isolation when unexpectedly the Russian tutor, tapped him on the shoulder and offered him a sherry and the opportunity to...

"Have a chat."

They wandered over the bridge and finally arrived at the public house where they first met and began to speak in Russian as if it was a natural act between old friends. He had a message and the inference was clear: he was more than just a friend of the Soviet Union .

"Mandel, may I first of all, after all these years, call you by your first name (he received literally a nod in response). My few true friends call me by my adopted patronym which you may now address me but not in public."

He quietly mentioned the name which made Mandel smile since its literal English translation he thought most apt for a man who was slowly exposing his true loyalties and nature.

"Our friends in Moscow have asked why you went through such a transparent charade with your friend Kashkarov, who unnecessarily suffered such appalling injuries to create an obvious false illusion and why, more importantly ,did you not report to the headquarters of the N K V D where your cover story had been already prepared to facilitate your repatriation back to the British embassy?

I am instructed to inform you that Lavrenti Beria received, via your uncle, your short letter and recently a copy of your statement. The messenger from Yerevan was imprisoned for fifteen years as a precaution, just in case he read the contents and I regret to inform you that your friend was severely cautioned, but because of his major wounds and his bravery at Kursk was only demoted and that finally, some time ago, a representative visited the British embassy in Moscow with a file detailing your work in the Ukraine and apologising that through an administrative error, which had been rectified, ongoing enquiries concerning your where-abouts and the purpose of your mission were not given, as they should have been done.

I have for you a private letter from your uncle and I believe, other than his interest in you and your career, concerns your parents. No doubt you will to read the contents in private.

You are to continue uninterrupted your life and career in England, until you receive instructions. Now let us return and have some excellent fish paste sandwiches."

He had subconsciously, for some time, harboured the sense that his parents had not survived the war since he was reasonably confident that they would have, somehow, made contact or returned to the United Kingdom (or even the Soviet Union), but his uncle's sympathetic words and his memories of his mother still could not console his grief or ameliorate the shock of the truth.

In January nineteen forty-seven, rather unexpectedly, he received a request to visit the local police station in Southwold. He was therefore most surprised to see Duggan, who ignored him. Two local detectives requested that he join them in an interview room where they produced the two five pounds notes bearing his signature which they asked him to identify and upon his confirmation, one of the officers stood up and left the room, shortly returning with both Duggan and Goodacre.

This time the interview and interrogation was more formal and certainly less amicable. Goodacre asked him to verify his where-abouts on September the eighteenth the previous year and, not unreasonably, he had to coax him to remember the day.

He was then asked with a clear sense of malice by Duggan:

"What information was contained on the sheet of paper handed to the Russian diplomat?"

Later that day he was permitted to make one controlled telephone call which was to his friend in Southwold probably less than a mile away, as the crow flies:

"I have just been charged under the Official Secrets Act with offences that I absolutely deny and also having in my possession forged British currency."

END OF VOLUME ONE